The Particle

A Novel

G.A. Chamberlin

Titles by

G.A.Chamberlin

The Handmaiden Legacy
Cultural Attache
Rare Earth Element
Outbound
Somma
Unintended Consequence
The Particle
The Kneeling Woman
At Auction

~

Kathleen The War Years

The Particle
Printed in the United States
ISBN 978-0-9904027-7-0

Crown Eagle Publishing

Distribution by Ingram

Cover Image: Courtesy NASA

Rare Earth Element

...climate, culture, commerce...Too important to ignore, too well written to overlook. And too technically suspenseful not to wonder about...

* * *

The Handmaiden Legacy

The Handmaiden Legacy is a contemporary thriller full of corporate interests, beautiful seas and ancient legacies...

---G.A. Chamberlin is an International Thriller Writer!

"International Thriller Writers ...that will surprise "
--Agent, Thriller Fest, New York City

Cultural Attache

"...Amanda Wells is lecturing on the historical integrity of medieval works at the University when she is informed that the original manuscript of a major work...has been stolen from the vault.

The Particle

"…Amanda Wells, once at the top of her game as a reliable Researcher, discovers from an unsuspecting expedition the disruptive force about to unleash a catastrophic threat to national security –

…With only a team of economically displaced, unemployed joggers at her beach house, Amanda Wells must save her daughter from the murderous fate of an international malevolent…and solve the mystery of the cause

...The Higgs boson, identified by the CERN Institute in 2013, is a tiny particle that researchers only suspected existed. Says astrophysicist Stephen Hawking:

> *"The Higgs potential has the worrisome feature that it might become metastable at energies above 100 [billion] gigaelectronvolts (GeV). ... This could mean that the universe could undergo catastrophic vacuum decay, with a bubble of the true vacuum expanding at the speed of light. This could happen at any time and we wouldn't see it coming."*

2014, CERN

The Particle

A Novel

G.A. Chamberlin

Prologue

September 2, 1851

On the east coast of North America it was sunny, even as children returning to school knew summer was over. Along cobbled streets the oak and elm, vivid in rich red and translucent yellow, hinted at imminent change.

At the Franklin Telegraph Company, the operator entered the building and took his place in the Telegraph Section. He commenced his day with transmission traffic moving across new telegraph lines. It was his job, and he did it well.

Boston, the operator knew, was at the center of banking and factories, absorbing Europe's able men and women engaged in developing infrastructure, transportation, newspapers, manufacture and shipping.

When the disruption occurred, it did not appear to be alarming. Within the first hour or so, some messages got through, if garbled and incoherent.

The operator and his co-workers at the Franklin Telegraph Company scrambled to find solutions. Notification was dispatched immediately to the company proprietors.

Courier messages came back swiftly. Had conductivity sources been interrupted? Did the Telegraph Company inspect battery charges in the building? What about the Operations center?

Hours passed and the situation did not ameliorate. From American Telegraph a supervisor came down to the Franklin to find answers about their communications.

It was hard to explain, they said. The supervisor said he would make outside inquiries, returning often to ask if there was any improvement at the Franklin.

By mid-day it was known all over the city. The matter was disrupting discussions at chief banking and business bureaus. How could the telegraph communications be down? Newspaper wire services had failed. All issuances of bonds and transfers had to cease…Finance was to halt.

The weather turned cloudy.

Could the engineers repair the lines? Perhaps the municipality might explain.

Agencies sent delivery boys with direct enquiries to the Telegraph Company: Traffic on the streets was now mixing up. They asked if the short-line locomotives were still running into Boston.

Outside the sun waned, and a wind swirled in from the sea. Temperatures plunged.

By afternoon, the Mayor sent a messenger over. *Government offices could not get heat in the building because the boilers were without coal and wood supplies…Without communications, how could they expedite their autumn deliveries of fuel for the boilers? What was causing the delay?*

By late afternoon, the telegraph service was still inoperable and the streets of Boston emptied of people, the wind gusting.

At the American Telegraph building, fuel was also in short supply, and a chill set in as rain poured against the brick in raging folds. By now, the Front Office had sent word that all workers were dismissed - the payday closed.

Only the operator sat at his desk. Perhaps the telegraph lines would become operable. Possibly he could help once the storm abated. The room became silent, grey and dank. He opened his desk drawer where he habitually kept a wool scarf, and he wrapped it around his neck.

He was worried. He tapped into Portland Maine - a substation that was always of concern due to its remoteness.

To his surprise, Portland came back.

He tapped as if nothing was amiss.

"Please cut off your battery power source entirely for fifteen minutes."

Portland responded. "Will do so. It is now disconnected."

He paused, alarmed.

A *current?*

He sat, the room still, then he tapped out a message, making an assumption.

Boston: "Mine is disconnected, and we are working with the Auroral current. How do you receive my writing?"

Portland: "Better than with our batteries on – Current comes and goes gradually."

Boston: "My current is very strong at times, and we can work better without the batteries, as the aurora seems to neutralize and augment our batteries alternately, making current too strong at times for our relay magnets. Suppose we work without batteries while we are affected by this trouble."

Portland: "Very well. Shall I go ahead with business?"

Boston: "Yes. Go ahead."

For two hours they transmitted messages.

Numerous explanations came forward. A geo-magnetically-induced current came alive from an unknown electromagnetic field, producing conductivity. That was one theory. But nobody knew.

The incident was reported in the *Boston Evening Traveler*, its many editions later assimilated in 1912 by the *Boston Herald*. The archive remained packed in storage for over fifty years. When the *Boston Herald* ceased operation, a delivery of its editions went to Washington DC to be conserved as a collection at the US Library of Congress.

In 2016, the article was reviewed by a Researcher. He signed off on his name, then entered his agency. NASA.

* * *

Chapter 1

Sandra's hair was afire.

In polar brightness, it was red for the summer, and it fairly glistened under the indoor blue-light that lit the lab.

"Hey beautiful!" said Mike, closing the door to the hangar behind him.

She looked up and waved. "Hey!"

She studied his appearance with a sweep that suggested a good "looking over."

Then her eyes refocused into the white telescope from a chin-rest where little black flakes of mascara had already left their mark.

Looking over was mandatory protocol. For every person entering or preparing to exit the hangar, they were to be "looked over." It was the Buddy System of survivalist training at the North Pole.

 That, plus First Aid course accreditations; swimming tests, endurance tests, fitness training, nutrition education, strength building, mental testing, meteorology readings, geographic and celestial navigation technique courses, ski coaching, deep submersible testing, animal management and self-defense training. Add a fair smattering of IT knowledge related to communications; signals and climate-impact response training; if not weather conditioning, then you just might, *might*, be invited up!

Academics, and the log and journal entries - by way of recording the expedition, were essential procedures. That was the keystone function: To record every sector of their day and their findings at the North Pole Research Expedition.

Not many redheads made it, as Mike one day had to remind her. None made it into the Program. Period. And none with the looks of Sandra McDonnell.

Her eyes were blue, the Viking-color of ice that came from faraway lands, and her Nordic colored hair was in fact as natural as the day she was born - leaving both her parents to wonder at the creature before them. Only her Scottish grandmother recognized the genetic throwback to an ancient legacy of descendants that might have once landed upon the ragged shores of their world and populated the mountainous regions of the Highlands.

But that was Sandra. Always mystifying people, and always observing the world as if it were a mystery to explore.

"You want to go *where?*" asked her father, Trevor MacDonnell when she announced she had applied for the University program to conduct research at the North Pole.

He looked at his wife accusingly.

Amanda threw back her head with a smothered smile, saying nothing. Clearly, there was a streak of her own personality in Sandra.

Both mother and daughter had the same features, if not the same coloration. But it was Trevor's height that put Sandra much taller than her mother. And with that light blue-ice look on her face and soft voice, there was little Sandra could not command from her parents, it would seem, both of whom would align the stars for her if she so asked.

But this was Sandra. Never a thought for herself, only for the good she could offer.

Still, Trevor was worried. Had she gone too far this time? Sandra's application to join the University Summer Expedition to the North Pole was totally unexpected. Was it safe, he wondered. He turned to Amanda, anxiety now shading his face.

"Does she know what's she's doing?" he asked plainly.

Amanda smiled.

Her head was bowed, a piece of embroidery absorbing her attention, and her posture suggested an exclusively maternal role. Yet nothing was further from the truth. Certainly, the item of antiquity at hand was made from a needlepoint tapestry of Scottish clan arras which hung from a stone wall of their Castle home. It required delicate handling with special skill and reconstructive conservation, matching dye-colored threads of the middle ages with modern silk. Amanda was meticulous, and she was a working professional.

"Dad" said Sandra. "You yourself know the Pole well... *You* have been there for a period under the polar cap?"

"That's different..."

"No it isn't" insisted Sandra. "At that latitude and longitude, it's the same. Even if you were in a submarine enjoying the comforts of the Royal Navy..." she giggled.

Trevor looked at Amanda for rescue.

"But just as dangerous..." she said.

Sandra didn't have to be told how easily a liquid sea could turn into solid ice and crush a vessel like a child's toy.

Polar extremities remained a frontier unknown. Submarines beneath the ice caps provoked risk to navigation even with advanced technologies. This they knew well enough. That Trevor survived a Specialized Mission was a tribute to the mission's leadership, he insisted.

Still, Sandra insisted on explaining herself.

The Polar Expedition quest was presented at University Orientation night. That is, before the rigors of training began and before attrition thinned out most of the student applicants, leaving those that survived endurance tests a small chance of making the final list of candidates. From that even fewer were selected for the expedition team.

In the weeks that followed, Sandra discovered that she made it. She had been invited to join the Expedition team. As was Mike. Also two others – one French, one British, plus a native-American Inuit student attending the University of Toronto.

They were excited.

Once they got to know each other, preparation training couldn't have been more fun. For the few requisite hours of scholarly work, there were hours of toboggan races; geothermal bathing in Iceland, skiing in Alaska, Canadian mountain climbing, survival camping, sailing, snowboarding and ice-skidding on power jet skies.

Trevor and Amanda knew Sandra's athletic capabilities. They insisted on receiving periodic mission reports and communications on a regular basis.

"We leave tomorrow!" said her final message. And it soon became clear that for Sandra, the expedition could not have been more stimulating.

From her initial messages home, it was certain the drills were routine precautions. But when it came to cataloging expedition findings and observations, there was little Sandra found routine. Her record of small accomplishments which, at normal latitudes would be uneventful, were remarkable because of location. Each goal accomplishment was significant.

For Sandra this had settled into a routine.

* * *

Chapter 2

She sat there and took a big breath, muttering.

Bloody Hell. What was his problem: This obsession to monitor the polar *bearings?*

Regardless, at the North Pole today was no different.

Sandra looked up at the overhead clock showing several time zones.

It was Fall-like on the Arctic Circle and the sun was at approximately 66.5 degrees of Zenith, or about 23 degrees above the horizon, barely perpendicular to the equator on the equinox. They were enjoying twelve hours of daylight and twelve hours of darkness. It made for a lot of time to play and exercise outside between good stretches of time indoors in the lab to examine collected samples under a microscope.

One weather report left a momentary furrow on Sandra's face. No worries.

Summer had been too wonderful, and too fleeting. They had entered already that mild transitional climate between the extremes of summer and winter, and there was a prediction of a winter storm brewing to the south east. But nothing definitive. Not that they were unprepared. You were *always* prepared on the North Pole. Even if you had your bikini in your backpack for a touch of sunbathing on the ice cap. You were always prepared.

No, she decided. This weather forecast came from an email she received. Her father was watching the weather conditions with a daily email. Even if Trevor MacDonnell was retired from H.M. Royal Navy after underwater expeditions in the Arctic circle, it was annoying. Especially since he was elsewhere occupied with official celestial observations from his telescope atop the hills of his own lands in Scotland.

Occasionally she sent back an abrupt response designed to deter further monitoring of the very spot on the planet where she was presently enjoying an Internship for University research!

Did that deter him? Not at all… This storm, he was saying, could come up so fast as to turn the sky into a sweeping ice eruption in a matter of hours.

Not that their survival training did not explain that. It was just the suddenness that was dangerous. It could quickly put humans in a vulnerable position, she knew. And out here, it didn't take much to perish. Still, with summer just barely behind them, surely October could not be a threat?

Ok, she looked up.

They were all grinning. They had enjoyed three weeks of bliss up here. And the guys wanted to go jet-ski racing again today. This, on the way to the Western grid where they were collecting the last of their sub-surface ice samples.

Just one more excursion, they pleaded. She turned to read the weather on their satellite information imaging service.

"We'll be back for dinner.." they insisted "Come on! Suit-up and let's go!"

"Yeah!" said Mike

"OK!" said Melinda

"Right then!" she heard herself say, glancing just once at her laptop. It was Sunday, after all, a short something by way of saying hello to the family was prerequisite.

"I'm coming!" she yelled back at Chris hailing her from outside. The computer was slow. Interference of transmission, apparently.

'Sandra, Come on!.."

> … *"What is your polar bearing?"* her father had asked in his last email.

She ran over to the main lab magnetic chronometer and made a note of their polar bearing.

> *'No change: 90.0000° N, 0.0000° W.*
>
> *Love to Mother"*

She grabbed her knapsack, drilled a wool scarf around her neck and flew out the door to mount a snow ski ride behind Chris.

He gunned the motor. Off they went.

Two hours later, the Lab building shook. It was barely a tremor.

Inside, the magnetic chronometer shifted two full degrees.

* * *

Chapter 3

They had made a nice track. Large, like a horserace track, oval so that you could count on good curvature taking the bend.

Twice, Chris had won the race, once Mike. But the heat was softening the surface and the snow began to look granular, porous like a mature watermelon, if white.

Everywhere was white bordering on blue or grey. It was truly magnificent, all that space uncluttered by others. A freedom of unmitigated possibilities rested within their souls as they played on a field created by them, students playing on top of the world - an academic expedition of unadulterated intellectual privilege!

Sandra looked at her watch. They would want a few lab samples from the field today, by the way, she told them.

…Then they could go home and microwave one of their delectable hermetically-sealed gourmet salmon feasts, as they called them: Pre-cooked and waiting in their freezer at the field-station cottage - complete with a small bottle of Chianti, it was always good food. Today would be bean-salad with lasagna and garlic bread…That had been their choice for the day. Preparations and menus were all elected the week before on a planning grid.

She called out... Food never failed to entice them home, thought Sandra. It had started snowing.

* * *

Nobody saw the crack.

The fissure had opened up beneath the ice pack, and ground cover filled with fluffy flakes. Rising wind smoothed over the surface, turning it into a glassy reflection of sunlight. Their jet skis had been moving fast...

Mike pitch-poled as the sled-rail dipped into the lip of the break, and while the sled managed to rev itself forward, if on its side with the motor still running, he was too stunned to know where he landed and he slipped quickly down the fissure, the wall of the ice a sheer cliff either side of him.

He dropped twenty feet, his body tipped to rest on a ledge surface. Bits of ice and a shower of snow obscured his vision. His breathing came to him slowly, the shock of his fall so sudden, and he raised his head to look around. His shoulder had taken the brunt of the fall, and his body felt heavy on his arm. But his hands were tight and stiffly pushing out - breaks against a gravity motion that instinctively he knew to resist before further sliding down. Whatever held him up was unmovable, though the sound of cracking and slothing told him his tension-hold was unstable. He looked down and could see very little that defined the beginning of one surface and the end of another. He looked up and recognized blue sky.

He wanted to yell. He wanted to stop the pressure against his hands. His lungs filled with air.

"Help!" he managed to say.

* * *

From above, his clothing was whitened by falling ice, debris and snow. His vest was neutral colored and his hat black, which gave the only hints of his presence through the flakes that settled on his head. But he was hard to spot.

They were on the verge of panic, and would have screamed out in shock had they not had the training to know that one false move, or one needless over-exertion might shift a precarious state of imbalance on this shifting icepack. Nature had her measure of miraculous tension, but it was a tenuous existence at best.

Or was it Sandra's voice that remained calm as she called out softly Mike's name as if calling her cat home. "Mike?...*Mike?*"

"I'm here!" he bellowed from somewhere.

But they weren't fooled.

When the ice opened, you were sitting between the fingers of a god who could spread out his hand without warning.

They approached cautiously. One step at a time. Then crawled, calling gently.

 "Mike…We're here!"

It happened very fast. There was little they could [JC1]asses, less do, but it was as if time stood still.

Twenty minutes passed quickly. Mike responded twice. They knew they were approaching the threshold of weighing the risks of a recue, something that in its calculations, could take them all to their death.

Relief came long before they could hear anyone or see anything. Sending out an alarm signal had been their first action.

He was an Inuit Rescue Ranger on a Jet Ski who arrived towing a small sled of Emergency gear.

"Everyone OK?" he asked, lifting his heavy visor.

Standing on top of his gear was a heavy furred huskie wolf hound. She waited.

"Rexy!" he said, by way of introducing her as she then bounded off her post and started sniffing the ground around every student in the party.

"We saw the tremor monitors going off the chart for this area and dispatched immediately" he continued, unpacking his gear.

They told him. Mike was down the crevice…It had been a horrifying moment, it happened so fast, they said…

"Is he the only one unaccounted for?" asked the Ranger.

Yes, they were not sure how he was doing, they said, and it happened so unexpectedly.

"We don't see him…" said Chris, his voice small.

"Please stay away from the edge of the crevice!..." he interrupted, pointing his monitor around them. It reflected density differentiations of surface vapor that delineated the fissure in wider perspective.

A radio transmission crackled and he unbuttoned the leather pouch at his chest.

"This is Andy. I am arrived at the North 36th Quad. Four parties accounted for, one absent in a fissure…" He dug out his compass "Extraction possibility at bearing 000.03 and 0.4 degrees. Request air aid for injured party, unstable surface. Repeat, surface unstable…"

"Roger" crackled the radio.

They all talked at once, and repeatedly he held up his hand to focus on his task.

"Roxy!" he called.

She came bounding back, and he tied a rope to her breast harness.

He pulled out a set of binoculars with filtered mounted lens and examined the surface from where he stood. "I want everybody to stay close to this area. No wandering, please!"

He dialed on the lenses of his binocular and saw a sharp break in the surface. He followed the opening above and below them, and calculating a breach of no more than four feet wide before them, he put down his binoculars and turned to his sled.

He opened two boxes. One contained a loosely coiled rope of light-weight high tension nylon. He anchored a small drill spike in the ice, and set the box back in a cradle beside it.

The second box contained something that resembled a large tree twig, rubber, weighted at both ends. He hurled it into the air and sent it way across the fissure where it landed. He peered through his binoculars and shot a gun of dye that stained the surface of the fissure opening.

"Roxy, Go!" he called.

The dog leaped forward to followed the twig across the ice with a force that thrust her in a motion that barely touched the ground. The rope tied to her harness followed her, weightlessly uncoiling. The dog, leaped easily across the breach in one giant stride, had calculated its width which was clearly visible to her. She reached the twig. There, she stopped, two feet from where it landed.

The Rescue Ranger unpacked a drone which lifted up and hovered exactly over the twig. It landed slowly, drilling a hard spike from beneath its motor, and fixed a peon anchor into the snow.

"Roxy!" called the Ranger, shooting two large rings, one to the left of the anchor, one to the right by ten feet.

Roxy got up, found each ring and went through it, her leash threading itself to the peon anchor. Trained as a rescue dog, she knew the routine. She turned and travelled again into the other ring, her leash fastening against the anchor, and she waited.

The Ranger tied off the rope at his end.

He clipped on a gliding rip-grip anchored across the fissure by Roxy and walked to the edge of the fissure, then lowered himself to the snow.

The Ranger lay down on the ice belly down, arms and feet wide open. He inched forward and looked over the edge. He switched on his flashlight.

Sandra was besides herself, yet she spoke softly. "Will he be alright?"

Chris held her back and Tim came to stand closer.

The Ranger edged backwards, stood up and advanced towards them.

"He's alright. He has a broken collar bone, and I'm going to extract him with a harness. But he's perched on a ledge. So I'd like your help, there'll be just one chance to snag him: I'll have a cradle sled beside me attached to a rope. When I give the signal…Like this,   then you pull on the cradle with this rope. That way you can take the weight off his purchase as I hold him to... Got it?"

The transmission crackled.

 "How long has the party been exposed?" it asked. The Ranger ignored the transmission and quickly unwrapped his sack.

From a large pressurized canister he sprayed the snow with dye. Then he answered.

 "75% of time-exposure."

The Ranger looked up only once before spinning back to the crevice.

"In that bag is water…" he called. "Open the zipper, drink, then seal up the pack. Also a small thermal pouch. Understand? Everyone OK?"

They said yes.

He turned back to shout. "A chopper is scheduled to arrive shortly. This dye in the snow will mark your position. So don't be alarmed. You all stay together. You understand?"

Unfurling the tow line, he reattached himself to the rip-grip. "Nobody approach the fissure. You stay here at this spot. Got that?"

As he began lowering himself down the crevice, the dog was barely visible.

It was long in the waiting. Minutes. Stillness.

There was snow, a whiteness came about them. The ambient Arctic blow that was always like a low whistle, was menacing.

"Oh my God…" whispered Sandra.

The signal came. They hoisted with steady rhythmic pulls.

Mike emerged first, his body hoisted by a harness system rigged to the cross-line.

The Ranger emerged behind him, and set him over the top. He rearranged Mike's position into the cradle. He raised his arm, and with both Day-Glo sleeves extended straight up, they knew to start pulling in across the snow...

Behind them, a chopper was hovering with a ground line, two Rangers crouched to leap off.

Mike was in shock, but he was safe. He was the first to be loaded. The party was next onboard. The pilot was clearly anxious to lift-off.

The rescue Ranger turned to his sled and re-stowed his gear.

With a remote controller, he aimed at the dog and released the clip on Roxy that had attached her to the anchor. She was free. He whistled, and she deftly leaped across the fissure and stood at his side, her rescue duty performed. He leaned over and patted her on her head behind the ears, then passed his hand assuring below her belly. He opened a pouch of liquid from which she drank. She retook her position upon the jet-ski sled and waited for him.

The chopper was ample. Her rotors never ceasing and her imaging camera following the length of the fissure for the record, they passed over the crevice.

The Rescue Ranger had leashed their jet-skies together for towing back.

She was beginning to feel dizzy and nauseous from the cold. She looked out the porthole as the chopper ascended. She tried to look down the fissure in the ice. How deep was it? Mike, she sensed, had been lucky. She sat, and she discovered that the name of the Rescue Ranger was Adam.

Then at less than twenty five feet altitude, with the rotors roaring, a loud boom echoed across the landscape with such force as to develop an impact wave. The chopper shuddered.

 The pilot knew a sound-wave could sweep him out of the sky like a child's toy. The ice pack beneath the surface had cracked open.

He kept the chopper bow-on, if never above one hundred feet off the surface, and all tracking systems on. He retraced his route to the rescue station at Physton Point.

Sandra never got a good look into the fissure. But as they sped away, she saw it widen into a darkening chasm that would have been unassailable to any   rescue. Something had happened. The others remained vaguely unaware of it.

Dark winds gusting and whipping up snow the chopper landing was rough, and they were ushered into the hanger. It was an oasis.

With Leed-Platimum certification for innovative technologies, the vault-shaped design of the geogrid structural system of diamond-shaped fiber arches infilled with translucent ETFE pillows was built atop a permafrost substrate, its bulkheads penetrating the icepack.   The effect was a light-filled atrium with open circulation and natural artic sunlight. LED lights, combined with northern lights of the artic night sky illuminated the ETFE pillows with bright shifting colors.

Furnished with modern surroundings of soft ambient corners for easy comfort, the Artic Depot for Rescue and Recording Operations was able to sustain them under extreme conditions, and warm air permeated their environment. The place was never dormant.

The Depot also served as a field monitoring station for high latitude Communications - a listening post of sorts, transmitting endlessly to US satellites and high speed data collectors with vast capacity processing all that passed across northern cap hemispheres. The staff were abundant.

Two officers manned the communications center; two of the Patrol Units remained at their desks logging in status conditions and monitoring flight and radar.

In quasi lab-like conditions, equipment hummed with incoming data, computer monitors, busy facsimile machines; seismic monitors; heating unit fans and even some music.

From one window of their warm office, Rangers could view the interior of the garage hangar parking equipment including Jet-skies, trucks, salt, sand and gravel heaps, even space for small planes. During the day, the hangar was filled with mechanics and specialists checking equipment and stock for rescue operations: Between them, the passageway offered a locker room for donning gear, oxygen and heavy weather clothing before stepping into the ambient temperatures of the North Pole.

Sandra and the others were examined for exposure in medical quarters, followed by food at a small cafeteria, then shown accommodations with warm cabin bunks in private quarters.

Mike would recover, they heard. He had been transported to the Main Arctic Transport Post less than twenty minutes away. In the lounge they gathered and chatted, feeling safe and fully recuperated. Here, stretched out on comfortable seating, they relaxed with coffee, snacks, TV and laptops.

Sandra decided against informing her father. Later, perhaps. Later, when the storm that closed them in would clear away, bringing them back to the bright artic sun; their happy realities and with Mike fully restored…

Yet Sandra knew that wasn't possible. They had been changed, if the forces of the region remained hidden! So far their expedition, she realized, was child's play.

What was unexplained was the booming echo that reverberated across the surface while being airlifted out. Sandra had said nothing, but she noticed the expression on the faces of the Rangers and Pilot of the plane. She recognized it as fear. This was clearly something alien and unexpected even to them...

The next day, after breakfast, Roxy found them. She sniffed and nuzzled. There was no end to the need for comfort and thanks they could express over the dog. At the door stood the Rescue Ranger Adam, smiling. The storm, evidently, was still closing in, no travel today. So it was to be a day at the rescue station with Roxy!

Mostly, they played video games. Waiting for the weather to clear the next day presented the same dilemma. Weather grounded all air-born transport.

"No worries…" said Sandra. "At least we're safe and warm!"

By day three at the station, Sandra was walking around and becoming acquainted with all Rangers. She was curious. There was more up here than anyone was fully appreciating.

An assortment of coffee, donuts, and few life stories and rescue accounting passed the hours. Including the events that led Adam to take his training and be posted to North Pole Ranger Station.

He was an ex-Marine, he told her. His mother was Canadian.

"I spent my youth skiing and skating not far from the family home in Montreal. I went to the University of Toronto to receive my degree in engineering before joining the US Marines, like my father…"

"No yearning for the tropics then?" asked Sandra.

He laughed. His duties were chiefly related to Artic and cold weather training and skiing, he explained.

Sandra was interested. She found him soft and comfortable with the daily challenges that faced him as a Ranger. He seemed earnest, as if tasting each day to its very fullest.

Whatever tension lay just beneath the surface up here did not faze him, she noticed.

"Up here…"he said "its peaceful, you might say"

"Yes" she laughed. "I'd say that! *Isolated* and peaceful… no question! Why humans should force themselves upon such an inhospitable environment is not even questionable, right?"

He laughed too, entirely comfortable with the choices and dangers he chose for a life. She watched him drain his coffee, his upturned chin firm and smoothly shaven. Neither was he uninformed and hiding from the realities of the world, she liked that. It was a self-assurance that would carry into everything he would do, she felt certain. This was the kind of man satisfied with his every accomplishment.

Shortly after mess that night, they watched a movie together. Adam especially enjoyed telling Sandra about Montreal. A place, she said, where her father had interests. She had never been there, she told him, but her mother had…

"What made you take a second tour of duty up here?"

He thought about it, then grabbed her hand.

"Come outside!" he said, heading for the suit-up platform just before the station doors. It was dark, and the temperatures were plunging, no question.

It was definitely cold, the thermometers reading well below zero. But it was windless. And it only took a few feet away from the lighting of the station to be totally lost to the Arctic night.

Bundled up like to pillars of cold-weather voyagers in thermos-clothing, they stood, almost undefinable as humans. Then he pointed upward.

Suddenly surrounded by a light show of colors, a corona of tints refracted like rainbow beams in frosted shades of translucent blue and green, and the night sky was radiating as if the heavens were opening. It was a stunning display that seemed surreal. Sandra held her breath.

"Aurora Borealis" he said.

"I've never seen anything like it…." she said between her teeth chattering in cold.

"Come inside now!" he said authoritatively, his arm steering her shoulder.

She turned to look up once again. The night sky was displaying such magnitude of force that she felt she could actually hear a harmonic frequency.

"My God" she said, once inside, her lips numb. "What *was* that?"

"…Amazing, wasn't it?" he said, smiling. "At this high latitude it's the natural light display of solar winds passing over the planet and releasing magnetospheric plasma, mainly in the form of electrons and protons into the upper atmosphere."

"Solar winds?"

"Yep! Ionization and excitation of atmospheric constituents emitting light of varying color and complexity. It's the aurora occurring within bands around the poles…" He paused. "You look blue. How about some coffee?" he laughed.

"I take it…. that wasn't exactly authorized procedure out there?"

"Strictly forbidden!" he said "Just too dangerous for human exposure…"

"But magic…" she said.

He looked at her gravely. "Yes."

They chatted over warm drinks. He led her to the Weather and Charts room. "We're in the Auroral zone 3° to 6° at Latitude from the geomagnetic poles. Sometimes it moves in oval patterns closer to the earth's surface mainly when a geomagnetic storm causes the auroral ovals to expand. This is the best time to see it, magnetic midnight."

She followed.

"As energy dissipates, oxygen emissions are green or orange-red, depending on the energy absorbed. Nitrogen emissions are blue or red; blue if the atom regains an electron *after* it has been ionized; red if returning to the ground state from an excited state…"

 "Night dragons…" she mused, thinking to see them skipping across the sky.

He was watching her again. "Yes?"

"Oh, err… I've never imagined it could be so…fiery.

 "Well, it's a power source related to the earth's magnetic fields. Particle density of matter is the very stuff of beginnings. Best not to trifle with… "

"Wait…You're conducting research on this?"

He looked away, but his eyes flickered. Whatever it was, he was not about to say.

"Come on! Let's get a real drink!" he said finally.

"How do I never forget this?" she asked, later in the evening.

"Your celestial name can be Aurora" he said softly, "Aurora is the goddess of the dawn, renewing herself every morning to fly across the sky, announcing the arrival of the sun."

"Shakespeare?"

"Yes! *And…* ancient Roman mythology."

Finally, news arrived that they were cleared to leave the station. The team was relieved, the ordeal had been taxing. While easily absorbed as part of their expedition, there had been deeper levels of anxiety that nobody wanted to articulate. They gathered their stuff to pack up and vacate the base.

They walked down past the office Administration area preparing to suit up into thermal wear and climb into a rugged terrain vehicle. Sandra thought she spotted Adam in the Rescue Ranger Mission Room.

"Wait, just one second.." she said, turning off down to hallway.

"Officer….Adam?" she said, seeing him talking to another man. He turned to her.

"I want to thank you for your swift response and your bravery out there…"

He smiled. "You're welcome!" He extended his hand.

"We were very lucky, I think" she said.

"You were!" said the second officer behind him. "Adam and Roxy spotted the tremors on our Monitors and they took off…Just in time!"

"Mike… that is, our student you rescued…he says thanks, too!" she added.

She would have liked to hug him. Or at the very least touch him, but there was no privacy.

"No problem" he said "We used a mountain climbing technique…"

Behind him, the Superintendent's office door opened. "Mr. Muir will be fine…" said Senior Ranger Jeff Troy. "I just received a report on his recovery!" He turned to Sandra. "We appreciate your expression of gratitude - it's not easy work that we do up here!" he said "And we were glad to help."

 He re-entered his conference room, obviously expecting Adam to follow him in for a meeting.

Sandra smiled, her hand in small wave, catching only a glimpse inside the conference room as the door closed.

She joined her friends, and as if nothing had happened, they returned to their station one day later, the storm long passed, to collect their gear and prepare for transport back home in two days.

It was good to be back in their familiar surroundings at the Student Research Station. If not entirely as bright and adventurous, it was at least slightly less sterile than the Ranger Patrol Station.

It was the end of the expedition, to be sure. They logged in their final entries, annotated the incident with Mike as a medical emergency, and wrapped up their concluding notes and observations. Back home, it would crafted into a final paper and presented for grading. Sandra felt satisfied that she had amassed sufficient data to deliver a decent report. There would be graphs, images, data charts, photographs and…and so many memories, she decided.

That night, in her dorm cot, Sandra lay there unable to sleep, her hands behind her head. She thought about the events of the trip. The rescue was a terrifying experience. Sure, she felt a profound relief that Mike would be OK. It was all so surreal, so dreamlike – all of them on a polar expedition on top of the world with everything white and crystal and reflective and beautiful. Yet the realities were harsh and real.

A broken collar bone…?

Damn, but he had played hard all day, she decided, thinking of Mike. He would doubtless add the event to his adventuring, with bragging-rights!

Gradually, the anxiety finally started to recede into plain fatigue, even if Sandra remained worried. And the day or two at the Research Station allowed them time to process the accident and tone it down with a measure of closure, if with much relief. But the horror of that day was never far beneath the surface.

Not so much the damned crevice that Mike fell into, but the unexpected way the snowpack just…*opened up!* That was the topic that nobody talked about yet. Why? Because it was unexplainable, that's why, she decided. Not your normal street-crack in the icepack, exactly. It was a fissure! What was *that* all about?

Only later did it occur to Sandra that there were more official questions than official answers. *Mountain-climbing techniques?* That had been part of their training for inclines, slopes and fissures on uneven surfaces.

But they had been on flat ground on an ice sheet at the North Pole.

And it opened up!

Why had nothing been said about the cause of the break in the ice, she wondered. Not even Adam…Come to think of it, when Adam Stewart walked into that office, just in that last glance as the door opened for him to follow his commanding officer, there was something about it that she noticed. That was no office! That was a Conference Room. And it was filled with at least a dozen men seated around the table - all *waiting* for him to walk in and open a staff debriefing of some nature. Perhaps to hear an *explanation* of what happened, perhaps something that the public should not be alarmed about?

Otherwise Adam would have mentioned it with insouciance. But no! He remained silent, as if cautious. Or *cautioned.*

She was puzzled.

An anomaly?

Clearly it was something highly unusual. What he had witnessed, being the first responder to the incident?

"Dear Dad…" she began, in her final entry from her computer station. "You'll never guess…"

* * *

Chapter 4

Trevor already knew.

Trevor was skiing. He looked up - as if anyone was coming down from above him on the slopes of this mountain, and then pushed off. Good sports practice he called it, when skiing with Amanda and family in Switzerland.

There had been little snow this year. It was January, and only 70 inches had fallen in Scotland on the lands of his ancestral manor home. But the snow drooped from fir boughs like powdery mittens, and at dawn, when the run rose over the peaks, the snow offered nothing less than a blushing invitation to test the delights of skiing.

And test it they would, he and Amanda over the years:

Frosty mountain air, touching their faces with the hint of faraway mists, had drifted upon Scotland across the northwest seas. Wearing heavy coats and ski gear perhaps less updated than most, they had on many occasions arisen from bed for a drive to the top of the mountain - above the tree line, to ski back down through thickets of fir and birch, coniferous pine stands only to come screeching to a halt at the Oak Lodge that marked the snowline of the Glen. Then trudging back up a few hundred feet, they would find the Land Rover to open a flask of hot tea and scones before returning home. It was a special treat they shared together, especially as a family with young children when in Scotland assembled: If little white snowflakes appeared in the window, glee would ripple through the house since not often did it snow - the temperate maritime of their coastline keeping them warmer than any tundra landscape. With a clustering of excitement at the center of this clan, none of the Scottish wilderness had *ever* frightened them in wintertime! It was a landscape that was both challenging and awe-inspiring, urging them only to be good stewards of their lands as Lairds.

Trevor's wife, Amanda Wells had thick ash-blond hair. Touched by a passing silver angel, he remarked once, leaving a few strands of grey under sunlight, and it adorned her blue eyes and earnest face like a corona. As far as Trevor MacDonnell was concerned, no crown could add to the regal looks of his wife. No. This family was a monarchy writ upon their hearts, like any other…

Today, Trevor told Amanda he was going up to the mountain, and she prepared for him a small snack. Then she called Victor, the gardener.

They left her in the kitchen, typing on her laptop and returning calls on her cell-phone, busy as she was these days. She had found a way to communicate with the local community. It had a long relationship, all of them insisting she was too American to understand much; and she puzzling over Scottish brogue. Most difficult was their brand of humor and teasing. That is, until she pulled a few American jokes on them that left them speechless. So a relationship ensued of sorts. And it was a convivial one of mutual respect.

Today though, she felt concerned. Neither was there sufficient snowfall to guarantee total surface coverage for skiing, nor was Trevor the athlete able to hike back up the mountain.

This, both Victor and Charles knew as they drove him to the summit to ski down, and then to leave parked the Land Rover for him at the Oak Lodge below.

Besides, Amanda knew there was no stopping him.

Trevor had loaded up the Land Rover and was driven to the top of the mountain. He wanted to get to the Oak Lodge for a different reason. In the small hunting Lodge he kept a veritable Library and Laboratory of his own, a place that served as an Observation post. There, he examined the stars, posting an Entry Log on any anomalies of the celestial telescope that he might observe. It was peaceful work, a study of the heavens, he explained. And it had sustained his curiosity for years.

Amanda looked up. Anything that brought peace to the soul was worth pursuing...that was the magic that held them together. Where wisdom and knowledge came first, wealth and favor followed, and it defined the richness of their life. Amanda, Trevor knew, would not stop him!

Trevor did run out of snow 1000 feet before the Lodge and had to walk the rest of the way to the parked car. But he was determined. His thoughts were with his daughter Sandra, now at the North Pole.

* * *

Chapter 5

Trevor walked around the desk in his library. Filled with books on shelves that lined the walls like the logs of a cabin, the room was an old place. It had known the works of his father and grandfather; his great uncles and it had seen the Justice of the Lairds of the Glen for centuries, Trevor MacDonnell connected by lineage. Yet here he stood, pondering things as they had, developments new and alarming.

 Retired know, grey at the temples and pacing the bearskin rug that ran the length of the room, he traversed the space above which hung sturdy hunting lodge trophies of his ancestors; his fathers and his grandmothers.

Here, variously dressed in the eras of their day, his family had contributed to the heritage of the Glen, finding solutions in times of dearth, times of wealth or times of war, each telling their story from the depth of their eyes in a portrait.

"…I knew the Indian physicist Satyendra Nath Bose" wrote George in his mellifluous hand from his Post in India.

"…a brilliant man with the class of particles "bosons" now called, because of him, (although the Astrophysics book calls it God's Particle). I find his assertions fascinating, and being most generous, he explained all. He invited me to the local suk. Over a cup of tea with sugar in a glass… he told of a particle physics, specifically elementary particles that we classify as objects of mass…

Trevor looked up and saw the valley turn grey, then bluish until dimmed by rolling fog.

"In physics, the behavior of these particles interacting constitute the "Standard Model." In mathematical terms, this model offers the framework of all that we know about invariance; symmetries, and now, even gravity…"

Trevor smiled. His great Uncle George had assisted the Viceroy of India. He would inform his brother in correspondence all that he found there. In this letter dated 1940 saved in the collection of family papers, he identified the first of a phenomenon that was today presenting itself with baffling disruption...

Trevor had seen the letter long ago, but now examined it with greater care.

There was much talk. Published articles defined the possibilities of a cataclysmic pole shift, suggesting the earth's axis of rotation has made geological rapid shifts recently.

Other hypothesis suggested that similar calamities - like floods and tectonic-driven events, had been described in antiquity...

But there was more that was worrying Trevor.

It came from more credible findings in scientific journals, including the venerated *Physics Review Letters*. The Higgs boson particle was making news!

At the CERN Institute in Switzerland, research had been ongoing for years on Colliders to examine particle-research. But a new and strange discovery had been made on July 31, 2012. Data, coming from a third channel of collaboration, offered hypothesis that mystified them. *"Observation of a new particle"* Or, as the press release said just eight months later *"A Higgs boson of mass ≈125 GeV is now tentatively confirmed by CERN."*

The date was 14 March 2013.

Trevor saw the Addendum. *"It remains...unclear as yet which model the particle best supports or whether multiple Higgs bosons exist."*

The citations were many.

Trevor paced. CERN, he knew, was one of the most advanced research laboratories on earth. The hunt for another unknown particle in the universe had been on for forty years. It had led to the creation of extraordinary experimental facility: The Large Hadron Collider, designed to split atoms at high speed velocities.

The particle that would define mass was significant.

This, however, was different.

Trevor unlocked the doors to the Observation cage, and he set to work. But his mind never left the Higgs Boson findings.

Particle physics had its scientific roots in the creation of the universe, its properties still visible only through telescopic observations. Yet its understandings were just beginning, decided Trevor.

In the greater scheme of things, it was simple really: In the Standard Model of Particle Physics, all basic forces of nature were embedded in laws of symmetries - symmetries transmitted by particles known as *gauge bosons.*

Certainly, all things of substance on earth had a *mass.* A weak force symmetry, for example, might reflect a zero mass and interact with the other forces in mechanisms that had other mass shapes. A strong force symmetry might reflect a mass that interacted through mechanisms of different shapes. That was standard physics, Trevor knew. It was a mathematical way to describe mass in atoms and other substances.

That is, until 1960. The weak force symmetry "W" and "Z" bosons as they were called, should have shown their boson to have zero mass. But experiments started to show that the weak force gauged-bosons were actually interacting with mechanism shapes that were very massive and very short ranging. Mathematically, it was unexplainable. Mass particle theory was held in the palm of planet life.

Trevor remembered the questions:

Was there a new "field" interfering with the symmetry laws of nature?

What "field" was breaking symmetry laws of the electroweak interaction?

What could possibly be out there that could *change* particles and, under certain conditions, alter their *mass?*

Whereas math showed bosons could articulate particles as having massive density despite their governing symmetry, here was something radical.

Like a magnetic or electromagnetic pull of polar force, now the Higgs Boson mechanism defined the new "field" as being able to alter the shapes of mass!

What did that mean?

Alarm was recognized, but few said anything for the moment, Trevor knew. Yet something out there could alter the density of mass!

For scientists, the mere existence of this alien "field" as a trigger to the Higgs mechanism was shocking:

The consequences of something that could alter gauge bosons of a *weak* force into a *massive* density – and in very short range, was catastrophic. On earth it would easily be an Extinction event.

In the word of particle physics measuring only fragile tensions that held the tiny constellation together was remarkable. Particles, in an unending and unknown universe, held together staggering forces of nature.

More specifically, scientists scrambled now to know, was the *density* of earth's gravity. That was the primary question above all others now.

But few could utter those words.

Trevor had been with the Royal Navy collaborating with exploratory research vessels examining the magnetic pull upon gravity at certain places of the oceans. In some spots, particularly where fermions were prevalent, they knew it had important significance, especially to the well being of human life on earth.

It also had implications for national defense. And those results were kept secret. Tampering in those fields was dangerous business.

Yet the research was clear: Electromagnetic fields high in magnetic-pull changed the heaviness of gravity, especially where magna resided closer to the surface mantle of the earth.

In areas like Bermuda, the magnetic-pull was known to alter the magnetic bearings of a compass, hence the mysterious disappearances behind incidents caused by flight instrumentation in the "Bermuda Triangle."

In military records of the US Air Force and the US Navy, documents in archives showed phenomenon in logs, reports, rescue sightings, rolls, minutes and briefings

But so far, it was all conjecture.

With the Higgs boson research however, questions were arising about finding, even, a new form of physics. The Higgs field was slowly dawning upon scientists as being an astounding suggestion. The Higgs was filling the universe. This was not just one planet, or one galaxy, or even one universe that could be affected!

How could this possibly be true? What about the Big Bang theory of the beginning?

"*Inflaton,*" a hypothetical field of *dark energy* —from those first few fractions of time was a cosmic residue moving out from that that Big Bang moment.

Now they should be asking at what speed is the force of that field in the universe *moving?*

If was a force field, how would it affect the earth?

Many wanted to silence the issue. It was too alarming.

But how?

Already, the most famous physicist of modern scientific discovery, Stephen Hawkin, had issued a controversial statement on the matter. He had to disclose the new thinking. It was his duty to speak.

> *"The Higgs potential has the worrisome feature that it might become metastable at energies above 100bn gigaelectronvolts. This could mean that the universe could undergo catastrophic vacuum decay, with a bubble of the true vacuum expanding at the speed of light. This could happen at any time and we wouldn't see it coming."*

There was much speculation. Some went to early ancient writings for evidence. Was there any written record showing instability and disruption; anomalies through recorded history; catastrophic events on earth described in ancient rock and fossil analysis?

So far, no human record showed evidence of the phenomenon known or imagined. Even storytelling through the annals of times and the mythology of ancient writings. Yet Trevor knew that it was only a matter of time before something to corroborate was discovered that would amplify this theory - even if on an ancient Stele perhaps.

This, Trevor was sure of. And he told Amanda.

Above all, Trevor felt that the true test of the magnetic anomalies were most evident beneath the polar caps. Had the electromagnetic field of the poles been reversed, perhaps?

* * *

Chapter 6

At the Medical Facility, the emergency capabilities were little more than rudimentary. First Aid was dispensed to those on station; to disparate Innuit communities and when needed, and to occasional International expeditions lodged at the North Pole. But it was a far cry from a fully operational medical depot. All procedures, if serious, were rerouted to advanced medical treatment centers.

Moreover, communications were less functional than usual. Wireless connectivity usually had to synchronize with satellite orbital systems on a sporadic basis. Thus, back-up reports were written up and transported by Courier pouch using flights coming in and out on a regular bases to replenish supplies, weather permitting. ..

At the Artic Medical Center, student Mike Currigan had fully recovered and was scheduled for release. In fact, his chopper had landed, and he was about to be airlifted out of the region to a Canadian outpost on the Pacific side. From there, he could take a flight into Alaska and then hop a commercial flight home to Chicago.

Mike's medical recuperation had gone well, and he was held back now for observation only. He had been sorry to see his student team go, but he knew it was their time.

Further, he had made the most of his stay getting to know the routine up there. He knew all the staff by name, Adam, his rescuer, had come to visit. And the others, Steve, Rob and Col Dexter, head of the Ranger and Patrol Station of the North Pole had sent him mail.

At the medical center, he was popular.

He had Innuit tribal ties in his blood, he once told them. And though Asian by descent, he had heard some stories about his early ancestors - Mongolian, he said, and they had traded with the seafaring Innuit.

Still, it was his time to leave now. He had his stuff packed. Dawn was when he'd leave, that being first light, which at these latitudes meant sunlight most of the night. Yet it was a much anticipated event and many had said their Farewell to him already.

He watched the staff prepare for the incoming supply flight, the same chopper that would transport him. There would be an outgoing Courier pouch, he knew. It would carry his own case-file, like all other case-files and observations from up here.

In fact, he saw his own case-file records get stacked into a couple of boxes ready for the Courier pick-up at the staging bay. Yes, of course they could be uploaded digitally, but not yet for a few days until the files were signed off and the uplinks opened up… This he knew.

For now, all medical case-files were designated for a final examination at the main clearinghouse for registered scientists before release to the general US data medical records: For reasons of security, medical observation at the North Pole were considered sensitive material requiring first screening. It was a general funding regulation for research at the North Pole and required to pass through this mandatory procedure, Mike knew.

Mike had had extensive tests following his accident. His case included results of his blood work and tissue sampling. Physical data; Xrays and scans. He had also been subjected to preliminary psychiatric test. None of this phased him. Except for one thing.

Mike didn't exist.

He had to eradicate all possibilities of his identification. No tracings, no data and no identifications, whatever they were...

Nor could he be entirely certain about security. He was not sure about sedatives and the effect they might have had on him. He knew one thing. He felt he had altered.

He was not the same temperament as when he came up. To him, these people were suspicious beings. Of that he was certain.

A doctor came in to give him his final clearance, and the nurse followed cheerfully to inform him that he could get dressed and was free to go.

He waited, dressed, his bedsheets covering his body.

In his hospital room bathroom was a security officer, dead. The gun from his belt was beneath the sheets in Mike's hand.

Only when the nurse leaned over him did he deliver two shots into her chest at point bank range from beneath the sheets.

With the chopper blades rotating on the roof of the facility, Mike made his way up the metal steps to the upper landing. Behind him was a trail of doctors, nurses and personnel whom he had killed. They had all examined him, at one point or another.

Also, he knew, the oxygen tanks were all opened for a slow release of oxygen, waiting for an inevitable spark. Combustion would occur the second the door was opened, and a conflagration would ignite to devour most of the facility.

He hopped onto the chopper. Seated not far from the boxes containing his own medical examination records, he buckled up.

"Hi!" he said, and they lifted off the pad.

Without looking back, he knew that within ten minutes, the base would be vaporized.

His timing had been perfect.

As soon as they got within range of a military base close to the coast of Alaska he flipped open his cell.

"Hey beautiful!" he said.

"Hey Mike. Nice to hear your voice…" answered Sandra.

He smiled.

* * *

Chapter 7

1850 BC The Ancient World.

The night air, which had crossed desert sands, whispered mysteriously as it swept through the open curtains. It felt good, the breeze, caressing the young body that lay on the reed mat, her veils opened and discarded by the hand that touched her now.

The room was warm, and there was little she could do to resist his embrace. As he became more insistent, her body responding in ways she couldn't even imagine…*It was too much for her. Oh! Oh!..*

He was gone before dawn, leaving only a vapor and a saying that would be read by biblical scholars for centuries:

" *For the dew of his kiss was still moist upon her lips…*

Jacob built his house in Succoth in Shechem, in the land of Canaan.

No question that Dinah was a beauty. Like her mother Leah, his first wife to whom he was wed under false pretenses, the girl was displaying the beautiful features of all the women in that family.

Most of all, the girl resembled her aunt Rachel – the woman whom Jacob loved more tenderly, and for whom Jacob had to labor as an indentured servant another 7 years! It brought back memories. But as Leban their father explained, how else could he marry off the oldest daughter if Jacob only wanted the second?

Yes. The girl Dinah had made friends with the locals. Easily!

The event occurred when she went to hang out with the daughters of Shechem: That's when he lay with Dinah, the son of Shechem.

The maiden of the chambers presented the evidence to the Stewart in the morning, the veil and lace filigree of gold charms still scented by sweet oils. He reported it to the House Manager, who decided to report it to the Chief Chamberlain.

They awoke him. The Chief Chamberlain could not believe what he heard. He got out of bed, incredulous at the information, and dressed. He said little, his thoughts trying to assess the situation and its consequences. Finally he stormed out, the House Manager trailing him.

They passed through the languid palms and white pillars of the courtyard toward the Lord's House.

"Will you tell the Master, Sir?" pled the House Manager.

"You goddmaned fool!" said the Chief Chamberlain, turning on him. "You couldn't keep watch for the night and make sure he didn't slip away?"

"We monitored his activities all night…Sir. He..he.." said the House Manager. "She, she…"

"I don't care…*who* she is!" barked the Chief Chamberlain. "But *he* is the *Prince* you… idiot!"

The Chamberlain paused and rested his hand on the balustrade to steady his breathing, he had to come to terms with the matter himself. He looked at the House Manager "Who *he* makes love to…. is critical to the reputation of the *entire* establishment. Don't you understand?"

"Oh No, no, no. Wait! She comes…She is of the tribes of the Abraham…" began the House Manager

"I don't give a goodgoddamne *who* she is. If she's fertile, our bloodline has been tarnished with….with…"

"Perhaps we negotiate a good marriage then…?"scrambled the Head Manager, his words a stammering mix of thoughts.

The El Haikim, stewart over the Houshold came to a sudden halt and looked at him. *"Marriage…?"*

His brow deepened and his breath came hard and full of fury. "Are you dreaming? *Marriage?* The minute the bitch let him touch her she signed our death warrants! *All of us!* You understand that?"

He could not fathom this turn of events, he felt terror. The city-king's son, the *Prince!*

What to tell all the wailing women at the next feast? *They* would not stop! For this they lived, and died. Fertility was the progeny of the tribe!

He strode, his robes thrashing at his legs. What to the tell the other attending Lords and Princes Leaders sitting at the City Gates, those whose accounts… He felt suddenly as if the breath of God had whispered in the wind and the world had suddenly been brought to a standstill. It was the hot sand air winds blowing, of course. And the gold trimmed curtains flailed at the colonnade bays. The Chamberlain shuddered, then pressed on.

"Maybe…err…Maybe we can *salvage* the situation. A little *diplomacy*….?" persisted the Manager. "Wait, m'Lord…I plead with you, please! If they are people of skill and trade, that might be not such a bad thing?..An alliance?"

"Get out of my way, you scum! If you had done your job of chaperoning the Royal Prince instead of letting them *play*…You don't understand."

"Our people will understand, Sir…If she is fruitful then…"

"*Our people?*...Our people?" He stopped. "No. You imbecile. It's not *our* people. It's about *her people*! The minute he laid eyes on her, *we are all dead*!"

 He walked on in order to breath and clear his thoughts.

"You don't know those people of the One God…The people of Abraham. *They,* they are devout! They are honorable in their accounting! *They* have trade Agreements and networks to be upheld…*everywhere!* They are trusted as moral, their signet seal is creditworthy in all places of the highest transaction!" Despite of the breeze from the garden porches and waterfalls, he could feel the sweat trickle down his back.

No! The more he thought about it, the more he felt outrage. He grabbed the House Manager by the shoulders and shook "You imbecile! You and your lewd minds, playing gambling bowles all night! *You could not keep Watch by night?*" he spat.

The danger was obvious, a cultural breach of the worse kind had been committed. And with devastating ramifications. One thing the Lord Chamberlin knew: You don't make important trade alliances with other states through a…a… *harlot!*

The Chamberlain was right. It was a scandal, compromising the very progeny of Jacob, direct descendant of Abraham to whom God promised a pure people of his own…

Later, as Jacob thought about it, the consequences of that sexual encounter where horrific. Her brothers took umbrage. They had killed the entire tribe to avenge Dinah's reputation. And the bloodshed was more than Jacob himself could fathom in the end: They ransacked and burned all, razing the city and leaving no ramparts, killing all that lived and defacing their culture, burying all their treasure and leaving no stone unturned.

So now, in the aftermath of the city-state slaughter and diplomatic disaster caused by Dinah, Leah's daughter, Jacob's entire household camp had to move.

Again!

He had pleaded with them, her brothers, to show forbearance! Dinah's sexuality and her act of with the city-king's son had caused them embarrassment and brought disgrace to their reputation as a people separate and apart from the locals, a tribe of Abraham.

Certainly, her act had been sinful. And for that there was recourse. But to go beyond that and kill all the sons of the city king and his court was without mercy and prideful…

No. They had shown none. They had killed the entire household. And worse of all, they had blemished the name and reputation of Jacob in ways worse than any infraction by their sister. They had compromised, in their intolerant and vengeful act, the security and survival of the entire tribe…

Still, it was for the best, decided Jacob.

The decision was made to move to Bethel. But there was much clean up to do first. There had been much trade. And they should purge themselves of all secular acts and sin of local integration that might displease the God of Abraham.

Jacob asked his household to bring forward all locally purchased items, like memorabilia; relics, trinkets, jewelry, icons and items of recent purchase. Anything they had brought into their household was to be deposited with him before he departed Sechem.

It took days. God had blessed him richly. He was a wealthy man with a prodigious household. Most trinkets would be valuable.

Most of all, at least his soul was at peace. Not only had he remained faithful to the Word of God as a tribe of Israel, but he was now to reconciled with his brother Essau.

This he would do, if he was to be faithful to his God in earnest.

* * *

Chapter 8

College Park, Md.

The image on the screen was an ancient censer. It was beautiful, redolent with the homage of an ancient people who worshipped the God of Moses, and if fairly glowed.

The houselights came up on an Auditorium filled to capacity. The lecture came to a close and Diane Thompson switched off the overhead digital screen. Her class in Ancient Studies with its magical images of archaic artifacts still held them in wonder, and her students stretched and yawned in a daze.

Diane unfolded a map the size of a poster. "For those of you coming on the summer archaeological Dig…" she said "This will be your location and altitude: This is the chart that shows the road system. So, come to my office if you have an questions, please!"

Several came up to talk with her.

"We may find nothing at all, but it will be a wonderful experience for us all…" she was saying "*These* are types of finds we should look for. Mostly, brass… perhaps some beaten gold; remnants and trinkets of various shapes, possibly household utensils, icons, or even dress-ornamentation, though It's highly unlikely given the circumstances of a wilderness existence. But mainly, *this* is a sample of what we are looking for…." She held it up. "This was found at a nearby dig, some three years ago…"

That evening Diane Thompson got a call from Amanda Wells.

 "Hi Amanda!" she said enthusiastically.

"Dora! How exciting…"

"Yes. I know, I can't wait! It's the chance of a lifetime, and the university had to pull a few political strings to achieve the dig.

But it's worth it, an almost new uncovered site for archaeological dig, and I am the first to go with my class!"

"How wonderful for you! I can't say I envy you in that heat, and at that altitude…"

"True. But hey, if the children of Israel managed, then so must we!"

"You have all your support systems in place?"

"I do. Thank you for asking. Yes. We're all set. I've even laid on some extra security by the host country, I'm told. But I wanted to say Goodbye before I leave in the morning. And I especially wanted to thank you for the Recommendation you gave me to receive the grant!"

"You're most welcome!" said Amanda. "I can think of no one more deserving than you. Your work is wonderful, Dora - *always* a pleasure to read up on your findings…They add richly to the perceived wisdom of scholarship."

Dora chuckled.

"Look, you'll have our number here? Trevor and I are in the UK should you need anything. Or, if anything unexpected arises… Remember, keep you phone batteries charged for communications to your Basecamp managers, right?"

"Right!"

"And your daily log, right?"

"Right!"

"Right!"

They laughed at the check list drill.

"I can't wait to read your published findings…" said Amanda

"It's a wilderness experience, and the students love that!" explained Dora "The Rebellion of Korah is what I seek to find revelations on. So, even if we find nothing, it'll be meaningful to them. Further, it's the procedure of things above all else, I want them to see. That's at the heart of the matter…"

Later that evening, with an after-dinner cup of coffee in hand, they sat in Trevor's study. Usually, they enjoyed cool breezes from the garden when the veranda doors were open, but tonight it was drizzling, and Trevor was absorbed in a report he was reading at his lounge chair beside the bookcase.

Amanda told Trevor she'd had a call from Diane.

He looked up and smiled. "Oh? Where is the dig?" he asked.

" 'Ain Kadis, Kadesh Barnea located about 130 miles north of Sinai. Mount Paran, when defined by Palmer as the Desert of the Exodus, is where the Rebellion of Korah took place."

"Umm" he said, sipping his coffee.

Amanda punched in for more information on the laptop computer. Diane, Dora or Dana Thompson as she was sometimes called, was a good friend.

"University of Chicago…The Elmers Trust Fund"

 "Umm" he looked up. "Isn't it the same Grant Foundation that's sponsoring our daughter's summer Intern project?"

Amanda laughed. "The same! We are a fortunate to have a nation that offers scholarships and grants for those interested in exploration…"

"Umm" he said from behind his report.

"From the polar cap to the deserts!" she asserted.

Trevor did not respond.

Later that night, Amanda took the time to examine the parameters of Dora's dig online at the University website.

It was an archaeological excavation scheduled for a place known in antiquity and in Biblical texts.

Ideal for those interested in ancient studies, she thought: What an opportunity to approach a site venerated in old and sacred scriptures.

There, according to the historical account, the Children of Israel had camped during their epic journey across the wilderness, and having sinned against God, they were reprimanded in what was known as the Rebellion of Korah.

 She read the background information.

> *"Then Moses rose …saying, 'Depart now from the tents of these wicked men! Touch nothing of theirs, lest you be consumed in all their sins…." And Moses said: "… if the*

Amanda shuddered and pushed back from the screen.

No such thing had been heard of in the modern world of science, she knew.

* * *

Chapter 9

The beach was perfect.

It was September, and the mid-Atlantic region of the East Coast of North America was still steaming hot. The summer air was humid and unrelenting. It suited Amanda fine, trowel in hand and wearing a large Tully canvas hat that fluttered in the sea breeze.

Not that gardening was a prerequisite for a beach home, exactly. But flowers blossomed everywhere people tended to them, and Amanda was always one of those people.

She and Trevor owned a wide sun-bleached home on Bethany Beach, and she could see the ocean from almost every window on each of the three platforms of the sturdy shingled structure. It had seen a few storms over the years, but sited back from the surf and behind an acre of sand dunes and tidal grasses, the old cottage had survived many a tale of terror from the sea.

In the morning Amanda prepared her morning brew of coffee and toast, then ran for half an hour, waving and grinning at families and students that swarmed the community beaches in the summertime.

It was a festive time of the year; inclusive for all visitors and always full of excitement.

Carrying beach towels, deck chairs, fishing rods and toys for the pilgrimage to the roaring surf just over the dune, parents came with children squealing in merriment as they raced up the guided beach ramp to observed a spectacular Atlantic ocean.

The shoreline consisted of miles of white sandy beaches.

If icy, thunderous waves surged onto the beach as children shrieked with joy. It was a windy combination of salt-air and umbrellas propped up like multi-colored mushrooms becoming the only shelter against a blazing sun and unremitting heat. Later in the day when the heat abated, tiny sandpipers gave chase to lacy white ocean-froth back and forth, delivering sand crabs, sea shells and tiny crustaceans…

Amanda smiled. The sea had a way of mitigating all earthly problems, it seemed. Whatever inhibitions cloyed to city dwellers were here ground to sand and sea.

Every season was a wonder; every family enjoying the summer treks to the ocean year after year. Sometimes, Trevor and Amanda leased out their beach cottage. She and Trevor had enjoyed their beach summers as the children grew up. But more recently, it had remained unoccupied, if managed by a Security service.

Their home was situated in one of the most private wooded compounds of the beach. Over the years, it had grown a stand of pine trees and oaks that spread shade and over their zone, even if it had fallen into less usage.

Occasionally, the management Firm arranged for renting out parts of the house for weekend stays and occasional friends. It was a limited arrangement, but as Amanda said, such an arrangement helped with maintenance and security upkeep. Thus, rather than sell it, it had been there and available for them all since when they needed a break from Washington DC.

Amanda had asked to have the place opened up rather than return to Washington for her temporary stay in the United States.

It was a choice she made because it was summertime, and because of Trevor's decision to remain behind in the UK - their days together in Washington as diplomats long behind them.

Further, the city as a nation's capital would be probably vacated by most of their acquaintances during the hot months.

More importantly, it was for Sandra. Earlier in the year Sandra had expressed an interest in planning to go to the beach during the semester break with friends. Certainly, she knew the place well enough; she had been taken there as a child for summer weekends by her parents Trevor and Amanda when they lived in Washington DC.

Above all, it was one of Amanda favorite places. She was somewhat excited, even if saying goodbye for trips was never easy.

Trevor, it had been decided, needed to remain in Scotland. Even in retirement, he was preoccupied with affairs in London as an Advisor. Especially now, he explained, if not fully amplifying the reason: He would join her later on, he said - for some summer sailing.

Of that she was delighted.

Amanda completed her gardening and finished her ice tea drink. She glanced up their entrance road where she could get a brief view of the street - sandy and gritty as it was with perambulating pedestrians.

This was an older beach community, and many young families today still owned homes bought by earlier generations in their family. It was a favorite resort before the war. Little hand changed it.

Some homes from the 1950s were still modest beach-huts with additions holding notions of faraway romance and adventure. But most had been updated by storm and weather safety requirements, often built on stilts and breakwaters.

Yet, as an augmented construction industry evolved into lavish seaside homes sited amongst landscaped sandy pine trees and ferns – even with insurance policies, there was little that could withstand storms sometimes known in two days to reshape the sandy coastline of this continent. If a violent hurricane made landfall, it could clear out every stick erected for miles, as it had done to the coast of New Jersey positioned between the Mid-Atlantic and the North Eastern United States.

From her Look-Out at the top deck of her beach house, Amanda could observe the force of nature take its aim and direction. None, as far as she could recall, had come inland directly.

She often wondered at the role of the gulf stream. It was that mysterious serpentine swathe of tropical water that caressed the east coast of America barely fifty miles offshore, bringing with it blue seas and tropic species whose strange remains often washed up on the beaches for beachcombers.

Yet an awareness to sudden change prevailed, it came with the territory so to speak, to watch for the weather - and for others, like fellow sojourners sharing an island, a coastal-state modern weather response systems for early alert warnings and evacuation routes.

As she looked out, Amanda knew of early accounts of sailing shipwrecks just offshore. This shoreline had been the blight of colonial settlers trying to find refuge and safe landings on the new world.

Amanda showered and settled to her laptop in a sun-flooded, cool room situated at the upper floor deck where she kept her office.

From years before, it was their "watchtower. She and Trevor would watch over children playing outside on their grounds. And many a howling cry had brought both parents tearing down to kiss a bruised bump delivered by a sibling's beach toy... From these windows were vistas of blue sea and white sands in all directions. Equally so the night storms, such that they used the upper deck as a viewing gallery, Trevor often said, to herald the unfurling of clouds as they scudded off the coastal shore.

 His lighthouse, Amanda laughed.

Yet from the start, she and Trevor had favored the room to keep up with the requirements of their various careers while on vacation: It was a safe place for documents under lock and key.

Today, it held every precaution and security measure in place for Internet access and peer-to-peer international-telecommunications. It was off limits to house guests; friends and visitors who came to the summer house. And it was private - up its own flight of stairs carved from bright teak and varnished pine treads. Mainly, Amanda found it a quiet place to work.

And she loved her early mornings: At that time of the day, few joggers would be about. Except for beach walkers who walked the beach early in the morning, it was deserted, and she loved to watch the beach walkers. They came out just after sunrise to watch the mists roll off the coast leaving litter along the shoreline from thunderous waves delivered of a night full of marine treasure. For them, it was a magical wonderland of surprises, and they would collect and inspect the morning beach - a gleaming mother of pearl here; a wet conch there, a string of seaweed …

Still, the area had a seasonal crowd of tourists and visitors who swarmed the area. There was much to manage by the local municipalities.

Bethany beach had a Coast Guard Safety station. Less than 50 miles away was a major east coast Military installation known universally as Dover Air Force Base, used chiefly by the US Airforce for troop deployment overseas. Below them at Chincoteake Island was a NASA launch site for rockets. Otherwise, there was little traffic and satellite interference for the security access systems.

In the months that followed, Amanda would look back on this moment. She would be asked, in a debriefing in Washington, about what happened that day.

She met him on the steps to the beach, she said. That is, the access pathway at the top of her street that led to the beach between the houses.

He was just hanging out, she said, watching the waves with a cup of coffee in his hand, McDonalds.

At that hour of the tourists' day, the combination of a night moon fading into the vast expanse of an early blue sky made for a natural beauty that left few unmoved.

And that's what he was looking at, he said.

She often said Good Morning. It was the way of people in the beach community.

He was still there on her return from her morning jog. She went into her home, refreshed herself and put on the coffee pot.

He was still there, she observed, when she emerged topside on her deck with a coffee in hand.

He waved.

She waved.

Clearly, he was staying at the beach for the week. As was customary for this time of the year, he was in all probability a paying houseguest at a nearby cottage.

On the third morning, she lifted her mug and called out to him.

"Care for a cup of coffee?"

He waved back.

She brought it down.

The next day when he appeared, she stayed to talk. He was a student, he said.

Her cell phone was ringing.

"Hello?"

It was Bill Arguetta, a friend of the family from their Washington days: Could she join them for the weekend? He wanted to talk with her, and they were having a sailing regatta in Annapolis. He and Mary were having a house full of guests…

Amanda agreed to visit them for the weekend, sure. She had strolled off and when she looked back, the student had gone.

Amanda sat on her porch that evening sipping a glass of wine.

The sun was behind her, a soft pink glow reaching for thin clouds closing on a darkening sea. The day was spent, and yet it seemed unreal that the sun was behind her, setting in the West!

Only two months ago, she was facing it from the East, from the other side of the Atlantic where the landscape of Scotland was a far cry from the landscape of the American colonies, as they said.

The affairs of the last two months had taken an unbelievable track. How could life play such tricks, she wondered.

How had everything happened so fast? What was she doing here?

She would call and thank Eileen for having her for the weekend…

* * *

Chapter 10

The gold that was wrapped in leather pouches was also coated in chainmail - as if that helped the effect of preservation, thought Ivanovich.

Fortunately, the desert air was without humidity and that went a long way to delay deterioration of ancient artifacts. That much, the study of Egyptology had taught him…

Jesus!

In any event, the deal was done; the item delivered, and the task done…done…done. Thank God!

It had taken no less than six months to arrange: He had positioned himself as a tourist in *Elat*. From Israel, he had crossed the border into Saudi Arabia and then drove the rest of the way himself. Easy.

But he took no chances.

Dressed in the robes of the fellaheen of Cairo, he met with herdsmen at the local village…

Now that he had possession of the items as per the university grant specifications, he could return home. He was to deliver the items to the Director at the Museum of Chicago, and if there was any mercy left in heaven, he would be goddamnwelldone with his Dissertation presentation!

Shit! It had taken *too* many years of his life to get this Phd. And now he was finished.

He was packing the last of the wooden crates into the Jeep, straw and string still peeping through the seals, and he counted all the gold and treasure from the archaeological site. He was sitting on a gold mine of wealth.

It was a long day of driving, the crates jamming together and squealing in protest over every dirt road bump and rock the Jeep negotiated.

He had decided to get on with the process with some haste. Academic accolades could come later. Get home fast…So fast in fact, that he had left for the trip inadequately prepared. He hadn't anticipated a full mountain traverse over such a barren stretch of the Arabian landscape.

Jees - no wonder the Children of Israel were trapped in the wilderness for forty years…

No kidding!

He was fatigued, if amused. Actually, he felt very pleased with himself. Even if had lost 30 lbs; aged by ten years in appearance, and wanted to get the hell as far away from this godforsaken world as he could…

It was the tribesmen who had told him.

Everyone at the dig had been slaughtered. They wanted to bury the dead, they said, but they decided to tell the police about instead.

A very Western thing to do, they told him…Normally, they would have just buried the dead and left with the loot!

He asked about the authorities.

Yes, they said. They came. They told of everything…

But as Ivanovich discovered, what the police did *not* know was that they had already gathered most of the artifacts and placed them all in a locked bunker not far from the excavation...

Not that there was much, the tribesmen insisted. Two days before the incident, a lorry truck had pulled into the camp and taken out much more. The Director of the archaeological excavation, a woman, was the first to die…

So, they took the remainder of the loot, well most of it, as Ivanovich understood.

They would resell it on the open market, they said. But having informed the police, they were fingerprinted - another Western procedure!

He could have the loot, they told him. They had family taken in as Refugees by Turkey and Greece, they said. It would be not good for them…

They wanted to be clean of such matters, without implication of any kind…So yes, he could take it.

Besides, it was poisonous material, they said.

He gave them all his grant money. Only one account was left with his name on it, and a credit card could get him home now. And he paid them two thousand dollars.

They left shortly thereafter. Before leaving, as an afterthought, he asked a question. Who had killed the party at the Dig?

They shrugged, and drove away.

The engine sputtered. He stopped.

He opened the hood and led the steam clear. The distributor cap had worked free of the housing unit from the jostling and rough road. He pulled it out, cleaned off some grime, and refastened it securely. He checked the water in the radiator, and pushed down all the hoses and clamps, then slammed shut the hood.

The sun was just above setting, and the sky was cloudless. It was still, and but for a few pebbles, tossed by shifting sand in the wind, there was no sound for miles. No clouds. No birds. Just hot wind.

He checked the tires, walked about the entire car, relieved himself and checked the cargo and his baggage. He pulled a fresh shirt from his duffle, doused water on his white T shire which he had pulled off. He added a tab of soap from a diluted squeeze bottle and gave himself a refreshing sponge down. He washed his face in the moist toweling, his head, neck, shoulders and down to his waist. Then he pulled on his fresh T shirt and put away his gear. He topped the tank with gas from a canister strapped to the rear bumper tow-crib.

He returned to the driver's seat, and with a long swig of water from a water-bottle, started the ignition which ignited instantly, and he proceeded. Roadside sand, now turning into a reddish brown in the setting sun, whished loosely just off the hard-pack surface of the road.

He drove, knowing that he could only log distance on the map since there were no other roads to take. He was riding the ridge of a mountain basically. And distance was distance. That's all he drove for, his body jostling from side to side in endless rocking...

As the sun approached the horizon, the angle of declination was getting low, and his thoughts strayed.

He drifted into an almost somnolent state of mind, pondering this, that and the rest of his epic journey. Yes, it was epic. But he knew he could hardly call it that. They would laugh at him. Yet, what did he have in the back of the Jeep?

He drank more water.

Well, it wasn't exactly the *King Tut* collection of treasure, but coming from Sechem, it would at least get him the final approvals he needed to receive his doctorate degree diploma.

He hit the steering column. *Finally!*

The sun was almost gone, giving the desert mountain a reddish rawness, and already the temperatures were dropping.

Deserted. Silent. Nothing on the horizon…for as far as the eye could see. It might be days, maybe weeks before anyone travelled this lonely stretch of the desert mountains, he knew.

He debated whether to pitch a small tent for the night. Then he would leave at first light. Or, he would press on down the road that was not much more than a hard-pack stretch, flanked by occasional human-painted white boulders, milestones, along which modern passage had taken place for the last century or two.

 The headlights worked fine.

He pressed on. Night driving was no more tedious than day time driving, other than the wind. It sang, almost harmoniously in the night breeze, like a languorous soft beckoning as desert wind rearranged the dunes.

What was it E.L. Doctorow said, *writing a novel is like driving a car at night. You never see further than your headlights, but you can make the whole trip that way.*

So, follow the headlights!

The sooner he got off this mountain and into the Plains the better he'd be, he decided.

Followed by a flight back with some carry-on luggage; a stiff on-board whiskey soda, and he'd be in Canada. From there, he'd catch his last leg to O'Hare Airport at Chicago…

His headlights began jaggedly piercing the dark for only hard biting mouthfuls of hardpan road, he had a flat tire.

He let out a stream of invective that fell into silence.

He was tired, and he regretted not having chosen to camp. Now he had to change the goddamned tire in the dark.

He got out.

Yes it was black — a dark blackness of silk and scarlet shadow off dry hot sand, but what the hell… The road was the same.

At least there was roadside milestones placed at intermittent places to mark the perimeter of the road, even if its slopes sometimes vanished down hills of sand that shifted and stormed about in the warm air of the desert.

Clearly, he had been approaching the calmer slopes, closer to the plains. By dawn he might be seeing civilization. That, he realized was what deterred him from taking his rest at sunset. Instead, he had decided to press on.

Besides, life was good. He had the artifacts in the rear of the Jeep. Especially that ancient statue, perhaps a deity of some kind worshipped by a pagan tribe. He would procure it for the museum. Not that it amounted to much in the world of the sacred, but it was contemporaneous with his research. *That* was sufficient to satisfy his Academic Advisors to decide on the acceptance of his dissertation, he knew it...

It had buoyed his spirits, if a little too much perhaps. He should have rested. He felt tired now.

The Jeep was older, and easy enough to fix. Out came the spare, the jack and the lift. His flashlight was not the greatest. God knows he had changed enough tires on diesel trucks working in military Reserve Units!

The wind was softly blowing sand about. It got into every nook and cranny of the lug nuts as he pried them free, one, two, three...

He placed the jack under the rear axil and started to hoist up on the ratchets. The old wheel rim with the deflated tire lifted gently of the ground. He braced his footing to pull it off the wheel housing and replace it with the new tire. The jack collapsed in a softening of its footing.

Godamit…Godamit!

Again he mounted the jack. This time two notches higher, for sure, with a good purchase on a base.

Again it failed. The jack was slipping because of weight distribution as the front end of the jeep dipped: If the bow-end of the vehicle could be kept steady and level with the ground - then he could pump down on the jack and the rear *should* hold steady…

The sweat, which should have coated his skin with moisture was quickly vaporized in the hot air. He sat on his haunches catching his breath and decided to angle the Jeep so as to use front ropes as pulleys to prevent counter-rising against his efforts…

He re-fasted one or two easy lug nuts, backed the Jeep sideways; dismounted to shift the crates in the cargo and remove the statue which he set on the ground beside the Jeep.

Satisfied, he walked forward to the front of the vehicle, pulled on the front-end towing gear and threaded the hawser through a crude grip embedded in the roadside milestone and he winched it in.

That should keep the front-end from lifting, at least!

The rope tightened and the Jeep held. Even if the sand under the tire was slipping and causing the Jeep axil to dig in a few inches. But it worked, and he replaced the tire.

Now he could release the front tension and pop the Jeep back on its four wheels to reposition on the road.

 He walked forward and sat in the driver's seat, turned on the ignition, released the brake and inched forward to slacken the tension on the front rope.

It snapped suddenly, lurching the jeep into a small bounce off its rear tires, and, sending it backwards into a fall off the side of the road, rolled and overturned gently down the slope to settle upright with its headlights still on.

Under the safety of his roll-bars, Ivanovich rolled with the Jeep, letting out a shout. The Jeep had rolled off the side of the road!

He noticed no damage to the forward section of the hood over the engine, not even a crack on the windshield. All looked normal.

All he had to do was rev the Jeep back up the embankment and repurchase traction on the road. He was adjusting the four-wheel-drive gears when he realized the jeep was sinking.

He flung open the door, and was about to leap out when the Jeep tilted and the sand seemed to swamp him like water, swallowing the whole vehicle…

* * *

Chapter 11

Paris, France

The Torraine Gallery was a recognized House of Antiquities.

 At L'Avenue des Artes, the gold embossed plaque above wrought iron and beveled glass doors marked the entrance to a granite building of Beaux Arts architecture.

The Gallery Exhibition had been a great success. For three days the media had crowded the streets nearby as playful flags added excitement to the tree-lined Art district. There had been official openings and showings of the Auction; evening gala celebrations, a fancy-dress ball, two all-day concerts on the Green attended by tourists, artists, strolling pedestrians and students, even all-night gatherings at the local Parisian cafés delivering expressos, music and alcohol.

Jacques De Torraine was a wealthy man in France. His had connections in every city of every culture. He sponsored events with precise focus to advance his reputation, and it paid off. He was known as the leading entity in Europe for valuables. Recently he had been approached by a large commodities' corporation for his affiliation, but he had turned them down. Others too, including those with gold mining interests; DeBeers and traders of diamonds -even oil drillers from the larger drilling companies. No, he always said. He was interested in artwork that could shape new markets and make new consumers! It was a currency in humanity, he once told Amanda Wells.

For all the stories, incidents and events associated with his trade, there were few people he trusted. One or two had become personal friends, that is, only because of their graciousness.

Amanda Wells and her husband were considered friends. Not because it had been easy to know them. On the contrary, they had induced great stress and some painful restitution for criminal activities in his earlier years. But they had been courteous and honorable. Something he valued. Thus, even if it cost him some political capital over the years, he had remained close to those he could trust only.

He picked up his cell to talk to Amanda.

They were retired in Scotland, he knew. For this, he would take a trip. He was always welcome in their home, and he could count on their hospitality for a week, such was the size of their estate and interests…It was always a pleasure. In fact, they were his family to him.

This, therefore, worried him.

Sandra their daughter was under the same sponsorship program as that of an archaeological dig that had recently come to his attention, and both were from the University of Chicago.

The archaeological dig in question was unusual. Loot coming out of Sechem was circulating in Europe. And the haul was enormous. Even beyond the trove found by Heinrich Schliemann who unearthed Priam's Treasure in 1876 at Hissarlik – a site from the Illiad's City of ancient Troy.

This discovery was of the same caliber. But there was something troubling, and he was alarmed.

The laws of private ownership of artefacts were long and complicated. Essentially, while costs did underlie every find, the ownership of an artefact belonged to the local sovereign state of the land on which it was found.

Selling, marketing, fundraising and investing in antiquities had its legitimate place in the marketplace, most often related to museum acquisitions. But in this case, a strange anomaly was evident from the sponsorship of the dig. Somehow, it was diverting all ownership to a corporate underwriter which not only added value in financial terms, but offered huge tax deductibility. Who was behind this?

History was rife with undocumented finds and wealth diggers. But here was an accounting of artefacts where almost everything was described in ancient texts. Yet most of it was going undocumented on the market by a private seller.

Worse. Such actions were not only socially irresponsible but illegal. Jacques was an experienced dealer. He knew. For one thing, he recognized some the names of the brokers associated with the treasure. They had not the best of credentials. Either way, it was a dangerous circle in which to involve Amanda's family. He would warn them…

Besides, he was curious. Who was engaging in this kind of work? Who had the kind of money needed to float this kind of loot, then to dig it up, transport it, and redirect it into the market. There must have been considerable money to competed with scholarly institutions; state bidders and museums. Who was managing this? Where did the money come from?

Was it European? American? Even if Jacques felt a twinge of envy, it was unusual that he had not been briefed on this intelligence. For some reasons, it was occurring in very quiet ways. Especially with its connections to the Soviet Provinces, he knew.

Yes, he decided. It was time to warn Amanda and Trevor about Sandra's sponsorship.

"Yes…Hello Amanda?" he said. He leaned back into his office chair, the sound of that voice of hers brought back memories. He smiled. "How nice it is to talk with you my dear! How are you?"

"Yes, yes" he said finally. "I would be delighted to accept your kind invitation to come to Scotland. There is something I want to discuss with you and Trevor…"

* * *

Chapter 12

Chicago, IL

Bill Sanders was young for a college professor. Especially for an institution as world-renown as the University of Chicago. He was not particularly demonstrative. Yet his disposition suited his job.

He'd been a professor for three years, and his success had been visible from the beginning: His student following was large; his scholarship recognized and his publications prolific. But like many in the academic world, it was easy to get lost in the popularity of daily business when teaching. Dozens of meetings, notes, reminders and requests pending; always a full box of emails; administrative decisions for class assignments and papers to grade; academic advising duties and departmental staff events. There were days when he could entirely forget a promise or an obligation, and they loved him regardless any oversight. He was tall, playful and popular.

Today he sat quietly, looking down at the page in his hand.

It was a message from Amanda Wells, once his professor in London! She had steered him into a profession of richness that he could never have imagined possible. For one thing, where else could you live in the past and bring it to life for modern teaching? Because of her, he loved his work...

But a shadow crossed his face. This was no social call. She wanted to talk to him about his student Ivanovich, he knew.

He looked up. Two students buzzed for him. Instead, he got up and locked the door.

The Department of Justice had already talked with him. He said he knew nothing. And to a large degree that was true. But at the same time, it *felt* untrue.

Ivanovich was *this* close to completing his Dissertation – he himself one of the three Advisors on the boy's Academic Advising Committee.

The other two, God knows, had strung him out rather than endorse his dissertation. They used petty demands really, mainly for their own recognition in the work of the student if not holding him back with a touch of professional envy.

But the boy had written copious notes, and while the final chapter was to be written upon his return with a relic from the El-Paran, the leads, innuendoes and suggestions were intriguing…

His assertions would shake up conventional scholarship about the ancient world, in fact. How could Ivanovich have just *disappeared?* Then again, that area was full of mystery…

And what of the artifact?

That was the real question.

Amanda Wells would do well to get to the bottom of it. True, she was cognizant of the expedition, just as she was with the second party that disappeared, Dora Thompson. But this was dangerous business, he felt sure.

What was going on, he wondered. Never would he admit it, but something about this was off. This was his student!

He gazed out the window, tapping the message against his thumb.

How he would have enjoyed talking to Amanda again! No, he decided. He would not. No! This was not a good time.

He tossed the message.

Instead, he texted Ali Enders.

"You have your goods. Deliver the money!"

* * *

Chapter 13

Dinner was delicious.

They caught up with news, family and the years of remembrances shared between them. The conversation turned inevitably to the topic that brought Jacques to Scotland.

"What concerns me, " said Jacques "is the frequency of these artifacts surfacing in Europe. I have no idea where else they are trading... In Spain, they are found in catalogues, with collectors sending emails, and with shops advertising their wares for tourists!"

"And you are sure they come from the same site?" asked Trevor.

"Certain. It's consistent with the biblical stories that buried all iconography of the classical period."

"So, it's a trove of the same kind?" asked Amanda.

"Yes. Definitely."

"What are we seeing here?"

"We are seeing either a mass theft or an archaeological discovery. Because it lacks official provenance, these items are devalued on the markets for resale."

"To say nothing of the ethical issues or the cultural significance it poses to Western Civilization!" said Trevor.

"*Precisement!*" said Jacques.

Amanda smiled. She knew of Jacque's flirtations with the less-than-ethical market valuations. It had caused them all some grief. But in the end, Jacques was a solid citizen. And now a good friend.

"Worse..." continued Jacques. "In almost all the documentation, the trail of provenance goes cold with the death of the finder; the source diggers, the *originators* of the treasure!"

He looked at Amanda sadly. "I am so very sorry…I heard of your colleague"

Amanda lowered her eyes. Certainly, Dana Thompson had been her friend.

"Has the government made any suggestion of foul play?" asked Trevor

"*Non*!"

"It sounds like the ownership to the treasure is also the perpetrator to the malfeasance…"

"Yes. I believe it is a smoke screen. It hides something deeper. By dispersing the objects into such a scatting for resale, it keeps from revealing any real items of value."

"Meaning?"

"Well, it's a theory I have. In my experience, usually when little items circulate, its only hiding something more eventful."

They finished their dinner and moved into the next room.

"What is the archaeological dig ascribed to?" asked Trevor.

"Sechem. It is related to the site of the summer dig conducted by Professor Dana Thompson, Amanda's colleague. Hers was nearby to another site that we know was robbed. And I assume that she too was the victim of the same perpetrators… "We don't know that…" interrupted Amanda. "There is an Inquiry as to her cause of death. But it's still uncertain…" she said, her eyes full of concern, close to tears.

Jacques and Trevor looked at each other. They knew better.

Amanda wiped away at her face and then looked up. "No. I'm fine!" she said "We must hold it together if we are to be any use. Carry on Jacques. The dig site. Please amply on any information."

Trevor got up and refreshed the drinks.

"Yes. Jacques…" he said, handing him a scotch. "You were saying that both sites were sponsored by the University of Chicago. By the same Foundation that also sponsored the Arctic expedition this summer?" Trevor sat down.

"Yes. Sechem is the site of enquiry. It is known by the story of Jacob when he had to leave Bethel. Before doing so, in an act of purity and obedience to God, Jacob asks his family to bring forward all treasure from local pagan cultures - a sort of cleansing redemption from their sinful behavior.

It is the result of what happened with Dinah, the ravishing beauty of Rachael's daughter, who slept with a local prince. Dinah's brothers murdered his tribe for it, and the incident caused trouble for the people of Israel and for Jacob whose mandate was to remain pure and stay separate from others.

So, as a token of their penance, they buried all their local merchandized possessions. All memorabilia from those parts of the ancient world, local relics, trinkets, jewelry, icons and items of trade…"

Amanda was looking at him intently. She knew him to be sincere, and she knew he was moved by this moment.

Jacques sipped his drink then sat back.

"Yes" he said quietly "If it is true, and if this is the discovery, then we are looking at this biblical account." He paused, his thoughts far away. Then he looked up, his professional voice returned.

"A mismatch of items may have been found: Jacob, son of Abraham was on his way to reconcile himself with his brother Essau. He wanted God's forgiveness for his earlier duplicity with Essau. Yet he was by now a man of trade and of some wealth. They had accumulated much. And yes, it was all buried in one place!"

Amanda sat up, a deep sigh of air whistled through mouth.

"My God!" said Trevor.

Jacques nodded. "Yes."

"So…To plunder this site" said Amanda "is…"

"an affront to the sacred biblical text of the human lineage of Abraham, Hebrew children of God…"

"And to the moral significance of all that we hold sacred today …" added Amanda. Now she understood Dana Thompson's interest. Part of her training was in theology.

The room was quiet and the night advancing as the three of them contemplated the horrors visited upon such a site by perpetrators.

Trevor put down his glass.
"It may be politically motivated…" he said "given the
conflict and military landscape of the Middle East."
"Possibly" said Jacques.

"But that's not necessarily the way of Islam. By nature, they
are a peace-loving people!" insisted Amanda.

"That may be true. But in this conflict, radicalism can be a
destructive force. Cultural iconography is something that may
be targeted for political purposes…" said Trevor.

"Of course! Cultural decimation is the root of territorial
conflict" said Amanda, standing up.

"We need some coffee" she said.

When she returned she found Jacques and Trevor talking.
Jacques was saying that he heard a rumor of another missing
student from University.

Trevor was interested.

"It's a desperate situation out there…" nodded Jacques.

They lapsed into somnolence, sipping brandy and coffee,
allowing their dinner of beef, garden vegetables and delicate
soufflés to satisfy their apprehensions. Together they sat in the
great drawing room of the historical home, long shadows from
veranda fenestration succumbing to the fire-glow of the
hearth, their thoughts penetrating all possibilities. Trevor
spoke next.

"You know…the nation of Israel sitting in the middle of all
this …they are the first to tell you that ancient relics, while
holding intrinsic value with cultural meaning, are not the
source of their faith…"

"it's so *frustrating*!" said Amanda. She got up and prepared to
retire for the night.

"So, who exactly sponsored this dig?" asked Trevor.

"An American Foundation apparently. We don't know who
exactly …But it is a trail of mishaps and lost people…"said
Jacques.

Amanda thought of Donna, her friend.

Sandra had nearly gone with her.

***

72

Chapter 14

If there was one thing Ali Enders understood was the power of suggestion. Such sentiment embedded in evocative words could touch the human heart. After that, he knew, he could reach for the human wallet. The speech that he was about to hand to his publicist was a knock-out. *No, a blow-out.*

He smiled and squared up his shoulders. Not a bad looking guy for his age; tall, slim with brown hair, and the prerequisite brown-rimmed spectacles of a thoughtful executive. He was everything a statesman should be, especially standing on a platform giving a speech for a fundraising event that cost over $500 each plate to attend…

First, he would express the circumstances of his legitimacy as the new candidate for the vacant seat in the Senate. Based on his record of civic functions and public involvement, he would show his *entitlement* to the post.

Not that it was an election, because the post was vacated by a serving Senator who died suddenly. Thus, he was to be selected by appointment to fill the vacant sea by the State Governor for the duration of that term of office.

Then, once he became an incumbent…

The electorate. His constituency! The notion thrilled him: To campaign for such a seat to represent a region as his constituents required a full political campaign, which, after the public had voted, might declare him the winner for a term in office in Congress.

But it was arduous, a tenuous ambition at best.

Still, speaking to a room full of sponsors never hurt to advance his brand name.

He would be mirthful. He would tell them that he deserved their support because he had participated in every chartable Marathon ever invented for New England - from the Irish patriots football team to the saving of souls half way around the world…

He walked to the window and saw rain. He hated jogging for stupid charitable Marathons! The goddamned weather never let up long enough to enjoy a few paltry weeks of sunshine up here…

He reached for another drink.

1638, he mused. No wonder Lord Baltimore petitioned the King to leave the colder climates and re-settle with a Princely proprietary title in Maryland…

The phone lit up.

It would be his publicist, from New York. *Always with the questions that woman!*

He knew what she wanted to know. *How did he plan to pay for all this?*

Well. He wasn't about to tell her: What he could tell her was that he had a plan. Of course he had a plan, he'd tell her. That's what strategists and politicians do - They make plans!

"Yes" he said, answering.

They hung up, and he returned to his drink.

His plan, if different, was a never-ending source of supply. That is, if he played his cards correctly. First things first, he thought.

First, he must get himself instated. Once on the payroll of the Federal Government, then the rest…was easy! So. Instead, redirect her to work on his political vision for his programs *after* his reinstatement. And there were many.

He would cite a re-arrangement of taxes. That always suited a voting constituency in your district: You re-designed the budget! Easy on that one.

Besides, he wouldn't be with them long…

Anyway, that's what he would assign to Barbara - that publicist whom he was told to commission by his Advisors at the Party Platform. Evidently, she had a reputation for successful publicity for all candidates.

Next, he had to deal with the questions of Defense. That that was no problem: Keep the work coming. As far as he was concerned, paying for all those military operations; fleets and tanks and privileges overseas was nothing more than a profit center. *Who goddamned cared about foreign policy anymore?*

He sighed.

Now, turn it all over to a dynamo…and he was home free! Then, bring on the family; the honors and the sociability of the candidate with a few well-chosen speeches, and voila: Party-playing at his Senate Appointment!

He drained his drink.

Only one small thought left him uncomfortable, but just long enough to get him up from his seat and walk to the window. More rain, if tapering off to the sweet scent of freshly wetted soil and marshy grass - the smells of his tender years, if only for a fleeting remembrance to honor and dignity – those things he once cherished as a college graduate. Even as a law student… That is, before he met Tom Brewster.

So. All that remained, was a conversation with Caroline his wife. Anything for saving face, and her reputation…Of course they could live together if they had to. She wanted that anyway.

He picked up the phone.

The thing is, Tom Brewster had it coming. All that pomposity and fancy language that he could lay on as a Senator from New Hampshire…

To hell with it, he decided.

Drowning was a common occurrence in these maritime parts. The accident could have happened to anyone! He felt little remorse or conscience. The goddamned fool always bragged about his boating anyway. Especially his fishing trips down to Florida in the winter…*Really?*

Now he could run for his Seat in the Senate.

Served him right!

* * *

Chapter 15

Ali Enders made it to Congress. In using the same kind of rhetoric that nourished an activist population looking for answers from Washington DC, the Governor offered him the Appointment: It suited the State to be disruptive, mainly because it achieved more in Federal dollars for state projects than most other states. Thus, as far as the Governor was concerned, Enders' ability to deliver a few key speeches with the promise to lead well and promote the interests of the State made him ideal for the post.

It felt good to be in the United States Senate. Washington was good to him. Certainly, he played the part as he walked the halls of Congress.

Ali Enders was a politician like no other. Some would say he had argued his way through law school - and through one marriage; now working on this second. He had argued his cases in court as a defense attorney with clear thinking; evocative logic and effective results. If there was one criticism that came often from his foes was that he was able to skin alive opponents…and to do so gracefully.

Thus, in Congress he was effective. But few had any delusions about him serving his constituents with any measure of sincerity. His interests were his own.

While Ali Enders announced that he could run again for office as the incumbent in the next election and challenge any opponent, he knew very well that he had no intention of running for election once the seat came up for re-election. His plans were to resign long before then, and place his hat in the ring for other, *higher*, office as a public elected official.

He liked those words. *Public Servant.* They made him sound like a man with a legacy or contribution to society in his service to his country. That, in addition to enriching himself, because to make money and remain unknown was no fun at all…

He paced his summer veranda, pulled a cigar that gave him the air of a victor, and he puffed. Even if he didn't like the job, he thought he had done a damned good job for the first Session in Congress.

Of course, his brand of politics easily achieved friends and followers. They came to him - except for public platforms and deliberate gatherings - mainly because they were attracted to his stature of confidence. But most people felt ill at ease with him.

There was something about him that was a little rancid. Still, he knew his laws.

"Nichomachean Ethics V.1 Gentlemen!"

The room hushed.

"Here is an excellent opportunity to bring reform to the tax laws of Bond and Equity holdings!" said Enders.

He spoke to a caucus of freshmen Senators, mostly lawyers, all of them newly elected from rural regions and recently ushered into the hallowed halls of Congress. The Speaker of the Senate had made them all welcome, even as they were guided through various orientation lectures by veteran lawmakers like Enders. This, with the aim of indoctrinating party-loyalty if ever voting on a bill as a block became necessary, perhaps down the line…

"Let's examine the way we write this law: It could profit the country greatly and allow enrichment to those willing to invest in America!"

He looked up, his face determined. Lawyers by training, true business-entrepreneurs they were not!

"Now, as you all know, unless I have a few closet socialist Democrats seated amongst you, inducing trade is the foundation of nation-building!"

A chuckle rippled through the room.

One hand shot up. "My Dad's a democrat!" he announced a young man.

They smiled.

"But YOU are not! Right?"

They chuckled.

The meaning was not lost on the crowd. Many had campaigned - and won their nomination on a party ticket that marked them as Republicans.

"It's a matter of how you interpret the law…" he proceeded. While we wish to *reward* a certain moderation from extremes with our tax code, we know that this country cannot afford to be a nanny state. Richt?"

They nodded.

"These precepts, if property administered, are rooted in early English laws that smooth out the extremes of the tax laws, or the *extremes* of the claim that the Third World is entitled to a free share of the earth's resources…" He looked up. "Now, certainly, charity has its place. But socialism and hard-work incentives are NOT equal virtues!"

They laughed.

"If that were true of course, we would have no ten commandments and the Children of Israel would still be wandering the deserts, right?"

A chuckle.

"Of course it is the foundation of all ethics that hard work and honesty are rewarded plentifully, right?" again he paused.

"…But many of these activist extremists expect Justice to come from reason tempered by sympathy and popularity. Judgments without adherence to the greater laws and statutes by tradition!"

 "Right" they all agreed.

"As Aristotle pointed out, justice is shown by reference to what is *unjust*. Do we believe that justice comes from the careful calculations inherent in a game theory model, or from weighing arguments and evidence in the mythologized courtroom, free from rhetoric and appeals to emotion?"

He looked up. They were in agreement.

"What does this have to do with the tax code you ask: It has everything to do with the tax code. We reward those who make money as the fruit of their labor!"

" …But what they want Gentlemen, is for justice to come from ire, *thumos*, a sense of what is wrong with the assumptions and biases of *contemporary* society. Therefore the ability – if not the right - to overturn decision by mob rule, as they see fit, and to redistribute wealth by law!"

They nodded.

"The source of justice came from the original ethics of God's morality."

They applauded. "Are we agreed then? We vote on this Bill as a block in favor?"

Enders was on his way back to his office when Barbara called him again.

"We've been hacked. The entire body has their emails and addresses posted by a hacker."

* * *

Chapter 16

"Good Morning" said the Janitor. "Excuse me Sir. They say to me the building empty…"

"Oh it is, *it is*, my friend!" said Bill Sanders.

 He gathered the research materials in the Department of the University School for Arts and Sciences. It was Saturday.

"Please carry on…I am on the Faculty Board, and I was just picking up some files. I'm finished!" he said.

"And they gave Jacob all the strange gods which were in their hand, and all their earring which were in their ears; and Jacob hid them under the oak which was by Sechem." Gen: 35:4

He knew those biblical verses.

Today he wore his speckled tie. It was a bow tie, which, together with his round turtle eyeglasses made him look like a professor. Only he was not. He was a lawyer by profession.

Still, this was his old haunt. As Endowment Director, it was here that he did a special research project with a team: It was an exploration of the Artic, and before that, an exploration expedition to expose a find of the first century in the Middle East.

He looked again at the first pages of the file before him.

"And they journeyed: and the terror of God was upon the cities that were round about them, and they did not pursue after the sons of Jacob." GEN 35:5

The treasure was vast, he knew it. Why? Because it a pivotal moment. It was the final act of compliance to God's wishes before God changed his name.

"..thy name shall not be called any ore Jacob, but Israel shall be thy name; and he called his name Israel. And God said until him, I am God Almighty: be fruitful and multiply; a nation and a company of nations

shall be of thee…And the land which I gave Abraham and Isaac,, to thee I will give it, and to they seed after thee will I give the land." GEN 35:12

Yes. Definitely, yes. An important find. And it was huge!

The treasure trove that was by historical account to be found *"under the oak which was by Sechem"* was the last frontier of the old order before God changed their mission.

Of course it made sense to establish an archaeological dig for the region. Any student worth his salt in ancient history would know that…Some would say biblical truth was laced with myth. That's why he endorsed the Dig as a Board Director of the Foundation. Hell, he recommended it!

The cache of gold and wealth that they might find there - if he was right, and if the sands of time had preserved well the relics of that age, would be an accumulation of all their gains.

The more he thought about it, the more he realized that this would be a vast collection of the ancient world gathered in one location!

Here, they had buried their treasure as unsacred. It was an act of obedience. At this point in their journey, they were to deny their ill-gotten gains and leave behind items to be buried and abandoned so that the children of Israel could proceed….

Did it matter to Bill Sanders that they would be considered items of antiquity with sacred meaning?

Not at all…

Besides, Israel's mission was now promised as something else *"to thee I will give it…"*

So what was buried in Sechem was discard. Stuff without value, he rationalized.

Many a discarded trash heap had been investigated for forensic examination. It elevated the status of learning.

The only thing that the student body did not know was the name of the donor that underwrote the expedition. Some things, he decided, are best left unsaid.

The overhead lights of the front office flickered on in a brilliance of fluorescent lighting as he passed through it. Behind him, they went dark again, electronics by motion-sensitivity.

He left the building muttering. *If only that idiotic dissertation had been finished!*

Ivanovich reported that he had found something 'intriguing.'

Jesus! Could that be possible? At Sechem?

What a fool, Ivanovich!

The University didn't have a clue. Still grieving, and with students and friends posting their sentiments about his loss, the University was conducting an investigation about his disappearance. That was the best the police could do, much less the Department of State making enquiries abroad about an American citizen. There were few answers about what had happened to him out on the dig…And his absence was overshadowed by that of another, a noted and respected Professor Dori Thompson. While the two events were unconnected, the University was striken by both events simultaneously.

Sanders felt annoyed. You'd think this University could do better for all the endowment money it received from US taxpayers!

The goddamned fool Ivanovich got himself killed. Well, that's what the Israelis said in a report they forwarded to the US Department of State, implying that the scholar had failed to follow procedures for archeological digs in the Middle East. Neither did he comply with safety precautions, nor did he report his whereabouts. *Really?*

Sanders felt even more annoyed. The government of Israel was *always* interested in the region's antiquities, especially academic expeditions – war zone or no war zone.

He walked down the wide granite steps that descended in splayed architecture to the main foyer of the building, everywhere students lounging about - mainly cramming before the end of semester final exams.

He would meet with the patron of the arts, a distinguished board member and sponsor of the expedition later tonight. Outside, he climbed into his car, and staring into the darkness of the parking lot, his thoughts raised his anger…

* * *

Chapter 17

Amanda was thrilled to get a call from Barbara.

"You'll never guess where I'm calling from…"she began

"OK. Where?"

"No. You have to guess…" said Barbara, always the playful one in the crowd.

"I'm on the road…outside DC and travelling to the ocean to come and see you!"

"Hey. That's great, where are you now?"

"I'm two- hours away from a cold beer and a nice BBQ dinner on your porch after a quick swim?"

"You're on!"

"What brings you down from New York?"

"Well, it's that idiot of a boss. He's got me going in ten different directions on the Hill, and now's he's flown out of town for the weekend. So I need a beach-break. Is that ok?"

"Sure it's ok" said Amanda, more relieved than Barbara realized.

Truth was, Arguetta had asked her to do some work, and while Amanda wasn't exactly prepared for it - nor did she have her Research staff available, she responded to his plea on the grounds of it "being a straightforward report…" as he put it. And, "because I need to give it someone I can trust with intelligence that might be sensitive. It's something I need to get to the bottom of…"

Barbara, as it just so happened, might be of help to Amanda, especially on Capitol Hill now working for Enders. She was trustworthy, as she always had been when she was on staff for Amanda's Research Firm years ago...

So the call was timely.

She thawed some ground beef for tacos. No problem!* * *

The bronze statue of the University Founder stood upon a plinth draped in the flowing gown of learning, his arm upraised in exhortation.

Enders looked up wryly.

He walked around the iconic monument and made his way out into the sunshine, wondering if it wouldn't have be more apt to build a water-fountain outside - a fountain to represent the endless flow of tax-free money that ran through this place

 Anyway, he wasn't entirely disappointed. He had made a copy of the entire file That was his prerogative on the Board. He found it unnecessary to notify anyone of his actions. This was Chicago, after all. Besides, the files were already gathering dust…

Outside, in the Quad, students smiled at him with a slight nod. Especially the smooth-haired girls.

He looked like a professor.

* * *

She was gorgeous. There was something savagely untouched by the way she wore her platinum hair, straight and smooth down a porcelain skin and a face of Danish blue eyes… and red, red lips.

But that was it.

Her only make-up, those angular features were her only adornment. If she wore earrings, she wore one – her touch of rebellion, as it were, and it drove him crazy, that attitude.

Today, walking towards him down the hall of Congress she was a classic young Intern wearing a dark Simon suit; Lauren bag and shoes, plus a Valentino computer case. That languid walk was panther-like, her eyes holding him as captive prey.

It was all he could do to act normal, trapped by this woman.

"Hello" she said softly. "I got the call…" she said, raising her cell phone slightly.

"Oh yeah?"

She smiled at him. She had just received permission to download the files for him.

"Really? You got the Intern's Research pass for only assigned Congressional staff access?"

"For only today: I get all the time in the world…"

"Well. You'd better wear overalls and sneakers! It's dusty as hell down there in that metal cage that they keep around the records…" said Enders.

He grinned at her, lifting a hair off her forehead. "It's a noble cause, remember – worth of getting disheveled. It gives me the scope of the amount of funds needed to submit a decent budget to the House Appropriations Committee."

She laughed. As if anyone as gorgeous as her would ever get dusty or dirty. No. Not this girl. She'd been too well disciplined an athlete to know about personal management; hygiene or endurance effects could be defied. Downloading files off old computers and databases was something she could manage quite effortlessly.

They walked around the marble colonnade of the upper chambers. He touched her elbow.

Having her from a shared pool of congressional staff assistants -usually working Interns, did help him to write decent legislation proposals, he told her.

"God knows, they've had little updates since WWII, even if Veterans are the only ones who care…"

This one, he explained, was a government agency that nobody had bothered with or wanted to champion. Nobody! *Especially* the Lobbyist whose efforts were richly rewarded by industrial clients.

 No. These records were from the Office of Personnel Management that was one neglected dinosaur needing updated technology and funds to upgrade, he told her. He would draft the Bill himself and give it to the Speaker of the House. They stopped.

 "So…" he said finally. "The Coastline, at 5?"

"I'll be done by then" she said. "Bring your hard-drive!" She pouted and moved on, almost as if she never saw him.

He was Chairing the Subcommittee Hearing on Agriculture today. They had been at it all day, and the gavel would shortly be adjourning the Hearing, he knew.

They gathered at the raucous bar The *Mexican Coastline*, a primitively decorated corner restaurant perched off Capitol Hill in Washington DC between the House of Representatives and the Political Convention Office Buildings - a place filled with suits; tourists and Moms and Pops showing the Nation's Capital to their kids.

Here, you could talk, laugh, throw popcorn, eat nachos and swallow marguerites as the overhead screens showed the House Floor recording the Vote Count for any Legislative Bill at any legislative hour. Here, between bouts in the halls of power, it was where Interns needing a touch of reality would gather for air.

Even popular for lobbyists and politicians doing duty, it was where you could let your hair down, under the radar and off the record...

He was with her. Or rather, with them.

Five Interns, two women the three men, all of them had been all day under the intense deliberations of proceedings and televised Hearings, each of them describing with a beer their awe at moment-by-moment drama of the day…

At least they could eat something here. And drink. The food was in abundance, and cheap.

Ali Enders ate snacks with them, dipping into the salsa and Mexican crèma.

 In his oxford blue shirt and tie, he looked not much older than the rest of the lawyers with jackets appended to their seats for a quick return to congressional staff quarters.

It was hot, the humidity high, and the summer temperatures breaching 100 degrees in Washington DC. A long evening pinkness resting upon Capital Hill, still aglow from the Anacostia river, and cool angular city shades fell from over abundant trees and townhouses. It would not be long before nightfall.

"Ready for some dancing?" he asked casually in her ear as they reached for a new round of Nachoes and shuffled around bar stools.

She looked at him, insouciant.

The ice blue of her Scandinavian coolness was almost unnerving him, like a challenge, and he felt quickened to his core.

"Only…if it's the tango!" she said, the smile was barely there.

They cheered loudly, at the bar, a football catch on TV by the Ravens.

 "Oh yeah" he said softy, " A *Dark*…tango!"

She looked away, inclining towards the others. It was time for her to go…

"I'll be ready at 9. Pick me up out front then!" she whispered, collecting her briefcase to withdraw.

"Bye!" they nodded cheerfully.

He slipped out behind her, and finding her already hailing a taxi, turned out of his spot on D street in his Porch, determined to keep his eyes forward.

Once back underground of his building, he sat in his car.

Suddenly his hand slammed the driving wheel in savage frustration. Before turning on the ignition he made the call.

* * *

88

Chapter 18

Admiral Arguetta was in a dark room at the Pentagon. The small conference of personnel who were viewing the screen were receiving a briefing from a Lieutenant Commander from R&D on a scientific matter.

 It posed threat to American defense.

"Who would want to manipulate this?" asked a Colonel from the Army Intelligence.

"We have a number of people identified with this kind of research. Their findings might be appealing to unfriendly parties. It's a case of scientific development that any rich buyer might purchase as a weapon of some disruption against America. Chiefly to cause harm without too much collateral damage, if you will, in terms of mortality"

"More like a total meltdown that generate chaos from within!" said the Colonel. "Society in *any* great nation has a way of disintegrating, once law and order breaks down."

"Not so fast, Dr. Samuels" said Arguetta. "I beg to disagree. I do believe in the American spirit of independence and endurance. We are a nation of great people, not a nation of society channeled solely by law and order."

They nodded, all of them in the dark seats around the great table. "So what options - in a worse case, would the average citizen have if faced with this situation?"

Arguetta looked up at the Lieutenant to continue.

"Well. A lot depends on the timing… and the location of such an occurrence. If it's a global assault, then we are looking at something of a catastrophic event. If it is regionally targeted, then we can develop certain counter-measures and awareness guidelines for early detection and containment."

"Then perhaps we examine the conditions that foster reliance on this method of survival" said the Colonel wryly. "Only my daughter thinks the world will come to an end without cell phones!"

They laughed.

"Truth is, the digital age has made an industry – and a very lucrative capitalist industry – to wean people away from conventions and into the global digital age of inter-dependence. It's a policy decision at the highest levels embracing modern technology…"

"Bullshit" said someone at the far of the table. It was a man called Jensen of Military Supply Command, arguably the most critical of all military functions on the ground. They all turned to look at him.

"It's a disruptive means to boost sales and profitability by Silicon Valley!"

"What's this Jensen? You've got something against free market capitalism?"

"No Sir. It's just that once we identify one source of innovation, it's a target for disruptive competition. Ergo, a profit center for the next shop!"

They laughed.

"Well that's Wall Street. So, let's hear more about what this phenomenon is and what we are looking at…Even if the case rests on funding and research."

The screen lit up.

Arguetta was concerned.

He had already heard from Trevor MacDonald in Scotland. And he knew Trevor said little without consulting with CERN.

The Lieutenant proceeded with his presentation.

"Had this happened fifty years ago, it would have collapsed civilization. Put it that way. It is the weakening and reversal of the magnetic poles."

"You are joking, right?"

"No Sir. A Polar shift presents real dangers to Civilization!"

Today, because of our dependence on the Cloud and all matters technologically electronic and relevant, we are better off to explain the issue: The problem is the centrality of data stored either on separate computers, or *interlinked*."

"What are you saying?" said once voice from the darkness.

"It is like the chip of a computer knowing all commerce; all necessary functions; all distribution and data containing critical information - being rendered suddenly useless. "

"Like some electromagnetic impulse attack?" said another voice at the far end of the table.

"Sort of... But worse, because it is global, sudden and *intelligent!*"

"Hello... Here, what's this? A scenario where an entire planet with 7 billion people is without technology?..."

"...Right. Tell me another fairytale..." chuckled someone. They all laughed.

Arguetta gave them a moment.

"Carry on!" he said.

"OK. Take vehicles, they would stop working. Banking would freeze. Security would be as useless as a rusty key. The financial world would go dark. Manufacturers would be slammed, distribution would be blind. Public transportation...state, local...hospitals...Well, you get the idea."

"Now I know I'm a duck..." said someone.

"Traffic lights would shut down. Police and safety signals would go. Telecommunications, computers, agribusiness, processing plants, electrical generating plants would collapse: Globally, we would be rendered just about as useful as the block we're on when it happens..." finished the Lieutenant

"Presumably..." said one sceptic "That would take out the enemy too, right?"

"Not if you have invested sufficient Eyes to survive the Fall out..."

"the *Fall out?*"

"Yes. This could quite possibly be a case of mass destruction, with only a few winners..."

"And who is this monster wanting self-annihilation?"

"Not who. But what."

Arguetta took over.

"It goes something like this, and the signs are unmistakably in place and visible, I'm afraid. It's a natural phenomenon for which we are totally unprepared!"

"Explain!"

"This chart shows that we're about to enter a storm...a weakening magnetic field exposing us to intense solar storms. Radio, television and communications would be knocked out for weeks, maybe months, rendering us to the conditions of a Third world nation. And it could happen in a matter of hours."

"Right!" said someone.

"Please Jim!"

"At key points in the solar cycle, from minimum to maximum activity, the geomagnetic field within the earth's core begins to intensify as it comes under bombardment of solar flares."

He paused.

"Worse. The evidence from certain science suggests that at a time of increased exposure to solar flares, we historically have demonstrated societal stress as a collective, with distinctive changes also in animal behavior. That suggests decidedly aggressive in nature."

They were not fools at this table. Science was one thing, its effects on the human race never to be under estimated.

"That means wars and combat over critical and diminished resources..." embellished Captain Rogers, his post listed at the US Air Force Information and Science Center. He put down his pencil and spoke for the first time. Evidently, he too had done his research on the matter.

 "Magnetic field electrochemically driven human brain has an adverse affect upon deep-rooted psychological responses. That includes abnormal hormonal swings and significant mutated brain-wave activity."

"Yes, that is true" continued the Lieutenant. "The Research of Becker and Freeman is disturbing, if isolated in historical narrative..."

"Their work confirms that of Russians Chizhevsky and Wheeler, specialists in biological electricity - twice nominated for the Nobel Prize out of State University of New York" finished Rogers.

"And…err. What's behind all this?" said someone.

"So, let's go back to explain the magnetic field within the earth's core?" asked Arguetta.

"It is a dynamo deep within the center of the planet that retains a magnetic field that protects us from potentially dangerous charged particles from space…"

"*Space…?*"

"The magnetic field flips as you know, on an irregular basis. Geologists and geophysicists are uncertain as to why. And it is infrequent. Usually evidenced in geological formations suggesting some 780,000 thousand years ago…"

The room went silent.

"More recently as you know we see a complete reversal of the poles 41,000 years ago. But that change only lasted for about 440 years before it flipped back: We do know from subterranean striations that as the reversals took place, the strength of the magnetic field protecting Earth declined by 95 percent."

"How strange is this, and how imminent is this a danger?"

"Imminent" said Rogers. "High altitude flight tests show increasing anomalies amongst our pilots. We are on an increase that's alarming us. We want to know why, and what this is…"

The house lights went up, and Arguetta stood before them.

"Gentleman. There you have it. It is considered high priority so as not to cause alarm. We want scientific suggestions and proposals to mitigate our exposure and options for this kind of calamity. Strange? Oh yes. But plan we shall. Plan we must! Get back to me with reports and more research ASAP!"

Arguetta left the building searching for Trevor's phone number on his Contact List.

In-house research and examination was highly reliable. But to be sure, he wanted an independent and private contractor to also double check and collaborate, if necessary. It was that important, even if the science was singular.

Trevor's network had contacts to intellectual content in Europe that most governments envied. He was the listed Executive Director of a Research Firm respected by many in the professional world. His group held DoD contracts for work of the most sensitive material needed by Western Governments. He and Arguetta were good friends, and if there was a need for expert research, Trevor's firm would be the one to provide it from top scientists.

Moreover, Arguetta knew Trevor's wife Amanda Wells. Over the years, they had become friends. More importantly, the British had intelligence that the Americans needed.

Amanda Wells was in the United States at the moment. And though she no longer managed one of their offices in Washington, he knew he could talk to her: The task would be one for scientists and technicians, he knew. But Amanda would expedite the contract, for certain.

Meantime, he had his own in-house meeting to conduct.

* * *

Chapter 19

The roses delivered to the office of Ali Enders caused a response. *For my staff*, the gold rimmed note said.

Two dozen long-stemmed red Costa Rican roses came out of their box in a sensational display of elegance -fruits of success for working in this office they implied, some unpacked with a petal-rim of gold-leaf glitter.

The secretaries and aids were aglow. At least half were put in a crystal vase that adorned the Senator's front office. A nice place to work, they all said. Word got around, *such a thoughtful boss.*

Ali Enders was attending the Subcommittee Hearing for internal reform when the cell phone purred in his pocket.

He reached discretely for the electronic device and turned on the Text Message from his office. U, for urgent.

It was Thursday, a weekend break approaching.

In Washington, long weekends were useful breaks to regroup; refinance, or retool, as the political agenda went. But it always wrapped up the week, ostensibly to avoid city-exit traffic jams on Fridays.

He was annoyed.

It wasn't that he couldn't stray far from the leash that held him close to the office where the paperwork was generated, but he couldn't quite respond immediately.

The Representative speaking now was the sponsor of the next bill coming up for a vote, and it was the last Bill on the Clerk's Agenda. Walking off in the middle of his Statement was just bad form. He watched the cell carefully for more messages. None came.

He did return to the office one and a half hours later. His staff were gathered around his desk, as if attending to a central menu, their posture stricken and pale.

"What's this?" he said.

They looked at him, embarrassed as if betraying collective secrets.

"What is it?" he repeated, all of them melting away but one.

His Administrative Assistant looked down, unable to look him in the eyes, unable to trust her own voice.

Victor Durant, Senior Aide from the Speaker's Office walked in.

"Bridgette Unger is dead. They found her body this morning in her apartment. Heart failure!"

His face was blank, his voice gone.

He could have said something. Perhaps he should have said *take time off*... But he did not.

Ali Embers was a married man, a man about to run for re-election with a political campaign of his own.

His staff understood, they said, patting him on the arm. One by one, they left him to himself.

"We'll see you here first thing Monday morning, boss…" they said, kindly. Or, "she was a great Intern…"

All except his Administrative Assistant. She took his instructions before leaving.

"We'll need to notify her family," he told her. "I'll call them. Also, please write-up a note of sincere condolences commending her contribution to our efforts in this office. Be prepared to manage all arrangements for a suitable ceremony here before repatriating her body …Call our personnel; State, and her Embassy."

"Yes Sir" said Helen, eyeing the roses on her way out. Bridgette Unger was a foreign student on their staff who had cultivated quite a following...

Later that evening, Ali left his office and went home. He had a townhouse off Maine Avenue. He walked through the place, fiercely picking up a few overnight provisions; dialed his cell to leave a few brief messages then locked the front door. He climbed back into his car, his tie still on.

He would not stop driving until he reached home in Connecticut. There his wife and family were waiting.

* * *

She had assets. Vineyards; timbering and orchards in New England were considerable land holdings. Add copper-extraction units; a utility company in the Midwest and fracking operations in Pennsylvania, and her family was owner of a small fortune in commodities, all of them tax paying and lucrative.

Founded by her father, the company had long ago assumed its own corporate brand identity and was growing like any other successful mining operation.

For Bridgette Unger, there had been a gap in continuous residency over the years. Her mother, following the death of the father, remained in Sweden and was too entrenched in a social hierarchy to consider returning to the United States.

Her elder brother, the heir to the family company, had died in a car accident. Her elder sister Yvonne and her Belgian husband were too involved in banking in Brussels to be able to absorb further family responsibility without it becoming a liability to his career. Certainly, they had already spent a fortune in contesting the audit by the IRS.

That left Brigitte. And while she had applied to college in the United States and finally accepted an Internship, the company had been registered without a family residency agency for too many years not to be considered a foreign corporation. The taxes, or rather penalties, were astronomical.

Never mind that they would have to liquidate. The problem was the liability of debt that the US IRS would hound them for personally. And the sums were staggering. Certainly beyond what any individual could repay in one lifetime of working!

Hence, when the new Tax Reform Bill offered amnesty to tax evaders caught in such a predicament - and there were many since much wealth in Europe had fled to America during WWII, Brigitte was delighted. In fact, it was where she had first met the young Senator from New Hampshire.

As she made the rounds to petition for the passage of the Bill, she had been offered several jobs; one internship – which she accepted, and more than one Letter of Recommendation for reference purposes.

It was what she lived for, these days, knowing that the entire homestead and family business back home would collapse in a day if the payment was made without some measure of mitigation.

Ali Enders remembered the day well. How could he forget the impression she made on him walking through the door and into his empty office. They had all gone to lunch.

"Excuse me" she said in her languid voice "I need to petition for the passage of a particular bill…"

He smiled. "You're not from the United States are you?" he sat back, pencil still in hand.

"Not yet!" she said simply.

He promised her the world. The Bill, he said, would be passed in the House, and before he was done, in the Senate too.

Of course it was not his intention to get involved with an Intern when in Washington DC. That was not the plan at all. But when something like this just happened out of the blue and without any filters or introductions – or much risk, for that matter, it was an easy promise to make.

How could he ever, *ever* forget that chance and charming beginning: After that, she believed every word he said.

Rather, he was trapped by hers. The weeks turned into months, and the months turned into almost the next session before the Bill could be introduced for a vote.

Much happened in the meantime. Chiefly, elections. And the public was disenchanted with reform, or amnesty. There had been too much Administration progressive expense on the national budget, leaving too much unemployment and lack of capital for progressive sentiment. The political climate had changed. Washington had turned sour, and most elected seats were overturned in a sudden force of protest by the voter.

That left him with a promise he could not keep…

He stopped for coffee. It would clear him mind of all memory: The New Jersey Turnpike was moving at high speed.

This evening the roads were not particularly populated. Yet by the time he approached New York, *Exit 10* had a traffic jam that lasted five miles.

He called Caroline. He'd be back home tonight, if late….

He drove through the night, headlights leading the way along Interstate Highways, up secondary roads and into the mountainous granite roadsides that marked the landscapes of New England, now so familiar to him.

He turned on the radio. The music was good, if fleeting in reception. That was one of his enjoyments when travelling across multiple states. The car radio picked up regional stations and picked up from wireless towers eclectic music, reflecting the tastes its local community of residents. Here, he heard a Latino song, a vibrant beat to a strong radio reception. He lingered on the station, and the traffic slowed to a crawl.

Then suddenly a song-beat filled the car that sent adrenalin coursing through his system like a bolt of lightning. It surged with ecstatic energy that almost left him breathless...

How could he ever forget that night...

The Tango, in the basement of one of Washington's most exclusive hotels, the *Mandarin* off Main Street off the waterfront. It was what they did that night after dinner at the Coastline Restaurant.

How could he ever forget that night

Down, down, down they went, deep in the bowels of the hotel's floors, darkly lit, and into the *Loose Tie*. It was precisely for the night crowd that migrated to the Nightclub after a black tie event. It was not a place erotic, or distasteful. On the contrary, it was exotic and attended by those in formal dress, coming from events of the body politic of the Nation's capital who chose not to be recognized. Secretive, heady and dark, it was always hot where you be yourself with uninhibited verve.

Oh yeah!

A dance - not far from the bar beside the band - and the hot, slow savoring-intensity of a Tango could permeate the crowd with sudden excitement.

Ender's yanked at his collar, only now aware of his office clothes, and he was sweltering with body perspiration.

They could not wait to get to 909, the two of them. It was where she lived, her luxury apartment building on Capital Hill, afterwards… They had sex in the parking garage first, she against a dark bulkhead in a silk dress yearning for more.

"You're very excited…" she breathed into his neck, up against the cold concrete pillar.

"Oh yeah? *Who's* talking!" he pressed.

She breathed hotly into his collar. "It's just that whenever you're aroused….you have such a high threshold…" she murmured.

"And you - the girl with ice in her veins…look at her now!"

"I'm sorry. I can't help it…" she breathed.

He smiled, her face under his breath "Yes." Her hair was falling forward over her face.

Then later in her apartment; he, intoxicated by her body perfume and pressing touch…

They dozed intermittently.

"I got a call today…A call from the President!"

She lifted her arms to push his off.

"He wants me….to advise him on his next campaign!" he said, pulling up her arms.

"Oh wow!" she managed to say.

"I have a few tricks up my sleeve, it seems, that he likes!"

"Oh?" she said, interested.

"Like all those Vet votes…" he said, succumbing to a surge that pinned her down. She uttered a muffled cry.

No, he decided, that night was not forgotten. But he would recall with that he had looked into her eyes, and he knew. He knew instantly. He knew he had lost her trust right then - she, on the bed beneath him, with a trust put in the wrong hands…

Well, such intel could be… dangerous!

Oh yes. He remembered the night at her place. It was wild and exciting, the hours of drink and lovemaking in her luxurious apartment, the windows open to a panoply of stars above city monuments and traffic sounds. From below, through the hot summer night reflections from a building swimming pool refracted shadows in blue and silver. How could he forget that night?

Or the other nights following. And that was the trouble. He was a married man and did not need this for his political career. And it was never the same. No. Not really. She found him odious. He knew it.

Yet that was beyond him to control…

She had taken on the dimensions of a goddess in his life, an obsession. And he could hardly carry on through the day without thoughts of her that night…Her touch, her hair…He was transfixed.

She, always willing.

 And only once did they discuss the upcoming agenda that she originally had in mind. The Tax Reform Bill. Nothing had changed, he told her.

It was a lie.

That evening, he had made arrangements for everything. He would be photographed with her at the *Loose Tie* Nightclub.

The photographer understood, and he waved when the shot was taken, a young Oriental man, known around these parts only as Kim.

That was the deal. The photograph for identification purposes.

And even then, he was almost sucked into her seductive breathlessness again before he refocused. And there was plan.

So when he was approached at the Nightclub, he had just enough presence of mind to agree to be imaged. Rather, imaged by the photographer with his arm around her shoulder, Brigitte Unger. Even in full view, and with others in the photograph. But his arm had to be around her neck. That was the deal.

So that there would be no mistake, later…

A half dozen roses would be sent to his office as confirmation: If yellow, then On Hold. If red, condition Completed. The Florist would add the billet-doux when taking the order by phone.

* * *

102

Chapter 20

Amanda found the large box on the kitchen table. The two ancient copper plates were cushioned in soft tissue paper and conservator's felt cloth. Jacques had offered them as gifts. She sipped her morning tea.

It had been a long night after all, the two men had been discussing the matter for hours.

She poured herself another cup.

Yet this morning Trevor and Jacques left early for the Lodge. Of course Trevor would want to share his world with Jacques. They had become old friends!

But what happened last night worried her. Less for what they concluded than what it all meant. She sat down by the window, buttered some toast and tapped the shell of a hard-egg.

Outside the kitchen window a hazy sunlight was burning off the morning dew from the tips of multiflora rose.

The copper scrolls, as Jacques described them, had particular interest to him. He said he had bought them from a Turkish Auction House.

Most people, he said, would have found them unremarkable. In fact, they were texts quite revealing.

Amanda could hardly keep her eyes off them. Specifically, they were a scribe's texts - someone who would have worked in the Temple - keeping inventory lists and items of note for their records...

In the silence of her home, she could contemplate on them at leisure, and she could hardly believe what she was looking at.

She finished her tea, cleared away some items and returned to the large oak table - scrubbed clean and clear, to reflect on the box entirely.

Codex and scrolls were common in the ancient world, she knew. The most notable were those discovered in terra cotta jars and known as the Dead Sea Scrolls. Those were the books of Isaiah written by scribes.

But these words inscribed upon copper plates were permanent indentations as if for inventory; special symbols indicating items of value. Mainly for record-keeping and durability.

It was a remarkable thing to behold, considering its age. Jacques knew that she and Trevor would value an item with historical integrity.

He had been concerned, he said, about the dispersion of the trove of relics flooding the market without explanation or provenance. This, he suspected, was from that trove. Perhaps Dana had seen it. She couldn't be sure.

For Jacques, this was a copper scroll. He assumed it to have been found near Sechem.

She thought about what Jacques said. If this was an accounting or inventory, it might have listed the items perhaps laid forfeit at the feet of Jacob in Sechem.

But that was pure speculation.

Still, being an inventory of some kind, it might help date things as a provenance: That was the challenge of all archaeology. To date things accurately. This might shed light on the excavation event. And it would have been what Dana might have done.

Yet, what he found, instead, was a deeper puzzle.

That was why he wanted Trevor to see it. Perhaps Trevor's interest and research in astrology might guide them. Because on one scroll was an astrological chart marking the positions of the stars!

It was impossible to believe. Yet there it was.

Trevor was thrilled.

"It is a calendar of the ancient world inscribed by the heavens!" said Trevor, smiling in awe.

The passage of the earth's position against heavenly stars were clearly recognizable.

On the copper plate, where the stars had been punched through the copper in a celestial pattern, as if to denote a historical event, it was carefully charted and marked with recognizable features, like the shape of the moon and its angle of elevation against the horizon of earthly trees.

In recording a celestial positioning of the orbiting star pattern, it could yield an approximate date, like a pictograph.

The day was full of surprises, and as tired as they were, they gathered at dinner for more discussion. Later that evening, it was Trevor who surprised Jacques.

"If this is any astrological calendar of any accuracy, it suggests an early date of some cataclysmic event that occurred…" he said. "We may never know of course. But it's an attempt to give us a record."

"Clearly, it was a record of value, the dating of an event possibly included in the Sechem collection, *perhaps* referring to the burial of material items for spiritual purification" offered Amanda. "But that's entirely speculative. We do know they marked events to dates, not dates to events, as we do in the West…"

"I agree. Though I can't make it out at all. It must mean something important happened, for sure."

They thought about it, examining the relic from every possible angle.

To have something so old in their hands seemed unreal. As if the past were calling to them to see the world as it was then.

"I'm taking picture of it, of course" said Jacques. "And I'll send it to the Museum for their records. That way, it's visible, and digitized for scholars to study…Who knows?"

Gradually, as the evening firelight reflected upon the copper plate, it glowed with incandescent shadows flickering as if to presume an organic likeness.

Of one thing they could be sure. The cosmic date drawn on that ancient chart showed clearly the heavens and the moon placed on a time spectrum.

Jacques pulled out a black book - a relic itself, teased Amanda.

Jacques scowled at her admonishingly. Clearly, she knew not what else lay within its covers.

She giggled.

Actually he was consulting his notes from a phone call he had received from an antiques dealer in Turkey who told him he had a codex. The words inscribed on it were given to Jacques over the phone. He wrote them down.

"The hearts of man were twisted for the time of the change..." it said, below a chart.

Jacques had done some preliminary research. It implied some kind of metaphysical disturbance, if not mass demographic shifting, Jacques was saying. It referred to lore and history.

"These codex' can be quite explicit" said Jacques. "For example, in one it described the floods, and it suggested that they had been told of them by early records passed down, like oral history. During that period, it spoke of strange things in the heavens and strange things in the "hearts of man.""

Trevor leaned forward.

"They certainly went to some effort to describe the celestial configuration, as if to give a date..." he stopped suddenly. "The description that you got from you man in Turkey, is it the same as this one on the copper scroll?"

"It is" said Jacques. "He described it precisely!"

"Wait a minute...I believe I recognize this...One second, please!" he got up and moved to the far end of the drawing room and behind a desk carved long before his lifetime.

He ruffled through papers and opened files.

"Normally, I keep this stuff up at the Observation Lab in the Lodge. But this was correspondence from CERN regarding some research they asked me to confirm with my findings..." His thoughts were wandering, he looked exhausted.

"I left the file here...It was a simple exercise of walking backwards in time counting celestial orbits...if you will."

He looked up and grinned. "It is quite mathematically possible, you know, to plot a date to a celestial configuration. Ah...Wait just a second..."

"CERN?" asked Jacques "What has that to do with anything?"

"CERN, the European Organization for Nuclear Research is one of the largest and most respect centers for scientific research. In trying to identify the building blocks of the universe, they have the Large Hadron collider, a particle accelerator which measures time in space…"

"You're a scientist now?" teased Jacques.

"No" laughed Trevor. "I send them observation data from my telescope, that's all. And they ask me for a few simple queries from time to time. Scotland is an ideal viewing post for a telescope! The moon being so close to the horizon here…Ah, *there* they are!"

He placed a number of charts on the table. "I'm retired, remember?"

He turned to Jacques.

"The topic in question was the possible configuration of tectonic plates at that time: The astrological dates straddle this…this copper plate celestial configuration that you have. That is, if we are reading it correctly! So, roughly speaking I'd place this date as somewhere around…Well…Umm…" he rubbed his temple, hesitating.

"When?" asked Jacques, his face darkened in the shadows of the crackling fire.

Trevor turned the item sideways. "These features are recognizable. But here…It's a matter of understanding what these two orbital stars so close together mean…."

They gave him time.

Trevor was unsure. But he had long ago learned never to apologize for astrological clues and evidence in the time spectrum of space. Planets and stars could be plotted with synchronous measurements once identified and positioned by their pattern of orbit.

"Umm…"

Amanda had to smile at his face so overwrought in thought and possibilities.

 "Well…If I were to use paleomagnetic dating, I'd say 60,000 years ago!"

They stared at him.

"Not bad for a man retired" teased Jacques.

"A date as possibly having some early human societal ancestors…" added Trevor.

"When?" asked Jacques again.

"What happened then?" asked Amanda.

Nobody had spoken. Except for the words on the copper scroll.

"The hearts of man were twisted for the time of the change…"

It was restful in Scotland, all of them taking some time to collect their thoughts and consult their data-base records - an occasional nap in private quarters; a tranquil bench out in the garden. Trevor and Jacques actually made it through a few rounds of golf.

The next evening however, was the last night of Jacques stay in Scotland. He and Trevor had spent wonderful days in Scotland together. Only later, however, did they come to reveal their darkest fears. It came after a fuller accounting of the missing student from the University of Chicago.

"The icon that was recovered on the side of the road suggests that the student came to a sudden incident that took his life. But the statue and the gold shows clearly that he had been to the Sechem dig, and was possibly the same perpetrators who killed the team, including your friend…" he said looking at Amanda.

"Diane was *murdered?*"

"My Darling…" said Trevor "I know you were friends."

"Murder…" said Jacques softly "has been the motive for much less in antiquities! Let alone the gold and icon in that sack, I'm afraid we cannot rule it out…"

"No" said Trevor

Jacques leaned on his elbows, folding his hands, but said nothing.

"Then…*everyone* was killed at that dig?" said Amanda.

"Your husband and I have been discussing this for days. I'm afraid we've reached the conclusion that it was a premeditated job, and that that the treasure was stolen…"

"for a sack…" began Amanda then she stopped.

"Oh! There was more. Much more, right? How much more?"

"Possibly the entire treasure trove of Sechem. In today's markets that might constitute pure gold in terms of value up to a billion or more…"

"Dear God!" she said. "But *who* would do such a thing?"

"It's probable that the Foundation that funded the project was informed. Perhaps they still consider it a matter of missing persons. Or rather, just missing students on a travel jaunt before returning to University for the semester. So we don't know anything" said Trevor.

"Or perhaps there's an investigation?" insisted Amanda.

"It is a non-profit group under the auspices of government inspection, after all. So perhaps there is an enquiry already under way… We'll need to find out" said Jacques.

They added nothing. But they all knew how close a decision is was that Sandra attend that very archaeological dig. Instead she chose the North Pole.

So they spent their last evening quietly gathered in the by the fire. They chatted about possibilities, and strategized on a plan to make fuller enquiry.

Jacques, being in the business would keep his ears open on the European markets.

Trevor would make enquiries of the various governments.

Amanda would check her academic connections in the United States. Surely some clues were turning up amongst friends and families of those who went on the dig…

Further, she would look more closely at the Foundation that funded the expedition.

* * *

Chapter 21

The meeting was set up in the office of his Attorney on K Street. It was a routine visit on the matter of an enquiry as a procedure, they said, since the Senator was known to the diseased.

The DC Police Homicide Investigator was not easily deterred.

"Michael Abrams" he said, offering his hand.

Formerly with the FBI -and before that in the Secret Police, it was immediately clear on his face that nothing in this city was too alarming for him. He remained unmoved in the presence of politicians and influential men, he spoke in normal flat level, as if routine and uneventful.

But he was still man of note-taking. It was his way of taking his eyes off the staring gaze of experts accustomed and trained to defend some of the toughest case before some of the highest courts of the land. All of them lawyers sharp, iterative and focused with their statements and inferences.

He had to ask, was the way he phrased it. Or rather, be *on record* with his asking…

"So Mr. Enders. Did you know that the young woman Brigitte Ungar was taking pills before she died?"

"No. I did not" he said flatly in denial. In keeping with the tone established by his attorney at the conference table, he sat calmly, waiting for the next question.

"When was the last time you were together?"

"Officer Abrams…" interrupted the attorney. "Are you accusing my client, and if so, do you intend to arrest him for suspicion…?"

"No. Just questions, that's all. So, Mr. Embers…"
"Enders"

"Enders. When was the last time you saw Ms Unger?" continued Abrams.

"About a week before she died…They told me in my office when I returned from the Floor of the House."

"Did she call you, at all recently, since you last saw her?"

"No."

"Oh? You had a dinner dancing date last Thursday, yet no follow-up call? No sociability communications?"

"It was an apres'office-party event. I believe she had gone out of town, or so I thought. I did not expect to hear from her."

"When?"

"Prior to the party…She told me she was going to New England for a few days…That's all"

"But she showed up?"

"Yes. She showed up. I volunteered to drop her off…"

Abrams, the police investigator totally ignored the explanation without so much as blinking.

"What time did you leave her apartment at 909 the last time you saw her?"

Enders averted his eyes. It was a shameful thing having to admit being in her apartment for the record.

He looked at his attorney. *Carry on!*

Of course, he would have to talk with Caroline. He hesitated, and knowing that his attorney advised him to be honest in all things so as to avert any further suspicion, he looked up finally and said.

"About 1.30 AM"

Abrams flipped a couple of pages back, and paused.

"Yes. That's right. The CC monitors see you exiting the elevators of 909 at precisely 1.45 AM on the morning of the 9th. Correct!"

"I think we can call it a day…" said his attorney. "That is, if there are no further questions Inspector?"

"No."

He was ushered out of the office.

Enders knew he would have to talk with Caroline. Even if separated, they had agreed to work together for the campaign. This did not look good, neither for their relationship nor for the local media.

His attorney re-entered the room. "Not much more than a security check verification. So relax."

Enders was tired.

"Ali…" said his attorney. "There's nothing to report. Nothing to be written on any record about you that is averse. You knew her. So did a lot of other people. Now go home! OK?"

Ali Enders looked up at him. "Jesus Tony, I'm a Senator and I knew the girl…How bad will that look in the Media?"

"Don't worry about it. She was a working staffer. It was an unfortunate medical condition. Heart failure can happen to anyone. That's all. Everyone was routinely questioned as a procedure. Nothing untoward has been suggested. All were questioned about her just to close the books - those who knew her at work; those she knew her in her building where she lived -including residents, guests, staff, janitors - all were asked about her. That is, all but one who got himself in a car accident two days later…"

"Who got himself ..." began Enders.

"So. There is nothing to suggest foul play. Now go home… It's over!" insisted his attorney.

"And if my wife finds out?"

His attorney rose and began collecting his papers. He looked directly at Ender and let him absorb the gravity of his words.

"Then that's between you and your wife, a personal matter. Nobody else needs to know. Nobody. Period."

Enders got it.

* * *

Enders changed the radio station. This trip was getting long. He called Carolina and told her he'd be home in an hour from now. The road home was familiar to him, and for situations like this one, it was a comfort to be going home...

Even in the dark and after hours, Interstate 95 through Connecticut could get cluttered. All six lanes might slow to a crawl in one direction, perhaps it had to do with the steep mountain-side flanks, carved through to accommodate highway construction across the region, its effect on drivers inducing slower speed and caution. Otherwise, the lanes were filled mostly with tractor-trailers delivering cargo from the ports of Boston with goods manufactured overseas.

So Enders drove down the last leg of the journey in silence, his thoughts still swirling in his head.

In his mind he replayed the interview. His discussion with his attorney were aimed at damage containment, he knew. Assurances, perhaps. But it was not good.

It was all bad business, he decided.

He was seen leaving the building.

That's what bothered him.

Blocking out the noise from the highway, he closed his mind to all the clutter, he centered his feelings, concentrating deeply, inwardly, on what was most important to him. That which was important to him, and that which was not.

Yes, by then, he knew the building well.

And there it was. The truth that held reality for him.

Fortunately, he had made the call before leaving the underground garage. Send red roses.

* * *

Chapter 22

London

"This dwarfs NSA information-gathering…" said the Minister, his white hairline visible for a polished look and his business suit stylishly tailored. He wore his glasses to read the report he was holding.

Trevor was surprised at his tenor. This was not a man given to hyperbole.

"The problem is tricky or us. It could potentially hold the government hostage" he continued. The Minister picked up the small assortment of newspaper clips.

"Even the liberal *Washington Post* labels this *cyberburglary* and I quote '…*an even greater intelligence catastrophe than the Edward Snowden Affair*'"

Trevor waited.

"This breach of security contains the records of all U.S. Military personnel including the long form SF 86…" he looked up. "What if this happens to us?"

"It is cause for concern, I agree" said Trevor.

The Minister continued to read further down his page. "For an innocuous agency called the *Office of Personnel Management*, this breach contains critical records of all American '*brain-talent as a national resource*'" He looked up "Jesus, Trevor…who thinks like that?"

"We do!"

The Minister took off his clean rimmed glasses.

"I can understand why it was the target of highly focused hacking" said Trevor, taking his seat across from the Minister. " To explain the Long Form SF 86? It's an in-depth disclosure of a very personal nature for every man and woman employed in sensitive work in the US Government and overseas! It

114

contains Social security numbers, private information on personnel's credit history, jobs background; contact information, family, friends in the US and abroad. It even lists for each person their non-American affiliations, including every foreigner ever contacted - every place lived; every person who can verify *knowing* that person. It is highly sensitive and personal data. It is a profile!"

"My God!"

"And with a digital management system that updates every medical, criminal and parking ticket infraction, every updated profile, browsing history, telephone call and every possible proclivity and personal judgements the subject can be responsible for is potentially listed!" said Trevor. "Oh, its intelligence-gathering alright. Of the first order, if you want to know how to blackmail someone…"

"My God, what have we come to in this Orwellian age?" said the Minister.

"I suspect that's what Snowden objected to as well when he pulled off his caper. It's an extreme infringement of privacy and human rights. But in his case, he acted illegally."

"True. And of course we have the same intel. But the Americans are such damned apologists about their security. It puts us all at risk."

"It's politics, Sir. It's the American way!"

"Well. This certainly isn't politics. It compromises our intelligence as well. This information, in many ways, is used to recruit an individual as an intelligence officer – or any officer of the law for that matter. It's the basis of civil law and order. And it's a routine *personnel* file?"

 "Collecting such information is the whole point of the form: Regardless their level of security, their exposure to sensitive material or their need to know, these are the screenings and filters that use government-to-government for assessments."

"What is regrettable is the filtering of intelligence that would sort out and separate the routine from the sensitive…"

"I agree" said Trevor. "Only commercial applications have that refinement. Especially for intellectual innovation and research and development."

The Minister put down the report. "Worse of all, it compromises the intelligence also of all Allied countries and assets in the Western civilized world. Bad enough in the hands of potential enemies of the state, but in a sense this kinds of intellectual content hijacks our advantages in any technological and commercial competition trading in markets, industry and military defense!"

"Their system was dated, Sir."

"I should say so!"

"I'm certain their updating their security systems now Sir!"

"What do you recommend Trevor?"

"Personnel records are one thing. Data mining across digital platforms is standard operating procedure. We do it a lot ourselves, and it has its uses. But we can be more careful with our digital architecture, that's for sure."

"Oh?"

Trevor was loath to indulge too much to anyone. His way of communicating was to reveal only what was necessary, a tradition that transcended politics of the day; party affiliation or gossip as fodder for table-talk. Somehow he had the uneasy feeling there was more to this conversation.

"Who is the source of the hacking?" asked the Minister.

"For now, we are uncertain. Worse of all, it exposes all our assets around the world, too."

"Is there any stated purpose yet declared?"

"No."

"One official…" said the Minister, without mentioning whom "has called this cyber-burglary hacking as a heist of data that is the 'crown jewels" of intelligence gathering?"

"That may be true. But in less than 12 months, it's dated. So it's ageing data, if that's any consolation Sir."

"Hmm" said the Minister, somewhat appeased.

Trevor prepared to leave, but he stayed, in a companionable way. He turned to the Minister "By the way, how did they access the Passwords and security thresholds to reach this office?"

"Well. That's just what I wanted to talk to you about, privately. It seems, Trevor, that your wife Amanda Wells has a research office in Washington that was traced as the first source of password access! After that, they reached us through you."

"My *wife?* …Amanda? But she hasn't been running her business research firm in years!"

"True. We know that. But it appears that one of her personnel did…A woman by the name of Barbara Rubowsky, who worked at her New York Office, and is now in the employ of a certain politician Ali Enders. It was *her* password that opened the key access in her new position with the politician. It was a signature key code that she had received while working for your wife, years ago!"

"My God… I'm sorry Sir."

"Moreover, she's treading on topics that are sensitive with her findings….Things that…well, are best left unsaid. In particular, its stuff that is controversial in the United States, and we do the sorting for them…"

He stopped short and said "There's a project called HAARP, High Frequency Active Aural Research Program. The idea is to deploy an electromagnetic beam into the ionosphere. It's supposed to control world-wide communications…"

He continued walking, the sentence unfinished.

"But it has military uses?"

"It does. As it turns out, we were doing some joint tests in the Sinai desert with the Israel. Enders was attempting to steal the technology and sell it to the highest bidders."

Trevor waited, concern etched about his brow. "Did he succeed?"

"Under the guise of some scholarship fund or other, the damned fool who was sent to do the errand lost the test evidence. He disappeared" said the Minister, "but electromagnetic signatures on the grid tell us that the key frequencies of that test have been appropriated by another…"

"Is Amanda aware of this?"

"No. Not at all. But the thing is, she may be onto something, a lead perhaps that will reveal who has it. Needless to say that in the wrong hands, it's potent weaponry. She needs to be warned of any danger, report her position, and stay out of the way. These are menacing people with deadly intentions. ...So we made the decision to pull her credentials to all further access."

Trevor looked down. The implications were not lost on him. *That's* what all this was about.

That'll be all Trevor. I'll be in touch..."

* * *

Chapter 23

It was 98° on the Chesapeake Bay, and humid. But the newscast was upbeat, announcing "Lots of action on the water today…"

At dockside every sailboat imaginable was moored at a boat-slip or anchorage just off the peers. They had come for the racing event of the Bay.

By four o'clock in the afternoon, Admiral Bill Arguetta stepped up onto the podium, and, wearing his usual salamander blazer; chino yachting shorts and sun-bleached hat accepted a silver-inscribed Trophy for his win of the boat race.

The crowd on the lawn cheered. He kissed the reigning Yacht Club Princess; said a few words of appreciation to the Commodore of the Club, then returned to his boat crew gathered on the lawn.

Off-shore the breeze had accelerated and winds began gusting at twenty knots velocity: This was not a bay to trifle with, they all knew, but the event was mercifully over.

"Congratulations Bill…" yelled a supporter from the applause "You won with that yacht of yours!"

"Hey Look!" chortled another "What's that our there floating?…You lost your crew?"

Laughter.

Historic Annapolis was a popular sailing town, and it was where the US Naval Academy trained its best naval officers for military service. Admiral Arguetta was one of them.

After a career in the Pacific, it had been his choice to retire to this town with his wife, he said. But it also gave him easy access to the Pentagon where he still retained office hours for consulting on sensitive material.

His crew were pleased with the trophy. Arguetta handed the trophy to Bill, sun-burned and exhausted from the day on the water.

"That was a lot of work Skipper!"

He put an arm around Eileen and announced "So who's hungry and up for a Crab Feast?"

They faced him with mouth-slurping sounds, fierce nodding and laughter.

"Right then. Our porch! 1800 Hours. Five blocks due-East. That direction: *Walk!*"

Arguetta strolled on towards his house at the water's edge of the street, his wife Eileen and Amanda Wells at his side.

"Any bars along the way Sir?" asked Jimmy deValario, his white nose coated with greasy sunburn balm and his arms laced around Susan and Tammy.

"Euw!" said Tammy, pulling away.

"What?" replied Jimmy "*You* gals look pretty crisp yourselves!…" he nudged at their burnt shoulders from their day on the water.

"No…" called Arguetta, walking away. "No bars that will let *you* in, son!"

The Midshipman and the girls was standing outside the Club House.

"…Oh?" said Jimmy, edgy "Because I'm Latino?"

"No!" giggled Susan. "Because you need a shower!"

They all burst out laughing.

Later that evening, the house porch was definitely cooler. Amanda sat amongst friends, a tall cool drink in her hand.

"To Victory!" she toasted.

"And sweet it was…"added Arguetta "Bill worked his ass off!"

They laughed.

"Poor Bill" pleaded Eileen "He is a Midshipman.."

"Hell Yes!" said Argueta, "But he's got to learn how to sail sometime: I've met skippers who don't know how to steer a boat worth a damn…" he chuckled.

Eileen indicated to Amanda with a nod. *Man-talk!*

"So, tell us more about the discovery, Amanda?" asked Ellen, the three of them sitting in the torch-lit glow of a dark summer porch.

They sat, quietly and waiting.

The circumstances of Amanda' visit to the United States was not lost on them.

Amanda was grieving.

She had come for Dora's funeral. Or rather, a memorial service, since none of the bodies were recovered or flown home for burial. Dona and six of her students had vanished from their archaeological dig.

"I talked to the parents…" she began, the events still redolent. It was the least she could do for Dona Thompson, once her own student!

Ellen reached over and touched her hand.

Amanda's thoughts went to that afternoon when her own daughter argued about going to the North Pole for her summer Internship. Sandra had nearly signed up with Donna Thompson's expedition!

"Well…" she said, clearing her mind to answer Eileen's question about the discovery that turned up.

"It's an ancient icon, really. Dona was to write up a professional paper on it of course. But it's a archaeological Find they never thought possible in that part of the desert." Amanda's voice trailed off.

"Do you suspect foul-play?" asked Bill.

"No, not really. At least, I don't think so. We don't know much. Just that they went out for the day's dig. Then vanished!"

"Any sign of *visitors* to the dig?" asked Ellen.

"No. No mention online. No log entry. No communication with Director in Authority in Cairo. Just some debris from a picnic lunch, that's what they found. The screening artifacts, such as they were, were absent. That is, those she had reported on. She had emailed me…"

"Were they significant?" asked Bill.

Amanda hesitated. She knew that he asked for purely security reasons. He was, amongst other things, an attorney in the military man with forensic experience in intelligence gathering. His unit was exclusive and he was a trusted Advisor at the Pentagon where he worked all day and often nights overseeing matters of security and defense strategy.

She appreciated his asking, especially since she knew he and his wife highly valued the sanctity of their home as a place for peace and quiet to get away from it all. Above all, she hated to immerse him in matters that could become an official diplomatic enquiry by the US Department of State involving US citizens on foreign soil - and already the Justice Department was asking...

"No.." he nodded. "Carry on!"

"Maybe this discovery will provide information about a motive?" Eileen added gently.

"Well…Ohm. As far as I can tell, the artifacts appear to have commercial value since the University Museum received a summary. But they were shipped off. So, that rules out theft. But it's the location and *significance* of the scholarship that might be of interest in other ways…" she said, her voice fading "I dunno, anymore…"

Her thoughts perceived a world of prevailing and counter-culture orientations including multi- faceted doctrines. She was hesitant.

 "You'd be surprised at *what* passes for significance to True Believers" said Bill. "Usually it's a cover for disruptive and deviant behavior who mean it for harm."

"I realize that it is academically unpopular to consider the ancient wisdom of conventional authority, but the cultural items they found in the desert seemed, I think, to be redolent with symbolism that would ascribed to counter-legitimacy of Authority; a treasure showing obeisance and adulation and worship of a different authority than the one true God of the ancient scriptures. They represent themselves, because of their symbolism, to be a new liberating force with doctrinal beliefs used as new defensive weapons; - complete with challenge to icons advocating separation and ethnic cleansing of the ancient peoples – those of the ancient scriptures chosen by God to recognize his authority alone…"

Eileen let out a muffled giggle. "Sounds like the just the stuff Madison Avenue would give a modern politician running for election!" she said.

They laughed.

Arguetta looked admonishingly at his wife. "Self propagation is precisely the stuff of a Reformist movement." He picked up his beer. "Little changes over time. We are all human. We use the same strategic tools of persuasion for disruptive endorsement. Even if we have a hidden agenda for a new societal order!"

"Forgive him…" smiled Ellen. "He's a spook!"

"That I am, ladies. My job is to keep us safe from harm…" he said, getting up. "And if you'll excuse me, I must retire for the evening. I have a long day tomorrow."

"Good night Bill. And thanks for picking me up from Reagan Airport last week ..." said Amanda.

"Not at all. You and Trevor have done much for me and Ellen" he said. "I'm just glad I get you to sail our boat on race day!"

* * *

Chapter 24

For the few days that Amanda had left on this trip into the city of Washington DC, she would use the time selectively. It was what she wanted. That is, after completing a few official visits, events and entertainment invitations that Trevor and she would be expected to have made. But as she thought about it, their tour of duty in Washington was long behind them. Besides, without Trevor at her side, things were less formal, and her socializing would be kept to a minimum as tokens of respect…

Still, there was always the list of prerequisite friends who would insist on a call; those acquaintances who had become friends over the years; and then former colleagues and professionals - many of them now retired.

She'd make a few calls, she decided. Especially to pals like Simone at her Gallery in Georgetown - her father now passed away. Mrs. Carlos, formerly their housekeeper, now the proud mother of two sons in the US military.

Mainly though, it was her former staff at her Research Firm that she called, most of them in serious careers all over the country, some of them expressly flying into Regan Airport for an impromptu reunion, they told her.

And Barbara. Well, what could Amanda ever say to Barbara that she didn't already know intuitively? Older now, and gracefully aged, she was just the same inquisitive New Yorker you could count on, but never for a secret! That's only because Barbara *always* deduced the truth from people before they talked. "Insightful" was the way Amanda had described her once.

Amanda smiled. Barbara had done well for herself. She had a shop in one of New York's popular districts. A dress shop, for which she and Amanda had had to scour the earth to plan for, years ago.

"And now I have two boutiques" said Barbara. "I'm even eyeing a third in New Jersey!"

"Well at least you have your list of loyal followers!" quipped Amanda.

"That I do!" laughed Barbara. "But none as sincere and honest as you Amanda Wells! We had a *hell* of lot of fun changing the world, didn't we?"

"Yes we did!"

"So, tell me. What are you up to know? How is Sandra?"

Amanda told her. And it was long in the telling. Barbara wanted to know details. Not the social stuff like the boyfriends, the prospects and the connections that might have arisen, but the real details of her work; the professors she worked with; the details of the Internship project. Barbara was being…Barbara. And Amanda knew better than to cut corners, corners that, in their professional history of working as a team, they both understood. That was the nature of their occupation - often related to intelligence. They talked on a different level, offering deeper understanding and analytical observation than most people cared about. In research, they knew, it was the mundane; the details and the undiscovered that mattered. Especially if required – as they often were - to advise on policy issues with long term goals and ramifications for key decision-makers in Washington.

"Thank you for all your interest…" Amanda said finally.

"Nothing. You know me to be that inquisitive. Plus, I'm just you know, err…direct…"

"suspicious…" interrupted Amanda

"OK *suspicious*" repeated Barbara "But we were the true Truth-Seekers, right?"

"Right!" chuckled Amanda. "So what's new in New York these days? That is, since you're too busy to visit me in London!"

"Ha! Now you've asked me something worthwhile. I've been signed on for this lawyer who is running a political campaign, he's a candidate who wants to run for election and introduce reform to Washington!"

"Signed on?"

"Well, you know. As Publicist for his high profile campaign— as a manager, like…"

Barbara was the best there was, Amanda knew.

"What is his platform?"

"Oh, I dunno. Nobody's even listening anymore. God knows how he plans to *pay* for everything he wants to do…he's promising a lot of unsustainable stuff…"

Amanda had to laugh. "Who is he?"

"Ali Enders."

"*Who?*"

"Ali Enders. He's running on an Independent political platform. He wants the vacated seat from New Hampshire in the Senate for the duration of that term, and then aims to run for the White House!"

"Umm"

"*Don't* gimme the *Umm* treatment, I know what that kind of non-committal stance means, it means Lets-Wait-and-See! But I'm telling you, he's a radical Reformist! He's *trouble!*"

"Are you working for him?"

"Yes!"

"Does he pay you well?"

"Hell yes!"

"So be grateful for the wage…"

"-and stop whining like a New Yorker?" interrupted Barbara

"Well, I was just …"

"Never mind. I get the idea…'*Focus on the best, ignore the worst…*" They both laughed at the adage from Washington days of working together.

"So I'll keep you informed as to how long I can stand this politician and his wife" continued Barbara "*Jesus!* Politics ain't what it used to be!"

Amanda had to smile at her friend.

"So. Tell me…What's playing on Broadway?" asked Amanda.

"Oh…I thought you'd never ask! Come up! When's your flight? Let's *Go!*"

The conversation had turned to fun.

"You're on! I'm flying out of La Guardia Sunday…"

***

Security was tight in that building on Capitol Hill. In it were essential personnel close to the call of power…So secure, in fact, that in the winter, when the nation's capital went dormant under a severe covering of snowfall and ice, the building became an underground city itself; generators, lighting, communications and sensors came aglow. Even a high-water military transport vehicle stood-by with personnel for communications, shovels and supply if necessary, to approach for support and protection.

The building's facilities were vast - accommodating any kind of administrative function or interaction network - barring catastrophic environmental collapse, for Essential Personnel of this legislative body.

Above ground were variously designed spaces for luxury apartments with recessed front-door lighting; elevators and architecturally toned hallways.

Certainly, they had guest spaces: For those at the Entrance Lobby level of the building, there were guest-housing facilities for member or special visitors. But they were visible on CCTV monitors during day hours. That area contained entertainment spaces, play-ways for children and pets, open terraces for grills and swimming and parking.

For residents at ground level of 909 there were sports lounges, conference centers, connection-to-wireless areas as well as social recreational lounges. At below grade were Fitness rooms, theaters, bar rooms, coffee centers – all spaces furnished with architectural lighting, artwork and live botanical floral displays.

 Below ground were accesspoints secured and separated for underground parking floors.

Nobody without an electronic security key had access the building. Neither by foot, nor by car. Underground parking worked only by electronic remote recognition.

Otherwise, to enter the building - including Janitors and security who came in before dawn for their duties, access requirements were stiff, by special vetting and pass-recognition alone.

Certainly visitors entering the building lobby could   be entertained by the Concierge. And the Concierge offered an assortment of services, like cleaning, deliveries, messaging and business platforms as well as a waiting lobby.

But at night, after the building was locked and at the main entrance closed, the building was dedicated to those serving on Capitol Hill and their privacy protected, especially for those working late when the lights dimmed; the music hushed and the elevators ran silent.

Had Enders not been in her car he might never have been seen entering the building.

* * *

Chapter 25

From London, Trevor took the train back to Scotland. It gave him the opportunity to travel in quiet comfort, especially in a private compartment where he could review his papers for work.

He had just visited with his solicitor in London. All affairs had been settled, and his business matters were in good order. He was pleased. All corporate taxes were accounted for; paid in full, and the family and corporate legacy of the ancient income licenses fully in compliance with all government regulation. Of this he was proud, as he was proud of his family legacy to his country. It was something that had been in place since the 18th century. It was his duty to review the accounts periodically.

Moreover, all his investments were doing well globally. He had been richly rewarded over the years, and he went to great pains to see that his children shared his values.

What was the point of wealth or wealth management if not to contribute to society? Those were the words of his grandfather, still etched upon his soul. Words often repeated in his home where his own progeny had heard them.

Still, it was good to record everything, and to check on the dates of issue and obligatory promises made so long ago, even as the modern world changed around him.

Hedge funds or no. These particular funds were secure and sustainable - all properly recorded and easily verified as the charter of a special Foundation Fund, as required.

Certainly, investment funds were circulating in the capital markets; and they were not cheap. Capitalism, at its core, since first introduced by his family with Scottish money brought to England for the creation of a bank of England, came with risk.

Risk implied possible loss, yet risk also implied opportunity to the individual to better himself. It offered hope that beat in every heart. This, Trevor MacDonnell valued: Hope for any individual to achieve success!

Whereas such individualism had been suppressed by the Catholic monarchy of Europe throughout medieval history, venture capitalism prevailed with the Tudors of England who encouraged trade by individual investors using private capital.

Grounded in covenants of trust - rooted in biblical precepts of the Judaic-Christian traditions, what followed was a Western civilization developing free trade economies as democracies, human Liberty being its greatest prize.

But it had not come cheaply. The cost of wars, greed and illicit behavior had shown its face throughout history, he knew.

Today, financial and investment banking dealt with risk by issuing Risk and Insurance premiums.

Still, the precepts never changed, and his own family trust had grown to such proportions that it was his idea - and his idea alone, to establish a Foundation that recognized the efforts of those who aided the cause of independent opportunity; advancing human liberties…

That was the Scottish streak within him, as he put it to his solicitor.

As far as Trevor MacDonnell was concerned, money was to be used for the growth of good, and to create opportunities for others. Simple as that.

Old or new, the tenets of justice; duty and honor lay within the grasp of every man in his lifetime, great or small. This, Trevor had determined to do with his Foundation.

He had discussed it with his wife, Amanda Wells. She gave him her full support, and he knew what he must do.

Satisfied that now the Deeds of Trust were held in the vaults of the Bank of England, Trevor felt happy that his trip had been fruitful. The letter before him was from the Head of the Bank of England, thanking him for his trust, and promising to uphold the charter of the mission with appropriate bookkeeping in compliance with all the laws of the land.

The sun was shining, and the train rocked him gently in his seat. The landscapes of England unfurled before him. They were beautiful, he smiled.

Before he reached Scotland he received a call from Switzerland.

"Hello Trevor" said the dark silk voice. "This is Sophie."

 One floor below the main Concierge, the place most popular was the Coffee bar lounge - a small surge of coffee drinkers 24/7: Here was the building's activity epicenter, they all said. Here they laughed, they talked, when coming in they glanced up at digital wall monitor managed by the Concierge above them, a digital display of any Packages waiting for them as they unlocked their mail-box besides the coffee bar, a side mail room of brass, marble and glass décor. Especially in the mornings.

Bridget was there this morning. She was wearing a tan raincoat and a bag at her shoulder, ready to leave the building, but not quite. Her hair was still loose, cascading softly across her face as she bent down for her coffee.

High grade coffee poured like silk into embossed cups. For this building, the automated commercial-grade grinding machine was supplied by imported coffee beans from Costa Rica. It was delicious, everyone stopped here before leaving for work.

"Hello Sheila!" she said absently, focusing on the need to leave for work.

"Oh…Hi Bridgette. How are you doing?" came the reply from a woman about the same age, equally distracted. She was stepping over a spill of coffee whose dark stain had spread on the marble floor at their feet.

The coffee counter needed constant clean-up or floor mopping by Janitors. They moved invisibly through the crowd, always with a pleasant smile. Today was no different.

They were a cheerful bunch, the personnel who managed maintenance; security and janitorial service. They were courteous, each wearing appropriate floor-level uniform and badges as they moved through the building mopping floors and sanitizing.

Those who had access to secure premises vacuumed and dusted decorative artwork; conference rooms and business centers, wiping clean desk surfaces, computers, re-arranging seating and emptying the wastepaper baskets. It was a routine building function monitored on CCTV, all highly recommended. Kim especially.

Kim was a part-time student of Chinese origin who worked at the near-by Baseball Capitals' Stadium. He had worked at Stadiums before, particularly the Baltimore Ravens' Stadium at Camden Yards. That was his home, Baltimore. His credentials checked out, so he was without event. Moreover, he worked hard.

Kim could be quick and unnoticed when he wanted to.

Kim was paid well.

The capsule opened quickly and dissolved in the coffee almost instantly.

Nobody in the morning melee noticed a thing as he mopped up the spilled coffee.

* * *

Amanda had called Trevor at least four times.

He'd be home before dark. That was two hours ago. She sent up Victor in the Land Rover to fetch him from the Mountain and bring him home.

Besides, there was a storm coming.

The Lodge. That was his favorite place to work these days.

Aging had suited her husband well, she thought. Grey at the temples, a little less tall than he used to be when he served Her Majesty's Government in Parliament, but those unmistakable blue eyes never missed a thing, and his generous smile remained his dominant features.

At that altitude, the Lodge was the ideal spot for observing the sky with high magnification telescopes He had installed the planetarium with remarkable equipment and mechanical adaptations for his hemisphere. Updated software gave him feeds he could deliver to several scientific labs and observatories. Plus, it had heated quarters for overnight accommodation when warranted, used mainly for long duration and low latitude stellar observations...

Trevor's work was significant, even as an amateur. It had filled his retirement days with careful scientific recordation; astrological discourse, readings, conferences and colleagues who compassed the globe. Once, NASA even consulted his data.

Time was the primary factor of enquiry in all things astrological, of course. But history marching through time and the developments of mankind held him equally captive. Hence his devotion to archaeology, especially Findings that proved evidence of ancient accounts. For Trevor, time and the story of humanity went hand in hand.

Trevor was not voluble by nature. It was with some reluctance that he accepted invitations to speak of his work at universities or places of learning. But he served on several Sponsoring Boards, and was Advisor to many academic endeavors across the globe. Mostly, he just turned them down. Especially now that he was working on his book. Rather, it was Amanda who had him working on his book...Certainly, it passed their time together with shared interest and activity.

Still, his life was filled with people, and more recently, it seemed that his observations had to be scribbled them down in notes for Amanda to decipher, their order and reflections harder to discern or explain. Never once, in years of his conclusions had he had to retract a position or override a previous observation. But he was not a scholar born, as he put it. And Amanda was the best "Filterer" he had: If it didn't get passed her scrutiny, he often told her, then it wasn't worth delivering as a finding!

They laughed a lot.

Recently, Amanda thought, due to years of risk and endurance that he himself had undergone as a working professional, he seemed to be slowing down. At first she ascribed it to his health. But it was more, she realized. There was unusual urgency to his observations. He was agitated, the data copious. He felt as if he had much yet to accomplish, he told her.

Trevor talked incessantly about Sandra's mission. Especially as she reported in on her Exploration Expedition at the North Pole as a graduate student. ..

Still, Amanda was concerned. His hours were too long, and the Lodge too isolated and cold for him to remain up there alone for the night.

She called him again.

"The Stars are right, darling..." he told her. "I want to be here observing the Norther Sky tonight..."

She knew better than to argue.

"Not without me to keep you warm, and hot drinks to keep you up!" she said tactfully. "So I'm sending up Victor in the Land Rover to see you!"

"Umm. Do you know..." he said, almost oblivious to what she had just said "That the Bowles theory of RB is rendered moot by the finding that there is no crust beneath the inner mantle and the outer...?"

"The Rotational Bending, do you mean?"

Of course she knew what he meant.

Bowles had a theory asserting that the combined gravitational effects of the Sun and the Moon pulled at the Earth's crust at an oblique angle, wearing the underpinning that linked the crust to the inner mantle. The result was a pull of centrifugal force on the Poles that if stretched would cause the magnetic poles to shift on the axis of the planet.

"True" she said. "Until they just discovered that there is no hard crust beneath the mantle! It's all one contiguous inner core of various degrees of magma viscosity, right?"

"Perhaps…" he said. "Perhaps not. The gravitation forces on the magnetic mass might be enough to tip the magnetic poles…"

She could see him now, surrounded by his paraphernalia and enjoying every minute. "So Darling. Do you think we could magnetically motivate you to gravitate yourself home?"

He laughed. "Yes of course!"

* * *

137

The National Press Club was filling with people. The event in Washington DC was receiving some attention.

On the 10th floor of the building, all dedicated elevators opened to dinning rooms, bars and studio broadcast sound rooms teeming with Media members. Reporters, anchors and camera crews from news agencies set up in the Press room. Commentators of various languages and stations using satellite uplinks for global broadcast spoke to their cameras by way of explanation. All hallways of the upper stories of the building was alight with transmitting for international press members, worldwide.

Flanked by pictures on the walls showing celebrity events through history, the procession moved into the conference center where the headlights and make-up made their final adjustments for cameras.

Finally, it was time.

"Ali, you're up!" called out his event manager.

Finally, the hour had arrived for an announcement in Washington DC delivered by a senior scientist at the University of Chicago.

The house lights dimmed, and a panel of Faculty took their seats across on a platform.

"We are proud to announce our Findings of what has to be the most comprehensive collaborative effort conducted in the Middle East by a number of Universities..." announced Professor Stevens of the Department of Humanities.

"In an remarkable effort by specialists and experts from academic institutions across the United States and around the world, we are excited to show you the results of *Sechem*, an archaeological dig of some significance. It is a place important to ancient scripture and culture. But before we begin, allow me to present the principles behind this Initiative."

"Professors Hallil; Jacobs and Thompson from Chicago University; Dr. Daniels and Swensen from the University of Holland; Theologians from Rome Institute of Religious Seminary; and others...too many to recognize. We add our thanks to their various governments and institutions who collaborated. But especially the Chair wishes to recognize *one* politician who wrote the necessary legislation to fund this project, and got the votes to ensure its passage through Congress. Congressman Ali Enders…"

The Media positioned themselves, their wires, transmission and communications pointing to the man who stood up. As international broadcast began commentating, a whispering began that would translate from English to various tongues the words uttered at the podium.

Enders took his bows to applause, and the presentation proceeded.

"We have uncovered the site where in the 19th century before Christ the patriarchs Abraham and Jacob worshipped, a place identified as where Joshua rallied the tribes of Israel, and where Amimeleeh was crowned as Israel's first King…" said the speaker.

The room hushed as charts lit up behind them on a large flats-screen.

"Here, in the old Biblical city of *Shechem* in Joran an alter and a sacred oak existed. According to a tradition preserved by the Hebrew culture for over one millennia, that is, 1000 years before the Bible was first written in the 11th century B.C."

"The *Shechem* sacred site was discovered below the courtyard of the city's temple fortress. The excavation which began in 1957 resumed in 1960 provided scholars with the long search of the sacred area. Was this legend? More significantly, are these the places of direct dialogue –as it is told, with God."

The screen went dark, and the panelists rearranged themselves. The TV cameras took a break.

Another scholar from Rome stood up and proceeded with the presentation. He was shorter than the others, middle aged with a hairline well groomed and a face that was broad and not deeply featured. "I am Ernesto D'Assuga, a biblical scholar from Equador. Allow me to continue"

"According to Ernest Wright of Harvard, this can be critically compared with the ancient oral traditions in an achievement not unlike the Greek legend of Troy by Schliemann's excavations in Asia Minor…"

"…Yet this expedition at *Sechem* is the largest archaeological dig in the Holy Land. It was, after all, one of the great cities of its area in ancient times; 4000 years of history now lie buried within a ten-acre mound, or "tell" as we call it, just east of Nablus in Jordan. "

The flat-screen came on.

"In this map…we can see that in Biblical times, it occupied a strategic position at the eastern opening of the pass between Mt, Ebal and Mt. Gerasim…

"Here, and here, you can see it is the site of the modern village of Balatah. On this spot is what we think to have been Jacob's Well, a place that must have supplied *Sachem* with water. It is cited by the narrative of the Samaritan woman who offered water to Christ when he approached her in 1024 A.D. The account of that parable…you know, I am sure."

"Shechem is the first city mentioned in the Bible; when Abraham and Jacob visit it, the city was a stronghold of an empire ruled from Egypt.

It was during this early era - at the very beginning of what is called the "Hyksos" age (13th century B.C.) that Shechem's inhabitants *enclosed* the sacred place within a courtyard. Rooms for priests and pilgrims. It was surrounded by a fortification wall, consistent with the narrative. They kept the sacred area - within the confines of the city."

From a longer historical view, we know that it was built about four times in the classical period. Finally, in early modern times it was abandoned 1650 B.C.

But as we know, it earlier once had a massive temple fortress built on the site with city gates. It remained under Egyptian dominion for about 400 years until the 13th century B.C. when the Israelites - under Joshua conquered the land of Palestine."

The audience was captive, and nobody moved. Only the *whirr* of cameras gave signs of life in the room.

"As you know, throughout this period, Sechem was the religious and political center of north-central Palestine before Jerusalem took over under King David."

Someone dropped their pencil, and it rolled the full length of the room.

"Here, after the death of King Solomon, Israel was assembled to crown Roheheam, the son of Solomon. But by then the twelve tribes had fractured into ten; and the Northern Kingdom of Israel made Shechem its first capital."

"The Samaritan capital was destroyed by John Hyrcanus, high priest and prince of the Judeans in Jerusalem in 107 BC."

He ended abruptly, and brought a small applause. Vaguely, the room lapsed and the audience dispersed.

The lights switched off and cameras cut out. All electrical devices were losing their battery charge. A cell phone rang, and the reporter left the room to speak to his Executive Producer.

A new speaker had taken the podium – a graduate from the University of Chicago. His voice commanded attention.

"They call us 'Post-Modernists' for a reason…" he began, smiling wickedly. "That's because we are seen as renegotiating the past as if by wizardry. But that's not true. We only examine more texts. Does this take-away from the truth? Or does it minimize the spiritual force of its original intended meaning? I believe not. Even as we examine other texts. There are a number of ancient texts, written and oral, known from the ancient world that overlap and corroborate what happened. The site that   Ernesto described is significant to us post modernists for a number of reasons. Some, significant as spiritual messages. Others, important in giving us context and legacy, anachronism and chronology. There are many, and I list only a few here."

"It is on this site that the invincibility of God is declared where He promises the land *'to the descendents of Abraham, and Abraham then builds an alter unto the Lord.'*"

"Here, Moses commands the people when they arrive here to build an altar to the Lord at *Mount Ebal.* This site flanks Sechem, it is here on the site that hold plastered stones inscribed with the laws of the covenant…"

"Later, when Joshua admonishes the tribes of Israel to renew their covenant with the Lord, Joshua sets beneath the sacred oak a great stone (the sacred Pillar) to serve as a witness of the covenant, *"a witness against you, lest you deny your God…"*

The graduate scholar completed his presentation.

The house lights went up and the audience gave an applause.

Reporters asked questions, a few were answered in practical ways; others were fraught with spiritual complications, or political nuance, to be answerable. Oone question did get attention.

"Sir. When the funding for this dig was approved, did it come from the Amendment to a Bill or was it appropriate as a cultural and educational line- item. And if so, which agency?"

The question came from a tall woman, a reporter determined to become visible.

"I'm not certain. You'll have to ask the Administrators on that one…Sorry! I don't know the answer to your question. All I can tell you is that the Bill was introduced by Ali Enders and passed…"

Budgets. Again! They rolled their eyes.

The rest of the Media covered her over quickly with white noise and general muffling over repacking…

Ali jumped up and wrapped up the waning presentation.

"So there you have it, Ladies and Gentlemen! One of our greatest finds that crosses all religions and all cultures! Thank you for coming…Yes, the bar is open!"

News feeds pouring from every wall of the Press Club representing every corner of the planet.

The evening passed slowly, a few drinks here, a good meal there. Gradually, the city night of the Nation's capital absorbed the dissipating crowd until all had gone home and the Club fell silent., except for a barman alone with echoing News feeds.

The Press Conference was over.

Done.

Done. And made public!

Only later at his home that night did Ali Enders turn to face the black sky from his desk window. There he sat in the dark, a drink in his hand. As for the rest…It was fair game.

He raised his drink to his lips, the echo of night traffic penetrating the stillness.

The Pillar, the *sacred* Pillar - they told him, had been discovered!

He had bid for it at auction.

It was his. Even if the scholar from the University of Chicago disappeared without a trace.

The relic was found on the side of the road by a passing tradesman. He gave it to an Antiquities dealer in the city. It was bought by a French Collector. And it was fair game…

 Now *that* was a legacy that would last him a lifetime, if not a fame unprecedented by any owner of any relic *anywhere*…

Still, he lingered.

Where the hell was the rest of the money that he had appropriated?

He finished his drink.

He'd make his calls in the morning.

* * *

Chapter 26

He and Jack met in a casual place, a most unlikely setting for surveillance or suspicion. Actually, it was amongst the confections, lunchmeats and cheeses in the marketplace of Dean and De Lucca in Georgetown where red and blue bottles lined up against high windows refracting hues across the cathedral space like mosaics.

They sat outside by the canal. When weather permitted, the parterre of the grocer crept the boundaries of winter awnings that enclosed tables. Even as cobble stones offered sparrows good pickings from petite pastries and fresh bread from the coffee bar along the old district city port.

Here, students gathered. Shoppers packaging boutique gifts from Old Georgetown also paused here, as did diplomats, bankers and agents mingling at the café in an amalgam of city activity.

Sitting in the open breeze overlooking a blue glittering river and shaded by Myrtle, this was the most innocent of settings.

Especially for Ali Enders.

Jack was from New York. A young financial broker trained at business schools and positioned in New York City for inter-agency cooperation, his job put him often between government and private enterprise. A well dressed young professional with a thin tie and tan narrow pants, he weaved between the two worlds with impunity, and he had a sense of humor that Ali found lacking in most Americans.

Jack read things differently, he once told Ali.

Jack would laugh at his perspectives, this man from New York sitting now at the heart of a city shaped by policy proceedings, political correctness and international sanction-eering, as he called it. Yet Jack was a man who dealt in precision and permutations; statistics, trends, billion-dollar computer trades across the globe in multi-second intervals. No wonder he could not define one cultural boundary from the next thought Ali, let alone sympathize with national interests.

This amused Ali Enders. Jack was an Argentine émigré who had been adopted through a Middle Eastern agency that failed to specify his country of origin, let alone his religion.

Jack suited Ali Enders fine. So the news that Jack gave him, in conversational tones, was level and uneventful.

Ali Enders knew they could talk freely without causing a stir, as in any broker-client confidentiality.

"So…" Ali asked, finally finished with his food. "How's everything?"

Jack wiped his mouth with a table napkin, a tab of sauce laced around his lips still.

"Umm. Good!" he said evenly, his head inclined slightly. "Yeah. It's all good!"

"Did the stock work well, then?"

"Stock?" Jack said. "What stock? I placed it all in bonds!"

"Bonds?" asked Ali, a little puzzled. "Well…Ok then. If you think it's good. What bonds and where did they perform?"

"An Emerging Market Fund based out of Asia"

"Asia?"

"Oh yeah. It's hot there, all those construction projects…"

Ali was getting impatient. "Look. I told you to invest locally. Not globally!"

Jack pulled back, surprised. "What's wrong with a better deal on the global markets?"

"It's just wrong. That's all. I took the money out of an Appropriated Bill that's funding a cultural project, and you put it in some overseas investment fund?"

"Hey! That's what I *do*, man!"

"Ok. Sell it! Bring it all home. Buddy…*All of it*. Repatriate the whole amount. You got that?"

"Wait…Now hold on!"

"No!" insisted Ali. "Now *you* hold on! You were instructed to make some sound investments with the capital for a while until the funds could be placed in safer accounts…"

Jack just stared at him. This was not the way it was supposed to work. You used your Stock broker to advise and invest on safe bets. Sometimes, for high-yield returns. The *highest*, in this case. *High risk premium grade investments.* Those had been his instructions from Ali Enders. Jack reminded him. "I have your directives!" he added.

"Never mind! Pull the lot!" said Enders.

Jack's face was blank.

"Well. There's a problem with that…" began Jack.

"First, the Volatility Index that I work with…I may not get it all back for you. Wait…with the Earnings you gave me to reinvest…What do you think all that QE is about? It's to stimulate reinvestment in the stock market, right?"

"Quantitative Easing is designed as a Central Bank Window for bankers to fill their vaults to meet compliance requirements, remember?"

"To say nothing of my Fee" Jack was saying "And then you have *Margin* calls that are nowhere ready for maturity…You'll take a huge loss. This is an early withdrawal. What are you doing Ali?"

Ali drank from his beer.

 "Look. What I gave you was different. It was funds appropriated for a government expenditure that I borrowed…I meant to invest it to make some money while it was waiting for deposit into a program!"

"*What?* You should have told me! There are plenty Shorts out there…I could have found a couple for you"

Ali's cell phone rang. He opened the speaker.

"Yep?"

"Hello Mr. Enders. This is Inspector Abrams. Just a few more questions about the girl at 909 New Jersey Avenue. Ingar?"

"Oh Yes Inspector. Fire away. Anything to help.."

"According to her office cohorts, she was working on a Bill set for the House Floor in a couple of weeks. A Tax Reform Bill, they said. Did she speak of it?"

The color drained from Ali's face. And he turned away. Especially from Jack.

" Yes, I do remember. She spoke of it once or twice…"

"She told her family that you had assured her of its passage with some lobbying, is that right Sir?"

"Possibly. I do that regularly for key bills."

"So this *was* an important bill?"

Ali paused, surprised.

"Yes"

"But according to her colleagues, she thought the Bill was declared a hopeless cause on account of some opposition in the Senate?"

"Well…"

"So had you informed her about its cancellation from the agenda at the time of her death?"

"Err…I'm not sure."

"Not sure?"

"No."

"Yet you say it was a major Bill…?

"Oh, you know how these things go on Capitol Hill. "

"Correct me if I'm wrong Mr. Enders, but in this town, when a major Bill comes through for Lobbyists on K Street, the newspapers don't close the doors for a week without pages of copy on the subject…"

"Your point?"

"This was a major Bill. Yet she was, err…what? *misinformed?*"

Ali did not respond.

"Had you and she had some err…discussion or conflict on the night she died about the issue?"

"No. Of course not!"

"Oh?"

"I hadn't seen her in days remember?"

"Right. Was she ill, when you last saw her?"

"No."

"She died of poisoning" said Abrams.

A silence ensued.

"I'm sorry" said Enders.

"Right."

Ali got up from the table, the speaker now off.

Jack waited, draining his beer. The river breeze was cooling. In winter, he thought, this popular alley would be a funnel for biting cold.

Ali had been walking around with the cell phone in his ear, and Jack watched him.

While talking, Ali had dislodged some dirt with his shoe from a wedged stone along the upper retainer ledge of the canal steps.

Judging from the look on Ali's face, Jack could guess how it was going.

He turned. "Certainly Inspector…"

By the time Ali resumed his seat at the table, Jack was standing and preparing to leave, his ears having politely disregarding any words overheard. But it was his name on his Trading License, and he had heard enough…

"Hey…I'm sorry it's been a bummer surprise for you on that investment" said Jack.

Ali enders was pale, his eyes dark and roaming.

"You alright?…" asked Jack.

"Yeah. Yeah. Sure" said Ali. "He wanted to know if the kid had any vested interest in an Immigration and Tax Reform Bill I was reviewing…As if I had anything to do with it!"

Jack nodded.

"As if I should keep people informed about the passage of a Bill…The damned thing was DOA in the House. No way was it going to get traction…."

"Err…the girl?"

"Didn't have a clue" shrugged Ali Enders. "Perhaps she thought she could influence me!"

Jack and Ali faced each other. Jack spoke squarely.

"I'll retrace my steps and withdraw the Put. I'm sorry. I misunderstood   your   need   for   the   money…"
"Hell no!" said Ali, his face pale and moist. "It's not so much …the money… as it's the *exposure* to accounts foreign…Just

politically incorrect, that's all. There's plenty of money for me to cover any losses, believe me."

Jack looked at him. It wasn't the way his investors normally responded when they learned of a potential margin call; or any sort of early withdrawal considering the penalties, let alone tax implications. He nodded, his concern shifting now to the integrity of his client.

"Hell yes!" Ali took a big breath. "What's coming in from an Annuity fund holds endless prospect.."

Jack looked down to the river, a ribbon that laced around this city of power and influence.

"It's a bottomless source of funds. Sorry I jumped out at you. It …err took me by surprise! You know how political campaigns can look like when they inspect your investment strategies, right?"

"Sure. I understand…" said Jack, glancing at the cell phone. A police investigative officer had just called about a girl-friend found dead in her apartment. That much had been made clear over the speaker when the call came in.

"Yeah, thanks! It's a wild trip, no question. Poison! But I'm cleared from the list of suspects. That's the way I like it to be, right?"

"Right."

"Ok. Then. Talk to you soon, yes?"

"Sure. I'll be in New York" said Jack leaving for the line of waiting cabs that passed through the old district and heading uptown to five star hotels.

Ali was left on his cell phone again.

* * *

Chapter 27

They were at the beach, he and the family.

Caroline looked lovely, if overdressed in earrings for a fisherman's jetty. But the kids were enjoying themselves, and though he would undoubtedly be staying at a Hotel further down the coast for the requisite ice-cream Boardwalk and hermit crab search that night, he enjoyed being a little lost amongst the locals.

The SUV had air-pressure released from its tires, and with a beach riding permit affixed to the dash, they broached the sand dunes of Lewis Point, ocean entrance to the great Delaware Bay and Atlantic ocean.

Caroline called out to him playfully. "Beach wimp!"

He laughed, and had to agree. All that was missing was a white bandana handkerchief for sun protection and a mosquito porch for grandma's beach chair. Caroline could be lovely, he decided.

The kids ran all over the sand and back, dunes thick with low lying dwarf shrubs, grasses and sedges of phragmites. The coastal region was a vast natural parkland, managed for shore-erosion control and storm abatement.

They fished, their line snagging on seaweed. Enders even landed a couple of sea bass with the help of Tony, their eight year old son.

She invited him, Caroline, to spend the night with them at the cottage rental. He reminded her of their conjugal truce – that he would stay away and she would act as his wife for political media. But she invited him to stay, and they made love that night.

By dawn, his mind was elsewhere.

Ensconced in his Kmart beach-chair and high-priced sunshades, Caroline found him reading the Minutes of the last FOMC meeting. She offered him coffee.

Last Tuesday the Federal Open Market Committee met in the offices of the Board of Governor of the Federal Reserve System in Washington DC

The list of attendees was prodigious. He made a study of them. The Chair, Vice Chairs, all thirteen with Alternate Members who represented a Midwestern bank; two Southern banks; one in Dallas and Philadelphia, respectively.

He knew them all.

The Administration's Secretary, Deputy and two Assistant Secretaries were present, along with General Counsel, Deputy General Council and three recognized economists.

A team of associate economists were on hand for support, and the Manager of the System Open Market Account. Under him came a Deputy Manager; a 2nd Secretary of the Board and Office of the Secretary of the Board of Governors.

Monetary policy was no small item. Its decisions shaped global markets, he knew.

The list of representatives at the meeting was prodigious. Present would be directors of the divisions of banking supervision and regulation; monetary affairs; research and statistics, financial stability policy research groups. Also senior special advisers, assistants and senior associate directors of the divisions of international finance; international monetary affairs and chief economists. Especially, he noted, there would be representatives from major key bank centers such as the Federal Reserves of San Francisco, New York, Boston, Cleveland, St. Louis, Chicago and Richmond.

He read fast.

> *"In the Manager's report, the developments in domestic and foreign financial markets …*
>
> *"The Manager updated the Committee on the plans and noted a soft floor for money market interest rates…*
>
> *"The manage also reviewed the reinvestment policy for maturing Treasury security, specially Treasury auctions…."*

Sand got in his eye. "Daddy, play ball with us!" admonished Tony, his hands filling the air with sand as he tossed it up and down beside him.

> *"...Desk rolls over the maturing securities held in the FOMA into newly issued security in proportion to the issue amounts of the new securities, and the Federal Reserves receives the interest rate ....*

"Daddy!"

> *"The managers updated the Committee on tentative plans to improve the calculation of the effective federal reserve funds published by the...."*

"A fish! Dad... a *fish*, look!"

Ali Enders got up. He fooled around with the rod, a few neighboring fisherman down the line chuckling at his son's response - which was more natural than his own with a rod and reel that he couldn't coordinate, and eventually, they landed a medium sized fish. But his mind was miles away...

Only later, after the day had been finally wrapped up, he decided that he had a plan of action all figured out.

The Federal Reserve System, the core of all banking money lending to all banks should be reeled into the control of the legislature. Even if for censure!

Already, there had been a few murmurings about it on the side.

Once he could do that...then he could reel in the rest!

He smiled, pleased with himself.

Congress, he decided, was a good place to be these days.

* * *

The Report that came to him was from NASA.

Under his privileges on a Senate Subcommitte able to call up Hearings for potential legistlation, he had access to some of the nation's most closely guarded secrets. T

This report, originally fostered by the Office of Science and Technology, has been sequestered by the Department of Homeland Security and considered a threat to national defense.

Why?

That evening, after a full day of reading he picked up the phone to his office.

"Hello Ms Jenkins, how are you?"

"Thank you, very well Senator…Hope all is going smoothly for your upcoming Hearing Sir" she said, expecting him to be at his home office, prepping for it.

"Well, not quite, exactly…" he said. "As you know, the Speaker of the Senate has asked to suspend my activities until the Ethics Board clear my name?"

"Yes Sir" she said, knowing the political ploys of two parties fighting for dominion on the floor of the House.

"… and you know how long that can be when it comes to a House of Representatives full of Republicans, right?"

"Yes Sir "

"Ethics can be everything from Moses to Moms!" he laughed.

"Right!"

"Anyway. I wonder if you could do me a favor, and ask Smith to make the rounds for me on a potential Senate Sub Committee Hearing from both sides of the Aisle. Have him take a pulse on their feelings. It's a Science and Technology item…It's costing us all a hell of a lot of money, and I'd like to know why…"

"Both sides of-the-Aisle?" she repeated, pencil in hand and taking notes.

"Right. He'll know what to do."

"Right."

"I   can't   just   sit   here   and   do   nothing!"
"Of course not Senator. You are much too energetic
and…*popular*!" she said, inferring his sphere of influence.

"Damned right I am!" he laughed "All that social networking
is not for nothing…you know!"

"No Sir."

"Oh, and Jenkins, when I get back, how about a lunch treat
over at the Mandarin?"

"That would be lovely, Sir. Thank you!"

"No problem. Thanks Jenkins!" he said, and closed his phone.

This was the biggie, he decided. *Definitely.*

* * *

Chapter 28

Timing.

He would wait for August. The last week in August was a good time... The summer vacation.

It was a week when children were having their last fling at the beach before school, and when parents indulged them. The city would shut down.

Congress, the White House, the Judiciary, State and Federal offices offered liberal leave benefits, and every lobbyist; lawyer and legislator would be pretty much out of touch: The President was nearly always seen bicycling around Martha's Vineyard with the family - world affairs seemingly dormant.

Thus, if there was a need for any Special Session action, it was left to one or two players to take charge in that somnolent state of the summer vacation.

The Plan was impeccable. To seize control of the Federal Reserve was to manage a crisis that left you in charge and with little room for Objections.

The stock market never slept; and with the central bank preparing to issue a rate hike in financing in September, timing was everything.

The stocks that plummeted that week were alarming. The sell-off was swift, no signals had offered warning.

Since 9/11, shock analysts had prepared the Americans for anything: If there was any cause for alarm, it was quickly subdued - demonstration that *nobody should panic.*

The President stayed away. The Vice President was in Aspen. Others were overseas.

Two days later, the stocks rebounded, and everyone gave a sigh of relief. Apparently, a flash news item that sent investors to the phone had been caused by a disruption in a production pipeline.

Ali knew better. The real damage was in US Treasuries. Bonds were selling off. A rumor persisted that the dollar was about to weaken in value…

Banks were getting nervous: If a currency valuation was about to happen, the holdings – and the debts - of the United States would be vastly altered. In theory, it could bankrupt the nation. But only in theory.

Ali Enders was in town. Thus, as a Senator on Finance Committees he had some standing.

* * *

Mom, you'll never believe what I've found… I don't know what to say about it. It's like, such new stuff…"

"Oh?" said Amanda, smiling. "You found the Snowman?"

"Mom!"

"O.k. I know what you're doing is serious, it's just that I'm just not sure it's your calling… You're still very young. Give it all some time - then decide! "

"I got it. *I got it.*"

"Sorry sweetheart. I trust you entirely, and I'm dying to hear about it. So go on. An Arctic Fox? "

"No. It's this plant life. Well, the Russians say there are no signs of any large-creature life. Only you'll never guess what we've found!"

"A wooly mammoth?"

"Hah! Almost! Only it's sea-like"

"A Polar Bear? A ringed sea-lion?"

"No! No! No!" said Sandra, laughing.

"So, didn't the Russians find some sea anemone from a deep dive? Shrimps and amphipods?"

"Well, yes. They did. But I'm talking about an ancient frozen discovery. Like an incredible, unbelieve…*Find*"

"Dad will want to hear it…"

"I will tell… I will. Only its *hush-hush* just now. Tim told us to remain quiet…"

"Ok. Then follow his instructions. Tell us when you can!"

"O.k. Only I wanted to give you a call."

"I'm so glad you did! It's always great to hear your voice Sweetie. Take care. Stay Alert and be safe, take every precaution with that climate at all times!"

"Will do. *Loveyoumom.* Bye!"

As Amanda closed her phone, she felt a little apprehensive. What could possibly be so serious for a bunch of kids on a summer Artic expeditions to warrant secrecy?

She moved around her kitchen, her thoughts puzzled. Perhaps it was for security reasons.

To them of course, *everything* they found would be a

discovery full of excitement and wonder. She smiled. And so it should be, though Amanda. At that age, such things were adventures.

But security about a Find in that Arctic climate? What was that all about?

And Tim, the one who told them to remain discrete was not just any Team Expedition Leader. Nor even her Professor. But Tim Beaverbrook. The Science Expedition's Director. He was the University Vice President.

What was that all about?

* * *

Chapter 29

"It was a matter of national security " said Enders. "It had to be done!"

"Congress doesn't like Executive Orders out of the White House" said one of his most loyal supporters "let alone out of one of its Congressional Offices!"

"Neither does the White House even like Executive Orders out of the White House!" admonished another "Especially when the White House is out on vacation!"

"Jesus Ali, what were you thinking?" asked his own lawyer.

"I'm a Senator, right? I was in town when the crisis unfolded. I had to do what I had to do to avert a national disaster!" said Enders

They stared at him, all of them. Each trying to figure out ways to reconcile his actions to the media and mitigate damages to their political party when they came. And come they would!

They were sitting in one Virginia's most luxurious Hotels across the Potomac River from Washington DC. Enders leaned forward from his leather sofa. "I explained myself to the President…"

"You explained yourself to the President?" mimicked the Majority Whip. "What does that mean?"

"I signed by Proxy an Executive Order for the Economic Continuity of Government."

"He approved?" asked the Senior Aid of the Majority Whip.'

"If course he approved…" interrupted Jack Heinenbaum, a devout opponent of the GOP. "Why *wouldn't* he? This gives *him* power over the purse!"

Enders smiled inwardly. *Atta-boy!*

It took several hours of explaining, a day of meals and a night of drinks before they came to terms with what he had done.

In the end they left, shaking their heads and recommending briefs and explanations that might stem further questions. But they left.

And now he was free to go.

Enders drove to National Airport. His flight to New England had been postponed, now he would spend a few hours in the Lounge. Travelling First Class gave him a few privileges in waiting areas…A place of separation where he could be alone to collect his thoughts.

He ordered a couple of drinks. It had been a harrowing few days.

Still, he was pleased with himself.

 He had set into motion a law that would divert all asset holdings by the Fed into the US Treasury. A secondary appropriation that was on his desk would now tap into the Treasury for special funds to service his affairs.

Simple. He sipped his second drink.

Essentially, his expense account had tapped into the US Treasury! He had appropriated funds for himself and for his Bills approved. Not all bills voted into law were automatically appropriated with funding.

The Federal Budget was coming up against a deadline. Reserved as a tool of negotiation and power brokering between all political parties, the budget was arrested to make no further expenditures until both Houses of Congress reconvened at the new session in the Fall. For now, they were all out for the summer.

Ali Enders had just signed the necessary mandate to continue government expenditures - and thereby guarantee the funding of his program!

It was a Takings of resources of sorts.

By any other name, it was the perfect Heist.

And that was just the beginning!

Already he had drafted some Legislation. It would make its way through the House, then the Senate.

It was a Congressional Bill requiring the Federal Central Bank to hand over all authority of autonomy and all its assets to the US Treasury. Monetary Policy would now be theirs!

Effectively, he was ending the independent role of monetary policy makers…Power, now   concentrated all in one hand…Well.

He chuckled.

What would the Founders of the American Constitution say now?

The separate branches, checks and balance of power in the Republic would be history! With the purse in the hands of the White House, the world would be its oyster, as they say!

Especially since he was slowly propelling himself into the White House.

Why not? He'd have the campaign   funding that could underwrite a media blitz campaign….

His Flight was called. His cell phone had four messages, all switched off.

Fortunately, he had the 'Good Looks' for a great campaign. And Carolina cut a nice figure too, when in the mood, that is. He turned on his cell briefly, to call her and let her know he was flying home.

* * *

Chapter 30

"Mom" said Sandra calling from Anchorage, Alaska.

"I'm devastated. There's just two of us here. We've been separated from the others and they've booked us into a hotel. I called Steve my Advisor at the University of Chicago. He told me to wait for instructions. They've suspended our research and asked us to put my findings on hold. I can't understand it."

"Why is that?"

"I'm not exactly sure. My Advisor says they don't like the topic of enquiry or something. The funding got blocked and the university hasn't budgeted for extending to unfunded projects. I'm getting the run-around…I don't know what to do just know."

"What were you working on?"

"Polar radiation. It's wasn't anything, really - other than for space flight exposure for Advanced Satellite Aviation Weather Products."

"Really? You're Dad would most interested!"

Sandra laughed, her anxiety fading.

"Yeah! Tell him it's related to his earth drifting magnetic poles!"

"Right…"

"Actually, you know what the funny thing is … We have been actually seeing this phenomenon currently shifting around toward Siberia at about 40 miles per year. It leaves no trace of polar radiation there…But we might be seeing evidence up there of a total magnetic shift of the poles…"

"Polar *radiation*? What's that got to do with it?"

"It is said in legend" said Sandra "that it can make people mad…and actually it is …."

"Hello, Sandra?" said Amanda. "Hello?..."

The transmission was less than clear.   "Yes, I can hear you now…."

Amanda raised the volume on her device.

"…So, I think I'll go back to DC and wait it out a few weeks…" said Sandra

"No!" admonished Amanda. "Stay where you are and see this through! If the worse comes to the worse, sit through your courses for the next semester and just wait until you get a clear answer from your Advisory Committee!"

No answer.

"Sandra?…"

The line seemed dead, or rather crackled.

"Hello?...."

"Hello…Are you still there, Sandra?"

"Hey! Yes, Mom…. Can you hear me now?"

"Yes. It's a bad connection…"

"My online server keeps cutting off…" Sandra said.

"Darling. Take Notes by hand if you have to. Got it? Stay close to the authorities there, and stay in safe places. Don't take off on travel right now, please!"

"…..Mom?.....Can you ….me….?"

"Sandra!"

There was no sound.

"Sandra. Can you hear me?"

"Hello?"

It was no good. The line was dead.

A message followed the call. Sandra's classwork was with her for the semester, but she was having trouble getting it downloaded to the University online computer server.

Amanda emailed her back.

> *Copy us with your assignment to Dad's secure server. We'll re-route it to your Academic Advisor , as necessary! Complete your obligation for your course-work. Stay put. Stay safe!*

Amanda paused, then added

> *"Keep at it, and don't give up! Love Mom."*

When Amanda opened her email the next morning she was alarmed.

> *They've suspended my registration of this class' research credit. Should I take a Leave of Absence? I don't understand what's going on, but I've been cut off and stopped dead in my tracks on this topic at the University...That's two whole semester's of work!..."*

Amanda was worried.

Two days later she received another message. She printed it up and went immediately up to Trevor's Lodge to show it to him.

> *Mom. We don't have any means of transportation to get back! We're stranded here. Help!*

By the end of the day, Trevor had been on the phone to Washington discretely making special arrangements for his daughter to be brought back to the University. He would talk to Arguetta later, he told Amanda.

Amanda was packed, her flight booked to Reagan Airport. But since they decided to remain out of the spotlight and keep a low profile, Amanda would not remain in Washington DC.

For now, and until they had answers, Amanda would stay at their beach house in Bethany Beach. From there, she was close enough to drive into the city, yet out of reach for security reasons.

Trevor and Amanda knew what the dangers were. Intelligence related to intellectual data was never off limits to the enemy, and clearly Sandra has strayed into potentially sensitive findings.

The possibilities that filled their thoughts were many, all of them treacherous. This, they understood. But where they could take no chances was with their daughter, Sandra.

She had just walked into an ambush.

* * *

Chapter 31

"I have some bad news, I'm afraid" Arguetta said on the phone. "Your colleague Diane… We believe her death was a premeditated act of homicide. We have some information that is disturbing… I think it best you come in."

She agreed, of course.

She called Trevor, there was little she could add. "When are you going in?" he asked.

"First thing tomorrow morning."

She stowed her sewing and her books, cleared away the dishes, her thoughts full of concern, questions and anxiety. Especially since it had proximity to Sandra by way of the same College. She need to think, and she decided to take a late afternoon walk along the beach before preparing for her trip in the morning.

Outside the house Amanda bumped into Kim who was carrying a container of pre-cooked meals. She was on her way down to the beach, she told him. Tomorrow morning she was off to DC…

By now, the student she had met weeks ago was a paying tenant holding quarters in the guest house of her beach house.

It was a separate structure, with its own roof and overhanging trees, but attached to the Main house by a garden pathway that led to a garage and a courtyard for private parking in the compound.

Tall, slim and of Asian descent, Kim was a Foreign Student with an excellent command of the English language.

Hong Kong was where he had learned English, he explained. His Father had been British, his mother Malaysian; earlier parentage were Chinese.

He had paid for his six months of rent in advance in cash, offering his Hong Kong Passport as Identification. The leasing transaction was handled at the offices of the local Real Estate

Management brokerage where he was given his receipt, and where he had completed an official Lease Application.

Sotheby's International Real Estate had managed the beach property over the years with services for cleaning; security and maintenance in their absence. Occasionally, they leased out her guest house for her. On this occasion, they assured her that her new tenant's credentials checked out.

He moved in two weeks later, and while neither Amanda nor her tenant were in occupancy at the beach house for much of the week, she declared him to be a tidy, quiet and a respectful tenant when they called her to check in.

The following weekend, she walked over to the guest house and asked him how he was managing.

They chatted.

What she discovered was that he was a student at the Culinary School of New York, and he travelled frequently to the Mid-Atlantic area to consult with Chefs at the Hyatt Hotel Resorts at beach locations. His specialty, he said, was Chinese cooking.

This, he explained, was the need for the occupancy of her place, if shyly admitting that he loved swimming and surfing on the beach. Adding, what he called a "cultural courtesy" of family respect – the privilege to cook for her meals that he would leave stored in the freezer in the garage for her convenience.

Amanda smiled warmly. "Of course."

Thus, to arrive at the beach house from Washington was for Amanda a treat in what-to-thaw-next when she opened the freezer door. Even if the labels in Chinese rarely explained the exotic contents within sealed bags, ready for the Microwave.

Between Amanda's trips into Washington to consult with Arguetta; her visits to New York where she spent time with Barbara, and her visits to Long Island before a flight to Toronto to meet with Trevor's staff on matters of corporate strategy for stockholders, she had barely had time to enjoy the beach house herself.

"I'm glad you've got a tenant, Mom" said Sandra at one phone call, now safely reinstated at the University of Chicago. "You'll have someone who can keep an eye on the place when the weather sets in. Especially if there's a storm coming off the coast. He can baton down the hatches!"

Amanda had to laugh. Plus, she knew, it was what the local municipalities advocated. Especially regarding security with so many beach houses unoccupied during the winter stormy months. And sure enough, Kim did so for one unexpected Hurricane Warning, when Amanda was away. He followed her instructions: He secured the storm shutters all over the house, especially those facing the sea. He watered the plants; chlorinated the kitchen and bathrooms to prevent mold; checked the garage locks, and later, when the storm passed, he swept the sidewalks from fallen debris and raised the blinds of the house for sunlight and refreshment.

He was both invisible and indispensable, she once told Trevor by phone when he asked.

Not than Amanda should worry. She kept few valuables in the house. It was a beach house after all, decorated with seashore color-tones and pretty rattan furnishings. Of course Kim had access to the house. Why not? If he needed to disarm its security alarm systems, then he knew what to do...

* * *

They were in one of the private conference rooms of the Library of Congress. A privilege that Arguetta had received from the Archival Chief of Research operations group that worked there.

Amanda knew the place well. She had spent many years in Washington DC and she had frequently been on Capitol Hill when working at her Research Firm in Washington. That was long ago, working independently at a time when Trevor was posted to Washington.

However, after she left, her work was continued as a branch of a larger firm that was based in the UK. Mostly a financial advisory and research center, it was registered as a government contractor in good standing to conduct scientific enquiry and defense contracts with full security clearances.

Now, her only research assignments were those that she picked, if she was wanting. Not that she was wanting, but she did come to the United States with a solid purpose to rescue and reinstate Sandra at her College.

The matter had resolved uneventfully, if with unanswered questions.

Still, Amanda did check in with her former office while in the city, and she did agree to look over a report before it was finalized. It gave her the access she needed to look into the matter of who might be behind the research that was suddenly arrested from the Arctic Expedition, and the foundation that sponsored the expedition.

In the meantime, it didn't surprise her at all that Arguetta picked the Library of Congress to meet her in lieu of the Pentagon. In essence, she had retired.

 But she wanted to stay low, she told him. And this suited her fine. This was a world she had left behind, she told him, and she was only in town for personal reasons.

 Arguetta placed the photographs on the table.

Amanda paused, then shrank back.

The scene of the dig showed total and utter disarray. The bodies of the students were littered everywhere.

"These are from our Satellite Imagery and Geospatial Data intelligence profiles…Can you recognize anyone?"

Diana was a meticulous scholar who would never have endorsed exposing people to danger at any archaeological site. Something had gone terribly wrong. Yet there was little to betray foul play for looting. This was a massacre.

"I'm sorry to revisit the topic of your friend's demise. But we have reason to believe this was more than a case of poisoned food. There had been visitors to the dig just days before she and her associate were found. A doctor and a visiting Nun. The doctor was General Duval from the W.H.O. - a Frenchman interested in her finds.

"I don't personally know these people. Her colleague is recognizable. I met him once at a conference. The students are unfamiliar to me. What are you suspecting?"

The villagers are saying something occurred during the night, like a paramilitary night raid of specialists. Neither the Nun nor the Doctor had any reason to believe the food or the provisions were tainted. They appeared to be healthy and well hydrated just before they died."

Amanda inspected the photographs carefully for any further recognition. Two other professors were in a couple of shots for a group picture of an Arriving Party. They were onhand to welcome them to the region and brief them on the site's history, University Professors Assad and Kedash, both experts in the ancient archaeology. Diane stood with them, each with an arm around her shoulder in the photograph. But they had not stayed for the excavation process evidently...

"Do you have any idea who might have wanted them dead?" asked Arguetta.

"None whatsoever...Diane was a fun-loving student, and careful with her scholarship when I knew her. After she became a professional she hosted several conferences and kept us all informed of her progress. But that was it. She was always courteous. I can't image any enemies…"

"In this photograph here, we notice that a couple of the local workers have been identified as international terrorists. They are linked to several incidents in Malaysia. They are formerly experts in business administration and worked for two banks in London and Zurich."

"Are you certain they were unknown to Diane?"

"No. She had many friends of course. But she never referenced them to me at least…"

Arguetta remained silent.

"How long were they around Diane, on the site I mean…"

"Almost every day. They helped as volunteers, never speaking English, but helping with the labor of sifting."

"Did they register for the dig anywhere…?"

"No. Just laborers. Trouble is, none of the locals knew them!"

"What brought them out of hiding now?" asked Amanda.

"A new incident in Malaysia. Two airlines have been downed, and we suspect they have ties to a mob of some kind within the Asian stock markets. We would never have known if Interpol hadn't sent their images for identification across the Terrorist threshold for US Intelligence. Diane's case was freshly opened, and the images still on file for digital examination…"

"Where are they now?"

"We don't know for sure. But we have our suspicions."

Amanda was saddened that terrorists should find her friend Diane: Ancient history should have been a galvanic for sacred knowledge.

"There is a third party that travels with them" said Arguetta. "One that has not yet been identified."

Amanda looked at him.

"Come on" he said "Let me get you a cup of coffee upstairs."

The view of the city from the Library of Congress at the lunch cafeteria was stunning. Not necessarily glamorous as a dinning facility, but bright, specious and architecturally uplifting with an unending view.

"You know Amanda" said Arguetta digging into his bag of potato chips "I've talked to Trevor about some work…"

Amanda nodded.

"He said you were too busy for any kind of research, but he's put his team on my Solicitation."

"Must be important."

"I take it you're out of the picture for other kind of documentation research down here?"

Amanda nodded, her teeth biting into her tuna-fish sandwich.

"It's just that I need some forensic comparisons from an expedition that was conducted some time ago, with possible relevance today…Know any Interns or students who might be able to help?"

Amanda was interested. What was he driving at? Might there be any connections to Sandra's expedition?

"Let me look into it for you." She said. "I may have a few names that I can work with. My team have all moved on, as you know. But I might find local Interns looking for work…Is that alright?"

He grinned. She would make recommendations to his Assistant at the Pentagon, he knew. And they would be reliable for work, he also knew. Amanda Wells was an excellent Research Historian. And Dana Thompson had been her colleague.

Their meeting over, it took her all afternoon to drive back to the beach.

Arguetta called to thank her - perhaps more to remind her that such knowledge of course, should remain strictly within the realm of tight security. This was international intelligence, she knew. Something she was cleared for in her capacity as a Defense Contractor for Research, previously registered with the Government. He said he would reactivate her pass.

Any by the way, Eileen his wife, wanted to see more of her in Annapolis when she had time.

"Yes…I will let you know. And I'll keep you posted as soon as I find out more about the investigation. I promise!" he said.

* * *

171

Chapter 32

The minute Trevor heard about the nature of the Research that Admiral Arguetta would be requisitioning, he knew he had to turn it down.

Not that it gave him pleasure to do so. Certainly, the men and women in his employment needed all the contract work he could give them; they would pay mortgages, expenses. It had been a highly inflated economy of late, he knew. But it was against his ethical standards to take on something that was outside his particular field, especially if it were already under enquiry by another client.

This, he realized, as soon as he the heard about magnetic polar reversals. He was already working on speculation theories about the earth's magnetic field and the effects of radiation. Especially if it had destabilized. Oh yes, the Americans were right.

But they were under-estimating the dangers by far.

He was worried. Perhaps it was time to share. He would. But not until they were certain, and only after they had conducted their own research.

He made a few calls.

There was some analysis of Hawkin's recent findings. The Higgs boson particle, if rendered unstable, might cause the universe, according to his latest book, to *"undergo catastrophic vacuum decay."*

This was no small declaration. Even in the face of contradictions and critics. Particles were particles. They were mass. They had density.

Trevor returned to his lab to deliver more observations. But his thoughts were fixed on the findings of Hawkin - one of the world's leading astro-physisists. They were troubling. And if he proved to be right, then this phenomenon was clearly cataclysmic if not an extinction event. Thus, the real question now was a matter of degree and timing… Hawkin asserted, in his publication, that the particle *"has the worrisome feature that it might became metastable at energies above 100bn giga-electron-volts (GEV)"*

What was he saying? That particles could *change* density? That they could change their mass?

Trevor's astrology dome opened to the heavens above Scotland. He anchored his telescope mechanically to view the northern hemisphere.

True, he was in retirement, and as a wealthy businessman, he would have ample time and activities to keep him busy. But deep within the heart of his family had been the legacy of unselfish dedication to exploration and enquiry for science and development. As his father and grandfather had done, he was making his contribution as a volunteer data collector! He looked up and felt overwhelmed by the panoply of the stars moving across a universe, the earth's constellation traversing its path in one fantastical orbit per day...

Even if his data proved to be insignificant, his resources, such that they were, would be turned to good use for data collections.

His telescope, occasionally repositioned with loud grinding mechanical levers and gears, would record items from his station at these higher elevations that might be useful. Maybe later. Or perhaps immediately. But he would show care, and be precise...

As the night wore on, he felt tired. He thought of his wife, Amanda. She had a name for all this. "My Dreamer" she called him. He would smile at her, then leave for his mountain trek and Lab at the Lodge, a kiss warm on his cheek.

It was getting cold. He rubbed his fingers.

He consulted his Notes tonight.

The vacuum decay "could expand at the speed of light and that could happen at any time…"

Certainly, Hawkin was too respected a scientist to utter such words without a caveat that this was *theory*. It was also Galilleo's theory that the world was round.

But… to keep put things in perspective, he also knew that a particle could not be accelerated to those speeds: Even an artificial particle accelerator that could reach 100bn GEV would need to be larger than the Earth itself!

Still, that was what CERN did. Their problem. Accelerated Particle Colliders had their place in research. And recently, even with their more recent acquisitions and instrumentation, the funding picture for the lab in Europe was gloomy.

More importantly, any kind of tampering could have dangerous effects on humanity, even at its most fundamental level.

Trevor had to be careful, he decided.

He would need to warn Amanda too about being careful.

What they had at their fingertips was intelligence and theory that could cause potential harm and change the earth's known world: If something was found, and if this data fell into the wrong hands, that is precisely what they would attempt to use it for...

* * *

It was a beautiful day.

The early sun had crept over the horizon and cast shimmering diamonds across the sea.

From her open window at night, Amanda had heard the ocean toss gentle waves on the shore, a moon traversing the sky in silvery brightness. Twice she got up and lookout out. She could almost see the night crabs, she mused. It stirred a sense of wonder in her soul when she looked at things this way, and the breath caught in her throat.

Later she ran on the beach, greeting her usual assortment of athletes who routinely jogged along these beaches. No Lifeguards today said one, in passing, as if reporting the beach news.

Truth was, they were displaced professionals running on the beach because they were out of work. Such was the appalling condition of the economy. At least down here they were "at the beach," they said. Amanda got to know them.

There was Mary, a former paralegal Administrative Assistant; her neighbor Phillipa who was a trained dermatologist who got a job working for a Law Firm and became the Expert on Taxes and Medical consultation; Tom, an engineer whose "Environmentalist" job had gone to a 26 year old MBA with an attitude; and Amanda - all of them jogging and meeting daily on the beach.

Occasionally they met at the local Coffee and Bake shop, talking cathartically about separation and unemployment with festering anger that bordered on anarchy. Amanda listed.

Then a thought came to her.

Actually, it was Mary who started the ball rolling. Amanda asked her if she might like to assist on some research. Then Tom and Phillipa joined in. Pretty soon, it was a cadre of researchers all adding to reports with data discovered by each, reports so prolific and exhausted that she had to work at getting them filtered. But it brought meaningful and professional analysis to the table, and pretty soon they were all over her house smiling broadly and breathing normally, she noticed.

More importantly, she paid them. Trevor would have insisted, even if it were a motley crew.

"I have a team!" she told Arguetta over the phone, later that day.

"Oh?" he said, simply.

"Yes. I'm not opening up the offices in DC exactly, mainly just working out of the beach house. But I have chosen a qualified team to do the research: We're a loosely formed network of professionals, and anything you need, under our standing authority to supply you with research, is at your disposal…if you'll permit."

"Great!" was all he said. "Have them each fill out a 171 Form for OPM, and I'll review the files. If I get a green light, then you're on! O.k.?"

"Agreed" she said breathlessly.

She sensed a little less than enthusiasm in his voice, ascribing it perhaps to the security clearances she once had in Washington DC that would require him a full and formal Request for Proposals. But on the on the other hand, this was hardly security content. Forensic research, rather, was what he had requested when at the Library of Congress. Regardless, she jumped forward to preclude any further objections and added. "Since the content is unclassified material, perhaps you wouldn't mind if I dropped off at your place in Annapolis, rather than drive into the city?"

He paused.

 "Overnight UPS would be better and it'll get it in DC if you don't mind." Then he added. "Still, if Eileen gives me any sealed envelope when I get home at night, I'll drive it into the office the following morning…"

Arguetta was a strict man, and he liked staying with procedures. But he was also a kind man, one who could elicit trust from those who worked for him.

"Have you consulted with Trevor?"

"No. Not about this project. He is busy with his own affairs at the moment in the UK, and he fully supports my contractual arrangements with the authority of his company here in the US. We are entirely independent and firewalled."

"I see" said Arguetta. If he was disappointed he didn't show it. Clearly it meant there was a conflict of interest, and that she could only qualify for declassified work.

She hung up and took a deep breath. It was the best she could do.

What she didn't tell Arguetta was that Trevor and she had talked. Trevor told her that he could not take on the research on account of a conflict of interest with a European contract he had with CERN. He would ask his government to share, he had said. But directly, the answer to the Americans had to be No. Not for the moment, at least.

"I told him yes!" she bragged to Barbara later that night.

"Oh my God. What if Trevor finds out?"

"For now, he won't…I have a small team of experts with me here at the beach! They're all highly qualified, and out of work…So. I'm good to go!"

"But what about Arguetta?" insisted Barbara, always the stickler for details and procedures.

"He doesn't have to know what Trevor does, right? He talked to me, remember?"

"But surely…"

"Barbara!" admonished Amanda.

"OK. OK… Just let me know if you need any help. And be safe, right?"

Amanda rolled her eyes. Always the grandmother, Barbara was.

The whole idea came to her on the way home. By the time she made herself breakfast and drank her coffee, she noticed that Arguetta had not returned her call from yesterday. She would try again later today. But deep down inside, she knew he knew everything. Including the fact that Trevor was not onboard.

She pulled out her laptop and found a shady spot on the porch. With soft jazz in the background, she returned to some material she had been working on for a book. The publisher had been very patient. Amanda looked up, the surf's windy rage a docile soft breeze by the time it reached her porch, and cool.

She sighed.

It was a man's world. A man's world of contracts, of justice, of legislation. Always the man's world with women following instructions! It hardly seemed fair. A woman could run circles around most men; women had multi-tasking skills… Easily, they could run a small corporation without needing a man's authority.

She paused. It was easy to draw anger.

A soft breeze sent a thrush off its perch, it screeched in protest.

Then again, did not men dedicate their lives to the comfort and security of their women, mused Amanda. Many had not, she knew. Either because life had treated them wrongly, or the lack of opportunity ….

But those in her family had. Where there was love in the house, there was self-sacrifice and little self-obsession. She sat back in her chair, closed her eyes to the here and now, to the faraway pounding of surf, wind and trees…

It was an old moral code, she knew, this idea of men leading the family: Dated and dusty - easily sloughed off by progressivism looking to hijack modern consumers…

But there it was, in the words of ancient and sacred records – truths about family patriarchs averting moral hazards to societal order…

Her cell phone rang. She went inside where the air-conditioning chilled the house and brought forward the semblance to professional quarters.

It was a call from Washington, confirming her paperwork. But not from Arguetta.

She would reassemble her files and set up the pro-forma schematic needed for a full Research Project. It was a lot of work: Discrimination needed for a thorough research project required an elaborate filtering of intellectual content - all of it leading to findings that should have anticipated every eventuality. There could be no gaps. She would be handling serious data collection and information. As project manager, it was her responsibility to set things up.

So much for women not taking the axe...

It was already late in the afternoon when she felt she had fleshed out a preliminary outline. And she was a little hungry.

She went outside, collected her work, called her publisher and asked for an extension. She would dedicate a good two months to the project, she promised. But for now, she had too much on her plate, she said.

What else did she have planned for her day? Oh yes...

With Kim away, she would go through the Garage and sort out stuff that had been left untouched too long. There was much that needed repair, refurbishing or just a good toss out. Beach wear like deck chairs and umbrellas that had corroded, fabric faded...

There was a coastal storm coming, they had warned. Better to secure things…

Moreover, they were all meeting at the beach house for dinner and for taking notes, her "jogger/friends from the beach," as Barbara called them.

Before long, she was rearranging the flower pots and by the time she returned to her desk and answered two phones, she was exhausted.

Upstairs in her bedroom Amanda opened her secure laptop, that which remained air-gapped from the Internet as a precaution, to glance at her Attachments received at the lunch table of the Library of Congress. She opened one or two briefly: Here it was, perhaps the topic of enquiry that must be informed by her research! She would return later…

Then she saw something. One file remained unaccounted for…out of sequence, and perhaps accidentally included. She was about to open the folder and annotate it for return to Arguetta! Tomorrow, using her server... But she stopped.

She would read it, she decided.

Accidental or not, it was pertinent to the meeting that she had with him. Clearly, this matter was of interest to him when he asked for her research.

She returned downstairs. Still no call back from Arguetta.

She called.

"I'm sorry Ms. Wells" said his Aide. His name was Eric Westergard, she knew. "He's unable to take your call."

"Is it possible for me to leave a message…" she began. The answer was terse.

 "I'm sorry Ms. Wells. He has appointments all day and is unable to respond to your call…"

"Eric..?" she began

He paused. "Your contact umformation is restricted Ms. Wells. I'm sorry."

Restricted? Since when did he put her off with that? What did that mean?

Perhaps he was in secured quarters and could not field outside calls? Perhaps he was just busy in conferenced all day. Perhaps he ….

Something was wrong.

Admiral Arguetta was her primary contact as a registered defense contractor conducting research services for the government. And while she was not currently fully performing services, Trevor had maintained the Firm's status as a security-cleared company for business. Amanda was on the list of approved personnel for communications and contacts with the government.

She called Eileen. A recording. Out Sailing…

Strange, though. Arguetta never neglected to call back within 24. That was the nature of the research she conducted for him at the Pentagon in years past…

She waited and called again later.

Finally Eileen came on the line.

"Yes. Amanda" she said, almost with a sigh of relief. "I'm sorry, but you're off limits for my contacts these days…It's difficult to find a way to chat with you! Very glad you called. So how are you?"

"I'm confused. What does it mean that I'm off limits?"

"It means your security clearance has been pulled for some reason. He is restricted to speak with only those with clearance, as you know. Something has compromised your standing…I'm not sure what it is. But I know he sent a message to Trevor."

"Really? I wasn't aware that Trevor had any information about the matter…"

"Yes. He seems to be aware of it. Apparently, he got word in London that your security has been compromised."

"Amanda. I want you check in with us here at the house on a regular basis. We need to know that everything is alright… That you're safe. That's all. Just a message - a couple times a week? Obviously, something has happened. Are you safe all by yourself at that beach house?"

"Oh sure! It's nothing to worry about. Just tourists and bikers…that's all. I'm fine. Thanks for asking…"

"Amanda, there is one thing I can tell you. Diane's investigation. It turns out she had unearthed quite a trove of treasure. It's missing. Someone has stolen her items of discovery. Perhaps that sheds some light? I don't know. Perhaps you could ask around your academic circles and let us know if hear anything?"

"Any suspects?" she asked, recalling the gallery of photographs that were presented to her for identification. People that might have been with Diane on her dig.

"No. Not really. Nothing new. They probably were responsible for the deaths as well…"

Amanda waited.

"I have no idea" added Eileen. "Look. I'll tell him you called. Keep in touch…"

Amanda hung up just as thunder exploded outside. The weather had turned foul, and a storm roiled the sea. Further thunder menaced, as if approaching to shudder the roof raters. House lights flickered, but stayed on. This was an old beach community, she knew. Lightening followed.

The doorbell rang. Outside, sea-surf was starting to snarl with anger and whitecaps, and there they stood, her motley crew — one lame bottle of wine in someone's drenched hand, and the four of them wet and wild-eyed huddled under a sou'wester shivering…The research team.

She smiled gamely. "Come in!"

That night, as they met in the dark at the beach house the storm passed over, and the power went out intermittently. A candlelight dinner, they laughed.

But later, as they compared notes, Amanda realized that she was working for Arguetta on her own. Trevor did not know.

Washington had pulled her security clearance, and her authority was gone.

Yet of one thing she was certain. Arguetta was aware of what she was doing. He could call her up and chew her out and stop her dead in her tracks, such was his authority. He knew she was working alone.

Clearly, this was important to him.

The file in her laptop was no mistake.

* * *

Chapter 33

Amanda Wells met with the Provost; several Administrators and faculty. They crowded to spend time with her, and by the time she was finished with her Lunch in the University executive dinning hall, she was pleased to go outside into the sunshine and walk about.

The campus was filled with students, many of them milling about on the Quad on break for the lunch hour between classes. Behind them the Cafeteria buzzed with excitement, young men eating pizza and planning a party; girls fixing their hair and talking into cell phones. On the lawns many had bagged their lunch and were soaking up the sunshine for a tan.

Amanda found one of the Instructors from her daughter's program. He was sitting on a bench.

"I'm not sure what the situation is, Ms Wells."

"We haven't heard from our Team Leader and I understand they are taking the whole semester up there. But it is usually a matter of funding in these cases. Many programs dry up pretty quickly when the funding has gone. Perhaps that's the situation here?"

"My daughter went on this Polar Expedition, and we are concerned, my husband and I"

"Of course." He rooted around his wrinkled backpack for a business card to give her. "My email address. What can I do to help?" he said

"When was the last time you communicated with the team?" "Last week, I believe. Now let me see… We'll need to check with the Department Administrator. I just assumed they all disbanded and went home."

Eric Westergard was not your typical stereotypical Program Director. Tall with a large forehead and receding hairline, his outstanding feature were his brown eyes emphasized by deep and dark eyeglasses.

He was probing, and hung onto silence in a way as to leave a person uncomfortable.

Amanda decided to take the high ground. This man too must have paid his dues to have earned his position. Perhaps years of post-doctoral positions before receiving a post as a tenured professor.

Still, this expedition was his, and his alone.

Yet he was entirely defensive about it, hiding behind the readings of the topic and holding fast to the boundaries of his academic position as protection.

Amanda had to penetrate his façade to impress upon him parental concerns for students.

Clearly, he had not expected a visit from Amanda Wells. She had stopped in Chicago, she explained, on her way back from Toronto.

He was uncomfortable.

Two calls came in; one pop-in-visit from the Front Office Administrative Assistant, and two students pacing outside made it abundantly clear to Amanda that he wanted this conversation to end. Being ever busy, she knew, was a tactic of diversion to throw her off. It was an old ploy amongst University academics.

She decided to take a different tack.

She smiled. Beneath those dark fuming brown eyes, she detected a large ego waiting to air his achievements.

She mentioned the loss of her friend Diane Thompson, and referred to her Archaeological Excavation. She asked him about the findings of Sechem.

"Oh My God!" he said, suddenly thrusting his hands high above his head and his seat pitching back. "What a find, indeed!"

"Umm" she said.

"We couldn't believe the treasure trove there. I understand it was one of the most remarkable of the ancient world. We've yet to see the full inventory. But it's even larger than the biblical account, and that was pretty amazing, as you can imagine: The gold worth of an entire tribe buried in one place - Imagine!" he said.

"By today's standards…I suppose it's worth a lot to a museum…?"

"And to any University" he added "Oh My God. It's gold weight alone is beyond anything we have in one place. The artistry and cultural value is priceless…"

"I can't wait to read about it."

"Oh sure" I'm planning a report on it for the Spring Issue of our Website. The Library and the Museum can be funded for twenty years with the sale of a couple items alone"

"Wow" smiled Amanda.

"Yes. I'm very proud. We have our sponsors to thank, of course. They get the lion's share of the finds as a reward…"
"Whose Foundation is the one so fortunate…?"

"Ali Enders arranged it all…He announced the find at a Press Conference in Washington DC. He is the Senator from New Hampshire as you know…Finding the censors was one terrific surprise! Imagine, the censors of the biblical story…"

"Umm" said Amanda calmly. "He…he also funds the expedition that my daughter is on, is that right?"

She faced him squarely, and the smile on his face faded. He came back to the moment only gradually and averted his eyes, realizing what had just happened.

In one line, the show had shut down. As far as Westergard was concerned, the interview was all over. He got up to open the door and motioned to some students outside, making it abundantly clear that his world was busy with other activities.

Amanda got the idea. She looked down at her purse, pulled out an item from a pouch and placed it gently on his desk. "My calling card, Mr. Westergard" she said politely. "I'll be checking in with you routinely for any news and updates as to their whereabouts. As parents, we'd like to be kept informed." She got up. "Thank you for seeing me!"

She left him almost as abruptly as she met him.

She was fuming.

If there was one thing she could not tolerate was the arrogance of academic instructors hiding behind their work. It was hypocrisy. The fiduciary obligation of Faculty was to the institution of their scholarship; their students and to their selfless dedication to the pursuit of knowledge: The essence of stewardship and intellectual learning – for the greater good, surely?

Amanda gave him a courtesy phone-message outside campus, leaving also a voice message: She thanked him for seeing her, and she reiterated her interest in hearing from him soon. The message, now registered, was to reaffirm the nature of their meeting… This, he would understand.

When she got in, she called Trevor. Westergard was not helpful, she told him. "He doesn't know anything!"

"No" came the unexpected response from Trevor. "It's not that he has no clue, my darling. It's that he's denying responsibility for the Team's disappearance!"

"He's hiding something..."

Yes, thought Amanda. *And I think I know what*

* * *

Chapter 34

Amanda was worried. She jogged down the beach, mindless to distance from the house. The waves had been augmenting in size, whitecaps dotting the surface of the sea and the wind velocity accelerating. By the time she reached the house she was exhausted and dehydrated. She paused to catch her breath.

Kim appeared out of nowhere.

"Hello" she said, seeing him behind the Garage. "I hadn't expected you back until the weekend."

He got in late last night, he said. He was sleeping in after two grueling days on the road. He was on his way to the Giant Supermarket for fresh vegetables. "Please, no seaweed!" she jested.

He laughed.

"Hah! No seaweed. Just prickly urchins!" he teased back.

Truth was, he was pleasant to have around. And as rarely as she saw him, it was always nice to exchange a word or two with a companion on the premises. Increasingly, her life had become isolated.

Still, today she had much to do at her desk. She remained in her Studio-loft for most of the day.

Finally she got up to stretch her legs, and with a late afternoon coffee in hand, she went out on the porch.

She sat, the tree leaves outside the beach house shimmering in a mixed breeze, now pink and soft purple from a deepening daylight. Sandy pine trees shaded the grounds like mechanical fans wafting salty breezes through the estate, hidden as it were by strong grown hedges. Everywhere craggy shoots of cactus pine, palm and even Pampas grass shot at random across rich garden soils.

Her thoughts were far away. Mixed with realities, near and present, and research from times distant. It occurred to

Amanda that history had an uncanny way of repeating itself. Certainly, humans never changed. And when under stress, they were capable of tossing conventions out the window for survival and self interests.

A cool breeze swept across the porch. She felt a shiver that left her feeling alone and afraid suddenly.

Not one to dwell on sentiments of no use, and with nobody in the house for whom to prepare a dinner, she fixed herself a quick hamburger and returned to the work at her desk. There were issues, darker than she imagined.

There had to be an explanation.

 Bad enough recovering from her visit to Chicago and finding opaqueness behind Dana's archaeological excavation; but the appalling disregard for students on the Arctic expedition bordered on breach of fiduciary responsibility…

True, both events were listed as off-campus activity.

"Remember, all students here are also consenting adults…" said Eric Westergard.

She had remained calm, observing his offhand indifference with the eyes of a prowling lioness about to defend her young.

Still, both events were University sponsored events, which, in the greater scheme of things, helped advance the reputation of any institution of higher learning. Especially if it were a venerated research university…

Was she missing something? One foundation had sponsored both events.

She was tired and decided to call it a day.

She called Scotland, left a message since it would the three in the morning.

Her thoughts were unsettled. She couldn't understand why there was not more open discourse about both expeditions at the University. Usually they were transparent. Increasingly though, under liberal and progressive pressure, they we becoming selective for political reasons.

Worse of all, could this be a cover up? If so, why? From what? And by whom?

This she would talk to Trevor about. Her chief concern for the moment was Sandra's safety: Get her back first, then ask the question...

For now, she would sit on it, and wait for answers.

She returned a few local calls, left messages, one to Barbara, then wrapped up the house for the night.

She took a shower, and was about to climb into bed when she saw her cell phone light up. There was a message.

Arguetta: *Stay in touch, don't leave town. There's something I wish to discuss with you.*

This contradicted her plans to fly directly back to the New York. She was annoyed.

She'd cancel her flight in the morning. Perhaps drive up later in the weekend...

Still, she was relieved to get a call from Arguetta. She'd been waiting for a response from him for days. That meant that his research was still necessary...

She watched a TV show, then switched off.

At dawn - with her suitcase downstairs packed to go, she put on her jogging pants instead and headed for the beach. No travel today.

She spent the day researching the details of the excavation in the dessert.

Dana had sent her material before leaving. Her published works were of particular interest.

Amanda read the full account of what happened at Sechem.

> *The Children of Israel had displeased God. His instructions in the Biblical text involved countless golden censors filled with oil to divide the tents of the disrupters from the faithful.*

It was an odd account - a tribe was swallowed up by the earth in the wrath of God.

No one had been able to explain the phenomenon, much less believe it. *Swallowed by sand?*

But the matter did not end there. There was apparently some other incident recorded.

If Amanda knew her Scriptures - not that she was a religious devotee or a theological expert, but the biblical account related to a different *era* near Sachem.

Here, clearly, the narrative held a different purpose - a different tale.

Sure, "censors" were cited as being used near Sechem. But not on this occasion. That is, if she knew her readings at all.

No! Westergard had it wrong. Sure, he could have indexed Sechem for a biblical account. A quick reference perhaps, and found an easy answer. But was it the right one?

Amanda sat there. Why was this troubling her?

She got up and made coffee, her third. Not that she drank it all, there were cups all over the place, unfinished coffee…She watched the steamer hiss like a steam engine, gurgle and spit before it finished pouring the …

There were no censors in this expedition!

 Not a one! Dana didn't mention them once…

Besides, that was not the purpose of the burial of items at Sechem: The censors were sacred. What was buried was something else, it was loot considered offensive to God, secular - not sacred, representing the mixing of tribes outside their own. Intermingling with other …

That was a mistake. What was Westergard talking about? Did he even know what was excavated and listed in the inventory? He was lying about something. Or just plain hiding something. Regardless, his vanity was getting in the way.

She started to sketch the notes into a time line when

Barbara called.

She wanted to know about the family. She asked about Trevor; the boys in the UK.

"And my favorite of all, how's Sandra?"

"Well, thank God I heard from her yesterday! At least she's in Canada at the moment. She has a friend she is meeting in Anchorage next Thursday. She said he was admitted into the hospital up there while they were on post."

"Anyone of significance to her?" asked Barbara in her non-inquisitive voice, as if she were hiding her inquisitive nature from Amanda.

"No. I don't think so. More out of a sense of loyalty really. Remember, survival training is based on the buddy system. But I understand he's taken ill again, and she wants to check on him …Or something like that. I'll let you know."

The conversation with Barbara was wonderful, it lifted Amanda's spirits, and she was about to tidy away the paperwork when she heard a knock on the door.

"House-keeping!" said Kim from outside the door to her study.

"Come!" she said.

He entered with a tray of soup and snacks. "For the woman who works all day in her attic!" he grinned.

She leaned back into her chair and smiled graciously. "You're too kind" she said simply.

"No problem" he said, and left.

Only later did it occur to her that having a student live in the guest house as a paying tenant was one thing, and having him serve her food in her study was a little odd.

Not that Amanda found it hard to express herself in professional terms about matters inappropriate or confrontational to working colleagues, in fact she could do so quite admirably and without offense, but this was getting a little awkward.

Kim's obsequious seemed oddly inconsistent with his presumptions somehow. He was *guarded.* One word of admonition might send him into retreat somewhere.

Perhaps it was her sense of open hospitality that encouraged him, she thought.

Or perhaps she should just be quiet.

* * *

Chapter 35

The hospital report that came into NIH from Anchorage was hand-delivered by toxicologist Ian Stewart.

The rules of reporting rare and unusual medical symptoms, if found on American soil, were strict. This report had a full analysis and was being courier-driven down Wisconsin Avenue and across the Potomac River to the Pentagon in Virginia.

Ian Stewart, a toxicologist at NIH, found Admiral Arguetta in his office with his Special Assistant for Covert Operations, Tom Ducas. He saluted respectfully.

"Take a seat" said Arguetta.

It was a comfortable chair by the window and Ian opened the file on a small coffee table before them. They had been waiting.

"Poison. Radiation, to be exact" he said.

"What happened?"

"Well, it's a matter of who's telling. The Canadians reported him as the suspect that left his medical facility at the polar circle in chaos and death. No question, it was premediated.."

"Premediated? A *student*...?"

"More than premeditated. It was a mission, and the worse part is that they can't find his records or the reports that showed symptoms of imbalance in his behavior. Which suggests some psychiatric reaction to something..."

They waited.

"Or, a planned operation" he finished

"So what is it?"

"At first it was thought to be thallium. He was loosing hair, and evidence was showing damage to the peripheral nerves. But his chemical levels were inconsistent. He was in transit from some academic expedition... Foul play might suggest a radioactiveisotope of thallium. He was treated with Prussian blue. But later, when the body was brought in, we found blood levels showing traces of polonium 210."

"That's only produced in one place!" said Tom standing, his hands in his pockets. "Source must be Russian in RBMK reactors."

"That's possible. In a highly controlled environment…" said Ian

"I doubt the Russians had anything to do with it. Probably, it was buried for a few years, then surfaced somewhere in the Middle East" said Arguetta, turning to Ian. "Anything else?"

"The symptoms seemed to show 2GBg which corresponds to about 10 micrgrams of 210Po. That is 200 times the mediam lethan dose of around 238 uCI or 50 nanograms in the case of ingestion."

"There is a connection to a similar reported event in the recent past."

"Yes?"

Ian hesitated. "I have a data record on file that's incomplete due to classified restrictions. But as you know, Polonium-210 has a half-life of 138 days and decays to the stable daughter isotope of lead, 206Pb. Therefore the source is reduced to one sixteenth of its original radioactivity about 18 months after production. This we can date."

"Not Russian?" asked Tom.

"Right. The finger-print source of production precludes anything Russian. We don't know where, exactly. Except that it came into the United States for sure, at about that time…"

"Traces?" asked Arguetta.

"Yes. American Airlines reported detecting traces of radiation on a fight from Frankfurt that stopped at Boston, then flew on to Chicago. It had potential carrier passengers connecting at Frankfurt with flights in from Athens, Istanbul and Cairo…"

"I'll check on this lead right away Sir" said Tom.

Arguetta traded in facts. He left discipline and conformance regulation to others…If the brains around him required relaxed atmospheres to best function, that, he gave them. He looked up. Then sat back, stretched his arms above his head, casual like.

"I'm very glad you brought this to my attention, Ian. It gives us a trail of enquiry, that's for sure."

Back to the basics of the coffee table. "So. What was the boy's connection? Any profile? Who was this kid…?"

"On it, Sir!"

At home that night, when Eileen his wife told him that Amanda called, he picked up the phone and called her directly at the beach house. They talked.

"Amanda, if you don't mind my asking, what exactly was Diane your fiend working on at that dig?" he asked.

"I don't know" spluttered Amanda. "The ancient relics of Sachem, I think. Most of the artifacts have gone missing. Why?"

"I have some intelligence that I need to discuss with Trevor's group in London. In the meantime, have you had a chance to do any research at the Library of Congress?"

"I'm coming into DC later this week…"

"Good. Make it tomorrow will you? You'll enjoy searching some early records, I know. By the way, didn't you say that your daughter Sandra was on a recent Polar expedition?"

"Yes. She was. The last I heard she was on her way to check on a colleague who had an accident up there and had to receive some medical treatment… She was on her way to Anchorage, I believe."

"Really?"

"Yes."

"Where is she now?"

"Chicago. Trying to patch together her graduate program now that her funding has been pulled!"

* * *

Chapter 36

In her email inbox was a message. Amanda went directly to the local Post Office to pick up a parcel.

She took it to her Attic-studio, closed the door and examined the package. It was from Dana, Dr. Thompson rather, forwarded from Barbara's office in New York for Amanda.

 By now, in her hand, she was looking at something mailed out and delayed by weeks from some place remote and unregistered. Amanda recognized the handwriting with a breath of regret. *Oh! Diane…*

She began to cut open the package.

There was a note.

I've got two of these stele. The text to both were imprinted in white plaster here at the site. I've asked Ed H to look at the cuniform and see if he can elucidate. Can you get this to the Smithsonian for me?

Gifts from the ancient past could be odd things to archaeologists, Amanda knew. Many a laugh had been shared about things old and venerated as gifts, some a little less venerated than others, they said. This, however, was more than a tourist trinket bought at a local bazaar and sent to Amanda as a gesture of scholarly courtesy.

Fragile. Obviously. The inner layers and found a small wooden container that was packaged more like a cargo crate full of straw than any pretty gift wrapping tissue.

The straw was not even particularly clean. Amanda knew instinctively that this had been packaged locally. No sanitary retail counter here. This was dabbed with dust of chaulky lime. God only knew where the merchant kept his packaging material, probably in a topical barrel of fermented pigeon waste, thought Amanda.

But that was the magic of dealing with history, wasn't it? The mystery of unearthing something that would cast knowledge upon man's past…

She pried open the lid and saw hidden in the straw an artifact. A small cylindrical tablet of clay with writing.

She picked it out and lay it down reverently, as if the item were sacred. Certainly it was old.

How wonderful…

But it reeked. It had a particular smell, the odor of anaerobic decomposition, and it was partly darkened by an ugly stain of moisture. Buried.

Amanda moved it to the sunlight of the window, its odor beginning to permeate the room.

God it smelled foul. She wanted to repack …

Downstairs the phone rang.

It was Barbara.

"Did you get the parcel?" she asked.

"Yes. She wants me to …err, *wanted* me to deliver it to the Smithsonian for examination!"

There was a silence on the phone.

"You realize, of course, that she mailed you that thing the day before she was killed?"

* * *

The next morning, as Amanda opened the door to her studio, her hand flew to her nose as she dashed to the window and opened wide. The relic was still sitting there, odiferous as before, yet somehow bleaching by oxidization.

She switched on the overhead fans. Eventually, a small sea breeze wafted around.

As she examined the small item, she realized that this was no idle artifact but a matter of some significance.

In fact, it was a clay tablet unearthed from her dig.

She had broken protocol to mail this directly to her.

What was she thinking?

The cuniform writing was visible, and as alarming as the matter was of receiving an original artifact from a Certified archaeological site without proper documentation, she sensed something grave and important.

Diane would never have broken the protocol unless it was urgent. She was too disciplined and respected a scholar.

Yet here it was, a small clay tablet with cuniform writing mailed out to Amanda on the day before she died.

Why?

Diane must have sensed something important…Or, an imminent danger. A threat, perhaps. Either way, she had mailed it out to Amanda at some risk to her reputation.

A message, perhaps?

Amanda knew Ed. She would contact him and talk to him about Diane. Also, she made a note to herself. Find out what was on this cuniform writing?

Kim called.

He was coming down this weekend. Could he do some more cooking for her, he asked.

Finally, she noticed that she had another message. The cat was weaving around her legs waiting for dinner… The message was from Arguetta asking if they could approach Sandra, when she returned, and ask her some questions in Chicago.

Amanda ran upstairs and replied by email. The cat followed and leaped onto her keyboard. She wrote saying that they had her permission to talk to Sandra, and that she would send her a message to inform her.

She began to dial Sandra's cell when the front door bell rang.

It was her beach crew: Ready and reporting for work, or, if not, then a dinner on the deck would do, they said. They hauled in a bucket of beer on ice; a 3lb London broil with a dozen ears of corn and four   locally grown tomatoes, then a child's red beach-wagon in tow squealing under the weight of a watermelon.

A white dog followed them in and growled at the cat which scattered into the rafters.

Where was the week going so fast, she wondered.

* * *

Chapter 37

Trevor received his confirmation, and smiled.

At least he was useful to the body of research now being conducted at CERN.

Sitting on the top of a mountain in Scotland watching the stars through a high-powered telescope on a low horizon was hardly work, he thought, reading the letter in his hand. He was after all, enjoying retirement.

Trouble was, people like Trevor never retired. They worked to contribute to society until they delivered their last breath. Small, large, the task was done with methodical care and devotion.

That was who he was…Whether serving public service - as had been his case in a long and active political career, or whether counting the bubbles on his buddy's breather system beneath the sea of the Artic icecap in a submarine, he was serving his country and contributing to the safety of society.

Still, this was troubling. Science was a peculiar friend and foe. If harnessed for the wrong reasons, or placed in the wrong hands, it could unleash a force of destruction with increasing risk in a modern world. His efforts these days were uneventful data points that he sent over to CERN. They were thankful of course, as ever. And discrete.

It was his own government authorities who kept him abreast of things and fully informed. This was one of those days. The findings coming out of CERN was troubling them...

It had been one thing to discover the Higgs boson particle that provided for its scientists the Nobel Prize in physics, it was quite another to go on to the next question of the existence of mass and its nuclear research properties.

Certainly, with its newly built atom-smasher in Switzerland, the upgrade of Cern's Large Hadron Collider doubled the energy at which it could operate. It could mean that the world's most powerful particle accelerator might demonstrate a "new physics" Especially if the particle constituted *dark matter*, the invisible energy that scientists said held galaxies intact, but a dark matter that remained elusive to scientific observation. Only those far-reaching astrophysicists who analyzed space/time dimension might anticipate such metaphysical eventuality…

Regardless, Trevor knew that the 27 kilometer Large Hadron Collider which lay beneath the Swiss-French border at a cost of a billion Swiss francs could shoot two beams of protons at each other at near light-speed, or more than 11,000 laps per second.

He also knew that superconducting magnets, kept at a temperature equal to space could guide beams to collide into each other precisely, producing forces of enormous power. And in so doing, release even smaller particles so dense that, if measured by a magnetic detector, contained more iron than the Brooklin Bridge of New York City. Such was the density of that mass known as dark matter…

CERN, he knew, thirsted for more knowledge: They were now thinking of building either a straight-line collider, or a 100 kilometer circular accelerator that would have to lie party under Lake Geneva.

Trevor knew them to be responsible scientists and physicists. But his government was worried.

They needed to monitor such plans, and follow any results or applications from such intellectual findings.

Japan, he knew was also thinking of building a super collider.

Membership to that venerated circle of scientists included nations whose top physicists were stable and reliable members of the community.

But he was getting concerned. Security was an issue. A number of questions had been raised.

Especially one member country whose regime was unstable and threatening the peace in its region.

Progress, indeed. But at what cost, he wondered.

His cell phone rang. It was Jacques.

"Trevor!" he said "I hear Amanda has a relic…?"

***

A small summer storm brought rain to the seashore. Possibly a weather front or a pressure system moving up the coast, thought Amanda.

She checked the outdoor awnings; filled up for extra water and emergency lighting, and returned to the kitchen to put the final touches on her buffet.

Tonight was definitely a work-night. But it was hardly an office 9-5 environment. No. Not with this crowd.

"We're back!" they sang out, raising a bottle of wine; Sangria and a six-pack of coolers.

"Come in, come in!" she laughed.

"Rain or shine, right?"

"Right!"

They ate.

"Spaghetti and meatballs…Umm, my favorite!" said Mary, licking her lips

"It is NOT your favorite!" interrupted Philippa, her neighbor. "You said it was your *only* college meal for four years!"

They giggled.

"Guys! Guys! Let's get back to basics" said Tom. "At least my only meal was Pizza."

"Yeah, and did you EVER graduate?" laughed Phillippa.

"Sure I did! Let me cite the ways, my darling: One undergraduate engineering degree. One graduate, civil engineering; and one PhD in…"

"So, how come you're still eating Pizza?"

They laughed, but somehow the room went quiet…

Amanda quickly realized what had been said, and jumped in "Well at least you guys are not eating Chinese food five days out of five!"

It broke the awkward moment, and they smiled.

It's not that any of them couldn't take a joke. It's that the economy had made a joke out of them. They were all unemployed. Pizza was the hallmark of their state, they concluded.

"What's wrong with Chinese?" asked Tom.

"Nothing" said Amanda. "Kim feeds me like his personal charge. I love his cooking. It's what he leaves in the freezer when he's done that gets me…"

"So why not throw it out?" asked Phillipa

"Hell. *Give* it to me!" said Tom

"Well…I dunno why. I feel obligated to eat it and report that it was good" said Amanda

"Why?"

"Well, he's a student chef, that's why."

"So why not be honest and say you've had enough?" insisted Phillipa.

"Because she's a wimp who doesn't want to hurt his feelings, that's why" said Mary.

"No. I'm not a wimp…I can tell people…"

"So?" they glared.

"It's just that I get tired of eating those menus all day long. I mean, I know it's his type of food and his culture, but honestly, give a steak any day!"

"We'll take 'em" said Tom, an executive decision for a corporate dilemma.

"Help yourselves!" said Amanda, clapping her hands.

Amanda thought she heard the door of the garage open. She jumped. If that were Kim, he might have heard her words…

Ruefully, she paused.

The food packed away quickly enough; wine, coffee and finally, it was time to get down to work.

She looked at them. Here was the circle of friends she had picked up on the beach, fellow joggers, now colleagues in research.

"So, what have we got?"

It took a half hour to define a strategic approach. The task could be divided into several components, she explained.

They looked like a band of merry pirates seated on the floor around the coffee table. Was anyone taking notes, even?

She proceeded. "When you get to DC, here's what we need to examine" said Amanda. "Nothing secretive or classified, just sleuthing through the records for scholarship and discovery. Got it?"

They nodded.

"We're looking for anomalies cited in archived documents. We want to find any open record, from any related source that reflected an impact on society caused by environmental change."

Mary looked puzzled.

Amanda went on "Now, that does not mean a one-time Act of God kind of thing. Just a tipping-point-event, any reflection of a fundamental change of some kind…"

"Ooh…" interrupted Tom "I *soooo* like mystery and mayhem!"

Amanda's heart sank.

"Tom!" elbowed Mary

"Just. Just…o.k.,o.k!"

Phillipa said "So, err…Like anything that led to anything in the record that might show nature causing an alteration in the progress of man…?"

"Hang on" said Mary "This is not a silly activist platform for climate-change and environmental obstructionism, 'cause frankly… if it is, I'm out!"

"No. It isn't!" insisted Amanda. "We're more interested in the course-of-human-events type of question in a collegian hypothesis…"

"Ok, then. I'm glad to help. It's just that environmentalism – while it has its place - cost me my job!"

Tom looked at her. "Oh, you mean the *Agenda* cost you your job. Because mostly, its competitive corporate cost-cutting bullshit that wants cheaper labor overseas that costs us our jobs…"

"Wait…" tried Amanda

"No. I am *pissed* about it" said Tom, red-faced. "They Foreclosed on my home and repossessed my car as a result of my job loss…It's making me angry as hell!"

"Too bad they don't make China and India pay for their environmental hazard before offering cheap labor…" said Mary.

"STOP!" belted Amanda.

They stopped. "If you don't want to do this…that's ok. Just tell me!"

They all looked at her.

"Ok…" she said, holding up her hand. "I know it hurts. Being unemployed hurts because it feels like you are unwanted and unworthy. Everyone wants to make a contribution to society…"

They averted their eyes, Amanda realized, to hide their frustrations.

"…And..And I know this is no corporate office, but you *are* important. You *are* qualified to contribute to this stuff! And you *are* all quite capable of getting over this …this…*issue*, and to move on, right?"

They nodded, muttering.

"Life if full of ups and downs, right?" said Phillipa.

"Right" said Tom, his chin coming up.

"Ok. So, Tom. You check out any judicial and legislative evidence that might shed light. Ask yourself: It if happened in the past, then it might happen again…?" suggested Amanda.

"Especially on public works projects and Congressional appropriations" added Tom.

"Mary, you check out the scholarship, and any academic anchor we might pursue. Also, epistemology. Got it?"

"Phillippa, check out any Emergency Contingency planning policy that might betray possible incidents on the charts of planning boards…It's a good insight?"

"Oh hey, plenty of stuff there. States too?"

"Yes. Can you do that?"

"Oh do I ever have access codes to reports; writings and data sources!"

"Wait. No cheating…" said Amanda.

"Huh?" began Tom

"I mean, we must use legitimate discovery, documentation that is verifiable, and credentialed. Otherwise, we're just an investigative body without authority. We need appropriate citations, legitimate references and legal access permissions. We need to do this research cleanly from authorized archives, a straight up research report. Got it?" said Amanda.

They nodded.

"We'll be looking at public policy and State Department history for international diplomacy as well, especially get background readings and references if we access any Academic Library, which I can do by the way…"

"Me too!" said Phillippa.

"Here, me too" said Tom.

"What do we say if we are asked?"

"Say it's for a Research Firm. Unable to divulge the name of its clients. Period. No details. Only stealth, professional standards and courteous manners, right?"

Tom was about to say something but Mary dug him in the ribs.

Amanda surveyed her group. They had not been vetted. They had not been hired. They had not been tested and their qualifications were only briefly checked by her. This was hardly a Research Firm under the firm guidance of an Administrative Assistant like Barbara in New York or Washington DC.

"Get an ID at the main entrance Front Desk, if you are asked. Be courteous to security checks, always! Be smart. Be efficient. Examine your material critically…"

Amanda looked at them. "Get a hair-cut!"

They needed the work, Amanda knew. Even if she picked them off the beach working out their anger.

She took a deep breath. She was on the right track. It felt right.

"Hey, Amanda" said Tom finally. "We appreciate what you're doing. We won't let you down…Promise!"

"Do you have a suit and tie?" asked Phillipa

"I have a suit and tie" answered Tom.

"Right then" finished Amanda. "I'll expect professionally written reports from you all…"

They grinned like happy children.

"Our next meeting is?" asked Mary.

"Next week." said Amanda. "Same time. Same place! And I count on your absolute discretion, care, security and professional ethics."

Before leaving that night, Amanda felt something of a grateful hug from each one as they left.

Or perhaps they were just drunk, she wondered. Still, she knew she had done the right thing. She gave them work. And she gave them purpose.

She cleared the table: This was a good first cut.

 After that, she would have them examine corporate data; geological surveys and mining anomalies for any forensic evidence…

Before going to bed she checked her email.

Barbara's message was the one she opened:

I hope you know what you're doing. Washington DC is not a place for amateurs!"

* * *

Chapter 38

The matter troubled Arguetta.

He would advise Trevor, he decided.

Their interview with Sandra made it abundantly clear that she was unaware of what had happened.

Neither could she have known who funded the grant, or why the Foundation was offshore. Certainly, she knew little of the matter as far as Washington was concerned.

Still, Sandra might be in harm's way if she had any association with the man who was poisoned.

His connections alone were worrying, if not his apparent actions prior to his death whereby he attempted to conceal his records and identity. Even as a student, there was no telling who sourced his actions, or why. What he did on that Artic Expedition was deplorable.

Worse, his death was finally induced by a third party unknown. Someone who had arrived in Chicago...That was most puzzling.

For now, he'd watch carefully the data coming in.

Yes, he'd advise Trevor.

This man and Sandra were students at the same school. Both had gone to the expedition!

From a judicial point of view, the boy might have witnessed something; or known something; or posited in Sandra some intelligence while they were on the expedition together that could make her vulnerable at best, a liability at worst.

He was about to leave for the day.

"Sir!" said Tom Ducas, his head suddenly appearing around the door. "I may have something of interest..."

Arguetta followed him down the hall and into his secured computer station.

I checked with international records and police identities on possible links and connections. Interpol had little; the British had most intelligence and we had…"he tapped a few keys "this!"

A hot graph and data filled the screen with intelligence portals, pictures and fingerprints.

"A hot cell in Chicago?" asked Arguetta. "You've got to be kidding me…"

"Yep. This stuff is a list of cells we know about; this is new" he said triumphantly. "I computed some cross correlations and this came up."

A closer examination of risk for a possible cell developing in Chicago had ties to Switzerland and the Middle East.

"Ivanovich is the name of a student candidate at Chicaco working on his dissertation. He was on a dig in the Middle East and supposedly connected with Dana Thompson. The locals say he had a lot of loot with him."

"In what context?"

"He vanished. Never returned to Chicago. He did file a report with the University of his find, or rather, the Director did, Professor Dana Thompson… "

"Can we make some enquiries about the source of funding? Check with the IRS tax filings."

"Yes Sir."

"It could be nothing, it could be something. You know academics, there's a lot of professional jealousy amongst them! They can be quite territorial about their funding sources if not downright defensive, even a motive for murder in one instance."

"Right. I checked some FBI Files with open investigations. It appears than when the Head of the Department was questioned by Investigative agents concerning the death of Ivanovich, the report cites the Department as being *'a little vague'* and uninformed about the official source of funding. They didn't know, precisely."

"What did the school records show about that student?"

"They didn't. There were few records about him…His financial aid records showed zero balance outstanding."

"Check the family…"

***

Amanda drove to the outskirts of Washington DC and took the subway into the city. It surfaced at the Freer Art Gallery of the Smithsonian Institute on the Mall.

She walked.

It was a bright, blue-sky day in the Nation's Capital. The kind of day that could bestow upon the city a coloring that reflected richly within the Potomac River basin at any month of the year, including the coldest. Little, on any postcard, could betray the time of year where the dome of the Capitol building of Congress was shown.

Here on the Mall, Washington's Reflection Pool lay as generous and enduring at the foot of the granite steps of the Capitol as any Corinthian column.

Amanda found a bench and paused before entering the Gallery. The clay tablet was in her backpack.

Ed was underground working on plasters, she knew. Far below the surface of the grassy mall, the Smithsonian connected its many operations and working lab centers to its Galleries, mainly for security reasons, but also for privacy and controlled conditions.

Ed loved what she gave him.

"I studied the images you sent, and the clay tablet is a beautiful stele of the fourth century B C!"

"Diane had asked me to give this to your keeping. You'll know where to catalogue it, and of course, to authenticate it. She shed little light on the place where it was found, I'm afraid."

"Here, I'll log it in, and I'll shelve in our secure vault sections until we understand it fully. Lunch? Let's walk over the Art Gallery and have a decent lunch."

Amanda nodded, enjoying the prospect of walk across the Mall to the Art Gallery on 3rd St.

He was a dapper fellow, this anthropologist whom Diane knew and trusted. Dark red corduroy pants, a blue oxford shirt under red suspenders, and a yellow bow tie. He resembled a canary in the coal mine. "To life the spirits of my colleague trolls…" he laughed when she complimented him.

"Well my dear. If it's authentic…" he said over his coffee at the Art Gallery "pending the outcome of the forensic testing, then I can tell you a little something about it. I just got back from a conference in Tel Aviv where we examined some similar artifacts."

"Do you think it elucidates anything recent?"

"Absolutely! It's got all the Antiquities dealers excited. And it is a stunning discovery." He buttered a scone.

"You see, the story of the Bible – the account we know from the cannon selected by the Holy Roman Empire in the first century, is the tale of the Children of God. It has moral overtones, admonitions for the walk of the faithful. Those narratives, known as the books in the Bible, reflects a period after the Children of Israel returned from their Diaspora in Babylon. That's when early Christians became fanatical about recording their history."

"So, what does it suggest?" asked Amanda

"Well, this seems to be identifying an incident of Noah's Flood which held moral overtones, too. The flooding of the Euphrates held special significance, in theological terms, we know."

He munched.

"But if any one particular flood was exceptional, including Noah's, then we're looking at a reference to an antecedent lore, or event, that is new to us."

"What is its contribution to the body of knowledge?"

" Well…let me see. Do you mean as a discovery that opens up new knowledge? Well, of course, that means untold commercial value. Mainly because while it has no moral significance, it is a clearly a pagan accounting of an event passed down several millennia…

Something astrophysical, which they ascribed to the stars, and to a change of seasonal animal hunting…I'm thinking. Can I get you more coffee?"

* * *

213

Chapter 39

Less than a week after talking with Ed, Amanda was listening to her posse of Researchers sitting at her dining table.

"Cool" Tom was saying about Mary's findings.

Amanda was unaccustomed to comments from fellow colleagues as if from a gallery of kids, but she remained silent.

Rather, her thoughts was wandering.

She had not divulged the matter of the stele sent by Diane. But she had discussed it with Trevor.

"he found it consistent with inscriptions in ancient glyphs that recount a catastrophic event, noted to be aligned with the stars."

"Well that's nothing new, is it?" he said. "There are Mayan accounts that suggests that Magnetic North was shifting…"

"Umm" she said, the phone connection between them less than clear with the split-second time lag between North America and Europe.

"In an article written by Robert Fusonans published by Taylor Francis and the American Geographers Association, there is an interesting proposition that shows a graph pointing to a conclusion."

"What's that?"

"In the study, they found the architectural orientation of ceremonial centers looking at man-land relationships in Meso-America. Physical surroundings were dictated by astronomical and cultural factors. This, they shifted about at widely separate locations, suggesting that alterations of structural positions, through time, indicated a *moving* reference point. It actually suggests that the Maya had a method of determining magnetic north!"

Amanda came back to earth and as the evening wore on, and the research or her friends yielded results, she found she had been richly rewarded.

She had mentioned, at one meeting previously, her interest in the search for magnetic north. And while she did not divulge the nature of her interest, or the reasons behind it, she told them she was interested in increased radiation."

"No kidding!" said Tom again. "Well, if that's right then, there are some remains of earlier ancestral man-made structures that point entirely to a different orientation. Like a Polar shift of the planet!"

Amanda smiled. Trevor would love to hear this, she thought.

"Wait" said Mary. "In Chicago Journals, I found an article about Turkish Mosque Orientation and the Secular Variation of the Magnetic Declination"

"Cool" said Tom again. This time Phillipa rolled her eyes.

"They reported on 333 independent determination of the orientation of 298 Turkish structures dating from the late eleventh century to the present, and the *orientation* defined a variation of the earth's magnetic field."

"You looked this up?" asked Amanda.

"Sure I looked it up. For you!"

"Wow! What standard did they use?" asked Amanda.

"A Koranic line which may be translated to orientation, the *qibla*, during the obligatory prayer, known as the *salat*"

"I know that the pole has played a mythical and cultural role in spiritual esoteric mythology..." said Phillipa "much of it rooted in the Persian culture of Sufism and Iranian mysticism. The "North" relates to heavenly places of purity and godliness..."

"What we need is hard evidence. Like geological tracings of a magnetic change?"

"That's easy enough. There's plenty of geo-spatial data out of NASA. And I've done some scientific research. There is nothing phenomenal about this phenomenon!"

Tom surprised them, even as he enjoyed his own alliterative speech.

"Meaning… that… whatever suggests an increase in radiation on the planet surface can rule out magnetic polar shift as a cause! There must be some other explanation if doesn't remain consistent with the data bases. If it's totally unexplainable, and its real, then it's a man-made threat…"

His eyes locked into Amanda's. For someone with a suntan who lived on beer and watermelon, this man was no fool, she realized.

In fact, he was alerting her to potential hazard.

"You're the one kidding now, right?" said Mary.

Amanda looked away. She got the message.

"He's been at his computer for days. Nights too " interjected Phillipa. "I was wondering what he was finding."

Tom looked up. "No... Yes I am mean, I've been researching this very carefully. You have to cut through the political bullshit and get to the real science. That's the thing!"

The girls rolled their eyes.

"According to multiple physics journals" he said "polar shifts are normal. They occur periodically. According to most scientists in recent writings the magnetic field has flipped its polarity about every 200,000 years. Magnetic fields move about gradually" Tom drew a sketch. Amanda was listening.

"…sediment cores taken from the ocean floors offer fossil evidence showing that magnetic polarity has no detrimental effect, not even to lessen the effect of solar radiation from the earth's mantel. However, the Earth's magnetic field – here - determines the magnetization of lava on either side of the Mid Atlantic Rift where the continental plates are spreading apart." He looked up. "So. As the lava solidifies, its creates a fossil record of the orientation of past magnetic fields. See?" He showed the direction of iron isotopes.

"Really?" said Phillipa, her patience thin.

"So, the last time it flipped was about 780,000 years ago in what scientists called the Brunhes-Matuyama reversal: Neither do they see any change in glacial activity, based on the amount of oxygen isotopes in the cores, nor evidence of it affecting the rotation axis of Earth – which would show up."

"Wow!" said Mary.

"Can you give me a copy of that info?"asked Amanda.

"Here" he said, pulling out a neatly typed document, and continuing "Finally, there is no truth to the hypothesis that a geomagnetic flip would affect solar activity. The magnetic field that protects us from solar flares and coronal mass ejections from the sun may have shown small increases in solar radiation, but the Earth's thick atmosphere also offers protection against the sun's particles…"

"Jesus, Tom!" said Phillipa.

"Well. That rules out a lot.." said Amanda. "Even a nil-hypothesis is helpful. That leaves us with fewer options to consider as to why radiation is increased, even as an academic exercise."

"Or *made* to increase…perhaps?" said Tom, warning Amanda that whatever she was after implied some foul-play or potential danger.

"Tom" said Amanda "You sure surprised us! Have you listed your readings with full citations and dates of literature findings?"

He nodded "Yep!"

"Wow" laughed Mary. "Not bad for a bunch of beach-bum researchers!"

"I'll drink to that!" added Tom, his face openly happy, a new man. He looked at Phillipa.

"Class dismissed!" announced Amanda. "Let's have a drink out on the sand…"

Later, Tom nudged Amanda aside. "You'd better get on the inside of this classified material and find out what's going on. This ain't no enquiry for an academic-review…"

"Hey Tom!" called Phillipa from the surf. "Over here…"

"This material is black ops…" he said. He waved back at Phillipa.

Amanda looked at him.

"The company I worked for? A software tech group with multiple defense contracts. Mainly, it was supporting intel for the US Air Force…"

* * *

Chapter 40

Trevor picked his schedule.

In October, the European Union was meeting. His destination was the Council of the European Union, which normally held its seat at Headquarters in Brussels, except during certain months – October being one of those months.

In fact, his appointment was at the Secretariat's office. One of many for the day.

Yet, as important as his discussion would be, he thought it best to meet casually, at a café somewhere. Where better to lower suspicion from prying eyes? The organization was rife with activists. For as respected as the coalition was, comprising of 28 nations created by the Maastricht Treaty, its roots, he knew, held closely to progressive policy and political power-brokering seeking everywhere advantages.

Prior to entertaining notions of defense, his choice of candidate for his meeting was a man he could trust with a matter of grave concern to the stability of the West.

Besides, the man seated across from him was an old friend. Herman was part Dutch and part Icelandic.

In the Netherlands during the war, Herman's father had been a scientist with unwavering allegiance to the Allies. His family had been incarcerated, and he had lost nearly all his brothers. Somehow, Herman was sheltered in place while his father fed intelligence to aid of the allies.

Today, Herman was a Luxemburg Banker consulting often with the EU dealing with European debt. A crisis which in all fairness had begun in the United States. The subprime mortgage crisis was a financial product developed by clever banks offering "teaser" interest rates for loans on homes. Many homeowners refinanced their mortgages.

However, as the loan matured, the terms of the loan accelerated interest rate which became unsustainable for average Americans, especially when the housing market values collapsed and homes found little prospect in resales. The banks were left holding non-performing loans and toxic debts on their balance sheets, thereby putting them at risk with the government.

Investment banking firms, engaged in brokering creative financial instruments, began "bundling" the mortgages and selling them as "mortgage-backed securities." Homes would eventually self-correct.

But as global financial systems became damaged, all overleveraged banks triggered a contraction of credit: Banks stopped lending, economies slowed and commerce stopped flowing.

Around the world, sovereign central banks had to step in to shore up financial institutions considered "too big to fail." It was a measure designed to prevent another banking crisis and open the arteries of trade.

Unfortunately, Quantitative Easing in the United States found its way only to beneficiaries like investors, large stock and public corporations changing money. It failed to filter down into the local economy of average citizens, and did even less to stimulate national economic growth.

An inverted socialism by the big hand of government intrusion, some said. Others disagreed, and led to the nationalization of financial institutions in some cases, and greater regulation in others.

Country after country struggled, some with issues of antiquated revenue receipts; over-bloated social entitlements or demographic changes. Some sovereign nations defaulted on their Treasury obligations and had to seek international aid.

Iceland, Ireland, Portugal, Greece and others were bailed out by others…

The greater dilemma was not just one of restructuring debt, or even debt forgiveness, but rather, the moral obligations of a contract: At its core, the issue of unravelling contracts that held together commercial ventures was like unbinding the contracts of civil law and order.

Trevor himself had been at the heart of many debates in London with his government over banking policy. It had not been an easy problem to solve...

The exchange and transactions of money was as good as any bond or contract that held society together. It was the underpinning of Western Civilization, if not the individual mandate of trade since the beginning of time.

Sadly, the seizing of assets by government also froze the assets of individual citizens and independent ventures. The power to regulate financial systems soon became political. And this was dangerous business. This, Trevor and Herman agreed upon.

As one country after another in Europe failed, the EU was dealing with a financial banking crisis of its own. It led to instability and disruption across Europe, leaving many to wonder as who was in control of what...Institutions that had prevailed for so long were now questioned.

The streets filled with angry voters. The guns of the Middle East changed from one despotic regime to another.

Herman was under extreme pressure, Trevor knew. He had a seat on the EU Commission, and as such, he was watched carefully for any pre-disposition that might favor one group over another.

Trevor had to adjust his attitude, as did Great Britain, now suspecting a power-grab by governments; progressives and over-zealous regulations from authorities beyond their boarders. Trade Agreements, largely induced by the United States, were unfavorable for smaller nations – with much of their world fed by large foreign investments needing assurances of return in free market trade.

There were difficulties, experiments, embarrassments as investors lost money; homes continued to be foreclosed, and populations aged.

"Did you not learn from my country Iceland?" said Herman. "Landsbankinn offered high interest saving accounts to citizens of your country and the Netherland through its Internet-based *Icesave* program. Iceland's financial sector assets ultimately exceeded 1000 percent of its total GDP, and its external debt topped 500 percent of its GDP..."

Trevor nodded. "A run on the bank triggered Landesbankinn's collapse."

"Then what happend?" said Herman "Iceland's government announced that it would guarantee the funds of domestic account holders - but *not* foreign ones!"

"The news rippled through the financial systems of Iceland, the Netherland and the UK" said Trevor. "Most of European investments - 350,000 British and Dutch deposits lost over $5 Billion in deposits…Iceland's overleveraged banks caused it to file for national bankruptcy, and the Iceland government collapsed in 2009!"

"Yes" finished Herman. "And their austerity measures were imposed by the IMF in Washington DC were harsh."

Herman owed Trevor a great deal of gratitude, for while allowing the Icelandic currency to devalue, the krona survived the inflation that followed as real wages began their slow recovery.

"Nobody knows how much your bank helped us!" he said quietly sipping his cappuccino"

Trevor smiled politely, his dark coat and white scarf keeping him warm in the Fall breeze.

"We did the same for the Irish.." said Trevor dismissively, his breath warm over his coffee, "but don't tell them that, please. They've harbored a dislike for the Scottish for a long, long time!"

Herman grunted irreverently at European history. "You know, it was a terrible thing we did to all those depositors, losing all that money. Especially the British who are not your big spenders in life."

"I know. We did all we could, I promise."

"That's good. The thing is, banking does work and is a very useful thing - given the time and patience of good honest bankers…It's so unfortunate that a few stupid bankers get greedy with playing systems…"

"I know. It's called disruptive innovation these days! We were amply compensated, at the end of the day, if that's your concern. The thing is to take the long view, I hope!"

"Of course. It is the right view, always. The test of time has proved that!"

They walked through the great park where trees flanked the city boulevard.

"I need to trace the money flow of an asset that is believed to have less than honest intentions, if not a hoard of valuables taken as collateral."

"Um" said Herman. "The bank was seized, and its windows sealed tight. Very tricky to find special exception" said Herman, his hands behind his back but his shoulders lifted to aim at the institution behind them.

"We suspect that is precisely what it is doing to shelter itself. Hiding behind the seizures of this crisis!"

"What is at stake?"

Trevor looking up casually at birds fluttering in summer leaves, his stance relaxed as if sharing a pleasant walk through the park with an old friend.

"We think its funneling money to a terrorist network playing with dangerous toys…"

Herman nearly stopped walked. Trevor kept him moving, noticing that the shiny vehicle tracing them moved gradually up the street.

Herman got wind of what was going on, and laughed artificially. He pointed at a child passing with his mother.

"Of course!"

"I'll give you the key codes of the account. It was opened in the United Kingdom. We believe it has intentions in the United States as well."

"What field of toy are we talking about?"

Trevor gave him only word before they parted with a hug and handshake, the taxi hailed and stopping.

"CERN"

Herman, he knew, was a scientist as well as a banker.

A particle collider of a new sort could offer bomb-makers an entire new universe of destruction capacity.

***

Chapter 41

"Gentlemen," said Arguetta "as we conduct our R&D for defense purposes to serve our national interests, there is concern about potential leaks." He looked around the room at the group assembled. "I know you are as concerned since you fully understand the implications of our advanced intellectual knowledge development programs. Keep your eyes open; your files closed and your data offline!" He was interrupted for a message placed into his hand by a Lt Junior officer.

"I just got off the plane from Prestwich in Scotland where I conferred with a number of UK staff. I must tell you Gentlemen, that I was sufficiently alarmed as to decide to share with you their concerns, even as we pursue our own investigations."

He moved to sit down "Lt Cdr. Thomas will give you a scientific run down, and after we're done here, I'm happy to meet with you each privately throughout the week in my office to discuss any matters pertaining to your particular R&D areas of specialization."

They all nodded. Clearly, Arguetta, was considered a fair man.

Lt Cdr. Thomas doused the lights and the digital monitor came up with DoD insignia followed by various fields and subsets.

"First, the basics.

CERN contains the world's largest particle collider machine for research of particle physics in its quest to discover the basic building-blocks of the time-space continuum in the universe. Officially, this includes the physics of planetary origin; scientific knowledge and its gravitational forces."

He switched to the next screen.

"CERN was the brainchild of the European Organization for Nuclear Research, by 2008 it worked with the collaboration of scientists and engineers from over 100 countries, including university laboratories and experimentation corporations."

Next screen.

"As you know, collision needs speed and distance so, it this machine was built inside a tunnel 27 kilometers in circumference; deep underground at 175 meters and lies beneath the France-Switzerland border near Geneva, Switzerland."

Next screen.

"Amongst its many recent discoveries in physics is the Higgs boson. And, if you don't mind, I'll let Dr. Simpson continue with her field of expertise here…" he said handing her the remote. She got up, and in the dark room, took over the presentation.

"So, these…new particles…"she cleared her throat "Excuse me…" she crackled, sipping water "are predicted by supersymmetric theories, including new and unknown particles. In fact, collisions of certain particles at high speeds of impact may describe the origins of the universe. This you all know, I'm sure!"

Next screen.

"In the meantime, data from works produced by the Large Hedron Collider (LHC) has created a computing grid that became, for its time, the shared network infrastructure connecting some 140 computing centers in 35 countries!" They grinned. "It was the beginning of the world wide web, the Internet, as we know it today." She paused, smiling at the happy-ending-story. Then she sipped water again.

"But herein lies the problem: Our inter-connectivity has become the subject of electronic innovative disruption; data is mined, and cyber security has become a new industry defending intellectual intelligence… "

She paused.

"In play: The Hadron Collider refers to composite particles of natural substance like quarks held together by strong forces (like atoms, molecules are held together by electromagnetic force.) Best known are baryons protons and neutrons; hadrons also have mesons such as pion and kaon, which as you know gentlemen, were discovered during cosmic ray experiments in the late 1940s and early 1950s."

Arguetta looked at his watch. He had a four o'clock meeting Downtown. He would call Eileen and tell her he'd be late. He'd have dinner in town, if necessary. He nodded at Dr. Simpson a thanks for her contribution.

Lt Cdr. Thomas regained the full attention of his scientists.

"There is no oversimplifying what this research is. Nor is there any apology for what it can do. We have to take this seriously. The Europeans think they're entitled to public access on the grounds of Fair Use Laws"

"We prevailed, using NATO as our authority!"

The room laughed.

"Let's face it, we are tampering with the basic laws of physics. Deeper and unknown structures of space and time are the relations between quantum mechanics and general relativity. This is tampering with atoms at the molecular level. It's an unknown science, let alone an *angel wings' whisper of balance* that we might be playing with…"

"So, at the most prescient, we may ask *simple* questions. Like, what are we doing to mass, since everything has mass? Or, if generated by the Higgs mechanism via electro-weak symmetry - does it break?"

They laughed.

"But we have critics. They ask probing questions: In supersymmetry, do particles have supersymmetric partners? Or, are there extra dimensions, such as the string theory? Or, what is the nature of the dark matter that accounts 27% of the mass energy of the universe?"

More grinning.

"Yes. We laugh. But there are more dangerous questions like electromagnetism and the weak/strong nuclear radiation of universal unified forces…"

Tom paused slightly.

"There are problematic vulnerabilities…Like why is the *fourth* fundamental force of gravity so many orders of magnitude weaker than other levels etc. etc. And I leave to your imagination what comes next?.."

He waited.

"So, how concerned should we be about the critics who are concerned? Especially on issues about symmetry between matter and antimatter? What are the real properties of quark-gluon plasma that we thought existed in the early universe only, but are now discovered in strange astronomical objects today?"

The house lights went up. It was lunchtime.

Arguetta said "So you see the problem. And the danger!"

They relaxed, laughing and chatting now.

"God, if only science could be left alone without Activist informants!" said Peters from his side of the table.

"Hey, I'll settle for a-political science alone!"

"Yeah!"

"We wonder… Still, with each of these collisions at Hadron, there are risks, huh?" said someone.

"Yep! We *may* be tampering with a topic that could run beyond us…"

"Right!"

Lt Crd Thomas pronounced one last comment for all to hear. "Chief amongst our concerns? This research might have potential to wreak havoc as a weaponry system…" He consulted his watch. "See you back in an hour and fifteen?"

Arguetta whispered something in his ear.

The Lt. Cdr turned to Arguetta. He nodded. "Right away!"

They disbanded for a Lunch break.

* * *

Chapter 42

Arguetta called Amanda.

Never one to let the sun set on a schedule he could optimize, he wanted to know how her research was coming. He knew she would talk discretely over an open phone, but clear enough to sketch him the outline. The words radiation poisoning would be eliminated from her conversation, if clearly implied.

Amanda told him that there was little in the National Archive records that showed signs of anomalies. Neither in scientific journals, papers, medical or the legal cases was there anything related to magnetically induced incidents, nor in newly funded projects outstanding.

"Nothing significant stood out as being eventful outside its predicted conclusions. Only one litigated case argued that a change in shoreline had occurred due to an anomaly in the northern hemisphere mid-19th century, but the case rested on a progression of construction. Army Surveyor Corps concurred. In that particular case, the Jury found for the defendant - a contractor who showed that a railway had been build nearby and caused the shift in shoreline!"

Arguetta chuckled.

"And finally, one insurance record shows that a claim was considered without merit following an Act of God at sea that caused a cargo to sink with the ship in a fierce storm due to compass anomalies."

"Oh yes. I know the case! Being a Navy man, we all do. The matter of safety and mission must come before commercial interests. However, that was not always the case in Admiralty Law!"

Now it was her turn to chuckle.

"Thanks Amanda. We don't need to be blind-sided by something fundament, so this research venue needs to be exhausted as a Null option before delving deeper."

"Right."

"Sounds like you had help?"

Amanda was unsure about disclosing the "help" she had.

"Yes Sir"

He paused, saying nothing.

"Alright then, he said finally. I do need to talk with Trevor on other matters, have him call me when you can please!

* * *

Amanda thought about his call later in the car.

He was obviously wondering how they were performing, her motley crew of researchers. He clearly had reservations about her choices.

They were after all, unaccounted personnel working on a contract! But then again, none of her work was classified since she had lost her security clearance. They could be classified at Interns.

She had told him earlier about her "unaccounted personnel" as she called them. They were professionals presently unemployed and in need of part time work!

She had explained in essence that her group was a posse of researchers, but capable. They each had professional experience which she would present in due course to Arguetta. Clearly he had received their files, and his silence, when he asked her the question, was tacit approval for their work without clearance.

However, she knew he would want their working names and addresses on the Report. She wondered how you address your jogging neighbors on the beach…

Still, she was very proud of them all, she decided. They had done way more than she expected. Then again, why was she surprised? Ordinarily, they were hard working professionals, even if now feeling like unwanted bums…

No question. It was awkward.

* * *

Chapter 43

Lt Cdr Thomas was still at it when Arguetta returned to the conference room and took his place. Dr Simpson was standing beside him.

"The science of physics is dangerous. Many scientists around the world worry that experiments with a machine this powerful at CERN might release into the atmosphere forces capable of literally in the decaying our ambient environment. We are declining any official comment at this time" he said. Then he turned to Dr. Simpson. "Please continue, Dr. Simpson if you will…"

She took over.

"Altering the…err… *density* of particles or the forces that keep our natural tensions in check are credible. Smashing hadrons, as the readings suggest, might produce tiny black holes so dense that they consume everything around them, growing larger and larger until they consume the entire solar system." The room remained silent.

"Or, the collider might produce a product of quantum physics called *strangelets* which could possess powerful gravitation fields that could eventually render the earth lifeless…" She paused.

"Then there is the theory about a magnetic monopole, a particle that holds a single magnetic charge instead of two: Such particles could pull matter and gravity *apart* because they would be totally out of magnetic balance." She stepped back and returned to her place. Arguetta leaned over and tapped her elbow in a gesture of thanks.

Lt.Cdr Thomas was speaking. "So, as I said earlier, out chief concern is that this stuff may have military ramifications." He paused. "The real strategic consideration however, is the functionality of cyber wars in our computing systems that may well constitute industrial warfare, if not national warfare by economic disruptions of our infrastructure or worse, larger destructive forces of nature unleashed willfully. This is way beyond hacking. Such acts of God would now become acts of Man!"

He sipped glass of water and lit up the digital monitor to show several men on Identification grids.

"It took us months to detect a computing bug that spied on sensitive industrial materials. Mostly, they crawl other content. But recently, we saw real incursions into our infrastructure. Already, we have seen failures within our own industrial complex…Globally, it gets serious. In the Fall we saw three different Airlines afflicted by the *same* malfunction in three different airports at *exactly* the same time!"

"A message?" asked someone

"Absolutely, a message. Bow shots!" said Arguetta.

Lt Cdr Thomas continued.

"A researcher at CERN was arrested because he had ties to Al Qaeda. He had been working there since 2003. Another person was interrogated who had specialization in centrifugal forces of nuclear reactors that he monitored from half way around the world!"

He sipped again and looked at Arguetta who spoke next, leaning forward from his seat and folding his hands on the table.

"We do have the Snowden's of the world who find such spying offensive. And to a point, it is intrusive! Especially if utilized as a defense profiling system, which is against our Constitutional values. We do understand that, and we are listening closely to Congress, as we must. But what have now are larger questions beyond hacking balance sheets and bank vaults…"

He had their attention, his voice calm.

"We are now concerned with a wider interest in world destruction by terrorist fundamental groups showing interest in the particle collider. Clearly, if it concerns destructive physical forces, they are dealing with doctrinal convictions rather simple conquest or economic advantage…"

Lt Cdr Thomas passed him a folder, which Arguetta opened. "According to our own *American Physical Planet* these particle collisions cause no threat since the elements involves exist already in a natural state.

"But we are concerned about research being conducted *outside* the collider that deals with magnetism and the bi-polar weakening of the field. And yes, we are detecting a foreign hand at play across our cyber electronics that power most of our grids."

Lt Cd Thomas continued.

"One theory put forward by NASA suggests that by placing three particular concentrations of magnetic pulls across the northern artic regions, a dome of electromagnetic blocking occurs for the transfer of signals and charge. It might interrupt a natural frequency. And it could shut down the entire North American and Canadian continent…

"Unfortunately, if such a theory were true, it would not take much of a force to effect its consequence. Shut down our hemisphere, and you shut down the world…A mono-culture outside the dome may seek to dominate with global supremacy. That's the theory."

He waited, sipping from a glass of water at the table. "Any questions?"

One hand raised slightly. It was Bill Pearson, senior Project Manager from Northern Operations and Cyber Defense systems. "What is the goal? To detect possible invasion of our data intelligence and patch holes?"

"Yes. And no. That's the conventional method against cyber hacking. Here, the real question is this: Can such an electromagnetic dome-field be possible to weaken natural bipolar tension? If so, how to counteract its effect and break its dome web?"

"In other words" said Arguetta "We must design a counter measure before such an event can occur!"

* * *

Chapter 44

Amanda returned from her morning jogging. Already, the ladies had completed their run, she knew. But she had not seen Tom yet. He lived next door at his Aunt's beach house. She walked up over the beach dune pathway and down to her house at street level.

She stopped suddenly. In her driveway was an Ambulance.

Out of breath, she asked what the commotion was about. Two paramedics were working on Tom, bundling him onto a gurney. They called in his condition to the Emergency Room and made ready to transport him. He was in shock, they reported. The Ambulance pulled away, sirens blaring.

"What happened…?"

Mary came forward. "Tom! It was Tom…"

Phillipa appeared. She was sobbing. "He was choking…frothing…or fading. I found him coming out of the house, his hand holding his throat…"

"Who called 911?" asked Amanda.

"I did" said Philllipa. "I was going to his house to make coffee for him…"

Outside they stood, the air still ringing with a siren alarm. Other neighbors came out, asking.

They spend the morning together going over the events that led to his incident. Amanda's kitchen was crowded as many came and went...

She called the hospital.

It was a long day. They had gone to the hospital and waited. Finally word came out that he was alright. He had a muscle spasm and been choking, they explained. It had cut off his air supply and low blood pressure put him into shock. Luckily, Phillipa called it in. He was recovering nicely, they said.

Last night the girls had met again.

"This will cheer us all up!" said Amanda giving them each a nice check for their work. Plus a bonus. "And this one is for Tom…" she added, holding his envelope.

They grinned.

Exhausted, they went all went home, arranging to take turns visiting Tom in the hospital the next day.

Later in the night Amanda had talked with Trevor. He had talked with Arguetta.

"Be Careful" were his words of admonishment to her. Not once, but several times he expressed is concern.

They talked of Tom mainly. While Trevor didn't know Tom personally, he had met his Aunt, a neighbor. He asked if there had been a family history of illness.

There was nothing they could figure to explain the reason for his condition.

Gradually, Amanda realized that hearing Trevor's voice assuaged her anxiety, regardless, and she was glad he called.

The windows were slightly that night, a moon trailing across its path leaving shadows and shapes on the wood pine flooring of the bedroom.

 She dozed fitfully.

Only later during the night, Amanda awoke to an unsettled feeling. In the mirror of the bathroom she saw a sleepy face, eyes swollen, and her neck stiff. She took a deep breath, and her chest hurt with a little pang. She felt itchy, and decided to take a small aspirin.

She couldn't get comfortable. Her throat was sore.

She went up to her office. Opened her computer, sent messages to Trevor, Barbara, Sandra…

Downstairs she poured herself a glass of wine and then went upstairs. It had been a long day, she could not have anticipated Tom's incident, and she was clearly behind schedule on a lot of things, she knew. It had drained her completely.

Why? How did all this transpire?

As she switched off most of the house lights, she noticed from the kitchen window that there were no outside porch lights on at the guest cottage. No interior security lights on, either. In fact, the place looked so dark that the place looked abandoned.

Earlier, in the turmoil of the day's events, she did notice that Kim was absent from the cottage. But it was clear he had been in there recently. This was apparent from the way he had cleared out the back yard; the trash containers; swept debris and leaves from the garden sidewalk. These chores he did habitually around his living quarters when he stayed, even if Amanda was away on travel or staying in Washington.

In fact, it had been weeks since she had actually seen him around, such was her schedule. In the morning, she decided she would visit the cottage.

She dozed off.

She decided to forego her jogging today, and instead, settled for a dark coffee and hearty breakfast. She cleaned up, made a few calls and easily recaptured her scheduled items on her calendar. Later, she would join the girls and visit Tom, she knew.

Outside, the sound of water sprinklers filled the neighborhood air, lazy clouds promised beautiful weather with little humidity at the beachfront today.

She walked over to the closed guest house. The cottage was sealed, secured and in top order.

She knew he was away, but she knocked on the door anyway as a courtesy.

She entered at the side door, calling his cell phone to ask permission to enter as she did so. There was no answer on the phone.

She walked into the kitchen and found on the countertop a letter addressed to her. She picked it up slowly. Typed, addressed and stamped, it was left there, sealed.

The kitchen cabinets were impeccably clean, almost untouched. Only a small forgotten white plastic fork lay in the recess of a kitchen corner.

Amanda opened the letter - a *Thank You* note of sorts. It contained a check for three month's advance rent, paid in full, with a line marked *Notice to Vacate*.

As per standard Leasing, Kim had met State requirement procedures for Tenancy Occupancy. His written notice to vacate included his full rent in advance, even vacant. Clearly, *Wear and Tear* provisions were waived since he wasn't there, and the place was left in full operating order and without blemish. He had added a few sentences.

He phrased it as a "severance token" with advance payments in full. This, plus his *Notice to Vacate* put him without further obligation, and in full legal compliance.

Overseas, he said in his explanation. It offered, at the very least, a gesture of civility, if distant and sanitized.

Amanda looked at it.

He would call, the note said. That was three days go, judging from the date.

The phone rang.

 It was Phillipa. "I just called the hospital and talked to Mary. She stayed all night. He's been taken back into ICU. So we can't see him."

"What changed?"

"Food poisoning!"

"*Food poisoning…?*" repeated Amanda.

"I'll be there this afternoon" said Phillipa.

"And I'll be there this evening!" said Amanda.

The sky took to a dark churning between two battling weather fronts, and the sea frothed between them in menacing anger.

 Amanda spent the day collecting her thoughts, pulling together the affairs of the last few days; her reports, her conversations; her notes and email, as if order brought sanity and concentration to new challenges. It was the way she worked. And the house was very still.

Later, in the darkening house, she stayed calm, and examined the affairs of her situation. Had she somehow neglected to understand something? What was missing in this development?

She was angry at herself. For someone familiar with crisis management; Congressional Investigative Hearings and forensic assessments, she could not believe how caught up in the present she had been! Stand back and think critically for damage control, she decided.

Why?

Why was Tom suddenly taken ill without it being noticed by the others?

Had she pushed them into taking unnecessary risks? Were there financial obligations that she had failed to pay in advance? Were her records and data in order; her research work and computer notes…

What was Tom working on with his research…? What had he said, that night at the beach?

Had she missed something?

Why in the world was Tom suffering from food poisoning…? The idea was ludicrous!

*Who could say they suffered from poisoned-Pizza for God's sake…*The range of cooking temperatures for the average Pizza oven came close to 900 degrees?

No!

Then a thought came back to her. The night of their first meeting…all of them laughing about food - and she complaining about eating five days of Chinese food…

"Give it to me…"

Tom had thought it hilarious and offered to eat her share of Kim's…

She paused.

A question took over her mind like a grappling hook. She opened the fridge door. The freezer was stocked with cooked food, frozen. Especially Chinese food…

 In one recess was a frozen cavity that had held a dish. A meal missing…*Tom had taken home!*

Never mind that he got into the house. He always did anyway: His Aunt lived next door, and over the years, they had often made special access arrangements between them…

Amanda stood there, stunned.

The thoughts that ran through her head could barely be processed. Then one thing became clear above all others. The food taken by Tom had been cooked by Kim.

It was intended for Amanda.

* * *

Chapter 45

Amanda felt like an intruder. It wasn't often that she had to file a petition to a government agency and ask to see their archives.

By definition, an Archive meant inactive and old content stored for safekeeping purposes only - useful records for scholars looking at historical facts and data for academic elucidation.

Moreover, materials held in the public domain were open to access for viewing by virtue of Fair Use laws, a basic tenet of democracy steeped in the tradition of freedom of speech and freedom of information.

Certainly, Amanda understood that not all information was open access. There was privileged material; classified material; restricted information; proprietary data, intelligence and intellectual content that held copyright protection, or patent rights of usage.

Moreover, there was always judicial discretionary protections, legislative, executive and privacy abilities, much of it subject to contractual arrangements or citizen entitlements.

Amanda had no problem with a government needing to function efficiently, securely and appropriately in the interests of national security and wellbeing.

Much of it, she knew was subject to privacy rights, contracts, and citizen entitlements But sitting in a waiting room for an interview about her research was not what she expected. Such tactics usually belonged to a secretive government and an insular society. Unless something was wrong.

True, there were other places for archives. There were libraries and repositories. There were online sites to make enquires; and there were public relations offices and agencies for every possible function of the Federal Government. The Founding Fathers who wrote the Constitution would be proud, thought Amanda as she sat.

Two young professionals walked by, engaged with their work. One held files, her pony tail coiffed neatly for a sharp look and fun colored shirt; the other holding a laptop and a cell phone. Not much older than Sandra, Amanda knew it was only a matter of time before her own daughter held a job of responsibility somewhere.

She waited, thinking that these were new days with bright people, bright colors and bright prospects all over the world...

So why did she have this sinking feeling in the pit of her stomach?

The Mineral Management Offices of the US Department of Interior was an imposing edifice located by the Trade and Patent Office, Virginia. Generally, it was a federal agency of generous information and open doors to all.

Except recently.

In ploys to embarrass the Administration, public agitators and disgruntled political activists disparaged the agency. It was a targeted campaign to inhibit opportunities for jobs on US soil and elsewhere – citing unfair entitlements to those most qualified; excess data to those asking, and public ridicule to those working.

Amanda was never one to care much for politics. Other than cast a thoughtful vote on election day, she was not one to notice divisions, disputes and disparities amongst politicians. They were all doing what they could to help. It was their job, after all, once elected to office.

She knew at what price such rights and privileges had been paid. Given lingering struggles overseas; efforts at stability in developing nations and global civil rights, Amanda held for a democratic process of open elections and free market economies.

There was little else she found worthy of testing. Besides, it was just not in her nature. She was neither a lawyer nor a political scientist...

Only Barbara had made it her business to inform Amanda on these things, whether she wanted to hear it or not. Barbara was Barbara.

And Barbara did tell her that the progressive activism and insurgent anger wanted access to the US Department of Interior chiefly for its resources; its intelligence and its tax collecting.

There was no arguing with Barbara. Risk assessments; education, moral hierarchy and legitimate trade were anathema, she said. Here at the US Department of Interior was the source material for a societal redistribution for wealth, as she put it.

Of course Amanda refused to believe it. But clearly, she felt like a suspect. Information was information.

Barbara was right.

Not that it helped to have lost her government security clearances for automatic access. But someone had seen to it that she had no further access to confidential material…

Perhaps Arguetta already knew this, she wondered.

Research. If there was one thing Amanda understood was the analytical processes of forensic examination: You looked under more than one lid.

Keep looking!

"You may come in now, Ms Wells!" said the receptionist. "Mr. Wilson will see you now. Did you fill out your Questionnaire?"

She glossed over her particulars and requested materials that she knew she could find at other repositories.

But he was asking, and she had to answer. He was an African American. He wanted to know more about her mission. Her reasons for research, even. What did she hope to find in these documents? He even asked about her friend Dana Thompson. Who wanted to know about these things…

Finally Amanda stood up, finished with his interrogation.

He read her resolve.

Only a few of the records were available, he told her, if she cared to wait, they would be brought out to her in the reception area to view.

He was treating her like a Media reporter nosing for a story. And he was running interference…

She waited.

On her way home that night, Amanda was fuming with frustration. Little that she asked for came out. A ruse to block any information that she needed was employed. By the time she reordered, the archive was closing. She would come back tomorrow, she told them.

Still, as irritated as she felt, she could hardly blame Mr. Wilson. He was doing his job. The question was, why?

Her thoughts went back to Sandra.

"Mom, we had an accident and one of the team fell down a bore hole we were drilling…He's fine. But it was scary!"

Well, that was the initial assessment. Actually, the situation had conflagrated since then, the boy went ballistic at a Medical Facility. That was two months ago. And while Sandra was safely back at the University completing the semester, this mission today for Amanda was something she had promised to do for Sandra to help her write her paper on the Expedition.

As far as the US Geological Office was concerned, the

matter was less about incompetence, or procedures. It was about a Fault Line in the ice-pack through which they had themselves recommend for study by students. The students went up to set their test bore anchors for a geological survey established by the government.

Sandra and her mother had discussed it at some length. She could work from old projections…

"That should all be in the US Geological Survey Records of the Department of Interior" said Amanda. "I'm in Washington soon, perhaps I can help and send you what you need to catch up for your Report?"

That was weeks ago.

Since then, it was clear that Amanda had lost her research privileges. No longer did she have access to classified information, her security clearance had been withdrawn for further research.

Mr. Wilson said as much.

Amanda went to the Library of Congress to garner older data, material cited in legislative governance related to US Geological Reports. It took much longer, and was less than current. But she sent it all up to Sandra immediately.

Two days later, she heard back.

"Thanks, Mom. But it's too late! My Research Funding has been pulled…We got our notice yesterday to terminate all our research studies... The program I'm studying has been shut down!"

***

Chapter 46

The place was grand. Amanda took Arguetta's arm.

They walked through a colonnade of paired columns, above them colossal arch-headed windows that for years, shed light into a warehouse basement, now refurbished as the great hall of a Beaux Arts structure erected in 1927.

Amanda looked up. The barrel vaulted coffered ceiling was freshly painted for the updated commemoration to those who had served in World War I.

With all the street lights on, the Gala event at the Van Ness Avenue War Memorial Opera House in San Francisco was a lavish event.

Tchaikovsky's Nutcracker could be heard emanating from the building, a stunning performance produced there on site December 2008 for a world wide telecast, and captured on DVD for subsequent events such as this.

Admiral Arguetta ascended the steps in full dress uniform, Amanda Wells on his arm wearing a formal evening gown and white long gloves.

"You know Sir, it is Eileen who should be here!" she whispered.

"Yes" he smiled, taking her cape. "And she would most certainly enjoy it. But equally, you are the wife of the former British Emissary here represented today, and I am proud to be your   escort"   he   said.
"Besides, as Eileen aptly volunteered, you are my chief Researcher, formerly under contract to the United Nations in New York" he patted her gloved hand. "So keep your eyes and ears open!"

They were greeted by the host committee.

Amanda's ball gown was grey silk with a gathered waist band. She kept it simple. She had wanted less to draw attention to herself as to be appropriate for this occasion. She was after all being accompanied by a US Naval Officer known for his diplomatic analytical skills; his decorated service and his distinguished diplomacy. Never mind counting his career in deployments and his operations in covert international intelligence assessments. They were on a mission.

Trevor insisted she go, and he trusted her discretion as to dress. However, with her stunning features of blue eyes, dark hair and exquisitely proportioned face, Amanda Wells was a show stopper. There were few who could divert their eyes from her face.

Amanda was introduced to countless agents from various nations. The Gala today was dedicated to a new commemoration - not of World War I, but of an event of World War II that took place here, at this spot, the drafting and signing of the UN Charter.

Arguetta was in full sway with his various alliances.

"May I present my colleague Ms Wells, wife of Minister Trevor MacDonnel of Great Britain" he said to the Chinese Ambassador.

"Ah Yes! My father speaks highly of your husband's family, Mrs MacDonnel. Please convey our respects…" replied the Chinese Ambassador, his wife standing beside him in a column of fucia and raw silk.

"I certainly will" said Amanda with a smile. "Thank you for your kind words!"

They circulated. Every nation on earth, it seemed, involved in WWII was here represented.

Drinks and cocktails were served by waiters, the conversation redolent with memories and epic offenses. Yet they toasted less the achievements of a military war than a world of trade amongst once-enemies, new freedoms and democracy.

Amanda was impressed. She knew her history, as did all who attended. Especially the Yalta Conference wherein the United Nations was established in this very building by Truman, in the end.

Roosevelt's dream was to create a United Nations body that, after the peace, would prevent other wars: For such had been the tragedy of WWI - inadequate peace-keeping to enforce the Treaties of Versailles, that resulted in WWII.

Trevor did inform Amanda of what his family had done as the British Minister in WWII. How difficult it was creating policy papers for the UN Charter with the world was in turmoil; the Armies in full battle and nations in recoil…Yet it was pre-planned in secret as a condition of the peace, and the documents were drawn during the period between the Dumbarton Oaks Conference in 1944, and the Yalta Conference of 1945. There was a contingency too.

Trevor told her about Roosevelt's greatest fear at he approached the Yalta Conference, his health fading.

There he sat, negotiating with Stalin and Churchill about plans ahead when he knew in his heart that America still couldn't win the war in the Pacific without Stalin *declaring* war on Japan - a secret Russian ally!

Europe, he told her, was not the Allies' darkest threat.

Asia was.

The week-long Yalta Conference in 1944 was calm and beautiful on the banks of the Crimea, he told her, all three Allied Heads of State staying at the former palaces of the Tsars…

There, the Delegates of the three Allies knew that the War in Europe was ending, and they worked hard crafting peace treaties for nation after nation; negotiating Armistice Agreements; redrawing the boundaries of Europe; drafting Restitution plans, new government constitutions, new rebuilding programs for populations, schools, industry and food supply, all of it levelled.

It was tricky, Stalin was telling Roosevelt in private. Russia had signed an agreement of non aggression against Japan. Russia had lost too many men in Europe already.

Moreover, Stalin told Roosevelt, Russia wanted more concessions as war reparations in Europe.

The United Nations were not a priority… Especially, since he wanted the four Allies to have dominant voice, vote and veto at the UN over universal membership.

But Roosevelt knew there was a greater problem, one the Russians could not acknowledge.

Russia had over one million armed Russian soldiers stationed in Manchuria. China was an ally.

But for how long, Roosevelt wondered.

Already, China could not guarantee safe passage for a Russian retreat, their arsenal included.

By 1945, China was under increasing encroachment by Mao Tse Tung and his communist People's Army of China.

Worse, as Roosevelt went home from the Yalta Conference feeling tired and depressed it was because he had read the report on Japan's capabilities and standing Armies across all Asia. They were fathomless.

Roosevelt realized, inwardly, that he was not going to win this war. And it was perhaps here that he made his decision to use the atom bomb on Japan.

Less than five months later, Roosevelt died. And only out of deep respect for Roosevelt's wishes, Stalin agreed to send the Russian People's Commissars Vyacheslav Molotov to San Francisco to represent Russia for the United Nation's Security Council Charter...

This, Trevor had told Amanda, his family having been part of the Churchill government at the time, negotiating .

Thus, the San Francisco Conference, formerly known as the United Nations Conference was an International Organization, a world wide body created to embrace political objectives defined by the Allies. 46 nations attended that first Conference, and they signed the 1942 Declaration of the United Nations. It was a stunning feat of diplomacy brokered by US Secretary of State Edward Stettinius; Anthony Eden of Great Britain; Molotove of the USSR, and T. V. Soong of China, their ally.

But as Amanda knew, it did not go well. The war had left smoldering embers...

As she looked into the faces of guests commemorating that achievement, she wondered how many knew of what happened...

The United Nation's Agreement started to fail in a Cold War. The Lublin Government of Poland entrenched as a Russian Communist colony, and the Iron Curtain fell between the Allies.

Gradually, the Allies' powers as permanent members of the United Nations' Security Council dissipated to include other votes from smaller nations, particularly those with petty grievances; many expecting hand-outs and progressive entitlements without making serious contributions to the world economies. It became a bazaar for populist regimes.

The result was a funding-drain. Much was already being invested to rebuild Europe. There was little left for less than legitimate democratic regimes, or potential enemies.

Neither were all enemies of the state foreigners, socialist movements budded internally.

The Chair of the San Francisco UN Conference himself, Alger Hiss, was accused of being a Soviet spy in 1948 and convicted of perjury in connection with his charge in 1950.

But this was a new day, and the modern Treaty of International Trade was today signed. They applauded. The event was clearly a success!

As the event drew to a close and the orchestra played for the ballroom floor, Amanda was offered a dance.

"Will you allow me a waltz, Amanda Wells?" said Arguetta.

"Certainly Sir!" she said, laying her white gloved hand upon his arm.

Where he led, her grey silk gown followed to the floor from a rear sash that shimmered with her movements.

"May I congratulate you on an evening well executed" he said. "You have my thanks!"

Recognized by all in the Ballroom for their national representations - he a party from the United States; she, a party from Great Britain, the dance was viewed as a public statement of solidarity amongst Allies. Applause followed their steps, and the orchestra complied.

"So, are you enjoying your evening Mrs. McDonnel?" he said

"Indeed I am Admiral. You're escort for this social event was most gracious!"

"Good, I'm glad" he said.

But under his smiling eyes, Amanda sensed a darker concern that he felt obligated to mask.

Two staffers, one a Seargent, approached. One whispered a few words to Arguetta, the other stood back, his eyes scanning the room.

He nodded.

The Seargant took his position at Amanda's side as Arguetta excused himself.

"Ma'am?" he said, "May I offer my congratulations on a splendid evening?"

"You may indeed Seargent" smiled Amand. They chatted as he escorted her through the ballroom.

Arguetta returned less than half an hour later. His face was calm for all to see, but she could tell from the darkened look around his eyes that his mind was elsewhere.

"All went well with the signing of the International Treaty for Trade?" asked Amanda as they prepared to leave.

"Yes" he said perfunctorily. "But I've just had the strangest conversation with a Japanese man who asserts that he has information that might backfire on the Trade Treaty Agreement. He challenged one of our assertions!"

"I'm sure you've negotiated an excellent trade deal…" said Amanda. "Trevor tells me that there is none more qualified than you to know how to transact for resources."

Amanda knew well the skills needed for negotiating good treaties. They required the knowledge to know which assets and opportunities to give away, and which to bargain for…

They moved from the ballroom, lingering behind an elderly couple of slow-moving guests.

"He told me that he knew I was mistaken in the valuation of assets conceded to the Chinese in our Non-Competetive Clauses" said Arguetta.

"Was he a party to the negotiations?"

"Yes. A Scientist. He is the son of a sea Captain who was liberated from Port Arthur after the war. He had been a prisoner of the Russians for his role in the Manchurian rebellion. That's what he told me."

"His father would have known the Chang Hi Check Regime before China fell to communism?"

"Oh Yes! He said his father served their Intelligence unit and was attached to Soong on his visit here for the UN Charter in 1945." He paused. "He seemed quite well informed. I've agreed to meet with him later."

"We had been discussing drilling options in the Middle East - the Euphrates. He said that while his was the vanquished nation, Japan had much to thank America for, and he wanted to give back with some intelligence that he had…."

Unexpectedly, the background music ceased and an announcement was issued from the main platform. All guests were asked to leave without incident. The police were approaching the building…

Later, as the limo pulled into the landscaped courtyard of her Hotel, Arguetta looked at her soberly.

"The thing is, Amanda, I have been less than honest. This man…he actually said he met with your friend Diane while she was on her archaeological dig! He said he had evidence of resources found lacking in one of Geological Survey Reports…"

Amanda could hardly believe her ears. Either flushed with too much Champaign; or bewitched by a ball-gown, she found it hard to grasp the gravity of his suggestion. What was he implying exactly?

"We have missed something, Amanda."

"Sir?… " was all she could muster.

"We'll talk again in Washington. I'm taking an overnight Army hopper back now. Are all your arrangements in order for tomorrow?"

She nodded.

"Right then. Call my office when you get back to work!"

The door of the limousine closed and she was left standing on the curb of her Hotel, a doorman waiting with an open Entrance.

She ordered coffee and sandwiches to be sent to her room.

Diane had been murdered.

Yes, it had been a lovely soiree. But when the event was cut short by the police because a man had been found killed downstairs she felt strangely cold.

It was the Japanese man. Arguetta's staffers confirmed it to him in the limousine by phone.

Worse. The implication was that he had critical intelligence for Arguetta which he had wanted to give. Why? What happened?

Strangely, he challenged certain information supplied to Arguetta's office prior to the Trade Agreement Signing at the event of the Commemoration. It was a ceremonial treaty, clearly.

Yet the information he had related to asset valuations and international assessments. Information, in fact, that she and her group had delivered in their research to Arguetta!

She felt a shudder from the past, as if a cold hand from WWII had just touched her shoulder.

* * *

Chapter 47

Alone in her hotel room, Amanda showered, ate up her refreshments and sank into large pillows. But not for long.

She opened her laptop. Much had transpired during the course of the evening. Carefully she gathered her thoughts, listing observations, analysis…

She looked at the time. A few hours before her morning flight!

A small icon on her laptop jogged her memory. The data, the geological data that she had produced for Arguetta had been edited for another use. Amanda had filtered all irrelevant materials; carefully redacting all sensitive information, and applied only those generic parts of research pertinent to a college paper – Sandra's!

She had promised to send Sandra some basic information on the Artic region. Dated mid-19th century, the data was listed in the public record of US Geological Survey. Remarkably void of information, it nonetheless completed her citations for her college paper…Harmless.

Yet Sandra was sitting on the data…

Amanda worked on, sleepless, exploring possibilities that might inform an error, or data, that would alarm a foreign national about their Trade Agreement signed today.

What happened?

How could her data have misled those making decisions about resources in a Trade Agreement? What was the motive?

When did he come forward? Why was this man found dead…

Who was this man? What had he said, in the brief moments he had with Arguetta?

What was he implying? More importantly, how did he *know* what was being negotiated…The material she gave Arguetta was confidential and proprietary.

Clearly, Arguetta would expect her to offer him her brief on the matter, if not explain what the meaning of it was, given the information she supplied…

Classified or not classified, surely there was more light she should shed on the issues.

Obviously, it was significant enough to get the man killed.

Oh yes. She felt certain he was killed.

That is, killed before talking to Arguetta!

Amanda got up to stretch her legs, her mind scrambling to asses the situation. She walked to the window. From the upper room of the Stockton Street Hotel, she took in the view.

Below twinkled lights of a city in slumber, its bay barely definable by buoy beacons, those harbor-markers and coastal channels rimming its contour as a place of safe haven. It's effect drew her breath.

For over a century this Pacific coastal town of San Francisco had seen the trade of sea captains crossing oceans with wealth, goods, immigrants and resources for a growing nation…

She thought about it.

Were there too many coincidences?

Here, the railroads had flourished, connecting a continent so vast and expansive as to fill the journals of Lewis and Clark, surveyors to Thomas Jefferson. From thence came prospectors and cities and industry and ideas and inspiration so abundant as to provide for natural resources and technologies that would revolutionized the world.

It seemed unreal, she turned away.

This evening had been a commemoration for a War memorial that, like this city perched on the Pacific sea, embraced foundations of a vision so enduring, yet so tenuous.

What made it so? *What had happened?*

The answer, she realized, was a new state of existence.

Trade was hardly a threatening word. Yet it could so threaten worlds! This was economic warfare…

How could she have not surmised this?

Following WWI, Amanda knew, agrarian economies still serving national interests were threatened by pressing demographics; industrialization, labor demands and technological advancements. Especially small nations…

Trade agreements between larger nations were leaving them behind. Old angers festered as the seeds of destruction spread from Asia to Europe, ripening for another world war…

The 1931 plot to seize Manchuria and its rich resources was conducted by Japanese men dressed as Chinese bandits who attacked Manchurian Railroad workers.

It was a staged act of provocation and resulted in the attack by the Kwantung Army, a Japanese unit. Its aim was to occupy the whole of the province of Manchuria by the Japanese.

The plot was exposed and caused a sensation of protest from all around the world.

The League of Nations, a global body of peace-keepers failed to react. There was no censoring. They did not protest or protect China from Japanese aggression.

Soon, a second assault followed. Within a year, Japan had conquered most of China's eastern seaboard.

Elsewhere, the Great Depression of the 1930s damaged all but those with strong Trade Agreements.

Imperial and Colonial world powers with international political and economic standing relied on raw materials; food and resources for sustainability.

Oh yes, decided Amanda. Trade was the strongest motive of all in any war amongst nations. Trade represented human survival…

WWII followed, and it would leave no continent untouched. The global toll was 7 million dead.

On her way to the Airport the next morning, her thoughts never left the worries addressed by Arguetta.

Data in the Trade Agreement could be misleading. When describing a resource, it meant a very, very large, bargaining concession!

Where had Amanda failed to provide accurate research?

She paused suddenly.

The Euphrates region…? It was a region documented as dry of resource material and minerals.

What did he mean, the Japanese man who approached Arguetta?

How and why had he met with her friend Diane while she was on her archaeological dig?

What was that about?

Did she know something for which she was killed?

Amanda stopped. How desperately Diane wanted a child! She did everything in her power, she and her husband to have a child. Her career came first, she always said, but Amanda knew that it was her career to whom she fled for comfort. Adoption was to be her next quest, she informed Amanda just before leaving for the dig.

Amanda made an abrupt turn and headed for the ticket counter to re-schedule her return flight. She was not flying back to Washington DC.

* * *

Chapter 48

Diane's family had a place on Lake Michigan. The home was an airy architectural modern structure made of timbers; stone and landscaping. Hidden in the woods, it had a stunning view.

Amanda was made welcome, but it was clear that the family were grief-stricken.

She spent the night, and together, they enjoyed a long evening of chatting and catching up with old tales. They talked of Diane's life and her choices.

"You know" said her mother "you had a tremendous influence on her."

Amanda smiled. Her mother was searching for connections with the past, she knew.

Eventually they came around to talking about her death. The matter of her death was too puzzling, they said.

Amanda made a request, and conceded willingly.

In the morning, it was Jeff Parks, Diane's father who insisted on driving her back to the airport. She left with a big hug of thanks, and offered them encouragement. She would keep in touch, she promised. And as per her request, she would return Diane's laptop computer to them in a month, if that was alright.

"Please, take it!" said Jeff. "The police never asked, and there is nothing on that that she'd be hiding on campus…She only took her person computer on the trip. So, please, do examine her work all you wish. We trust your discretion."

It was a painful and exhausting visit, all told.

But as Amanda gathered her thoughts on the flight home, she peeped briefly into the laptop on which Diane would have kept her academic notes. And she discovered enough to close it calmly and just sit there, trying to assess the full sway of the information at her fingertips. It seemed, somehow, unreal.

Especially for a scholar accustomed to the documentation of fact and science, not lore or legend…

She had gone to the Middle East with a head full of biblical narrative, it seemed. What she hoped to find was unclear.

Amanda landed at Reagan Airport late and took a cab to a hotel where she'd spend the night. The morning would take her to a couple of early professional stops in the city, then she'd start the long drive to the coastal beachhouse.

The hotel was comfortable, and quite. But sleep did not come easily. Amanda made herself some coffee and opened Diane's laptop.

There was information on Diane's laptop to rethink the Steele. She would tell Ed, she decided.

She would reveal it all to him, precisely because Diane had directed her to send the Steele to him.

However, it lacked the scientific underpinning that any scholar would require before publishing… Perhaps that explained why Diane had it saved in draft form only. Diane, or Dana, as she was often called, would about to cross into other disciplines of scholarship to support her theory. Where was she going with this? What was the hypothesis?

Still, even in its cryptic analysis, Diane was no idiot. Even academic publishing had its risks.

Amanda understood what Dana was doing. And she was not shocked. Rarely in ancient research do you uncover a crucial fact that might have changed the course of history – and find it correlating to something entirely different from its original precept.

What then?

Such profound reversals could be most alarming, if not targeted for ridicule or worse, retribution. There might professional envy, scorn by critics from universities deeply vested in that research and money; or reputations to be challenged, let alone theological and cultural tenants of ancient faiths…

Perhaps it was for this that she was killed, Amanda thought sadly. Ed would know.

But there was more… And it was almost dawn before Amanda ended her readings.

The explanation did much to help understand the events in San Francisco.

Perhaps this is what motivated the Japanese Delegate who approached Admiral Arguetta to speak up?

Amanda went downstairs to the Hyatt dinning room for breakfast. If there was one thing she believed in, was eating well in the morning. Especially after a long flight and a long night, a night which produced little more than a couple hours' sleep.

Before checking out, Amanda returned to the Report on Diane's laptop. There were some supporting entries she would need.

The report, written up by Diane, had been saved as a draft.

It was intended to be sent later, clearly when completed and spell-checked. It read like the furious and passionate words of an entry to a Diary.

"The concept of the Euphrates River rising and falling allows for local and regional flooding. In some cases, the flooding was higher than normal, sometimes catastrophic.

"Throughout antiquity, we have evidence of massive flooding due to ice melting induced by weather and climatic cycles…

"Certainly the fossil record is full of evidence of catastrophic changes. Climate could well have been altered by cataclysmic events like volcanic eruptions and earthquake tsunami. Rainfall and harvest is closely related to the survival of humans at various locations and cultural centers…

"Of the many narratives of the human condition, there is one that alters the survival of human colonies in ancient times: It relates to the era of navigability and transportation disruptions induced by flooding.

"Such migration pattern would alter, or breakdown the food and supply chain. This is likely to have affected the demise of known enclaves of isolated human colonies.

"Certainly, river navigation was a trade lifeline.

In the Euphrates, colossal flooding is many times recorded, perhaps even as part the narrative of the great flood…

"Other dislocations of one group from another may have been somewhere recorded. Perhaps shown as a motive that ended one grain-supply trail to places beyond the sea, as trade routes, like rice, fuel, tools to colonies of early dwellers in Iberia whose societal demise are now scientifically known related to weather, supplies and sudden malnutrition. This might well apply to the discovered forensic evidence of Neanderthal colonies…"

"However, what is particularly evident here is the shape of vessels, including those manufactured at the point in time of the Biblical Great Flood. For this, we have no evidence. But the building of the Arc, today depicted in narrative related to Assyrian cuniform told after the fact as memoires who have been subject to these conventions…

"It's shape, according to this Steela, is different from what we thought was the optimum form of sea vessel, even if primitive: It is here implied that a form of ship- building was round, circular, tub-like.

"Propulsion, presumably, was by paddle-oar or sail. But rotund nonetheless. Moreover its properties are identified. Properties that pertain to indigenous resources. Which leads to the following conclusions.

"This Steela section, discovered just prior to WWII, offers a cuniform inscription about early ship-building. Such ship building accounted for all navigable trade both locally, regionally and beyond the continents. This might well show up in Phoenician records - but for the traditions of an ancient tale!

"The vessel is manufactured by reed and wood is bound, and the pitch that binds it is described, essentially, when heated, as a sealant…

"Such waterproof primitive technology would have made it sea-worthy! A sealant from a substance readily found in the mud-flats of the Euphrates where tar and oil beneath the surface is viewed as having been in such abundance as to be seeping through the surface continuously….

"The Steela was sold to a German officer who gave it a Japanese man for passage on a vessel…"

"The Japanese sea Captain studied the inscriptions and found little value in it. This I was told by a recent visit of a Mr. Muna of Manchuria. It belonged to his family, he said.

"But it was his assertion that the region described is replete with underground mineral wealth, specifically oil under the river beds and sea...

"I suggested that he consult with Hebrew Antiquities Commissioners who have expertise in transcribing the Steela of its cuniform inscriptions" wrote Diane.

"He insisted that they tell that obviously, for the common man who was a shipbuilder, the region was 'dripping' with substance that is known to suggest massive oil deposits beneath the surface!"

"That implies oil fields today, he told me. In fact, Mr. Muna says that you can trace this ship-building evidence along coastal regions where vast areas of mineral wealth remains today unexplored!"

It took several days for Amanda to digest what Diane was implying. The breadth of the question was important to understand, its consequences many. Her conclusions could be logical. Amanda wanted to be sure that Diane's thoughts were appropriately interpreted. Definitely, she would need to consult with Ed.

Amanda took a deep breath. She realized that if this were correct, then the United States had just signed away concessions to perhaps half a continent of drilling rights!

The real question however remained.

How was it that no such data by the Geological Surveys showed up? *Or had it?*

* * *

Chapter 49

Kim entered the Korean Restaurant and ordered his meal in his native tongue.

Before long, he was being served by three different waiters. Two female Restaurant Hostesses came to have a few consultative words, a privacy screen now erected at his table for his dining pleasure. They bowed.

He finished eating won ton soup and a plate of seafood tempura, then got up and walked into the kitchen where he spoke with the head cook and his two assistants.

He was then ushered into the back staircase of a second floor and he met with the restaurant owner, an uncle. He bowed, even knowing that this man was not a direct blood relative, but a trusted family friend, the title of uncle inherited for his allegiance.

They spent the afternoon together, talking, eating, drinking and smoking cigars. At one point, he actually asked for a Starbucks coffee to be brought in. They complied, grinning, his modern tastes not lost on the younger generation of servers.

The elder man was given to bouts of native tongue but mostly spoke English. Clearly, his nephew was a strong and accepted professional American citizen.

"Your father was a great man!" he said.

The door opened, and a wave of waiters with fresh plates of assorted snacks arrived for their comfort.

They laughed. "You are most generous" said Kim "as always!"

Ordinarily, the reference to his father would be a passing compliment to the young man sitting before him, an offspring with great sexual prowess. But in this case, there was more significance to the comment made by the Uncle. It had modern connotations.

"...He worked on the Railroad. He was the leader of the Chinese workers because only he could speak English..."

Kim looked up, the room smoky.

The uncle continued. "He travelled with the workers of the Railroad through the mid-western region. He saw their ways, and he could plant dynamite. He met with the Native, and he even spoke a few words of Sioux and Cheyenne, understanding the ways of the ancients..."

Kim nodded.

"He was here at the time that the Chinese came to sign the Agreements!"

"A great honor!" said Kim.

"It was. A Chinese worker in San Francisco at the time of the United Nations Conference of 1945. He was invited, such was the high regard by his employers!"

Kim nodded.

"I am Korean only because they left me there with the military to defend the land from the natives. But your father, he...he was pure Chinese!"

They paused.

"He married a white girl, a Mexican girl. And you are the good looking son of them both, I say..." grinned the old man.

The conversation would take an hour of eating, lounging and chatting before returning to the quiet contemplation at hand.

"If it were not for the Chinese, the Americans would not have defeated the Japanese.." he said.

Kim, brimming with ripostes, knew of the day seized by Chinese communists to sway the ancient kingdom from its honorable roots as traders, and to yoke it as laborers for a socialist regime... But it was for the old man to tell it.

He waited.

"T.V.Soong promised the Americans that they could pass through Manchuria!" continued the old man.

Kim watched his eyes, glassy, and expressing words that would recount the inevitability of history.

"Ah. You say. But *did* they?" said his Uncle.

Kim waited.

"No. Instead, it was the *Russians* who stood in Manchuria!"

They contemplated the vision of Stalin's troops crossing Manchuria in a final declaration of war against Japan.

"Roosevelt, he gave to Stalin *Port Arthur* and *Port Darien* as reward for their troubles to cross Manchuria…"

The old man paused. "Why?"

Kim looked down, finding it appropriate at this time to insert himself in the conversation by way of a social exchange.

"Russia had signed a Peace Treaty with Japan" he said.

The old man smiled. "Yes! They had signed a Peace Treaty with Japan."

Kim spoke again. "Stalin would be breaking the treaty with Japan by sending his troops across Manchuria."

The old man grinned.

"*Oh. Oh. Oh!*" he rocked.

It was the mission of the elderly to reignite in the young a sense of meaning about the past, therein to offer a sense of direction about the future…

Kim understood, and he waited.

"Ports Arthur, and Darien. They were beautiful sea ports with warm water… and for trade on the horizon… as far as the fish of the sea could swim" said the old man, his hand unveiling a landscape across the walls of their confined room that stretched into China's past.

Kim watched him, as if waiting for a fairytale to arrive. But the old man was done imagining.

"Roosevelt did not think he could beat the Japanese. He may have won the war in Europe. But he knew more was needed to beat the Japanese!"

The dragon of his tale was about to enter the story, Kim knew.

"Yes. The Russians lay down their arms. But when the Russians lay down their arms, it was the Chinese communists who collected them. And in so doing, became the rebel communists!"

Kim nodded.

Modernized perhaps by modern standards of global trades, China remained socialist to this day, restricted without freedom nonetheless.

They both understood how it was that the old man now lived in America, his family having fled from oppression; and his exile the result of an unliberated China. He turned to Kim.

"But your father, he knew T.V. Soong who came here when they negotiated the trade Agreements!"

Kim smiled.

They ate, and talked again about matter unrelated. Only then did the admonition come.

"My beloved one, If you find any, ANY, that should compromise the trade Agreements made by Americans, then you must reveal that infidelity!"

They parted, Kim refreshed in his heritage and empowered by the memories posited in the heart of his ageing uncle.

Kim found a Hotel and took a shower. America was his home now. He looked deeply into the face in the mirror. Asian, smooth-faced and tall due to his Caucasian mother.

He did not survive two graduate degrees in Information Technology at UCLA for nothing! Silicon Valley found him without merit, however, since he remained still without work.

He appreciated his Uncle's sentiments, but he was a man for hire for the highest bidder…

Thus, if he was the next generation of intellectual cyber programming to be used for any purpose, then so be it!

Old men be damned…

He smiled at himself. Sure, his prowess in software intelligence was quite as virile!

For Kim, it was nothing to kill the Japanese delegate at the Commemoration.

The real victory, as far concerned, was what he had on his computer, frankly:

Access to encrypted data held in the software of a computer owned by Amanda Wells.

* * *

266

They were pleased with him in Hong Kong. Certainly, they had paid him well. He might not need not work again. In fact, he might even start his own Hedge Fund!

In the briefcase of the man descending the ramp from a Transpac jet in Hong Kong was an electronic device with a complete survey of the minerals underground found in a zone itemized in the Trade Agreement this past week.

A list of "Non-Competition" was used in the Trade Agreement just signed by Pacific rim Nations and the United States.

More importantly, a complete survey and composition of all resources beneath the surface were itemized with a detailed account showing commercial value by commodity.

One zone showed up as mineral-rich with oil and gas deposits. The source of the information, originally from the mineral surveys of the US Department of Interior, came from overseas cyber-reconnaissance. In all probability, it was from Russian sources, citing classified material issued by the Intelligence community.

For while the data showed resources on American soil and within its territorial boundaries, these resources cited those in territories in which the United States had vested interests.

Contrary to the representations made at the table by Admiral Arguetta and his party from the United States for these Trade Agreements, here was evidence that the Americans had been less than honest with their disclosures.

This act would surely call for retribution - if not acts of trade-terror designed to show the Americans that their trade partners were not without intelligence. They knew *exactly* what they had, and what they had been traded with…

* * *

Chapter 50

Sandra left a cell phone message. Amanda dialed in the server and entered her passcode:

> *"Mom…its me. I'm coming home! They cut my program funding. I need some time to think this through…Call me! I'll be landing in Philadelphia on Friday, spending a couple days there with Mike and family. There's a concert, and we'll go to the NFL game at the stadium. Then I'll be driving down to the beach house…Lov-ya."*

Amanda stopped the car for food. It would be a quick stop. Then she would press on, it was dark.

By the time she got in, she was exhausted. She had driven all the way home to the beach house from Washington after landing at Reagan National Airport the night before. But she was glad she had stayed over.

She picked her way through the weekend feeling as fatigued emotionally as physically. The events of San Francisco had been filled with glamor and excitement at the Gala event. But there had been stress. Nor had it been easy for Arguetta and his staffers.

The commemorative memorial had been picked as the site for the new US/Paciic Trade Agreements, and while the signing and ratifications had been satisfied for the media, internal negotiations had been rocky.

Security was tight; alerts littered their servers with notices; communications from various agencies including his own at the Department of Defense, the Departments of State and Commerce presented issues and matters of dispute. Last minute concerns and attendance lists were passed alone for discrepancies, change of venues, political posturing and protocol.

Amanda sighed. She sat on her porch with a cup of coffee.

Barbara called. How was everything…

Amanda assured her that all went well and that she could retired all her reservations… They laughed, shared details about dress and décor, but that was it.

What remained unsaid were the complications. Barbara, after all, was no longer on Amanda's Need to Know list of personnel. If anything, she might be considered to be prying. Still, she was a good friend, and Amanda kept it that way.

But as Amanda thought about it, she was disturbed. So distressing was the outcome of their trip that she worried on the flight home if there would be serious political ramifications for Arguetta and his team.

After all, a serious breach of security had occurred; a man died trying to impart intelligence, the data and integrity of the United States at the negotiating table might well be challenged by a negotiating nation…

No! It had not gone well.

She could barely think her way through the fog.

She knew she should call Trevor, and while they had chatted for a few words during her stop at O'Hare Airport in Chicago, he remained largely in the dark.

Perhaps that was the best state for him to remain, she thought. Uninformed.

She sipped her coffee…

The meeting with Diane's family left her with a trail of unanswered questions. She had work to do, enquiries to make.

Further, the message from Sandra was troubling! Clearly, there had been an abrupt ending at the University.

What was Arguetta finding now that he was back in Washington? What could she do to help mitigate the events of the Commemoration?

She must have sipped three cups of coffee. The sea was a cerulean blue, and calm. Then it occurred to her that Sunday was called the day of rest for more than obvious reasons. She decided to slow down. She would pick up the pieces Monday, if one piece at a time.

Still, she was glad she went, glad it was over.

Gradually, the sun shifted shadows along the beachline and a few more bathers showed up. To Amanda, the semblance of a normal life began to seep into a mental state of relaxation.

The waves, smashing the shore with seething froth withered harmlessly in retreat, and returned to an ocean glittering with diamonds. A few surfers dotted the tops of waves, but today, not many people were on the beach.

She walked onto the beach with her coffee in hand, her mind not really in focus.

Only gradually did she register recognition with the person seated on the sand and gazing out. It was Mary!

She walked down to her.

"Hi Mary!"

"Hey Amanda!" said Mary, standing up to brush sand off her pants. They hugged.

"We missed you!" she said, "how was everything…?"

Amanda smiled.

The simple thrills of beach-life washed over her like a balm that drained away her fatigue and worry.

They say down together and chatted, sandpipers running into wave froth and seagulls screeching in protest. On the horizon a surfer sat on his board, rising and falling with the sea, his perfect wave to ride into shore not yet arrived.

Finally, the events of their world came back.

"How's Tom?" asked Amanda, feeling suddenly remiss that his condition had been overlooked by everything else.

Mary turned her face to the sea and nodded. "He's back. And he's fine!" she said.

Amanda followed her gaze. "Tom!" she squealed.

Tom suddenly stood up on his surfboard, his features clear in a dark wetsuit, his wave swelling with promise for the perfect ride back into shore.

Off course Mary would be here keeping watch. That was the role of the surf-watching buddy system.

"Yah-hooooh!" the girls shouted, his ride a skillful balance on a long, long wave that rolled and pitched its way along submerged sand dunes and into the shallows.

He waved. They laughed. Tom paddled his way out to sea again.

"You all did a great job keeping vigil…" said Amanda. "He looks fully recovered!"

"Thank God" said Mary.

"So what caused the final medical diagnosis?"

"Poison" said Mary flatly. She did not take her eyes off him.

Amanda sensed a note of pique in her voice.

"Everything ok?" she asked Mary.

"No. He won't come in. He's been surfing every day since he came back. We're all watching him like a hawk."

"What's going on?"

"He's mad as hell Amanda!"

"He's…" She stopped.

It was Tom who was most offended at losing his job for budgetary cuts. And it was Tom who did the hardest work for her. Anything that might add to his distress was something that would clearly aggravate his disposition.

Mary spoke. "He's mad with you Amanda!"

Amanda knew what was coming.

"He was food poisoned from food he got from *your* fridge! Remember, *you* were complaining about Kim's menu and *you* offered it to him to take at will…"

"Oh My God! Surely you don't think I had anything to do with intentionally… "

"Perhaps not. But he didn't need this right now in his life. He was seriously in danger, I mean, really Amanda?…"

Amanda looked away. How could she have anticipated this happening…Whatever suspicions she had about Kim had only recently risen to the surface. How could she have *not* trusted this man with his good intentions…his food? It was a turmoil she couldn't reconcile.

Finally she turned to Mary.

"I'm so sorry. I would have never thought…I'll get to the bottom of this, I promise!" Amanda got up to leave.

"Yeah! They want a complete report from you at the local police station, Amanda…"

"Can you ask him to *talk* to me?" began Amanda, knowing that she had lost the trust of her friends.

Mary got up and waved at Tom.

Amanda returned to the beach house.

It started to rain.

Once seated at her desk, Amanda's thoughts became immersed in the issues before her, Tom's condition would have to wait…

That evening, she looked out the window of her third floor perch where she could get a clear view of the beach. She saw a desolate beach with no one around. The weather had turned foul.

She sighed deeply, and stood.

She felt as desolate.

If she slept fitfully, breakfast and coffee put on her feet and she knew she had work to do.

She climbed the three stories to her office just to look out the window. Few people were walking, only one or two were dedicated joggers moving down the beach, none of them recognizable.

At this time of year, the crowds had left and their children's summer vacation nothing more than a school-written essay.

Chapter 51

Splotches of sunlight illuminated patches of the ocean as clouds skidded to open up intermittently. But it was windy, rainy and grey, and the surf beginning to snarl into white caps and choppy waves.

She was about to turn away. She spotted then the little black wetsuit figure surfing.

Yes! It was Tom.

Mary was right. Whatever it was on his mind, he was not coming in…

She worried, and repeatedly during the day she ran upstairs to watch the weather and observe the surfer.

Finally, he was gone.

No. What that meant was that Tom had fatigued himself. In his anger and frustration with a life not going well, he had surfed until his energy gave out. He had come in, walked by, and just gone home!

The day was dreary, if productive. She came to terms with paperwork; catch-up and communications – all work necessary to complete her professional obligations and clear her desk where she was in control.

She made no social calls. She didn't feel like it. Too many unanswered questions; needs, hurts…

That evening she watched a game show, then made herself a sandwich and had a beer before going to bed.

But there was little sleep, no deep-rest of the contented who could snore through thunderstorms and lightening bolts on a hot summer night.

All during the night, Amanda lay in the darkness and wondered about Tom: Twice she picked up his document report. It was a masterful work, complete with analysis, quantitative surveys, research and intelligent observations.

Yet he would not talk with her.

She had called Mary twice; Phillipa once…

She felt hurt and puzzled. If only they could discuss the matter…

No, she decided. Tom was a stubborn high-minded young man who expressed his anger in odd ways.

All night she fretted, a full blown Nor'easter churning itself offshore into a micro gale with high wind velocity.

It was Wednesday morning when she awoke, papers still strewn over her bed where she had dozed off intermittently. She got up, ate and checked her mail.

There was nothing new.

She raced to the upstairs attic studio to spot him out at sea in the angry roiling surf. *Surely not…*

Yet there he was!

How to communicate? How to explain? She wanted to express how sorry she felt…

The sky turned purple and she leaped to her feet at the crack of thunder that hit the beach. Lightening followed, and there were no people in sight.

She ran to the third floor window. He must come in! It was dangerous. Nobody should be out on the water during a thunderstorm. He must come in…What was he trying to prove?

Please Tom!

She put on every light of the house. Perhaps he could see her lights. Perhaps he could understand…

The sea was too ferocious to discern if there was a surfer, or behind rising waves, or struggling…

She stood there, watching for half an hour before she decided that Tom was no longer out there. That was a relief. She finally turned away, miserable.

Only the next day did the storm pass, the sun heating up tidal ponds on a beach all flooded out and docile.

By evening the sea was producing soft waves, consistent, perfect for surfing in fact.

She did see him out there. And Mary was sitting with Phillipa on the beach. She decided to walk out.

"Hello" she said.

They looked at her, and she sat down beside them.

They talked of little, and ignored the surfer.

Then quite suddenly, he started to come in and walk straight up to them. Amanda stiffened.

"OK" he said suddenly. "I've decided to forgive you…"

She wanted to smile. Or wanted to cry with relief. Then she felt mad as hell.

"Tom…" she began, unsure of where her response would go when she noticed his frown soften and his blue eyes wander slightly.

"…I'm sorry Tom. I'm glad you're recovered, and I want you to know…"

"I know" he said vacantly.

She was about to answer when she realized he was looking over her shoulder. She turned.

"Hi Mom!" said Sandra approaching with a surfboard under one arm. Grinning, she approached in a bikini swimsuit designed for a body lean, tall and strong. A flock of seabirds scattered as she crossed the sand, her hand waiving at her mother.

"Sandra!" said Amanda, laughing suddenly. They hugged, and they hugged.

So missed-you Mom! whispered her daughter, her voice wavering in underlying distress.

Amanda held her squarely at the shoulders and looked deeply into her eyes: Here, the open blue sea, beach-sand and security of a summer place was clearly all around them, and she smiled calmly.

Sandra drew a big breath.

Amanda introduced her.

Tom was grinning like a schoolboy, and she slew him a look filled with reposts, the moment too happily filled with Sandra…

Amanda fed them all dinner that night at the beach house. For the meal, she had left them all on the beach earlier and gone to the Safeway, the local grocery store. She bought a Turkey, which she roasted. If her body was weary, her heart was merry. It was a wonderfully warm evening outside on the porch, a small brazier of coals glowing close-by.

Sandra was quickly brought up to speed on the exploits of her mother, each of them sketching out their contributions to her research and findings.

"I want you all to know…" said Amanda, setting down the platter of food and turning to her friends "that I'm…*furious* with you all …because I have better things to do with my life than entertain a bunch of beach bums…."

"and poison people…" chimed Tom, his eyes slit in suspicious jest. They laughed.

 Sandra leaned over and kissed her mother on the check. "Mom" she said "We're starved!"

They ate like hungry pirates.

Only later did they calm down at the dinner table when Phillippa tapped her glass to make an official announcement.

"I have a job!" she said, grinning.

"No way!" they laughed.

She told them. "It's a hire out of New York…"

"*New York?*" they chimed.

"… and I'm leaving Monday. Someone actually needs my services as a legal assistant!"

"Congratulations! So what do you want as a parting ritual?" they grinning deviously.

"A BBQ on the beach Sunday night!"

* * *

Chapter 52

"Hello my Darling.." said Trevor

Amanda's heart missed a beat, still, after so many years, the sound of his voice thrilled her.

With three thousand miles separating them, she told him Sandra was with her, and that they had not yet discussed plans.

Trevor suggested Sandra come back to the UK and start with fresh thinking before returning, or even to take a leave of absence for a year and regroup her plans for a solid university program.

The idea was solid. Amanda was tempted to comply. But as Sandra had said, these decisions were for her to make. Chicago was frustrating her, but she had a stake in the game, and she wanted to see it through. Amanda was less pragmatic. Instincts had a lot to do with how you shaped your life, and she encouraged independence in the life of her daughter.

Amanda gave Trever an account of the events of San Francisco.

"Yes" he said "Arguetta called me yesterday! I'm sending you some documentation that will help explain the motive behind any accusation of disparities in a Trade Agreement…"

Amanda was surprised at how updated he was.

"Arguetta has most of the data by now, and he may be getting in touch with you for more research once we reinstate your clearance. Please apply every precaution, will you darling, and keep the encoding protocols switched and monitored on your laptop…"

He got a "Hi Dad" from Sandra who came rushing up to use the bathroom, then disappeared.

She felt tired.

Still, the conversation with Trevor helped assuage any possibilities of failure on her part to supply adequate intelligence to Arguetta.

Amanda wondered now if she might not have been better situated in Washington DC with her staff in an official entity. Perhaps she had misjudged the scope of the work. Perhaps she had not remained as updated as she should have. Perhaps she should have just said no. Truth is, she was older now.

Those days of working 24/7 as a Firm in the Nation's Capital were over: That was a time of round-the-clock performance at high-levels of professional work, a world in which you had to be at the top of your game, – with Barbara running things, as she would put it! Amanda smiled, remembering so many good times together; producing content of some significance for decision-makers and policy leaders…

Moreover, the field of candidates willing and qualified to perform was ample, usually found amongst the spouses of those already working in government.

 It had its rewards, especially its social life. But it was also a ferocious life. Definitely behind her, she sighed.

She did miss Trevor at her side just at the moment. Together they had attended so many functions and fulfilled so many obligations that, as the years slipped by, even their professional lives began to merge. Such was their reputation, even in semi-retirement. Both of them strong and independent people, representing fields and constituencies sometimes in total apposition to each other, yet bound together in a strong sense of duty.

Perhaps she felt a little more needful of his reassurance and love. This, he gave, as he always had.

Yes, she decided. Theirs had been a wonderful relationship.

 Right now though, she felt like she was upholding three agendas on two continents perched in unsecured quarters in a rickety old beach house. And she sensed a storm brewing...

On the other hand, how else would she have been able to offer work to her beach-crowd?

So, Washington or not, this was where she was! And proud of it.

She turned to her laptop and downloaded the content Trevor promised. It would be read later. It would be classified, she knew, and she had to use special passwords to enter the data source of his communication.

She would get to work first thing in the morning, she decided, then call Arguetta.

For now, she heard her house guests downstairs. She had a beer with them...

* * *

They had just put the dishes away and settled to a TV show, all of them. Amanda noticed with a grin that very little was leftover from the meal. They had consumed half a case of beer and two bottles of wine. In fact, Sandra had even added a cake that was now baking for their late night desert, she announced.

"Come sit!" they admonished her.

Amanda was tempted to retire and get a good night's sleep. But they made a place for her at the end of the sofa, and the Late-night show held promise…

Fifteen minutes later, at just after 10 PM the doorbell rang. This surprised them. No one was expected.

Amanda realized that in a neighborhood of beach houses, it could be anything from a mistaken address to a kid searching for his dog. She got up and opened the door.

It was dark outside, and there was little to indicate someone was around, let alone a car with its headlights on and engine running.

It was quite, except for the eternal wash of wave action on the beach behind the house.

"Hello?" she asked several times.

Amanda was about to shut the front door when something caught her eye. It looked like a delivery parcel left on the front pathway to the house.

"Mom…*who is it?*" called Sandra from the crowd in the front room.

"I don't know…" she answered.

The wrapping was brown paper with a string loosely tied around it. No stamps, she happened to notice…

By the time she reached the parcel, Tom was suddenly at her side. She bent to pick it up when he swooped it up with a yell.

"Get back inside the house and take cover!"

"Oh my God!" said Amanda, suddenly realizing what might be happening.

"*Back! Back!*" yelled Tom running with the parcel.

"Tom!"

Sandra scrambled up, Mary and Phillipa to behind the kitchen counter.

Amanda stood at the door, eyes searching for movement. No sign of an assailant. No evidence of foul intentions. Just a silent street. Shapes and shadows of a night storm long and shiny on moist pavement, the neighborhood was deserted as a grave yard.

Tom had the parcel under his arm and he could be seen running. He aimed for the water. Powerful strides propelled him into the surf where he tossed it in the air, his body diving deep into a wave.

The explosion lit up the sky. A blast flashed into the contours of a fireball. Shockwaves pushed deep into the surface of the water. Impact levelled an oncoming wave. Fire magnified into a spray of white hot incendiaries. A flash rose 20 meters and burst open, it fell back down to the surface, igniting a driftwood that flared up and roiled in the sand. Projectiles sizzled and split into multiple oxidized bangs at the water, cooling and spitting into a darkened sea. Smoke and Sulphur vapors filling the air of the charred beach line.

"Tom!" yelled Amanda.

His body, made visible at impact, had been lifted by a giant wave that held him aloft in an emerald sheet of water before rolling. Now in heaving blackness, the sea yielded nothing.

"Tom!" wailed Phillippa, pointing.

The moon glistened just briefly off wet clothes as Tom surfaced, floating face down.

They waded in and retrieved him, Sandra the most powerful swimmer and reaching him first to float him upside and tow him in.

On the sand they administered CPR. Barely two breaths had him choking up and gasping for air.

"My God!" said Amanda, the shock of it all washing over them.

"What happened…?"

* * *

282

Chapter 53

It was well passed midnight by the time the police completed their questions and the Fire Department left the alley. More interviews would be forthcoming, they promised.

By the time she called Trevor, it was decided that their Attorney be apprised of the situation and make himself available to represent the family for any further enquiries about the delivered package.

Amanda remained concerned about Tom.

The girls had him back inside, he sat coated in a warm blanket and holding a mug of hot chocolate.

He was dazed, but unharmed. Mainly recovering from shock, he was physically undamaged. A deep wave had sufficiently sheltered him from the impact of the explosion at the surface. He had scraped his elbows and knees pushing along the bottom as he swam, but his reaction and alacrity had saved him.

The girls were determined to settle down with Tom in the house. He would be placed in the downstairs guest bedroom - each would take turns sitting in the room to monitor his sleeping.

Nancy, the local nurse who had attended to him in the hospital less than a week ago, was also in the house. She heard, and came over.

Tom was fine, he insisted.

When she was done, there was little evidence of any medical damage other than his scrapes. She dressed his abrasions. There were no signs of concussion. He had managed to avoid the effect of impact from the explosion by diving deep enough underwater at the moment of detonation.

"that was the idea!" he said, looking at Nancy with a sheepish grin.

"It was a lucky moment" she said.

She recommend he be taken to the hospital for a thorough check up. But Tom would have nothing of it, fatigued as he was.

Still, Nancy asked them just the same if it was o.k. for her come over after work and look him over the next day.

Finally, Amanda smiled. She found it amusing seeing Philippa, Mary, Sandra and Nancy all ministering over him with Tylenol; temperature readings and dehydration sips of water.

She left the room saying that what he needed next was a good drink, but that kind of vintage humor could get her cited for being anti-social.

Still, the shock of what happened was still redolent. In the morning, when Tom was absolutely given the All Clear, there would doubtless a lot more questions, she knew.

Amanda slept fitfully. She checked downstairs at her cabin of girls, and found them all nestled and slumbering. Tom looked comfortable and was deep in sleep.

During the night Amanda only dozed in her room. Fragmentary images surfaced with uncanny clarity. Something was stirring her. They had all been under stress, and she felt anxious. She couldn't quite make out the full picture.

Tom was grinning, that much she remembered. Then in one single swoop of arms, she saw his face suddenly contorted with instant recognition - he picked up the device and tore away at the brown string packaging until only a bulbous white bag wrapped in tape could be seen as he speed off.

Thank God!

Were it not for Tom's quickness, they might all have been dead by now, had the thing exploded in front of the house.

Only slowly did the horror of that implication sink in. Clearly, they were the target of an act of deadly force. Why?

Who…?

Downstairs, she checked again on the girls. In the guest bedroom Tom lay sleeping, a mild sedative keeping him steady, warm-colored and breathing normally.

What had he recognized? * *

Amanda answered her phone. It was the Smithsonian affirming her suspicions.

"…what we have, Amanda, is a steele that describes ancient uses of oil and petroleum in great abundance. In fact, it was used to waterproof anything that was made of reed, like boats, statuary, mortar brick walls, drains, stair treads and used mainly for shipbuilding.

We have citations from Herodotus and Diodorus Siculus - four thousand years of natural asphalt was employed in the construction of the towers of Babylon. This steele, described how it was used in ancient *shipbuilding*, including the vessel built possibly by Noah. It attests to the large deposits of oil and gas beneath the surface! Especially along the Tigris and Euphrates rivers. Some say that this is the mountain of gold cited in ancient Islamic prophesies."

"Wow" said Amanda. "that's most interesting!"

"Yes. It is a clear record of its usage on a written steele. Well done, Amanda! What a find. We have theories - tons of them. But what we want is real evidence. *This is it!*"

"It came from Diane" said Amanda. "She sent it along to you with a purpose in mind. Perhaps you could consider curating it and adding it to the record? She would have wanted that, I'm sure!"

"Of course! Actually I'm pretty excited. This is quite a find, you can't imagine. Clearly, there was a lot of seepage in the region. Petroleum seep is where natural liquid or gaseous hydrocarbons escape to the earth's surface, as you know. The resource has been exploited by mankind since Paleolithic times. Earliest records are Neanderthals - some 70,000 years ago with bitumen it is found adhered to stone tools at Neanderthal sites in Syria. Imagine, *pre homo sapiens…*" said the Director of the Smithsonian resource laboratories.

"So. It's recognized as bitumen, pitch, asphalt and tar. Its uses, since the beginning of time, have been for fuel. As the steele shows, the waterproofing of reed boats you say?" Amanda took notes.

Diane had been presented with evidence that the region reeked with a resource that remained absent from the geological list of concessions open to International Trade bargaining.

"I was wondering Bill, do you think you could write up a preliminary report on that steele for Diane's University Department? Plus, if you get to keep it at the Smithsonian, a sort of letter of recognition to her family, please?"

"I'd be pleased to."

Oil was already in full exploration and extraction in that region. Certain fields were already cited and listed on the surveys of natural resources.

Why was all this abundance different?

More importantly, why were these records missing from the Management Archives in Washington DC when she went to research the topic?

Someone was obfuscating a complete survey of resources negotiated for trade on an international level. Drilling rights and concessions or energy exploration and extraction represented large amounts of money for trade and commerce. History had shown that such disputes over resources defined the winners and the losers over global metrics…

This was beginning to sound political in nature.

As a researcher, how had she failed to identify matters essential to critical geo-political decisions? That was her job. To get the right information into the hands of those who made decisions.

Where had she failed?

* * *

Chapter 54

The sea was folding over the beach like blue sheets of silk. It was calm, warm and windless.

Amanda looked out across the ocean, not a cloud in sight. She sat, feeling at peace, relieved that all had gone well with Tom following the incident of the parcel delivered to her door.

She probed in her mind questions of why it happened, something possible to do forensically only when the danger was passed. She felt no imminent danger…

Phone calls had been endless: She had talked with Arguetta, Trevor, Barbara, the girls, Nancy, the police, the local sheriff and even neighbors who had come over, asking about things.

She assured her husband, finally, that she and Sandra were unharmed. Otherwise he was on his way, he said.

A barrage of other calls had come in asking for further details, mainly as the sleepy hollow community of the beach found its way to her door. Not even neighbors, just curious club members, realtors, commercial vendors wondering what had happened to their community. She would have like to give a Press Conference assuring them that nothing was amiss.

Others came on the grid, federal officials evidently sent by Arguetta. They asked permission to make agency inspections and analysis. At one point she found them taking finger prints off her kitchen cabinets! Enough, she insisted, showing them all to the door.   Amanda sensed that this was not going to go quietly away.

Certainly, the United States took the matter most seriously, any explosion was a critical matter that would immediately arouse suspicion of foul play.

She thought about it. What kind of device was it that found its way to her door…? A bomb? An oversized beach firecracker? An explosion that…that…well, burned up the sand and could have seriously caused some damage?

Why?

Come to think of it, what was the incident anyway? Terror, for the most part, belonged in the city where it doubtless received public attention for the media.

But here? *What was this?*

They all had questions. At the house a few wise cracks had been levelled at suspects from her house guests, including a wayward parcel delivered by a drone! Or it was a fall-away bomb from a passing plane…Or even a left-over WWII bomb wrapped up by an alien…Somehow, making jokes helped mitigate the shock of it all.

Certainly, Amanda did all she could to reinstate calm and safety in the minds of everyone at the house, an instinct of obligation that every mother carried in her heart toward protecting her young.

But now alone and gazing out to sea, Amanda was worried. There was more to this incident that she could fathom. She felt certain that her work might have something to do with it. And frankly, the sooner she was delivered of this crowd, the less exposed they would be to further harm. She even expressed this concern to Arguetta, not that he was entirely reconciled to her idea of…Never mind.

So, glad as she was that Tom had been asked to deliver a full report to the local Sherriff's office, she would go Running through the weekend, as promised, to practice for the Big Run-Off event next week along the beach park, she told them.

The others would each be going home shortly, the summer ending…

For the moment, Sandra and the others were still catching up on some sleep.

Amanda returned to her studio and opened her laptop computer. She worked for two hours, there was work to do, including reviews and returns needed for a final research report.

Plus emails with attachments from Trevor; Barbara, the Smithsonian; two university library connections and three agencies. Other email waiting were social in nature; a ton of policy positions and several charity invitations were left unopened. They could wait…

Sandra surprised her. She knocked softly at the door and entered with two cups of coffee.

"How are you doing?" asked Sandra. Amanda looked at her daughter and smiled, if with a little fatigue.

"…I'm Ok. You?"

Sandra nodded. "Bit of a shock, wasn't it?"

Amanda nodded. "Who would have thought…a bomb on our doorstep! My God…"

"You'll get to the bottom of it, I'm sure. It must be a mistake or something"

"You figure?" smiled Amanda "Just a wrong address or something huh?"

They laughed.

"You know, err…Dad wants you to join him ASAP. He's got some research that he wants to share with you…"

Sanda grinned.

"Funny you should say that. 'Cos I got stuff for him too! Like, this dude I was with on this Arctic expedition, he was digging for something else, I'm sure of it."

Amanda listened, draining her coffee and not betraying a shred of concern. She smiled, returning the conversation to her daughter's agenda.

They agreed on a Flight back to College for Tuesday morning. Amanda was going into DC then anyway, and she could drop her off. That way they could get to the Airport without any rush."

Sandra was easily refocused, and they agreed on a BBQ menu for Phillippa's beach party: Since the property of the beach house went all the way up against the sand dune that fronted onto the public beach, they would have an open fire pit with a grill and torches within view of the night surf. Romantic! It would be a fabulous Farewell party, they giggled.

Amanda walked to her window and looked out over the beach. Only a few people were about, the wind a little fresher.

Perhaps it was that time of the year that tourists had had their fill of the sun and sand. Some strollers, retired couples, walked easily; a young man, determined to enjoy every moment of his vacation was at his beach umbrella going through the motions of Yoga. Someone else, further down, was seated with a book in her hand, the wind blowing her hair in her face.

Joggers were sparse. Except one man who caught her eye. He was bouncing down the beach. Not that he was distinguishable in any fashion, but because of what ran with him. In his hand he had the leash of four dogs who bounced along beside him, each wearing muzzle guards and a red collar.

Dogs on the beach were strictly forbidden, Amanda knew. But with so little population about, an occasional dog walker was ignored, his pet only happy to tag along for the walk.

This man, she observed, was a very fit athlete accustomed to endurance training. His dogs understood him as they kept up with him in a manner of deliberate precision and pacing. If they were muzzled it was perhaps from a household along a beach community where children might be at play. She was about to turn away. Suddenly he stopped, pullout out a whistle and blew it.

They heeled at his feet. These were no pets! Perhaps a beach walk as training dogs? If these were military dogs, they were clearly well trained, she noted.

Their trainer, if anything was a paramilitary specialist, no question. Perhaps he worked for the government. He acknowledged his dogs, as reward, then just before turning back, he looked up. He turned his head directly at her window, he seemed to have observed her, not altering his motions, but in deliberate manner.

Definitely, he had looked up at her window…

Her cell phone rang.

Tom was coming back to the house. He was fine, he said. The report was done, and they were all to relax and not worry about it…

"Amanda…" he started to say "I wonder if we could chat…"

"Tom" interrupted Amanda. "How can we all possibly *thank you* for your astute observation and instinctive reaction. Please accept our sincerest gratitude…"

"No problem" he said. "We'll have a good time for Phillipa tonight."

"Yes" promised Amanda. It was the least she could do for the crowd. She laughed.

Good thing Arguetta couldn't see them playing, she mused. As researchers, they'd been a pretty good team!

* * *

The brazier glowed with coals and firewood, its hamburgers sizzling and hot dogs well charred.

They had played volley ball on the beach for the last few hours, and though booze was not necessarily an item, there had been a cooler of beer, wine and water available.

They were laughing, all of them gathered for Phillippa's farewell, and each offering their advice for a city job as if she were leaving hearth-and-home for the tortured captivity of concrete gargoyles.

"I'm going to get a new wardrobe!" said Philippa.

"Really? *Why?*" as Tom. "Your bikini is fine…"

Mary prodded him.

"Oh Yeah… And if you use Uber…be sure he ain't gonna hit on you!"

"No! Be sure *you* ain't gonna hit on *him!*" they squealed.

Amanda had come out. She ate a hot dog. She thanked them for their efforts across the summer. "Seriously, you were all great, and I'm happy to write any references if you need them going forward…"

"Are you kidding? I *paid* my wireless bill…" grinned Mary. The smell of slow-fire cooked food permeated the air. They sat, a circle of friends contemplating the events of the summer. Reflections from the fire cast a soft gold glow that shimmered on their faces. A small breeze come up from a Northwest weather front, bringing with it a cooler feel to the dark night.

No reference to the event of the bomb was made. But the incident remained close to their thoughts. On occasion they lapsed into quiet, their minds and heart full of enjoyment for their last night together.

It happened close to about midnight, just as they were making promises to keep in touch.

"Shhhhh…" said Tom.

"Huh?"

"Did you hear that?"

"Hear what…?"

They listened.

A slow deep growl came from twenty feet beyond the beach gate.

"What *was* that?" said Phillipa

Another low growling curled, as if from a creature of another world.

"Wait…" said Mary

"Jesus!" whispered Sandra.

There was something primordial about the sound. It needed little explaining. It's tenor pitched into their senses as menace, like the warning of a wolf.

The gate of the beach house was open to the beach, and while the food and fire was on private property, most of the activity had been just on the public side of the fence, such that there was open access across the party zone.

It was threatening.

A second deep growl was uttered from the darkness, the sea waves masking its direction.

"Don't move…" whispered Tom, as he reached for a piece of large kindling, red with glowing heat.

He jumped. "Yahhh!" he shouted, cinders flowing from the stick.

That's when they became visible.

Two dogs, their teeth bared, and their dark body crouched.

Sandra, Mary and Philippa leaped forward to wield sticks. Cinders landed on the black fir of one dog and it howled at the sizzling burn, the sound settling to a whimper in the distance.

Two dogs remained. Three, total, one unseen. Trained attack dogs. One circled, the other paced briefly, as if running interference by way of distraction.

Upstairs in the house, Amanda heard the yell. She saw them from her window.

She approached the porch door softly, the others aware of her presence.

She suddenly flashed powerful torchlight at the dogs, and they lowered on their haunch, momentarily blinded.

Tom understood. He took the opportunity. He took a step back, the girls ushered behind him, and he backed up towards the open porch door.

"Go!" he yelled, tossing embers at the dog closest.

The dogs lurched forward, but his gesture had bought them just enough time to pile into the screened porch, and slammed shut the porch door.

One dog backed down, the other followed, clearly conditioned as a response.

Amanda switched on the outdoor lights, and the place lit up like a theater.

Inside the porch they felt safe. But as the seconds passed they realized that outside, there were four dogs, each with a red collar.

Just as Amanda opened the French door to the house, the screen tore away from its frame and she realized that these animals were trained to lunge into structures and follow their target.

She turned to face them. "Lock the doors, and check the windows. These are trained attack dogs!"

They went through the house, and switched off all the lights.

"Shhhhh!" said Tom.

One dog had penetrated the house.

It stood as silent as a ghost. It waited, its head down, scenting. It had accessed an open window in the kitchen.

In the darkness of the house, moonlight pieced the shadows and reflected off chrome kitchen appliances. Amanda could see the dog begin to prowl, its reflection shifting across the blender's bowl.

They backed into the sitting area. Claws left a sound on ceramic tile as it took just enough steps forward to observe the door opening from the kitchen.

"Upstairs!" pointed Amanda.

Everyone had a clear view from where they crouched. The staircase to the second floor was a polished modern architectural design of wide Georgia pine steps without risers.

Flanked by wide balustrade rails, they would have ample space to vault to the first landing. Sandra began to move.

They were too late.

On the second floor stood the dog that had surged from the kitchen, hurling its jaguar-body off the dining table to leap through the air and attain the second floor landing. There he twisted, facing them.

In one leap he lunged at Sandra.

Amanda shrieked out and pushed away the animal that was flying through the air at her daughter. Sandra had just enough time to whirl around as it tore off her shirtsleeve which ripped away like straw.

Tom kicked him and the dog rolled downstairs, landing quickly on its feet. He turned to re-engage when Tom pulled the tweed woven throw rug over him, and it twisted easily off with a jerk of the dog's head. The dog growled low.

 "My office!" yelled Amanda.

Her mind was tumbling through the options. The dog could have lunged for Philippa, who was closer. Or it could have ripped into Tom's leg. No. This dog was after a target.

Sandra!

They scrambled up to the top floor and Sandra flew to reach them as Amanda pulled her in and slammed shut the door.

Mary was in a state of panic. "He's not going away! He's…."

The dog lunged at the door, the lock rattling inside the carpenter's well.

"My God" said Philippa.

The dog lunged again, and it bayed a ferocious roar, barking with a wolf-like aggression.

"Mom!" screamed Sandra.

Amanda tore into her drawer full of paraphernalia at her desk, knowing full well that by now, there would be no power, and that her cell phone signal had been blocked. If there was one thing she understood was that they were the targets of a deliberate assault.

These were fierce dogs deployed in a planned and premediated strategic attack.

"Is there a gun in the house?" shouted Tom at the door.

"Too late" said Amanda scrambling through her desk as the dog once again lunged. Screwdrivers, bottle openers, pens, pencils, rules, glue, paperclips, stapler…

Another lunge. Or was it *two* dogs now?

In the quasi-dark she found what she was looking for.

She flung open her window and put a whistle to her lips and blew.

It pierced the night air like a siren. A loud shrill that was one-pitched and searing, and the sound carried far above crashing sea surf and a howling wind.

She blew again.

Suddenly the room went quiet.

Mary, Philippa, Sandra and Tom, they all looked at each other, tensely waiting.

They flew to the window and stood by Amanda. All dogs were running. They counted four, all disappearing into the darkness of the beach, as if responding to the pitch of a call that only they could hear.

"My God…" husked Amanda, her mouth dry.

"Mom, are you alright?" asked Sandra, crouching.

Amanda lifted the whistle, and smiled lamely.

"Your sailing-coach whistle!" she pointed.

"How did you *know?*" asked Tom

"I saw their trainer earlier on the beach. He had a whistled that they responded to. It was a long shot…"

"and it worked!" said Philippa, thankfully.

Amanda wiped her pale face. From her arm blood was draining off in large drops.

* * *

Chapter 55

The next morning, Tom found Amanda not in the beach house but in the guest cottage.

She had been bandaged and medically attended during the night. Sandra insisted. A claw scratch that would easily heal, Amanda knew. She received it from the dog, a small defensive wound below the elbow.

As she explained it, the laceration came from a stray beach dog at their BBQ. She didn't elaborate, exactly. Nor was she prepared to report the incident until she had more answers.

She was standing in the kitchen, a kitchen now closed, its counters settled with a fine layer of dust.

"What is it?" asked Tom

Amanda said nothing. She was holding the waste basket of the Utility room.

She stood there, pale.

Tom snatched it from her hand and looked inside.

"Just as I thought!" he said. "We've got to file a full report on a possible infiltration…"

Amanda followed him back to the beach house.

He turfed the contents of his backpack searching for a book that had all the information he needed. There would be phone numbers, lists…

"Tom?" asked Amanda.

He looked up. "There is no way this is a coincident…"

"What?"

"You're Roomer, Kim. He was here right?"

She nodded.

"The contents of that basked…" he said "That's what you have, isn't it?"

She looked at the wrapping in the waste basket.

"He was here!" said Tom "He tossed out the unused string and brown paper used in the bomb packaging…"

"How is that possible?" she whispered.

Tom was rifling through his backback.

She took a step back to consider his words.

"*Infiltration*…?" she said, looking at him. "Tom. What are you saying?"

He stopped.

"Amanda. I'm sorry. But I've misled you…and err…the others, too. I'm a Federal Agent."

"You're a…?" she stammered, stunned.

They sat down, all of them. Tom explained himself. It took an hour.

* * *

Amanda and Sandra both understood. The government had been looking into possible cyber leaks. Hacking malware that posed a threat to our infrastructure. There were links also possible toxic and terrorist activity that we are tracking…"

"My God Tom. You could have fooled me…" said Amanda. "I'm sorry" he said. "But you were the leak!"

"What?" said Sandra.

"What … tracking?" whispered Amanda.

Tom looked away.

Amanda stepped forward. "Tom, please… The truth!"

"Plutonium. It seems your man Kim is not what he says he is…"

Amanda was angry, and to a large degree ready for his explanation. But she wasn't prepared for what he said next.

"Actually, to be totally honest. It's not so much you we're worried about…As it is for Sandra!"

They looked at him.

"*me?*"

"Sandra!" he repeated. "About your expedition!"

 "Well…*indirectly*, that is. You were in the middle of it. Mercifully, you blundered through it when your mother raised hell in Chicago and made you the subject of a public debate up there…which is what made the target lose interest in you!"

He finished his packing.

"For now, at least…" he said, gearing up to leave. "That's all I'm prepared to say!"

* * *

Chapter 56

Without a Lieutenant at the desk of Air Force Northern Flight Command the door opened and Captain Rogers entered directly into Arguetta's office.

"Excuse me Sir…"

"Yes?"

"You need to see this..."

They walked down the hallway of the building and entered with full security clearance Satellite Intelligence Digital Surveillance. The room was dark.

"What've we got?" he said.

"Your worst nightmare Sir!"

Two men came forward with clipboards.

"Someone is playing harmonics on the North Pole and causing some kind of oscillation with electromagnetic fields. It's blipping our network grids!"

Arguetta stood still. "..*harmonics?*"

This was no casual observation, he knew. Here was the full resource and talent base attached to the defense department trained to spot anomalies that link to all moving systems related to the security of the United States.

"Explain"

He was a lawyer, they knew. They approached him and spoke softly.

"In lay terms, they've picked the North Pole's magnetic field, that is, the area most sensitized - if human intervention were ever possible - to simulate solar-flare impact upon the magnetic fields beneath the surface."

"That's science fiction, right?" said Arguetta.

"You'd think so Sir. But all they need is a short duration pulse to disrupt our screens and grids."

“How do we know it’s man-made?”

“Because it’s too predictable and synchronized with our satellite orbital passage to be organic. It’s picking the moments where we have *least* protection coverage.”

Arguetta was not a man easily swayed. “How coincidental?”

“More than the odds. It’s *timed*, we know that. It’s *consistent*. We’ve been watching it for three, maybe four orbits. They seem to know exactly where we are, and what we’re doing…”

“So. Someone is inside the grid. Someone is receiving. And someone is tampering?”

“Pretty much, Sir!”

“Let’s find out who, what and why, shall we?”

As the day wore on, data analysts came down from Homeland Security; NSA; CIA and NSF. Finally it was confirmed. A danger existed.

Gathered in his offices downstairs, Arguetta was reviewing various briefs.

* * *

"Who is doing this?"

Captain Rogers responded, his reports in hand.

"Better than your average hacker…This is remarkably high capacity, and clearly underwritten by a force greater than some local club organization!"

"So, we should assume an enemy of the state."

"China?"

"Possibly!"

"But we've just signed a Trade Agreement with them, and nothing seemed amiss. Rather, in so far as I can tell" said Arguetta. "There remains some err…*misinformation* on the data exchange of that Agreement. Some irregular incidents that don't seem related, but we're working on it…"

"Anything else?" asked Rogers to the others in the room, including Dr. Jensen; a woman Naval Officer and two IT Directors trained in counter-cyber security intelligence systems.

"Possibly a decoy. An excuse for a third party?" said the one.

"Well, whoever it is, then this third party is about as powerful as the Puppet Master of the Wizard of Oz. He has at his fingertips the ability to disrupt our entire grid at will…"

The phone range. "We need answers within the next 24…" said Arguetta.

"What we need to discover is how this mechanism was made possible" said Rogers. "It could disrupt our signals in flight. Conceivably, it could redirect any cargo we deploy in defense action…"

Arguetta looked at Jensen from the National Science Foundation. "Any ideas Tony?"

"We're funding some pretty remarkable research in the development of digital technologies, true. And when we do, there's always the risk of exposure or leaks with outside research institutions. This sounds more like something from overseas. Worse, it's at the molecular chemical level. It suggests manipulation of an organic frequency delivery system, moreover."

"Damage level?"

"The highest!" he said "But nothing that is beyond the test ranges of scientific experimentation…All we need is time!"

"Andrea, anything to do with CERN?" asked Arguetta.

She stepped forward. Andrea Watters had trained there for one year. "Well. Anything is possible there. The security is lax, we can count on the minimum -few safeguards…" she said.

"I'll make some enquires" said Arguetta, thinking immediately of Trevor.

Arguetta turned to Jensen. "What logistics would be necessary to tamper with this kind of level of harmonic resonance…?"

"Actually, remarkably little. Perhaps a long tube between two insulated containers, even below ground. It might actually be possible to excite some particles with a high speed accelerator…"

"Particles?"

"A Metaphysical condition that alters the state of density *within* the particles, something susceptible to magnetic response. Again, all you need is a tiny impulse to disrupt our networks…"

"Ok. Same time tomorrow for a briefing… Gentlemen, Ms Watters!" he nodded respectfully.

Arguetta walked away knowing one thing for certain. The matter of the Trade Agreement survey was a distraction by someone pulling something else. Or someone else. This "third-party" world puppet master needed to be unmasked, for sure.

He needed the motive.

Some nations might qualify, he decided. North Korea was at the top of his list of possibilities.

Toys and games for trade for an emerging nation was one thing. Playing with national defense was quite another.

If the matter was occurring in the North Pole, he knew someone personally who had just been up there for some research…

* * *

Chapter 57

Ali Enders was in his office with two Senators. One, a member of the Foreign Relations Committee; the other Intelligence and Defense.

Outside Capitol Hill, it was raining. Washington's traffic was easily snarled, and an Emergency vehicle could be heard somewhere needing to pass through.

Ali could not have been happier with what he was hearing.

"They aren't pleased with the Trade Agreement" said Charles. "They say we gave them less than an honest survey of our reserves in certain commodities."

"How egregious is that? Are we not able to hold some discretion as to how much we reveal?" asked Enders. "Are they flirting with us or what…?"

"Not exactly" said Domini. "The Trade Agreement was good for both nations. We have what they need, and they had what we need to grow our economy. It's a good standing arrangement for all…"

"So they think we're playing!" said Ali.

"*Playing?*"

"They think we're about to make a better deal with their competitors. More like Japan and Korea."

"I'd say it's *them* that's playing. We're doing the best we can to pay down our debts and boost our economy" said Enders.

"The Europeans are doing the same thing…"

"True. It's a question of transparency" said Charles.

"And Money!" said Domini.

"Money?" asked Enders.

"Yes. There are less than veiled implications that we owe the Asians a lot of money and they may Call-In our Notes because of our debt exposure"

Enders tossed down his pencil and leaned back in his chair. "That's ridiculous! We are the world's currency, if not the world's bank!"

Both men nodded.

"As you know Gentlemen, I've just been nominated for a seat on the Fed. If it came down to such a threat, we'd seriously be talking about nationalizing our banks before letting another nation deplete our money supply!"

"That's a bit extreme, isn't it?" said Charles. "This is America. Nobody is going to put up with nationalizing *banks* – I'll tell you that!" he laughed.

"You think it's funny?" said Enders, one old-boy talking to another, "since when is the money, risk and security of your nation secondary to popular opinion? We're not here to reflect popular opinion but to legislate!"

"Well… honestly!" Charles guffawed. "That's referring to sovereign money in a primitive manner isn't it?"

"since when is money a *primitive* matter?" insisted Enders.

"Look…" said Domini, getting serious. "Let's put it this way: This is not something we want debated on the House Floor, that's for sure. So let's keep it under wraps and get to the bottom of all this…I'll meet with the Chinese when they arrive at State."

They agreed.

Enders was especially pleased.

He had waited for a long time for the excuse to nationalize the banks. This might well be the excuse he needed.

All he had to do now, was wrap up a few loose ends in the field.

Where the hell was his informant? What was holding things up? He had failed to receive the last deposit promised for his Swiss bank account.

What was up? What was the delay out there…?

* * *

Chapter 58

"Hey Mom!" called Sandra from outside the front room. "I've just booked my ticket and sent you a copy of the flight details…."

They were packing. There was a plan.

"Thanks Sweetie!" responded Amanda, her mind fairly scrambling to understand what Tom had told them.

There was so much to process.

But again, this was the plan.

Amanda's mind kept wandering back to what had happened in the last 24 hours.

She had to reconcile the fact that not only had Tom been in close proximity with them all - misrepresenting himself as a beach buddy, but he had *never* become food-sick!

Apparently, that was a ploy to flush out Kim, her tenant, who was clearly the target.

She felt angry. This was her home and she'd been played.

Jesus!

She realized she should have known Tom was a trained professional. Who else would recognize a parcel as a bomb with such quick response?

Yes, it happened that fast. He had swooped upon it with immediate recognition!

For that she was grateful. He behaved, after all, as he should in the service of his country…

"Thank you!" she had said, her voice weak. He had saved their lives and risked his own.

"Shhhh" he had said, taking her hands into his and stepping back. "Look, I'm sorry we had to mislead you. We knew you'd understand in ways that most people would not…"

She looked into his face, uncertain.

"You were a professional in your capacity as a Researcher, performing with honesty and integrity for those who asked you. We knew you'd handle it."

She nodded.

"We knew there was risk. But we had to anticipate his moves…People have lost their lives to this man, and his goals elude us yet!"

She understood.

"It was a risk we had to take. At the very least, it added pressure to his movements. He knows we know about him!"

"My God" Amanda had said, her hands up to her face, embarrassed at her gullibility.

The impact of that conversation was unnerving. She remembered the moment well.

Tom had tried to be delicate about it, she knew. But when he told her that her tenant was suspected of terrorist activity and that there was a high probability that he had accessed her office computer and seen all that came into her laptop…

For Amanda the surprise of Tom's identity was truly unexpected. He was a Federal Agent. She struggled to separate his real persona from his duty. Not only had she trusted him, but he had added richly to their summer existence, all of them keeping busy, jogging and sharing meals…Who would have known?

How could she have not known? She felt embarrassed somehow.

But she understood.

That was the essence of working undercover. Nobody was supposed to know.

More importantly, who sent him…And who would do such a thing without warning her?

When he told her she was shocked.

"Arguetta!"

She stared. He looked down apologetically.

"Trevor knew too…" he said. "It was for your protection. We knew he was monitoring your calls. We had our suspicions and we needed him to play his hand…"

"Play his…?"

"We knew he wouldn't harm anyone unless you became a threat. So I kept close."

It was all Amanda could do to console Sandra. She was devastated. "Is Dad alright?" she asked lamely.

It had been a difficult day when finally she and Tom spoke privately.

As he explained it, Tom had been planted close by to keep an eye on them, and to add pressure to Kim's movements.

"Sandra?"

Tom looked at Amanda gravely, there was clearly a danger. Then he spoke softly.

"Here is the plan. Get her on the Flight. Let her pass through security. Once she's through the gate, we'll redirect the passengers to other airlines and cancel that flight. That's just in case there's a watcher on the inside.

Amanda raised her hand to her mouth.

A watcher?

"Yes. That's right" he said. "The Airline itself will call the diversion and delay, and she can exit normally as if she were a regular passenger in the flight options…"

Amanda had tears in her eyes. The thought of something happening to her daughter was too horrible to imagine.

"You alright?"

She nodded, and then she smiled at him. If this young man was willing to risk his life for them, then the least they could do was show bravery.

"Yes" she said definitively.

* * *

Chapter 59

She dropped Sandra off at the Airport and pulled off down the Parkway to Old Town Alexandria. She saw a man cross the street with a newspaper under his arm. That was the signal that Sandra was under their protection.

Amanda was to proceed as per normal.

The Department of Interior was in Virginia. That was her destination.

Make like a normal routine, she told herself.

She and Trevor had talked, if carefully. Suspecting now that their phone conversations were being monitored, she responded without alarm.

Further, there were signals passed between them that her computer and data had been compromised. Trevor would know that already. Clearly, they both understood that a noose was being tightened around the family. Sandra included.

For that reason she was to act normally. There was a plan.

By now, the Department of Interior was accustomed to seeing her enter the building.

When signing in, after a routine frisk by armed guards, she listed the reason for her visit on a sheet just as she had always done. "Archival Research."

The Receptionist, a beautiful African American woman in her thirties now recognized her. "Hello Ms Wells!"

"Hello! How are you?" smiled Amanda, checking in her bag; cell phone and all. She retained her eyeglasses; locker key and Notebook which was inspected, stamped and approved for entry.

"Thank you" she said, passing through the turnstile.

Amanda recognized security cameras. Added measures of security in the Federal Building were visible. Many security officers were different, the faces calm, silent and watching.

Less the chitchat that most security officers engaged in when standing about for hours and waiting on visitors. No. These were trained military men, their posture resolute, their eyes penetrating.

Something had tipped them off. Someone had given the order for extra precaution.

Was it just in this building, or was it across all Federal Buildings?

She wondered if Arguetta had anything to do with it. Yes. When on the drive into DC with Sandra yet in the car, Amanda had stopped in Annapolis and left a note with Eileen for Arguetta. She explained everything about Tom, Kim and her new information.

But that was just today.

Arguetta might well have been informed before hand. He must have had other sources of intelligence alerting him to danger. In talking with Tom, she had told him to contact Arguetta. But she wasn't certain about anything. She had been essentially isolated and cutoff from inside information.

Still, for now, her chief concern was for the safety of Sandra. She had a small duty to perform. This she would do. Then she was to proceed to the next step of the plan.

"The same survey?" asked the Collection Desk at the Archives, a student from George Mason University doing a Internship at the Department of Interior.

"Yes. The Mineral Rights to these three regions, again!" she smiled, handing him her Request for Documents slip.

"Okay!" he said, spinning off like a tecky on his book cart to "Pull" out her requested stack and bring it out for her to read.

She would work for an hour. She would image the documents and the survey reports, she decided. Then she would leave.

She checked her watch. The "Pulls" for each research request came out every hour or two.

Sometimes, if the shelves were easily itemized on the Request for Research Documents chip, then it went quickly. These students knew their stacks and sources. But Amanda was feeling impatient, perspiration seeping up through her shirt and down the back of her hair.

It arrived. She thanked the student.

She bent over, immersed in the reports under muted lighting and with her digital Nikon imaged the documents. That was not her intention today, although God knows, she had invested hours in that pursuit for Arguetta's Research.

Today was a different mission. She too knew her sources and their content.

She had sent the student Intern on a wild goose chase. He would be the full hour hunting for her documents before coming out with a frustrated look on his face saying "Sorry…We couldn't find what you asked for…"

The time gave her the opportunity she needed. She waited, and she waited, not far from the desk. She watched others come and go, so that her face was getting closer to the log book on the Counter at the Collection Desk.

Repeatedly, the Interns wheeling out book carts of documents for Researchers. They would spin the log book on its pedestal at the Collection Desk, enter the name, slip number and time of retrieval. After that, every researcher would sign off on the documents and sit in the large research room under careful supervision.

Rarely were documents unfound.

In one quick moment Amanda spun the log book, ostensibly checking for her order.

She flipped back the sheets to the previous weeks and searched for the names of all who had retrieved previous documents.

There it was, her name listed from a month before - and the same documents reviewed by another name, just prior! The signature of the recipient was vague and undiscernible. She but knew. It was Kim's hand, even if a stab of the pen, it was his aggressive penmanship. She had seen it on a note in the kitchen of the guest house...

Not only had he traced her findings, but actually managed to steal them from a Federal Building! Few could manage that…

Entire sections of the Report of the Geologic and Mineral Survey had been lifted.

She left the building, her lips grim. He probably didn't even have to steal them. He might have just imaged them, then flushed them away, refiled them elsewhere, or tampered with the desk materials of another researcher reading something else from different boxes… The possibilities were endless.

Even if she were mistaken, and it was not his own signature, any other student might have worked on his behalf…

Regardless, the conclusion was the same. The research and information she had passed on to Arguetta was not accurate and had been tampered.

She left.

The drive back into Old Town was careful. She parked the dark SUV not far from the doorway and entered the Austin Texas Grill. She ordered a chilly bowl and tacos. She waited. Reagan National Airport was less than a mile away.

A young woman in a raincoat joined her for the meal. They had a friendly meal together, visibly seated by the window for anyone to observe.

Following the meal, they strolled to the parked SUV and drove all the way to Annapolis.

Sandra, for now, was safe.

* * *

Chapter 60

Charles popped his head into Ender's office. "He in?" The young Intern grinned. "Yes. I'll tell him you're here!"

Charles walked right through, gesticulating with his hand that it was alright. He opened the large oak polished door of the Senator's office and found Enders at his filing cabinet digging through papers.

"You heard?"

Enders looked up, a blank on his face.

"The Speaker wants a committee on what's happened. He's asking the Finance; Appropriations and the Intelligence Committees to send in reps. He wants to know if we need to write something..."

"Hell No!"

"He says the Fed called him!"

"I'll call the Fed!"

"No. Wait. You aren't a confirmed member yet. It would be inappropriate besides. Best let it come to you with an invitation and to remain unblemished until then..."

"What are you implying Charles?"

"They want a head to roll. There's been a complaint sent to State about a less than honest survey of mineral rights in the Middle East that changes the balance sheets of parity between the two nations in a tally of trade rights..."

"My God" said Enders "They have a nerve, don't they?"

"Shall I call Domini?"

"Not yet....He's in Europe. The Chinese were in street rags and running cumshaws yesterday..." fumed Enders, slamming the file cabinet and returning to his oak desk.

"...today they hold most of our debt!" finished Charles.

The door opened, and the Intern popped her head in "Speaker of the House on Line 2 for you!"

"If they get pissed they can Call-In their Notes…I know. I know" finished Enders reaching for the phone "Yes Senator Lions?"

He nodded.

"Err…Yes. I just heard." He looked at Charles. "At 2 pm today? Absolutely. I'd be happy to attend. Thank you Ted!" He put down the phone.

"He's trying to contain the situation before it becomes an issue for public debate!"

"Okay. That's not good. There's a whiff of malaise about this complaint. If word gets out, people will view it as a reason for banking instability. If there's a run on the banks…"

Enders looked up sternly. "Then we nationalize the banks!"

"My God, Ali…"

"Get a grip will you? No bank run! No nationalization! We'll deal with it like a foreign relations conflict resolution. That's all. And even if there is an issue, I'll be on the Fed Banking Committee, remember?"

"Right" said Charles, his eyes following Enders out the room.

∗ ∗ ∗

Chapter 61

The drive was long and tense. Gradually, from the Airport in Virginia, the city streets and police security of the nation's capitol of the District of Columbia gave way to commuter traffic heading for Maryland.

All US 50 traffic crossed from the Nation's capital to the major highways of the suburbs.

Finally, she reached the historic colonial town of Annapolis. That's when Amanda released her passenger, a look-alike to Sandra. She walked into the grounds of the US Naval Academy and passed the security guards and into the reception building.

Amanda was parked and waited. The girl was an ally of the security detail, a decoy.

Now on secured military premises, Amanda was obscured from view by outside surveillance and possible spying.

Suddenly Sandra appeared from behind the guard's post depot and climbed into the car besides her mother wearing a similar raincoat and boots.

That was the plan. She had not taken the flight. She was safe. Once Amanda pulled out of the military compound, the same profile was visible and identical. To anyone watching from afar, the identity switch was undiscernible.

They spoke very little, Amanda and Sandra. Their relief however, was held deep within their hearts.

 Amanda crossed the Severn River Bridge and followed US 50 until it merged onto the six-mile Chesapeake Bay Bridge. Once the Eastern Shore of the great Bay, she took a full long breath.

Here, Maryland gave way to flatlands and finally, as the sun set upon crop fields of corn stalks and soy beans, long dark stretches of coastal tidewaters stretched into Delaware and down farm roads with meager night-posted signs: Here, one could travel for miles without seeing cars.

The car hummed steadily as if knowing its own way home, and Amanda settled into country road driving for the last lap, and down the coastal highway to the beach house. It was long after dusk when they arrived.

Sandra would not be on her flight. She would be safely back in Maryland, returned to the beach cottage with Amanda if under subterfuge. After a week, she would return to the UK and fly out of Philadelphia. That was the plan.

They hugged. They made it!

The back of the car was loaded with food.

The house was a welcome sight, and Amanda eyed it carefully for any sign of suspicious activity.

The old house loomed in silence, shyly perched between shadows of the ocean and darkness of the night. She knew every curve and cranny of the old structure – its Dutch colonial roof-pitch shaped by traditional soft chimes and undulating eves, its weathered shingles bleached by sun, sea and rain. Over the years, it had held up well, as all traditional structures did in these parts. Despite the pernicious creep of tree roots and vines which, by virtue of hot humid summers flourished at every crevice, nook and cranny, giving it the impression not of a well manicured high profile beach house, but rather, a dubious narrative of summer intrigue and suspenseful delights.

For now, it remained still and undisturbed.

* * *

Chapter 62

There was definitely a commotion in the front office of the Senator's suite.

From his desk, it sounded like a party of fundraising lobbyists doing the rounds in the Senate. Laughter, jokes, a round of cheers and storytelling… Somewhere a few high pitched women delivering a line or two; his staffers could be recognized, even the jubilant giggle of some children in the surge, families no doubt. But he did not recognized them or know them.

They would pass on, the noisemakers, for sure. He returned his attention to the laptop at his desk. Mainly, he was sending email.

A Congratulations on an Award here; an encouragement there…Some needed recognition and stalwarts of the community making contributions to his political campaign…

That's what Congressmen did these days: Set up by his office manager, these were duty letter and messages from his constituents that needed responding.

A head popped in.

It was Mary, his Front Office Administrative Staff. "A surprise for you!" she said.

He rolled his eyes. If there was one thing he hated was to be interrupted and deal with aspirants seeking to petition! His tasks in Congress, as far as he was concerned, were far more important than anything his Constituents and voters could image.

The door opened fully.

"Hello Dad" said his daughter. Caroline his wife was standing behind her.

His face, once he recovered, was in a state of surprise, his irritability well masked.

"Caroline, what a surprise!" he said, finally. He hugged them all.

"Wow! What a shocker…You guys have totally blown me away!"

Mary maneuvered deftly behind him and closed his laptop.

"Dad" said Katherine "show me Congress!" she recited, the words clearly planted on her lips long before they arrived on the Hill.

Ali Enders turned to his wife Caroline, the expression on his face changing more presciently to one of disbelief.

"Of course!" he answered, blindly.

Caroline stood in a calm and glamorous silence. She was wearing a dark silk dress under a MILLY trench coat, vintage bag, shoes and museum scarf. On any bus, she might have blended in as a buttoned up passenger. But here, at close range, she was a bombshell with an edge. Enders couldn't take his eyes off her. This was hardly the Caroline he knew.

They passed through the halls of Congress, Katherine, Caroline, Mary and two staffers behind them chatting and joking about traffic; tourists and shopping in Washington.

As they walked down the hallway of state representative offices; Senator's offices and Senior Legislative Liaison offices, the procession became something of a parade, Enders introducing his family to politicians who would normally recognize a Congressman's wife from prior personal relationships. But not Ali Enders. They hardly knew him, more often the man they saw came surrounded by beautiful young Interns. But here he was introducing his family!

Caroline remained quiet but for a flashing smile and laugh – an indictment of a husband estranged.

They re-entered his office and found Mary seated at her desk.

"My wife Caroline, my daughter…" he said to her.

Mary got up and came around the desk to shake hands. "I'm very pleased to meet you" she smiled. "You're husband speaks highly of you to us and to his colleagues around here!"

Caroline smiled graciously, if looking around the mahogany lined quarters of her husband's congressional office, decorated with photographs of himself and his party leaders; executives and Washington leadership, she saw none of his family.

Enders turned to his wife. "Lunch?" he asked, sensing coolness.

"Oh yes…" chatted Katherine.

Mary resumed her work at her desk. The phone rang.

Ali Enders turned to Caroline. "Where are you staying?"

"The Hyatt, across the River at Crystal City. It's close to the Airport."

He looked down.

They had a townhouse on Capitol Hill. Ordinarily, that would be where she would stay as his wife. He understood. Even by asking her where she was staying was an obvious separation. He owed her an explanation.

Mary interrupted, the phone in her hand. "It's your five o'clock meeting tomorrow at Senator's Allen's office. They need to postpone a day, can you do that?"

"No" he said. "Please cancel. I'll catch up with them the next day!"

He turned to face Caroline, his voice clearly audible. "As you know, the townhouse…I've got the damned place for sale…"

He eyed Mary as he steered them towards his office door. "They're showing it this evening, and I've got a Maid crew cleaning it up to within an inch of its life…With the price of homes around here and the place being over a hundred years old…"

Caroline looked down. He, speaking with unnecessary force in a Washington pitch at his wife and child, was embarrassing her.

He understood. And he also knew that within two hours, Mary would have his place listed with the local Coldwell Banker Real Estate Firm; and have a Latino cleaning Maid crew on deck for a $200 cleaning service.

What Caroline might find in the house could lead to a suspicion of sexual indiscretion, or, as the tabloids put it, a political-career-ender.

The Cafeteria delighted Katherine. She found food to choose from a buffet spread that thrilled her. At the top floor of the Senate Office Building, the décor was elegant and suitable for any congressman and his wife. Caroline and Enders faced each other, Katherine had long been finished with her meal and strayed back down to Mary.

But if there was any surprise at the mea, it was for him. He should have seen this coming he realized, the moment the words came out of her mouth.

"I want a divorce."

She said it with such calm and smiling conviction that it had the feel of a menace.

She was at least being discrete. Especially when she produced images of him with the Intern Ingar at the Manderin's *Loose Tie* disco; and another showing them entering the lobby of her apartments at the 909. It didn't need to be explicit.

He looked at the image of Ingar. That he had her hand inside her waist band, or that she nipped his ear or had her tie in her moth while dancing was clear. There was enough blond hair, skin and inebriated body heat between them to leave the rest unexplained.

Hell, he be discrete too. "I'm begging you Caroline. Give me a chance!"

She smiled a gorgeous, beguiling and malevolent smile. The smile of one deeply damaged, and it frightened him.

"Look…" he said, his hand on the table to touch her fingers. But she curled up her hand to a fist.

"I'll be up home for Thanksgiving. Please! I'm asking. Give us a chance to at least talk about it? Then it's your decision. Just one conversation to discuss our options, I'm begging. Just one opportunity, I beg you… Caroline!"

She was a Catholic, he knew. She would try to save her marriage, he felt certain.

"What do you hope to gain by it?" she asked.

He looked at her gravely. "I make a mistake. I was wrong. I am deeply remorseful. *Please* allow me to heal, and give our marriage a *chance*…I'm committed to therapy. I can't bear losing you and Katherine….*Anything.* I'm pleading for a chance of making restitution?"

She hesitated.

He knew he had her.

"Two weeks, I'll be up back home then. We adjourn for the session. Caroline. I want a second chance. *Please...* I know I don't deserve your forgiveness and that I'll have to earn your trust. Therapy, counseling…anything, I'll do it for you!"

She barely nodded.

"Tell you what.." he said softly, now gathering her fingers into his hand. "This afternoon, I'm giving a speech at the National Press Club, and I'd like to suggest dinner and a show at the National Theater downtown?"

She looked up.

"At the *Hay Adams?*" he asked, peering at her.

"Why not eat at the Press Club? The Theater is across the street…" she said softly.

"The *Hay Adams* is a place I want to show-off my wife in public!" he teased.

Ali Enders returned to his office to check on his messages. He was on his way out for the day, he told his staff.

As far as Ali Enders was concerned, things were not going well.

Caroline had told him that she was meeting with her lawyers in Boston next week for a strategic planning session. In any other language, that meant a fine line between a man and his wife privately, and a politician and his wife publicly. In the eyes of his voting constituents that would preclude him from holding public office or much longer.

Clearly, attorneys in Boston understood the enormity of such a move. Aware of the PAC money that he had at his disposal for his election campaigning, they would understand his obligations also. Their concern would be to protect Caroline from any liability and exposure to his debts…That was the reputation of the Law Firm she picked. *Rowenstein, Kinkle & Boswell* were a formidable group of associates. For one thing, they could dig up enough dirt to shame the Puritan Pilgrims if they wanted to.

No, he decided. He could not become the target of their enquiries. Period.

Most definitely. Caroline his wife cannot and must not put her case under their management. Especially now that he was coming up for a nomination to the Fed; the US Central Bank Board.

If her meeting with her lawyers was in Boston was next Tuesday, then he had time…

Yes, the *Hay Adams* was good. It gave him a chance to talk.

The way he explained it, was clear. He a bill he was funding for defense. If he succeeded in defunding it, then he could sent large projects their way to oversea. Caroline's interest, in that perspective, would be minimized.

Yes. He would meet with them himself.

In the meantime, he could get himself imaged with her. Just in case he needed to send a message to his photographer asking for a delivery of "red" roses. But only if desperate, he decided.

Then again, desperate times called for desperate measures, and you just never knew who were your friends, and who were your enemies. Perhaps he should act to be sure.

The date and place however, would have to remain far distant from Washington.

Preferably, Boston. That way, there would no ties to him…

Most importantly, it must be done before she meet with her lawyers. So, he'd see how it went with his Congressional Appointment to the House Defense Budget Committee.

If all went well, he'd endorse the Congressional Bill for defense. If not, then the Bill would fail…

* * *

Chapter 63

They agreed to meet in person.

In fact, the call had lit up on Ali Enders' cell phone while having dinner with his wife. It was his stock broker. He would have liked to answer the call straight away. But the *Hey Adams* was hardly the place to discuss money matters. Besides, Caroline was with him. He deferred. What was another day?

It was two days, actually.

He and Jack could have met anywhere in the city. Certainly, he sufficiently able to handle any tab bill. But convenience was the choice, where they normally had coffee in the street-side closed-porch of *Dean & DeLucca's* marketplace. Ali jumped at the suggestion. Besides, it was a milieu in which to remain unnoticed.

They each chose a deli sandwich; sweet pastry and cappuccinos. Jack bought two bottles of wine and a gift to take back to his wife in New York, a chef's apron and a brand-market picnic bag. They carried their food outside and found a small round marble-top table.

"For the boat!" he laughed, yanking his package up, over and setting it down at his feet where they sat.

They ate, Jack coughing occasionally. He was not himself, he explained. The flu, he said. He had just returned from Hong Kong and he still had jetlag. "That, plus a hell of crisis up at Wall Street…"

Enders was interested, as Jack knew he would be. There would be jokes about travel; the food, the women, the lay-overs and then the intel that the trip provided for the Firm.

Enders liked to dig for as much information about finance anywhere as possible.

Jack sneezed as if Ali was the cause of his allergy. It allowed him to pause; catch his breath, and hold back his conversation. He apologized. Jack was clearly uncomfortable.

For an honest Senator, Jack realized that that Enders knew a lot about a lot of things. Perhaps he had access to intelligence or to underground operations - for all he knew. Especially today. There was something angry about Ali's demeanor today. He was pressing for information with less finesse than was befitting any client, much less a Senator with the public trust on his shoulders. Still, Ali told him much about his office. This was something new.

The Cafe was populated by students. Outside, an afternoon sun peeked through dappled colored Fall trees; inside, the music festive and promising – Halloween just one week away…

"So, I did as you told me and sold off all the Bonds" said Jack. "I invested the proceeds into this list of Stocks, all winners, and I increased the yield term for a longer period, giving you the optimum return on your investment, even a chance to make up for the loss of that margin call…"

Ali put up his hand. "Woah! Woah! Woah!…Did I say I needed a deficit reduction plan?"

"Well. Not exactly. It's just that most people…"

"Do I look like 'most people' to you, Jack?"

"No!" he chuckled.

"Wait till you hear the news! I'm a little concerned about an agenda developing on the Hill that has national security overtones. I'm afraid it may send the markets into the jitters!" said Enders.

"Oh?" said Jack, suddenly interested.

"Well, it's *related* to events overseas with possible threats on the Homeland. I just want to be clear about that. Not that I'm able to share intelligence with you. But it helps to have a client on the inside, wouldn't you say?"

"Oh yes! Absolutely!" said Jack, wondering if this conversation were about to stray into that grey area the Security and Exchange Commission might call 'insider trading tips'…

They tucked into their gourmet sandwiches. Thick spicy sauce oozing from the bread was licked off. Jack's sausage and liverwurst sandwich on Reuben dripped with melting cheese. They savored their food, quietly grinning.

"Best damned food in the city!" said Ali.

"Oh my God yes!" murmured Jack.

"So, what I'm about to tell you goes not further, right?"

"Oh absolutely!" said Jack, dabbing his napkin to his lips.

"Look. All hell is going to break loose. We may be reacting to things in a solely defensive way, once the media gets done! But don't worry. It's under control. We have a plan of action and we know what we're doing. But it's not going to be pretty, that's for sure."

Jack looked at him gravely, his appetite diminished.

"Be glad for the privileged information, my friend. You'll be the only one on Wall Street that knows. It's just roller ride before it settles down. So don't panic. You got that?"

Jack was not accustomed to being treated like a child. But in a city of power like this one, you went with whatever came your way as if it mattered. Or whomever it came from!

For Jack, it made the task at hand even more uncomfortable. Not than Enders ever made things comfortable for anyone. But this was going from bad to worse. In fact, whatever it was he had originally intended to discuss with Enders was fast losing its appeal. Jack swallowed hard and reached for his coffee.

"there may even be a bank run. If there is, then we'll call a halt to transactions, even trading, and close the banks. Especially the Central Bank…"

Jack could barely believe what he was hearing.

"*Close the Fed?*…" he repeated in utter disbelief.

"Like I said alarming stuff… But don't panic, it's just a precautionary move to keep the floodgates firmly closed on any mischief."

"So…err. How should we react?"

"Like nothing ever happened! Just don't panic and start selling *everything!* We need the money in place and secure. That's all.."

"Are you sure?" Jack said spontaneously before realizing that he was questioning a man in a position of leadership who wielded enormous power on key Congressional finance committees.

Ali evidently overlooked his outburst. He smiled. "Relax! We're good.."

They finished eating, the place filling now with late afternoon crowds stopping in from work to buy from the market some gourmet food; drinks or alcohol to take home for dinner guests, as was often the case in the city. It was already getting dark.

They were close to wrapping up, and Jack fulfilled his report with information on about recent stocks, options, markets and currencies overseas. The conversation was lively and informed.

Jack was finished, then he realized he forgot to say something.

"Oh, I almost forgot. I got a call from a Lieutenant Ferguson. He's the man investigating…."

"Yes, I know what he's investigating…I knew the girl who was killed, remember?. My lawyer has the matter in hand" said Enders.

Jack fell silent. They finished their coffee and assembled their trash to leave.

"Well? What did he want to know?"

Jack regretted opening his mouth. "He…err… he just asked me questions about you. He wanted to know how long you'd done business….How much etc. etc."

"I hope you cut him off!"

Jack nodded. "Of course! You know its our policy not to discuss clients. But my boss says we can be subpoenaed…"

"Your boss? You discussed *me* with your boss?"

"He got the initial call, Ali. I had to answer for you. They review all my transactions, as you know. Its SEC rules."

"Damned Right!"

Jack continued. "He wanted to know if you had any idea about a certain Immigration Bill that might affect your judgement relative to the girl…like…I'm not exactly sure."

"*Influence* me, you mean. Did she think she could influence me?"

"No! I believe you promised to 'review' the matter … or look into it for her or something…?"

Ali leaned forward about to answer. Then he suddenly stopped short. "The Lieutenant wanted to know this?"

Jack nodded. "I just thought I should inform you…that's all."

Jack saw before him was a man recoiling, a dangerous and angry man.

Ali chuckled. "So what's that got to do with anything?"

"Nothing. Nothing at all. I don't have a clue, really what it means. But my boss…."

Ali turned with a quick sidewise look. "Your boss again…?"

"It's just that we can't make trades for anyone under police investigation. It's a policy of the Firm, Ali."

"Oh. So, you're here to tell me that I can't place any bets with your firm because I'm a suspect, is that it?" "It's just Regulations, we are strictly reviewed to meet compliance regulations, as you know!" said Jack, backtracking his tone. "I'm supposed to ask you personally, then submit a written statement at my office. That's all."

"Oh. I see. So that's how it is?"

Jack nodded.

Ali Enders looked up.

Everywhere above them could be heard a finch chirping in the porch café, waiting for crumbs that fell from tables.

Jack knew that he had triggered an alarm in Ali's mind. Perhaps he was tumbling nervously through what had just transpired: Jack might be wearing a wire. He might be trapping the Senator. He might be *goading* him with trading intelligence…

Jack waited nervously. He was not without sensibilities, especially in his line of work making money on the stock markets.

Jack realized what has just happened.

Ali was stunned by the allegation that implied the girl was peddling influence. It immediately revealed a relationship that tied them together! *Enders had de facto implicated himself in a possible murder, if that was what they were now investigating.*

And the instrument most used, like a honey-trap, was money. Of course, Jack was his broker!

 "More coffee?" he said suddenly.

"Sure" said Jack, relieved. "Look. I'm sorry if I've offended you…"

"No. No problem!" said Ali, getting up. "Here…" he said, leaning forward to pick up both cups of coffee for a refill at the coffee bar.

Ali moved deftly through the crowd that was gathering, beyond the muddle of a band setting up for a night of playing at the Georgetown café. He reached the great cappuccino mixer – made legendary in these parts by a paid barista who manipulate the polished brass machine with great flourish and flavoring, and Ali placed his order.

Ali looked over to him, and waved cheerfully, the muddle of things a situation of fun...

Jack decided to relax.

* * *

Ali waited his turn in the line behind two students and a legal aid, his briefcase still in hand.

Behind the bar was alcohol. But Ali knew that Jack was not a drinker before 4 P.M. Something to do with keeping his license in good standing, he once told him. So, it was a coffee serving – straight up! He paid, diving first into his side pockets, then into his hip pocket for his wallet.

Ali then migrated gingerly to the side counter for the accoutrements that went with cappuccino and added some crème to both coffees. The sugar was cane and beautifully packaged, like the monogrammed paper napkins.

The music transitioned from overhead speakers as background noise to the musicians now tuning up. The crowd surged with a little fresh excitement as a casual quartet prepared to perform.

It was the ambiance of the place, an eclectic mixture of selections from baroque to hard jazz. Languages flowed freely representing several continents, and Ali recognized that this was an special event, a reunions amongst those residents greeting family and friends.

Ali Enders smiled, only his hand wavered. He was close to panic. But his mind was clear. And his pocket, that place where never he went, was now calling.

He moved slightly, Jack somewhere behind him.

It was a measure of desperation that caused him to reach into the pocket, open the purse, uncork the vial, and in the small gesture of stirring sugar, he let two drops fall into the coffee cup for Jack. He returned to the table.

It was easy to watch Jack drink.

The effect would not take hold until several hours. By then, Jack would have taken a taxi to Union station; settled into a train seat for Grand Central Station in downtown New York City. By then, he would have encountered dozens of people! And even if the day was closing, it was his custom, Jack had said, to get back home with the family rather than spend the night. This, he had told Ali knew.

Heart failure could occur strike at any hour, people knew this.

They shook hands, Jack and Ali.

"So Let me know how things go, OK? Anything I can do to help, let me know" said Enders.

Enders called up his own cab to return to Capitol Hill.

By tomorrow, Jack would not be submitting any written report, Enders knew.

* * *

Chapter 64

The phone call that Amanda received from Arguetta was puzzling. It was a message, suggesting that more lay beneath his parse words.

> *"Hello Amanda,*
>
> *Arguetta here. Could you give me a call when you get a chance? I received an enquiry about the incident of San Francisco. I was looking for some further explanations, if you don't mind, since you are implicated in some fresh information we just received.*
>
> *Thank you!"*

It wasn't often that an Admiral called. In fact, it wasn't often anyone from the government called. Amanda was working alone. She and her beach-cohorts were the only ones doing research on this project. To a large extent, she felt entirely isolated.

Arguetta understood. He knew it was hard on her and he relied on Trevor to breach the gap, a gap induced purposefully for the purpose of government deniability. It came with the job. Research findings had a way of raising awkward issues, and it served the public little to be exposed to unfiltered data.

However, since his message referred to the incident at the San Francisco Conference commemorating the United Nations inauguration of 1942, Amanda was on safe ground.

Little was said about its real purpose: The signing of the Trade Agreements was one thing, a fact-finding mission about covert threats to national defense was another. Searching for motive behind plausible threats was always of interest to the government, and public events were ideal targets for those seeking opportunities to vent leaks.

In San Francisco much had happened as far as Amanda was concerned. Not the least of which a stark awakening to the possibility that somehow her research findings had been inadequate for government work, if not misleading to decision makers crafting international trade agreements!

She felt awful.

Not that most people would consider such work profound. Trade was not hot stuff. Yet it was profound in that it affected the livelihoods of thousands of people at various stages of the economic delivery system in the West. Every-day consumers who trusted free-market capitalism presupposed peace and stability. Change one component, and the other suffered.

Moreover, if Amanda was correctly recalling her history, things like delivery, supply, labor-supporters and source materials were often *precisely* the targets of assault by an enemy. *Strategic warfare*, they called it. And it took career warriors like Arguetta to remain vigilant and suspicious at all times, even at a nation's most somnolent moments.

But still, it bothered her that she was called in on ….*what?* Fresh information? What did that mean?

Accustomed rather to receiving calls about the excellence of her work performance, this was new.

She called.

He spoke without hesitation. The Conference event was publicly open and the incident of a guest who died was a matter of news. No need for secrecy.

"As I'm sure you realize, there's been an investigation about the death of the Japanese Gentleman whom we met at the Conference, Mr. Gutolomo. We've been asked a few questions. I'm afraid it means bringing you in for some questioning. So, could you manage to come in tomorrow at say,   mid   morning   or   so?"
"Yes Of course!" she said.

She actually found nothing in the Media all night long as she searched for the broadcast.

Still, it was a restless night with worry and apprehension. Neither could Amanda reach Trevor. Thus, with all the poise and aplomb that had gathered over the years, Amanda Wells showed up in Washington DC the next day precisely as instructed, notes and research at the ready.

The Inspector had flown in from San Francisco, he said.

They were all seated at a modest conference room in Arlington. Adm Arguetta; Lts Thompson his Aide and Joan DePrima from JAG; and then Amanda.

She wondered what she had got herself into, and Arguetta's face was static. But twice she was interrupted by Joan DePrima when trying to answer a question by the Inspector.

Clearly, Arguetta had her shielded by DePrima who was guarding their responses to the Inspector.

These were leads too sensitive to transmit electronically, the inspector was explaining. "Just too many loose ends and the need for some security" was the way he phrased it.

"How is that Sir? - If you don't mind my asking" said DePrima.

What followed utterly surprised Amanda.

"Mr Gutomolo had certain sensitive information on his person that was purloined. In fact, he was killed for it." He paused "It was his intention to present this information to Admiral Arguetta after the ball. But he was murdered on the premises of the Hotel, and in full view, making it a very public event" he said, looking at Amanda.

"Yes. I remember the incident" she said, wondering where all this was leading. "It was a horrible tragedy for an event commemorating the sacrifices of WW II"

The Inspector nodded.

"Especially for a man whose parents would have been involved with what occurred during the war, and to his country's final surrender…" he said.

"Yes" nodded Arguetta. "But whatever else he might have felt about it, there is no doubt that he was a grateful ally on the day he died. He was trying to avert an impending disaster, he told the Porter, before entering the Hotel…"

The meeting ended abruptly with a call for the Inspector.

But after they disbanded, the discussion continued.

"Might you have any idea who that could be?" asked DePrima as they all walked down the wide halls of the Pentagon.

"No."

She turned to Amanda.

"No. I had seen him in the lobby, but not closely."

"We've had little specific intelligence .." said Arguetta, opening the door to his office. Two staffers stepped out.

DePrima put her briefcase on the table "would you mind Tom?" she said to Thompson, nodding towards the open door. He got up and closed it firmly behind the two staffers who left it ajar. Arguetta took his place at his desk "Please!" he said to Amanda, offering the seat across from him.

DePrima extracted two files. "An autopsy was conducted and we found distant traces of polonium. In this case, it was not what killed him. But his killer was contaminated when he left traces."

Amanda looked at them. There was little room for imagination here. Plutonium was the stuff manufactured at nuclear reactors and was highly regulated, she knew.

Her thoughts flew directly to the Conference as being the penultimate war-time conference before Potsdam, when President Truman had to drop an atom bomb on Japan to bring the war to an end.

"But that was over 70 years ago….right?" continued the lieutenant, anticipating their thoughts.

"And we've had a Cold War since then" added Arguetta. "To say nothing of the kinds of technology we now have at our disposal."

"Right" said DePrima. "So we examined his belongings and we explored further tracings... We discovered his movements for the days preceding his murder. There is no question that he was visited by another Asian man who was threatening him…"

"Who?"

"He is the killer, we are sure!" said DePrima, holding a photograph.

"Is…this man still at large with any trace elements on him?" asked Arguetta.

"Oh yes!" said the lieutenant, her gaze fixed on Amanda.

"He was last seen at an Arctic expedition…" she said.

Amanda's hand went to her mouth.

Arguetta spoke. "Carry on!"

"I've talked to your Staff Officer about expanding our leads already. And we may wish to go over a few leads with your team…" she said, addressing Lt Thompson.

But she turned her attention back to Amanda.

"This man… took a direct flight to Chicago, then on the Washington DC where he lives. Or rather, just outside Washington where he stays periodically."

The lieutenant sat down. "Do you know *anything* about this, Ms Wells?"

"No. Of course not! How should I know such a man…" began Amanda her voice suddenly raw and dry. The Lieutenant pulled out a second photograph.

"This man is Korean and his name is Kim Miu. He drove directly to your home Ms Wells. Do you recognize this photograph?"

Amanda froze. She felt as if she should stop breathing. "My God…" she began.

She looked at the photograph. There was an image of her beach house! There was the porch; the Guest House where the tenant…Even the flowers she watered on a regular basis. She might even have been standing in the tool shed when the image was taken! It was absolutely unbelievable. And there he was…her tenant. Kim!

He was unrecognizable from the first image.

Arguetta poured her some water and set it beside her, shock rippling through her when she felt his hand on her shoulder. "Calm down Amanda. Can you confirm that this man was at your house?"

"Kim! He….He…He's my tenant! A student, he told me, at a Culinary Institute….My God!" she tucked her hair behind her ears, her lips dry.

"We shall have a team test your place for any tracings, Amanda" said Arguetta.

"*What?*" she whispered, her eyes watery.

"If you don't mind giving us permission, that is" said DePrima.

"Yes"

"The substance, even in distant forms, leaves tracings. There may be traces left around your place, if he was involved as the killer of the Japanese man...We believe him to be of Korean extraction."

Amanda nodded.

"Your Security Clearances are temporarily suspended, is that right, Ms Wells?"

"Yes" she said simply, too tired to untangle that one.

"I'm afraid it's now a matter of national security. And we cannot keep you updated unless there is direct bearing to you, you understand..."

"Yes."

"But I would appreciate it if you just acted normally without raising any alarm? This could be bigger than we know, especially since he is moving about with impunity."

"I understand. But he's...he's left!"

They all stared at her.

Of course. By now he'd know that they knew his identity. She was the bait! She was a target for his next elimination!

The cell phone rang. Arguetta answered.

"Yes. Thanks! No. Not yet. Tell her to wait on that until I get there..." He eyed Tom who moved towards the door, the meeting ended.

"I'll walk you downstairs Amanda" said Arguetta.

"Why was the Japanese diplomat trying to talk with you in San Francisco?" she asked.

"Oh..." he hesitated.

"To tell you that there was oil in the Middle East unaccounted for in the Trade Agreements?"

"Well, err. Yes and No. It's the funding *behind* that dig that tipped us off. We know someone is tampering with funds to divert money. That lead gave us this man who was also funded by the same source. He aims to tamper with natural phenomenon at our polar magnetic frequencies..."

"Polar?"

"Yes. To a large extend, it is our most vulnerable border, the northern extremities. He is tampering with possibilities that give us cause for alarm."

"As in, a defense threat?"

"As in, infrastructure manipulation of a serious kind that threatens our homeland security…"

His cell phone rang. "I see" he said. After a pause he added "Thanks for informing me."

"The Defense Budget has been cut without passage of the Congressional Bill for continued government funding. We've been asked to cease from pursuing this enquiry… and hold off until further notice. I'm sorry!"

Arguetta led her to lobby, a center of confusion and distraction. Amanda imagined that others in the building had received similar calls - one department after another coping with the reality of shutting down critical defense operations.

Outside, Amanda took a big breath.

It was unreal. She felt numb, Arguetta at her side.

"I don't have to tell you Amanda that you may be under scrutiny since there is a link to your Kim…"

"A suspect you mean?"

"Whatever you do, remain calm. Just follow instructions, and stay off any electronic devices with any words …Right?"

"I understand" she said, hoping against hope that he would say something about Trevor knowing…He did not. And she knew better than to ask.

Finally he paused and turned to her.

"This man, Kim. He may try to contact you. Say nothing! If he does, we will know about it. Amanda, don't take matters into your own hands. He has no reason to hurt you. You were a good cover, that's all…"

"Until now, that is?"

"If you stay calm, there is nothing to cause alarm –Think of light switches in harmless ways: Just casually flip on the lights. The car headlights. The cellular flashlight…whatever. I'll recognize it as a signal.?"

She looked at him, her eyes full of tears. *"My God…"*

"I know…" he said. "But you are a strong woman, Amanda. This is the business we are in…We have enemies."

She nodded politely.

Arguetta leaned forward slightly "Don't worry" he managed to say. "I'll find a way to keep you out of danger…"

It helped to hear it.

* * *

Chapter 65

She drove home straight from Washington. No stopping. Two hours of choking back her frustration; bawling, pounding the wheel. She wept almost all the way to the beach.

Her mind thrashed about, every angle of the situation was appalling.

What of those friends who had come to the house? What had she done exposing them to an *anarchist?*

It was too awful…Her house!

Kim?

As the road unfurled before her, there was little she could think of that didn't run ablaze with hurt and betrayal. In her isolation, she felt disgrace, embarrassment; shame and anger…

She finally pulled into her driveway.

Kim Miu was just standing there at her front door. In his hand was machete. For a moment their eyes locked, as if he were scanning her brain for any sign of recognition.

Amanda quickly recovered. If there were any signs of shock on her face, she managed to mask the fear.

What a surprise, she had said. She said was thrilled to see him, she said.

He smiled, bringing forward a pike and an axe .

* * *

Arguetta moved through the building, his stern brow becoming a perpetual frown. Only those that knew him well felt safe to approach him, and he usually lightened up. But not today. Today, his thoughts were not only far away, but tangled in knots.

"I'm missing something" he told Tom, striding beside him "I'm just not connecting the dots....It's frustrating as hell...."

"Yes Sir! We'll figure it out..."

"And call a conference with clearance to all who attended the first potential threat analysis. CERN ain't no dormant puppy, it turns out. And to those next closest to matters of atomic reaction and defense..." Now Tom stopped briefly, surprised.

"And to those at NASA and NSA Cyber defense systems. Got it?"

"At what time would you call the conference?"

"ASAP I'll be wanting Emergency Contingency Plans..."

"1400 tomorrow?"

Arguetta stopped. "Today!"

"Yes Sir."

"Thanks. Limit exposure and call in security measures, too."

"Got it!"

"Do we go Executive Sir?"

"Not quite yet..."

* * *

"Gentlemen, we have a problem" said Arguetta "It poses a clear and present threat to our national security. Tom, if you please, proceed with your presentation!"

Tom doused the houselights and the display lit up in the dark.

"As you know, CERN holds the Large Hadron Collider (LHC) which is the world's most powerful particle collider machine in a complex experimental facility. Built by the European Organization for Nuclear Research at the turn of the millennium, it is today the single largest machine in the world…"

The image of the center came up, Alps behind it.

"Used in collaboration with over 10,000 scientists and engineers from over 100 countries, including countless universities and laboratories, it advances knowledge – the story of the principle creator of today's internet."

Next image.

"Here physicists test the predictions of different theories of particle physics; high energy physics, and in particular the theorized Higgs boson and other supersymmetric theories in an attempt to advance our knowledge base…"

An image of scientists showed up next. "You've all heard of the incomplete Kovacks Theorems, said to hold electromagnetic secrets. But this is something different."

"But as with all experimentation, we harness our knowledge to keep it safe and without unleashing destructive forces. Manipulation is one thing, unleashing physical change in a threat to human existence. So, our interests, for the moment, are focused on these people and guarding against possible intrusion into our networks; security and wellbeing as a nation – all of which is possible from CERN."

Arguetta took over.

"The Europeans balk at our interests, mainly for populist reasons, but their governments assure us of monitoring. We feel they are playing with fire under the masquerade of Fair Use access."

Tom continued. "At our experimental station, we find this. The spike is beyond the scope. It is not only astronomical, but we think it suggests tampering. These are very low electromagnetic frequencies. It is periodic, predictable and systemic. That implies testing…"

"I should mention here - just as a matter of conversation" said Arguetta "that there is a recommendation by the Pentagon to include all flight personnel as technically listed by the US Department of Labor as "radiation workers" like X-ray technicians and nuclear plant workers."

"Right" said Tom. "An assault on an Experimental Station, and at a close-by Ranger Facility showed tracings of Polonium. As you know, Polonium-210 has a half-life of 138 days and decays to the stable daughter isotope of lead, therefore its source is reduced to about one sixteenth of its original radioactivity about 18 months after production. As we know, since 97% of the world's legal supply occurs in Russia in the RBMK nuclear reactors, producing about 85 grams per year, they do remain in compliance with accounting for it: Most of it goes to U.S. companies through a single authorized supplier. They don't appear to be the source of this…"

Tom advanced his graph.

"But this showed up in San Francisco. Moreover, up here in this zone, we see tracings of high-intensity radiation that coincide with the weakening magnetic pole and solar radiation. Since the production of polonium starts from bombardment of bismuth with neutrons, we suspect someone is experimenting with the naturally produced energy sequence that accelerated particles during times of the Aurora circle…with the effect of simulating a Haldron Collider impact with particles that create enough atomic energy to control the world's power grids with one switch."

"How is that possible?"

Arguetta stood up.

"Based on what Patterson tells me with the data, two stations transmitting energy can harness the low frequencu electromagnetic at a latitudinal flow at precise points straddling the North Pole. That creates a natural flow of current at the time of greatest solar radiation into the earth's atmosphere."

"No way!" said Dr. Stephens. "that's out of science fiction!"

"Exactly" said Arguetta. "Two fishing vessels properly positioned would hardly be detected as the wizard pulling the switch from behind the veil on his fishing boat!"

"Who…?"

"Korea, possibly. We're not sure. Or a lone wolf vigilante out on a contract…"

Tom flipped up the image of a Japanese national.

"This man was killed at San Francisco by this man, Kim Miu who has ties with terrorists and anyone who can pay. He is still around, and we think he's being funded by someone stateside. The amounts of money are astronomical…"

"*Internal?*"

"That's ridiculous" said a voice "Who would want anything to do with that kind of stuff?…" said one official in the dark recess of the conference room.

"Someone with a grand flavor for world dominion. Power. Control. Wealth…" said Tom.

"Whoever it is, it depends on timing..." said Arguetta. "An event producing high energy is anticipated in the next two to three days, and overflights are being monitored…"

* * *

Chapter 66

Amanda had called Arguetta.

"I found him on my doorstep" she said "Then he was gone. He said he forgot his tools in the garden shed."

"A warning" he said. "He may be observing you. Stay vigilant."

Arguetta called periodically, but she could report nothing new. In fact, Amanda had to admit that her house tenant had added to the tools of the garden-shed. He had planted vegetables during the summer.

"Perhaps he left because he found nothing threatening?"

"Perhaps" said Arguetta.

That was almost a month ago. And somehow, the shock had worn off. The season had changed. Collecting your set of gardening tools seemed more plausible as the weather cooled, and the weeks passed uneventfully.

Gradually, Amanda realized that it was good to just be home. Today, she arose early and bundled up for a walk down the beach.

It was Fall, and the sky was crisp and pale, the moon still at its closest and biggest size in position to the earth's northern latitudes.

The sun was slow rising over the Atlantic, and Amanda paused as if to salute its appearance.

Dawn turned softly purple then pink and then blue, the sea its undulating herald.

It had taken her several days to regulate her routine. She had been grocery shopping, relishing every step of it as if nothing else were on her mind.

There was spinach, lettuce and bacon dropped into her basket of groceries. Not that she needed any of it, the family all gone and dispersed. Oh yes, and breakfast cornflakes; muffins, soups, crackers and spice from overseas somewhere. And bananas. Sandra loved bananas! Regardless, it all packed into the back of her car.

Besides, Sandra was due back this weekend. She had gone up to New York to watch the Ravens play the Giants. There would be a party or two; friends, shopping for her to do before returning to the beach house as promised.

She even picked up a jar of spiced fruit for a mince-pie, she thought, pulling into her bank. Next door she stopped for coffee; filled the tank with gas and even received a quick haircut. And now she felt a little drained. Chiefly because it was nothing more than a contrivance to keep up appearances - the semblance of a life untouched yet safe.

For three days she kept up her busy work at the beach house too. She hoed the garden weeds, cleared out the basement, tied the three bedrooms, replaced summer swimming toys with Halloween colored décor…chores that to keep her occupied and feeling satisfied.

Then a sort of ennui set in. She watched TV. She felt alone.

*If anyone is observing you…*had said Arguetta.

She was getting angry. If there was an observer, then let them follow her around to the local Library where she checked out movies; books and audios!

The house had five televisions and over five hundred channels for entertainment!

Music could be piped throughout the house. Three times this week she had turned to her kitchen for an intensive bout of Cuisine Art baking –including fresh home-baked bread, pies, cookies and…Enough!

Today, she took in a deep breath and watched the sun rise over the water, the rhythm of the sea an eternal assurance. No question. This was going to be a beautiful day.

She searched for beach walkers, thinking of her friends and finding them nowhere on the horizon.

She smiled at a few dog-walkers and runners, people evidently preparing for the day's festive events organized for the beach community upcoming...

How did she forget?

Of course! She had promised her colleagues that she'd be in top physical condition for the event. She smiled at the memory of that bunch.

Overhead, a routine chopper passed low along the beach. The local US National Guard Military Training depot was in full activation, she noted. Perhaps to coincide with the confluence of people arriving into the community, or perhaps just one of many scheduled training weekends for recruits. A larger plane followed.

All summer long large grey military transport aircraft could be seen flying into Dover Air Force Base, the largest military based of the Atlantic seaboard.

She missed the gang.

They had filled her life, in truth. Thoughts of them filled her mind as she walked along the beach with her small flask of coffee. She found a soft spot and sat.

Tom with his endless criticism of government policy, his over-reactionary litany of contradictions with one financial situation or the other; his politics that swayed from bad policy to anarchy. Yet he was always the one best informed, as if he were the designated timekeeper of the century: You could get a stock quote update from him by the minute.

Phillippa - and her girlish ways of charm and patience, silly and useless as she seemed, Amanda smiled. Somehow, she was the one who could put the brakes on their frustrations and coax them back to normal with her calm manner. Amanda paused to think about the many moments Phillipa had interceded, such that her ways were no accident but a skill acquired to restore the group's equilibrium. More than anyone, she was the most unappreciated, decided Amanda.

Mary, the alarmist, was always on deck at the ready to serve. Regardless the task, there she was! *Done*, was her stance. Prepared, whether a meal on the table – and cleared away inconspicuously, or the fully edited research report typed and ready for delivery. She was flamboyant and bright. And above all, she was focused 100% of the time. *Done.*

Yes. They each expressed themselves effusively in the end. They told her they were grateful for the employment during the summer months - each of them grappling with financial setbacks and loss of jobs, they said. But the truth was, they enriched Amanda…Had she told them enough times, she wondered.

It had been almost a week now since she had met with Arguetta in Washington.

She was beginning to feel neglected, if not forgotten. Perhaps the matter had been resolved. Either way, there had been no contact at all. She was alone. *Finished business.*

There was nothing to worry about, she could call Trevor. She could call Barbara. She could call…She didn't.

She had been up all night, especially since Sandra returned from New York at two o'clock in the morning. Actually, Amanda found plenty of work on her laptop.

She sent an unclassified e-mail attachment to Arguetta with data on her research and findings, as per normal conditions. So that was finished business..

And Sandra! She would call Trevor, she decided. It was so good to have her around.

She sipped her coffee.

Sandra was upstairs sleeping like a baby- certainly until noon. Up at noon, perhaps an hour to jog -or surf if the waves were up then shower, hair, late-lunch and either an afternoon of things to achieve, laundry, shopping or appointments for hair and manicure. Tomorrow she was taking the car for a day or two to Philadelphia.

Amanda smiled. Sandra was exceptional. Not the type who fell into the habit of staying in bed. Sandra could also be found studying all night; in labs at a University or preparing for an expedition to the North Pole…Sandra was a highly motived young women. So if she chose to be at home visiting her mother and sleeping until noon, then fine! Amanda was delighted to have her daughter around. She checked her watch.

So, this was the day, she sighed.

She got ready. She thought of skipping the whole race. She thought of…*Never mind.* She'd do it. How else to face a reunion this Christmas without the recount of that damned marathon she'd been training for all summer…

In an hour, she was due at the Start Line. The banners were everywhere, the mobs filling the streets with color and excitement. This was a charity Marathon. As an annual event, it was the main even of the year… Or, as Tom had put it, the *only* event of the year. True. Nothing else happened throughout the winter until the next summer season of tourists…

She parked her beach Jeep.

The beach road traffic was off-limits now, parkway sidewalks being monitored by police at checkpoints as the Marathon participants completed the full course.

She had signed up, and paid her dues.

She took a deep breath. The mob was thickening. They came from everywhere, mainly the city where another weckend at the beach brought them out in droves for a run for charity along the seaside.

The local tourist board who thought up this excerice to bring in tourists had also brought in the portable toilets; portable food trucks; police, ambulance and T-shirt kioks for flags, hats, kiddy toys and pin buttons. Music belted out from parked cars, trash was piling up everywhere and checkpoints backed up with pedestrians asking for bottled water reserved for contestants… They gave out penny shirts with numbers, colors, signals, instructions and bullhorns calling for the owners of the lost children… The temperature had climbed and everyone was getting cranky. There was nowhere for spectators…

Amanda waited patiently. Her turn came. She was given her running number; her shirt. Unseasonably warm, they had water on hand. But the supply had been depleted by spectators, they explained.

She had her own bottle of water, she said.

"I've made the Start" she texted Sandra before switching off.

Another half hour.

In contemplating the days ahead - plus the schedule she had to keep, she decided that completing the full race circuit wasn't needful. As long as she displayed her public spirit and effort, she could take the short circuit.

For now, she was suited up. But it was getting hot. She finished her drink. She would have liked another bottle of water. This, she could collect from the organizer's next kiosk...

The Start gun fired and they were off.

She paced herself. It was the least she could do for charity. The beach town had been festive and full of excitement all week.

The Librarian recognized her and waved. The Council beach community Commissioner was standing beside the Librarian and waved. They appreciated her participation, especially as a home-owner. The horns blasted as they all passed the first flag.

The pack she fell in with were not the fastest, so Amanda kept up easily and paced herself. Counting her breaths, her stride and her rhythm. Keep Time. Stay calm. Gradually, they fell away, and she was virtually alone, running ahead.

That's when she saw him.

* * *

Chapter 67

"You are running today?" said Kim.

She nodded, stunned by what she noticed beside him. The Trainer appeared holding the four dogs on his leashes. They were muzzled. But there was no doubt as to his intentions, especially since their foiled attempt at her house. The expression on his face was malevolent.

He suddenly joined her in the run, the trainer left behind as a spectator of the side crowds. Clearly, Kim was not officially a runner, but someone who had just jumped into the fray to keep up with her.

"Kim?" she asked, wondering if there was any room for chatting. Neither did he look at her, nor did he deviate his forward motion. He was a running footman in robotic discipline.

Not that she was in a shape to negotiate. She was jogging and burning up with heat and short breaths. Her mouth was dry and her sneakers scrapping the pavement with unmeasured stiffness.

There was no familiarity here. His face was stoic, his words darkly focused, and sharp. She could hardly believe what he was saying.

"You have done well so far Ms Wells…"

"*done well?..*"she echoed. He ignored her.

"But our plans cannot be stopped. Not by you, your research or your government! We have a plan of intention. And while we admire you daughter…."

"my *daughter?*"

Amanda stumbled, slowed down and almost stopped in surprise. As it was, she had to quicken to keep up. "Oh yes. I know she is sleeping…upstairs!"

"Wait a minute!..." she belted, shock shortening her breath and seeping down to heavy legs. She looked desperately around her. The crowd had thinned, the scrub terrain opening up for a stretch along the runner's pathway without room for spectators, and the beach beyond it.

There was no one to reach to in this melee, no way to reach for help or call attention to an assailant. She was vulnerable, wearing only shorts and a numbered penny in running shoes, miles of beach road ahead for a runner's marathon and nowhere to shelter!

He ran beside her, and he might as well have had her on a leash. Methodical, systemically, pulling at her with his threats such that she could not afford to lapse, her lips dry and her lungs pulling for air.

He had her, she knew. The sweat poured down the back of her head and drenched her shirt, her legs beginning to ache with pain. She was definitely dehydrated, and even her vision was stammering under the pounding of her feet.

Run. Run. Run.

Except she wasn't running. Her weight was lurching without thought, from one step into the next. She was in trouble, she knew.

This man was not the man she knew. He was strong. He was trained. He never broke a sweat.

It was then that she decided to harness her concentration. The first decision was to stay alert and not dissipate further reckless physical effort. She started to breath. She paced her stride and kept up, she refocused on running.

Keep Up. Stay strong.

Next, she pulled her feelings under control. There was much she could have said. But she was watchful, alert.

She ran on in silence. He was the first to speak.

"There is much I could do to make things unpleasant" he said "but this should suffice..." He showed her his phone, and she glanced at it.

There was no question. The dogs were in the house now.

"So, as long as your daughter remains in her room, she is safe. That is, until I give the word. You see, even attack dogs have ways of entering barricades! So, I need you to do exactly as I say…Understood?"

Amanda did not flinch, every nerve focused on the moment.

"*Understood?*" he repeated.

Amanda nodded.

The image darkened as he put away his cell phone. But he did lose his rhythm, she noticed.

So, he was not infallible.

Still, she was horrified, her mind a fog, ready to close in on her at any second.

Run. Run. Run.

How had she not expected this? What more could she have done to avert such a moment? Why hadn't she kept Sandra away…

She felt angry, and even stiffened.

The water kiosk appeared ahead. They slowed.

Arguetta had warned her, after all.

There was much she should have prepared herself for. So she steeled herself. And with Sandra upstairs, her energy began to focus on the resolve within to play along with this man who was clearly a threat. Just as Arguetta had warned her. He had already killed, she knew. The Japanese gentlemen in San Francisco.

They stopped, and she drank. He turned away, shaking one leg as if to loosen muscles.

She calmed her breathing, sipped more water.

She watched his face. Like so many faces of Asian extraction, they were difficult to read for emotion. His eyes in particular were small and dark, distant-like.

He would have like to press on. The kiosk manager nattering.

Amanda lowered her breathing, and sipped more water.

Kim smiled, like he had when he was her tenant - the student, the kiosk pressing them forward.

Amanda did not rush. She focused on a patch of grass lowering her breathing and her heart-beat, then she drank again to finish the water bottle.

The smile was gone now. There was no feeling on this face. This man was a dangerous man, she knew. He was off again.

The thoughts swirled in her head. She could warn him that he had already been identified. That his intentions, whatever they were, could be discerned by the tracings of his plutonium.

Instead, she looked forward, afraid that her eyes might betray her thoughts. He was a mind-reader, this man. Why give him anything?

 She could remain silent. For now, that is. God knows what lay ahead. He was menacing with his chest out, perhaps irritated at her, and she said nothing.

The road for runners stretched out ahead. It was long and isolated at this juncture, and free of traffic. The runners had staggered along miles of the course, and they were virtually alone, Amanda and Kim, the two of them running side by side.

Suddenly, from nowhere a dark SUV appeared on the side of the road - a road blocked to traffic earlier by the police protecting runners along the marathon. Yet here it was, stopped just ahead of them. Not particularly unusual in appearance, but unnoticed at this junction of the long beach pathway.

Perhaps it had emerged from the sand dunes. Perhaps it had special permission to attend to runners needing help. Perhaps a patrol monitor along the runner's course…

Then just as suddenly, the rear door opened and Kim got into the vehicle. "Proceed with your Marathon" he said. "And don't even think of calling for help…I need to get into your laptop and attain all the data I need to erase our tracks…"

Amanda realized he aimed to have reign of the house.

"You are being watched, of course!" said Kim, closing the door.

Her thoughts flayed in anger, she felt a need to lash back. She steeled her nerves. Stay Calm, she admonished herself.

Sandra was just too important to her to deviate from her instructions from a killer.

Think. *Her laptop?* What was that all about?

She thought about it. All she had on it was her research. Data from the Department of Interior was hardly critical information, let alone classified. Then it struck her. Her analytical report!

All her findings, her deductions about policy that might cause inequities in the Trade Agreement… It was intellectual content that someone on the outside might want to read. That was her input, and her input alone as an Analytical Research Analyst.

No. Kim was not interested. There had to be more.

Any expert on cyber hacking could have lifted her data from her computer weeks ago! Any nighttime burglar. Any paper-documentation that went through the paperwork process of any government entity was easily recovered. It wasn't that she had anything really important because she had little security clearance.

Then it struck her.

He wanted something else.

Run. Run.

Nothing. *Nothing!*

Without concentrating on your pace, you could get into trouble on a Marathon. You had to keep your breaching regulated. Not that she was hydrated, her legs moved rhythmically and without notice. Pacing was even and steady. She had panicked earlier, and ran like a jackass.

Slow down. Slow down.

What was he aiming for?

Pace. Pace. Run. Run.

Think!

She passed the second checkpoint, and waved at two police officers standing around. Half a mile up were another two police officers chatting at their bikes.

You are being watched…

Out here, who would that be?

That's when it came to her. Sandra had been up watching movies last night. She had wrapped herself in a cuddle blanket; cooked popcorn and plastered her face with cream as she watched the movie from the bar counter…

He was after *her* computer!

Why?

Sandra had perched herself on the bar stool and was working on her computer while also watching…

So what was on *her* computer?

All that Sandra had on there would be personal stuff; academic papers and whatever else students…

A thought suddenly struck Amanda that nearly halted her running.

Her Notes from the North Pole Expedition!

Something on her computer was the target of his attention…A report, a finding, an analysis.

Or, what if there were anything about the expedition that were *personal?* Like a name, an email…a point of contact…?

Jesus!

All that bullshit about her laptop being of interest was far from the truth.

Sandra was his target.

Amanda felt a deep fear begin to seize her. She wanted to stop, to think, to breath!

She was angry as hell that she had left Sandra in the house….

"Officer!…" she called, surging in pace a little. She needed to talk to the police officer.

Suddenly, she closed her mouth.

 Kim was beside him. He turned to look at her, his face hardened.

Like any other runner and now wearing a Pinney for the Marathon, he had been talking to the police officer.

Amanda approached.

 "You will find a young lady a half mile back in the beach grass along the parkrun. I'm wearing her Number. She has a knife in her chest." The police officer called it in, and they both left on their bikes to follow the trail of that direction.

Kim stayed with Amanda as they passed. "I told you that you were being watched…" he nodded, and he dropped back as she kept up her pace, the tumult in her chest almost unbearable.

Of one thing she was certain. He had just killed a woman.

* * *

Chapter 68

On the highway bridge where the crossover began,   a commotion incurred by a police held off traffic flow for runners crossing the highway, a U-Turn of the runner's course to begin their return to base along the other side of the road of the coastal highway.

Amanda made her decision instantly.

She veered. With two quick leaps she skipped out of the fray and jumped over the retaining wall of the bridge ramp.

Beneath it, the ocean surged into the inlet with a current, then funneled back out to meld into the rhythm of the sea ebb.

Amanda took a leap into the water and swam with all the strength she could muster. She would cross the inlet and climb out at the opposite shoreline, on the far side of the bridge.

It was insufficient, the tidal surge too strong a pull, and twice she was almost returned to her point of entry.

Though she could not see him, she felt certain that Kim would soon find her absent from the Marathon runners.

Again with one big surge, she pushed with all her strength across the tight channel, finding that only an outgoing eddy would give her the added momentum to cross the inlet. It did give her some buoyancy.

She was grateful for the effect, but as it picked up velocity, she realized that she was being swept out to sea, especially if she were to be wept past the bulwark rock jetty at the channel mouth of the Inlet where a small canal lay open for boats.

She swam, her energy dissipating, and her water mobility uncontrollable. She struggled.

She was pulled almost past the Rock jetty when a small side swirl, caused by a submerged obstruction, led her off the main stream of water flow and lapped softly on the Rocks.

She reached for some debris that that had wedged itself between two rocks and she clambered up. She lay flat against the rock, panting.

The sun was almost setting, and the wind calm. She slithered down between two exposed boulders for concealment and lay there, warmth seeping back into her bones.

Amanda peeped over the rock and could see the laste of the runners turn the bend for the their last leg to base. The Marathon coming to an end, and certainly the roads would be open again to traffic. But she was on the other side! She could spot nobody that she recognized. Of course she was wet, exhausted, bleeding from elbow scrapes and gritty all over, and she felt parched.

Sea debris had gathered at the rocks - horseshoe crab-shells, gull feather and bone, conch shell and seine webbing; 6-pack plastic collars and shattered driftwood, all choking and scraping between the rocks and leaving a foamy residue against slimy sea moss and barnacles. Soon, Amanda knew, it would all be washed out to sea with the outgoing tide.

More than anything, she felt pleased that she had evaded Kim. But with Sandra in his grip, there was no time to lose. She must get help!

She was, at least, on the correct side of the channel. For a while there in the tidal sweep, she could have been tossed backwards. But she had found a purchase and traversed to the other side, even it stretched for miles as a coast beach managed by National Park Service. At this time of the season, few tourists came. And few patrols occurred, she knew.

If there was anything on this lonely beach, there were occasional areas for sports fishermen in rugged-terrain-vehicles. No houses. No population. Only wildlife and nature to be enjoyed as a Park and accessible only at designated pathways. The rest was off limits to the public. For that she felt relieved. She would wait until dark. It was an hour before the sun began to lose its force on the beach.

And that's where she saw him.

He was standing beside his car which he had parked under the bridge, having crossed over after the Marathon, and by way of a fisherman's entrance!

She ran, the surf of the beach ahead of her. The sand dune was naturally uneven with bushy clumps of sharp marsh-grass and loblolly pine. It was dusk.

He followed, and she knew that very soon, he would catch up with her.

She made a decision, and headed straight into the dark sea. Mustering the sum of her strength, she swam as far out as she could, as fast as she could. Out there, she knew he would not be able to see her in the dark.

The sea was becalm, making her profile visible, she felt. She drifted in softly, came ashore and collapsed to the ground to look around, she could not stop shivering.

Under the reflection of a bright moon, she could see him. Obviously, he was out-waiting her. His features were pale and his eyes never left the water, she observed. Oh yes. He was waiting for her to return! She ooched herself gently a few inches into the sand, which served to warm her body. She waited.

There was nothing on this beach here. Nothing.

But there was one place that she knew well.

She knew what she must do. She untied her running sneakers and laced them to her pinny, still strapped to her chest.

She would wait for her chance.

His cell phone rang, she could hear it on the rising wind. He got up, and walked around to talk.

This was her moment.

She glided softly back into the water, and she began a quiet swim for half a mile up the coast. She kept a steady motion, no rippling or sound to the surface of the water, and she kept her relative distance by feeling for the sandy bottom off the shoreline.

Her arms began to ache, and she wondered at her fitness. Training on the beach all summer helped. Were it not for her cohorts, she'd have been too unfit to sustain this effort. She pressed on.

Sandra, she knew, was still at the house - the call to this thug just now was probably a report on Sandra's disposition. Amanda pressed on, the clouds concealing a shy moon above her with increasing fervor. The wind was rising, and the waves began to heave. She thought of releasing her sneakers from her pinney which snarled around her vest and made swimming heavy. But she decided against it. She might need her running shoes.

She saw the structure.

Years ago, Trevor had responded generously to underwrite the preservation of a landmark along this beach. It was an old structure.

The Delaware Lighthouses from WWII were iconic structures.

In summer, the beach pillars teemed with visitors who came to recognize their historical significance. The entrance to the great Delaware Bay, a waterway wherein lay dry-docks, ports, rail depots, armories and shipyards of Philadelphia, was protected by defensive watchtowers and gun placements against enemy vessels.

All enemy ships approaching the coastline came under their gunfire, including U-boats searching for opportunities to sink supply ships leaving America for Europe.

Amanda paused, catching her breath. The waves were getting rougher by the minute, the wind increasing.

Slowly, she reoriented her swimming and made her way into shore and held steady through the surf. With creeping advances, she moved out of the water from the surf and slipped darkly behind the large concrete tower.

She looked up the beach, and down. By now the wind was lifting sand and blowing noisily. She sheltered momentarily in the lee of the structure, untying her sneakers that had laced themselves into a knot. Her fingers were wrinkled, soft and uncoordinated. Persisting, and by using her teeth, she untangled them and put on both shoes.

Somehow, she felt she gained some agency.

The entrance to the tower was buried under four feet of sand - residue from a recent storm that had shifted the dunes.

She dug and tugged, swooping away armfuls, patting like a dog. She created a small sand-free channel to the great metal door to the structure.

The rusty casing unsealed barely from its framework, scratching against grit and sand. Inch by quiet inch she pried it open, holding her breath for noise, the wind now blowing loudly.

She slipped through the slot.

* * *

Chapter 69

Inside the ageing watchtower she found circular steps with occasional protrusions of iron railing. She knew it well.

She and Trevor had climbed the structure many times for occasions of public Open Fair events. It aided the local festive tourist industry. As donors, they were always invited, and Trevor frequently accepted their call.

Stark, lonely reminders, yet in a comforting way, they demonstrated freedom was worth defending. Thus it was, the monuments seems to say, that in WWII people had done their best in times of danger, even on the home front, to defend the freedom of the nation…And era long ended.

Now in the darkness, it was as dank and cold as tomb.

Amanda shivered.

She climbed steep steps angled like a lighthouse until her legs ached. She felt exhausted, gritty and was shivering.

 At the top, she knew she would be at least 100ft above sea level. Round and round she climbed. At the penultimate landing, she paused to rest against the a heavy bulkhead.

Her thoughts were in a whirl, her teeth chattering between strands of soggy hair and grit. She wondered at the insanity of being in this place. This was unreal. How could this have happened? She sank to the floor, her breath catching in her throat with a sob.

What appalled her was that she was up here in flight up when Sandra was the one in danger!

What was she thinking? For all she knew, her pursuer had turned his attention to Sandra exclusively. He might have abandoned his search…Was *she* actually the one running away?

Moonlight was passed over the structure and penetrated the shadows. She looked up at the walls made of reinforcing bars and concrete. It was an old construction, now brittle with age and flaking from salt and humidity.

Certainly it was off limits, a hazard of sorts. Its integrity no longer viable or managed for safety inspection standards. Iron protrusions, perhaps once the appendages for armament - now oxidized and rusted with dark stains of neglect and decay, thrust out from the walls. Even the Alarm-pull was a chain to a device long gone and unserviceable.

She realized that if she were found by the authorities prowling around inside one of these old monuments she would be cited for trespassing and vandalism. These lighthouse watchtowers were not exactly patrolled or policed for the public safety – located miles apart along stretches of beach. Today, they were only distinguished as isolated landmarks mapped on Federal parklands protected from modern development and population encroachment…

Then again, it was the Park Services conserving the natural beauty of the coastline which had decided to leave them for posterity. For that she felt grateful.

But damned if this isolated tower wasn't scary at night. Abandoned, hidden in the coastal sea sands, it could be lost to sight, yet up close it felt powerful and menacing.

Not items of beauty by any imagination, but rather circular battlements, they were intimidating pillbox parapets for turret placements standing as colorless and featureless fortifications along the coastline. At the very least, they could be used as lighthouses…

Amanda looked up. At the top level, there would be an endless vista. From that height, she could observe stretches of beach for miles, even in the dark, and as far out to the ocean as the eye could see.

From there, she would see how modern technology had prevailed in a world of super-vessel shipping with channel markers at the entrance of these waters. If viewed as fond landmarks on everybody's beach photograph, these zones were also known to modern traffic by sea and air, by pilots commercial and airmen military. In that, she felt a small measure of comfort and she determined to climb to the top.

She lay a moment longer to think… *Why Sandra?*

If Sandra's computer were indeed what he was after, then he would have achieved his goal, and even fled the scene. Sandra was either without awareness of their danger, or captive in her room. At least she had a chance…

If she was hostage, then what did he want?

Or, by now Sandra would be distraught. Her mother would not have returned from the marathon. There were attack dogs inside the house and an assailant making calls in a foreign tongue…

Amanda shivered.

She climbed to the top landing and paused against a rusty railing outside the Gun room. She moved unsteadily, the flooring less than stable.

There were levers and pulleys suspended from a roof designed to lift deadweight munitions.

From a small slotted aperture between shadows, moonlight opened up briefly, and faraway flashing channel markers rotated in dots. What was a breeze at ground level was a howl through the aperture.

The Gun room door was in all probability locked and sealed. If there was one thing museum preservation aimed to achieve was to leave things intact, she knew.

That's when she heard it.

A creaking of the door at the base of the tower was unmistakable. It was the cast metal entrance where she had slipped through.

She stopped breathing.

Peeking barely over the edge, she noted an ambient lighting bathe the vacuum below. A flashlight, the moonlight?

Had he found her and entered the tower?

Perhaps her assailant was inside the tower? Had he seen her or deduced that she was inside? If so, that meant only one thing. He aimed to kill her!

How to call for help? Who would think to find her in here?

She waited.

Arguetta has been vacuous and without reassurance during the week. Was he still on the alert, she wondered.

Certainly, she had been the bait that brought Kim forward, but was anyone even aware..?

She felt alone. Fear threatened to choke her. The entrance door creaked again and closed of its own volition.

She was mistaken, imaging the worst!

No one was there but the increasing wind. Relieved, she breathed again.

Good!

She got up and would give the Gun room door an inspection. Yes, it was barred across by an iron drop-lever and brackets. Even rusting they were strong. To enter, she would need a crowbar to lift the drop-lever from its brackets. Then the door could be unbarred, and she would enter.

She searched for a lever.

Above her spouted iron hooks for chains, pulleys; buckets and equipment. Beneath, a ledge of fraying burlap sandbags - sand mostly spilled out and fused like concrete from years of moisture and decay. Several tools hung behind veils of webbed dust. One, easily a crowbar, hung from a hinge wedged against the wall.

She managed to dislodge the crowbar and placed it beneath the drop-lever of the Gun room door. Slowly the lever began to lift off its brackets. She leaned into it for full purchase.

She lay the crowbar on the deck grid beneath her feet and pushed. Before long, even in the dark, she had lifted the drop-lever to a vertical position and unbarred the door. She entered.

An owl flew off, surprising her so suddenly that she stepped back in defense, stumbling onto the crowbar laying outside the door. It spun off the platform and went down the tower well with the sound of a brass gong…

She held her breath…

Nothing.

She entered the Gun room, the open air slits from the tower offered intermittent lighting.

Grateful that she had kept her running shoes, she stepped on shattered glass.

Before her loomed two massive mounted guns.

There they rested, silent, once the fierce cannon of WWII that would defend the homeland from enemy invasion. Amanda touched them lightly as she circled the platform where they were mounted on retractable wheels.

Two 16-inch guns, peeking out from their casing, were battleship grey of 45 caliper. When discharging, she knew, they could have a fearsome range of 20 miles across the sea to stop enemy combatants. They were imposing, testimony to the passage of peacetime, their duty done.

Originally covered by fitted leather, they were coated in white bird droppings, grime and debris. As unthinkable as those realities were, Amanda felt a empathy for those who would have engaged in the commitment of defense. She was glad Trevor had donated to this preservation.

Lest we forgot the price of freedom, he once told her. The opening of the gun turret was larger than ever she expected. The wind howled as if a belfry. Yet the opening was mainly stuffed by an inner rim of sandbags. Yes. You could see for miles across the sea and down the coast.

The platform for the gun placement was a swivel mount adjusted by levers that must have once run like well-oiled machinery chassis for those manning the cannons to point out the turrets. No other guns were there today. But much could be imagined about those fretful days during the war.

Lining the walls of the Gun room were places for sand buckets; paint supply for markers of yellow, red, blue and green to mark and signal. If fluorescent, it was new stuff for that period.

Amanda lifted her nose to see. By now it was probably a solid rock of hardened paste.

Beside it, gun-racks for arms climbed the sides of the wall; mounts for ammunition clearly evident. Along one side panel, an electrical grid showed switches for the search light gear mounted above the aperture. Others were used for telephone communications, even pegs to register blows logged.

Stacked also against these circular walls were sandbags, now mainly the domain of nesting birds and storm debris.

She was almost beginning to relax when she heard the base door scream out at the hinges.

Amanda froze, her breathing gone.

A tactical sense of survival took over her senses, and she realized that if she was the target of an assailant in this place, it would only be a matter of time before he found her.

They would ascend, as she had. They would climb the same steps…

Up there, she was trapped and alone. The only escape was through the aperture and a drop of 100 ft down!

She made her decision.

She barred shut the door, and she heard two gun shots. Definitively, gun shots from below at the tower. No question. Someone was inside the tower, even as she barred herself into the Gun room.

She pulled down a can of paint - red and dragged it toward a sandbag, half full.

She stuffed the paint inside the bag, as best as she could, and tied the fraying burlap ends together. Rotted, they would not hold fast.

She used whatever salvable threads she could tear from other bags, and with all her strength managed to haul it up to aperture.

If she could toss it overboard, who knows what kind of glutinous mess it would show at the base of the tower: Hitting the ground might dislodge some of the hardness of the paint and make it shatter. A red mess in a sandbag might look from the air…like…Then again, it may just shatter into two or three hard coagulated paint rocks.

She managed to lift it up to the opening and perched it ready to push.

Outside the aperture, tower walls descended straight down, weathered and decaying. A few reinforcement bars protruding like a balcony, having once served as a safety grid for the aperture.

The wind was at high velocity entering the tower's Gun room and shuddering all that lay within. Clearly, Amanda had pried free sealed openings and created draft holes with her entry, allowing wind to pass through and swirl about releasing new dust that had lay dormant behind sealed enclosures. And she was suddenly cold, the front line of a weather change had swept down the beach and up through the watchtower. Still wearing her silky running garments she had remained soaked and gritty and damp for hours. It was all she could do to keep from shuddering uncontrollably, fear gripping her chest and panic close to seizing her breath.

Concentrate!

She heard the steps outside, that clattering over debris that littered the way, pushed aside by the feet of a person climbing…

She felt desperate, eyes wide, her mind almost paralyzed.

She turned to the electrical grid. There was power, she knew. It fed the rooftop altitude beacon as an air-flight safety landmarks.

And there was something else she knew.

There were lights up there! They had been mounted and used for festive summer events…

Yes. The floodlights! Used only for Christmas as a coastal decorative gesture by the Park Services.

On such occasion, night-time commemorative lighthouses and ceremonial lightings were scheduled for tourists. Perhaps there was a chance that an electrician had been up…

Oh God!

What if they were inoperative…What if she were unable to…What if…

She closed her eyes.

Trevor was never one to take his donor obligations lightly: He made commitments to his obligations fully and completely with pledges of support and financial backing. There would be no neglect for things he cared about. This was the hope she clung to, the beacon that she had clung to throughout her entire marriage, the Trevor of integrity and hope that she so loved…

But here? While he might have insisted that the power grids remain switched on for the searchlight mechanism, he might have been contradicted by local authorities. He had received objections from the State, citing danger from intruders who might enter the premises and be exposed to power currents on a monument untended... And clearly, even with the Park Service patrolling the beaches, intruders had found their way into the tower recently because the entrance door had not been sealed.

Then again…

She heard the sounds outside, just one floor beneath her.

…It was entirely possible that the grid *was* serviceable.

Either way, she was taking a gamble.

She had no choice. She was trapped.

She *might* get attention outside – but that was *all* she could hope for!

She reached. Just one giant lever to pull down on the power grid, and the floodlight that once served as a night-time searchlight would come on with extraordinary brilliance and shine out through turret aperture of the watchtower on the Atlantic coast. She would, in essence, become a lighthouse.

She glanced furtively once again through the aperture, a dark sea roiling beneath a silvery moon. Between the town and the ocean, there was nothing but sand. Bleak, darkness.

As were her choices.

She heard the metal pull lever crack down and grind open. Yes. Definitely. It was her assailant.

Anyone else would have called out. Or used his cell. Or let out noises, talking about place, swearing…fearful and uncertain.

No!

This person was silent as the grave. Steady. Quiet. Methodical. She knew. She just knew she sensed danger.

She pushed at the sandbag and it fell out. She landed her full weight on the electrical lever and pulled it down.

Incredibly, the light spluttered and ignited a halogen beam that pulsed and whined within the Gun-room. She scrambled up to the rim and reached for the reinforcement concrete bars, wind threatening to toss her off like a leaf. He hesitated, buffeted.

The door opened just as she removed her foot from the ledge, and in the moonlight she climbed.

Up. Up. Up.

She climbed over rough weathered hard concrete and scrapped her body, her forehead and elbows, holding on where she could find purchase from the gusts.

She climbed to whatever she could find….

 Finally, she climbed onto the roof and lay upon it, sprawled, wrapping herself around the mast that held the Height Beacon.

It hummed and fuzzed like a drum in her ear, the wind gusts at that altitude strong.

She screamed out, in terror. All she needed now was strength to hang on…

She was getting cold.

How long she could do this, and for what, she wasn't sure. Her mind was tumbling, almost numb with cold, her fingers slipping. Her vision blurred.

 She would hold on until morning, by God!

* * *

It seemed like hours before she was rescued.

It might have never happened, even. But suddenly out of the darkness it appeared, a chopper with a search light scanning the concrete watch tower.

Amanda looked up, a man was propelling himself down a rope.

It took longer than she would have thought. She sank gratefully into a basket and glided through the life into the chopper.

Only in her imagination perhaps she heard about an approach to the North Pole with an assault team that deflected the plans of any coastal incidents posing danger. Or was it a message on ear phones placed on her inside the rescue chopper. Yes, it was Arguetta's voice.

But there was only one sound she wanted to know about. And it came shortly after the chopper touched down.

"Mom!" shrieked Sandra in the windy commotion at the base of the tower. "Are you alright?"

* * *

Chapter 70

It took two days of unravelling and processing.

Kim Miu had wanted to wipe out the computer drives and erase his steps. He clearly understood her role, and deduced her knowledge that implicated his involvement. More importantly, the involvement of the states in the Pacific that financed the plot…

Sandra, by watching the polar positioning of the north had logged in the critical data to transmitting a harmonic frequency across the Pole. She had it on her computer, and none that thought she might be the data carrier. Not her assailants, until they exhausted every other possibility.

He had been killed, it was told. But his communications revealed others, financiers, terrorist information networks, assassins, enemies of the state. One, in particular was within the government, a trusted representative from Congress.

Arguetta explained it to Amanda. But she got a more graphic picture from Barbara. "…homicide, fraud and few other technicalities of corruption, malfeasance and cover ups!" she said about her boss Ali Enders. "I could have told you so" she bellowed on the phone. "The son of a bitch…"

For Amanda Wells, all she wanted to do was relax. Sandra was happy to stay for a week, or ditz around town, shop, float and relax. Both used the time together to recover and debrief. They visited ARguetta and Eileen, called friends and caught up with their schedules. But only slowly. Amanda walked frequently down her beach, wondering at the possibilities of a major breakdown, one she had been part of. It was almost more than she could take, she told Trevor.

The days passed with less vividness the horrific events that had embroiled them.

Both were scheduled to fly back to London. Finally, Amanda and Sandra closed up the beach house and delivered it by contract to the management company to supervise for the season.

They were glad to be going home, Amanda told her friends…

They were on their way to the Airport, Amanda was at the wheel.

The ride was quiet. "Any regrets?" asked Amanda, eyeing her daughter for lingering after effects.

"None. I'm fine Mom. As long as you're safe! And…you know what? Thanks!"

Amanda smiled.

Sandra turned to her iphone.

"Mom" Sandra said "I just got an email…."

Amanda's cell phone rang. "Look…. If that's your father coming out to greet us with the Marines, tell him we're fine and that I shall explain everything…"

Sandra answered and chatted. Finally she said "Right. So Dad. We'll see you shortly…Yeah, ok. Bye!"

They drove on. Amanda turned to Sandra. "Oh, you were saying… *What* email?

Sandra was grinning, a beautiful grin that belonged only to people who shared something. She turned her phone to her mother to see.

"Hello Aurora…." it said.

"Who's Aurora?" asked Amanda.

Sandra threw back her head and closed her eyes, savoring a moment to herself that had lain forgotten and buried.

Until now, that is.

In her heart a tender blossom had just flowered.

END